BEVERLY LEWIS

SummerHill Secrets · 2

BEVERLY LEWIS

SummerHill Secrets · 2

BETHANYHOUSE
Minneapolis, Minnesota

Library of Congress Cataloging-in-Publication Data

Lewis, Beverly
    SummerHill secrets 2. / by Beverly Lewis.
        p.   cm.
    Summary: Sixteen-year-old Merry Hanson, living amongst the Amish in rural Lancaster County, Pennsylvania, relies on her Christian faith to guide her through such challenging situations as the childhood death of her twin sister, the disappearance of a friend's mother, boy troubles, a skating accident, and her Amish friend's newfound interest in the modern world.
        Contents: v. 2. House of secrets — Echoes in the wind — Hide behind the moon — Windows on the hill — Shadows beyond the gate.
        Notes: "Previously published in five separate volumes"—Tp. verso.
        ISBN-13: 978-0-7642-0452-4 (pbk.)
        ISBN-10: 0-7642-0452-1 (pbk.)
        1. Country life—Pennsylvania—Lancaster County—Juvenile fiction. 2. Country life—Pennsylvania—Lancaster County—Fiction. 3. Amish—Fiction. 4. Christian life—Fiction. 5. Conduct of life—Fiction. 6. Lancaster County (Pa.)—Fiction. I. Title.
        PZ7.L58464   Sume   2007
        [Fic]—dc22

                                                                            2007028933

About the Author

BEVERLY LEWIS, born in the heart of Pennsylvania Dutch country, fondly recalls her growing-up years. A keen interest in her mother's Plain family heritage has inspired Beverly to set many of her popular stories in Amish country, beginning with her inaugural novel, *The Shunning*.

A former schoolteacher and accomplished pianist, Beverly has written over eighty books for adults and children. Five of her blockbuster novels have received the Gold Book Award for sales over 500,000 copies, and *The Brethren* won a 2007 Christy Award.

Beverly and her husband, David, make their home in Colorado, where they enjoy hiking, biking, reading, writing, making music, and spending time with their three grandchildren.

Books by Beverly Lewis

GIRLS ONLY (GO!)*
Youth Fiction

Girls Only! Volume One
Girls Only! Volume Two

SUMMERHILL SECRETS†
Youth Fiction

SummerHill Secrets Volume One
SummerHill Secrets Volume Two

HOLLY'S HEART
Youth Fiction

Holly's Heart Collection One†
Holly's Heart Collection Two†
*Holly's Heart Collection Three**

www.BeverlyLewis.com

*4 books in each volume   †5 books in each volume

House of Secrets

To
Verna Flower,
whose loving hospitality
eased my homesickness
during college days . . .
and
who read
my first book manuscript
with editorial encouragement.
Thanks, Aunt Verna,
for your prayers
and love
all these years.

You spread out our sins before you— our secret sins—and see them all.

—Psalm 90:8 TLB

Eerie and still, the study hall classroom echoed my words. "What do you mean your mom's disappeared?"

I stared at my friend Chelsea Davis. Her thick auburn hair fell around her shoulders.

Her voice trembled as she searched in her schoolbag. "Sometime in the night . . . she . . . Mom must've written this note. And now . . ." Chelsea paused, staring at the folded paper in her hand. "Now she's gone."

She scanned the study hall cautiously, waiting until the last student vacated the room. Then she handed me the note.

"Do you really want me to read this?" I said, noticing how very pale her face had become.

Chelsea nodded, and slowly, I unfolded the paper.

Before you wake up, I'll be gone. Don't try to find me. I'm happy where I'll be.

My throat felt tight as I read the frightful words. Startled, I refolded the note.

I'm happy where I'll be. . . . Questions nagged at me, but I said nothing.

Chelsea's voice cracked, breaking the silence. "I guess you never know how important your family is until one of them is gone."

Her words struck a chord. I, too, had experienced the loss of a family member. My twin sister, Faithie, had died of leukemia at age seven.

But this? This was far different. Surely Mrs. Davis would return to her family. Maybe she and Mr. Davis had argued; maybe she needed space—time to sort things out.

"Give it a few days," I said almost without thinking. "I mean, your mom's got to come back home."

Chelsea sighed. "I hope you're right, but this morning I poked around in Mom's closet. She didn't take much with her, but she's definitely gone." Chelsea stared at the underside of her watch. "For no reason, she just walked out . . . left Dad and me."

I slipped my assignment notebook into my schoolbag. "How's your dad handling things?"

"Well, we talked at breakfast." She had a faraway look in her eyes. "You see, Mom had these new friends . . . a superweird guy and his wife. They were always whispering with her the few times they came to our house. They were into some of the same stuff Mom likes—astrological charts, seances, and stuff like that. Anyway, Mom went with them for coffee several times about a month ago, around the time she got laid off from work. Next thing I knew, she was going to their house for supper, and a couple of times the three of them went to some metaphysical fair in Philadelphia."

"Did they invite your dad along?"

Chelsea nodded. "Mom and Dad both went to a secret meeting with them at a hotel once." A frown crept between her eyes. "The thing is, Mom seemed awfully excited about these people—about their mysterious activities."

"What about the meeting? What was *that* all about?"

"Beats me, but after the first time, Dad refused to go again. Mom was furious. I heard them talking in the kitchen late one night, and I crawled out of bed to listen at the top of the steps. Mom was beside herself—nearly hysterical—trying to get Dad to see what she said was 'the true light.' Over and over she kept saying it—that he was resisting 'the true light.' "

Describing the scene really seemed to bug my friend—the crimped sound in her usually mellow voice and the way she blinked back angry tears told me more than her words. Somewhere along the line, Chelsea Davis had declared herself an atheist. I wondered if she resented her mom for this spiritual encounter—or whatever was going on.

I took a deep breath. "Do you think your mom's friends influenced her to leave?"

Chelsea shook her head. "All I know is that Mom seemed desperate to make some sort of pledge or oath, but she couldn't get Dad interested. From what I overheard, he thought the whole thing was ridiculous."

"An oath? What for?"

"I don't know exactly," she replied. "Mom wanted to keep attending the meetings. She pleaded with Dad, trying to persuade him, but he wouldn't go back."

"Did your mom ever go again?" I asked, wondering what on earth had really happened with Chelsea's mother.

"Three or four more times, I think. In fact, Mom was hardly home all last week. Oh, and something else . . ."

I cringed. There was more?

"She suddenly started cooking up these vegetarian meals for us—wouldn't allow red meat or pork in the house. And she refused to drink water or anything else with her meal. Crazy stuff like that with no word of explanation."

This was beginning to sound truly strange.

"But the weirdest thing about it—Mom seemed super relaxed. Content, I guess you'd say," Chelsea added. "And she'd been horribly miserable before and depressed about losing her position at the hospital."

I'd heard about the cutback. "Too bad her job was phased out. Your mom loved her work."

"The hospital only needs so many administrative nurses, and she had worked there the fewest years." Chelsea puffed out her cheeks, then forced the air out. "Then these people, this couple, seemed to appear out of nowhere."

"What do you think they wanted—I mean, isn't it a little bizarre?"

Chelsea gathered up her books and we headed for the hallway. "I wish I knew."

My heart went out to my friend. "I'll do whatever I can to help you," I volunteered, keeping pace with her.

"Thanks." She gave me a pained smile. "And, uh, Merry, if you don't mind, could you keep it quiet—you know, all the stuff I told you?"

"Count on me," I reassured her.

We walked down the hushed hallway to the long row of lockers. It was late. We'd missed the school bus, yet Chelsea took her time opening her combination lock, and I found myself deep in thought as I did the same. *How would I feel if my mom vanished into thin air?*

We dropped off our books and sorted out only what we needed for homework. I cast a rueful glance at my friend several lockers away. Chelsea had just confided a deep secret, not knowing I'd been praying for her all through junior high and now as a sophomore in high school. Sometimes she put up with my talk about God—the God she said didn't exist. Most of the time, she wasn't interested.

But what Chelsea said next really rattled me. Shook me straight to my heart.

"I'm . . . I'm scared, Mer," she cried, standing in front of her locker. "I'm afraid I'll never see my mom again!"

I ran to her and let her bury her face in the shoulder of my jacket. "Oh, Chelsea, you will. You will." I hoped it was true.

She clung to me, her body heaving with sobs. "I have to find her . . . I want her back," her muffled voice said into my shoulder.

I could almost feel the autumn chill, the cold, damp rawness, seeping through the cracks in the windowpanes as Chelsea cried.

Silently, I prayed.

After Chelsea dried her eyes, I gave Mom a quick call from my cell phone.

Mom answered on the first ring. "Where *are* you, Merry?"

"Still at school, but don't worry. Something came up. Could you come get me? Chelsea too?"

"I'll leave right now," she said without probing.

It would take Mom about fifteen minutes to arrive. We lived in a remote Amish farm community on the outskirts of Lancaster County. We weren't Plain folk or farmers, but most of our neighbors were. SummerHill Lane was actually a long dirt road that wound its way past fertile fields and pastureland owned by Old Order Amish. I must admit, it wasn't easy leaving the picturesque setting behind every morning, even to come to school.

Chelsea and I decided to wait inside the school's double doors, peering out through the window every now and then. To pass the time, we read our boring English assignments out loud. It was Chelsea's idea. "This way, we can knock down some homework before we get home," she said.

Soon, my mom pulled up to the curb, and we hurried out to meet her. Chelsea sat in the backseat, I in front.

"Something came up and we missed the bus," I offered as an explanation.

"Nothing academic, I hope." Mom's eyebrows flew up.

"Oh no, nothing like that." I was quick to set her scholastic worries at ease.

Off we sped toward the highway. Chelsea blew her nose. I hoped she wasn't crying again, but I didn't turn around to investigate.

"Everything okay?" Mom asked, glancing in her rearview mirror. She was like that—picked right up on things.

I'd promised to keep Chelsea's secret, so I ignored Mom's question. "What a hectic day. And the homework! I think the teachers have totally spaced out what it's like being sixteen. You'd think they'd try to ease their youngest students into the halls of higher learning. Instead, I think they have a contest going to see who can pile on the most assignments." I groaned for emphasis.

Mom smiled dutifully. "Speaking of higher learning, your brother called today. He sounded homesick, says dorm life is dismal."

I tried not to snicker. *Silly Skip. Probably misses good home cooking and his own bed.* He'd made such a pompous fuss about going off to college—managed to get top grades his senior year—and couldn't wait to show the world what a cool college man he was. Now he was coming home for the weekend—homesick! It was hard to believe my haughty big brother had actually admitted his weakness to Mom.

I flashed a superior grin. "Is this the same smart aleck we sent off to college at the end of August?"

"Now, Merry, you have no idea what you're talking about," Mom defended. "Skip simply wants to come home for the weekend. I think it's wonderful."

She would think that. Six weeks into the first semester, and he already needed a steak-and-potato fix. Truly disappointing to say the least. I just hoped Skip wouldn't make a habit of returning often. I'd waited a long time to have the run of the house—and all the parental attention.

Suddenly, my thoughts turned back to Chelsea. Here I was fretting over having to share my parents' affections, and her mom wasn't even around anymore. Overwhelming feelings weighed on me—worry and concern for my friend. What would Chelsea do?

Mom turned into the driveway in front of Chelsea's house, an old, two-story Colonial similar to ours.

"Call me," I said as Chelsea slid out and closed the car door.

"I will, and thanks for the ride, Mrs. Hanson. 'Bye, Merry," she called.

A lump rose in my throat as I watched my friend lean into the wind, heading up the brick walkway toward the house. *Please help her, Lord*, I prayed.

I pulled my jacket tightly against me and longed to curl up in front of a crackling fire somewhere, but not because I was cold. I was terrified.

Slowly, Mom backed out of the driveway and headed down the hill. I stared out the window at high, wispy clouds moving rapidly across a hazy October sky. Indian summer days were fast spinning into deep autumn. Flaming leaves of orange, red, and shimmering gold danced on thick, wide branches on either side of SummerHill Lane.

How could a mother abandon her family and her home at such an incredible time? How, at any time? I thought of Mrs. Davis tending her beloved flower beds, now ready to be spaded under for the winter. And her tinkling wind chimes, dozens of them, lovingly crafted by her own hands. How could she leave so much behind?

Most of all, how could she leave her husband, a charming man of forty-two with no sign of balding and apparently no hint of a midlife crisis? And Chelsea, too, their only child?

A horse and buggy caught my attention as it *clip-clop*ped and swayed up the hill toward us. I waved, recognizing our Amish friends in the front of the gray box-shaped buggy typical of the Lancaster County Old Order. "Look, it's Rachel Zook and her mother," I said, noting their matching woolen shawls and black bonnets.

Mom let the buggy pass before making the left-hand turn into our gravel driveway. "Must be headed for a quilting frolic," she observed. "Their potatoes are harvested by now, and most of the corn is cut and shocked, so it's time for visiting and quilting. Amishwomen live for such things, you know."

I sighed. "I wonder how Rachel likes going to frolics with her mother instead of school."

"She's following in her ancestors' footsteps, and she's already had a year to adjust," Mom said. "How would *you* feel about quitting school after only eight grades?"

"I'd miss it. Especially my friends," I said, thinking of Lissa, Chelsea . . . and Jonathan Klein.

"I suppose Rachel will be baptized into the Amish church next fall," Mom said.

"That's what she says. There's no reason for her to put it off. Rachel wants to get married and have lots of babies." I didn't tell Mom that one of the Yoder boys down the lane had taken Rachel to a Sunday singing recently. Not even her own parents were aware of it. Serious Amish courting took place under the covering of night—the way Rachel's people had been courting for three hundred years.

Mom glanced at me. "Have you heard from Levi lately?"

"Not for several weeks." Levi Zook, Rachel's older brother, had gone off to a Mennonite college in Virginia, turning his back on his Amish upbringing. Levi and I and all the Zook children had grown up together. Our properties shared the same boundary—a thick grove of willow trees. Levi and I had promised to write to each other this school year.

My parents hadn't been especially thrilled about the idea of Levi and me becoming close friends. I should say *Mom* wasn't too keen on it. Dad, however, was more easygoing. He'd even made attempts to get better acquainted with Levi on several occasions.

"Life is much different now for Levi, I would guess. He's probably busy with his studies," Mom said, attempting to make me feel better.

Truth was, Levi hadn't thought it fair to tie me down with a long-distance relationship while he was off at Bible school. He was free to meet other girls. I, however, had my heart set on Jon Klein, a guy in my youth group at church—also a sophomore at James Buchanan High.

Jon was a wordplay freak. I liked to refer to him as the Alliteration Wizard. Unfortunately for him, I was gaining ground—soon to topple his status. The two of us had become so consistently clever at conversing using only similar beginning consonant sounds that I'd begun to talk alliteration-eze almost automatically. Especially at home.

Today, though, a cloud of gloom hung over me. Chelsea's mom was in trouble, and my friend had asked me not to tell anyone. The secret burden was horribly heavy.

I looked back up at the sky. The fast-moving high clouds were a sure sign of a storm. Trees swayed back and forth in their dazzling costumes. There was so much Chelsea's mom would miss if she stayed away: the deep orange of the Pennsylvania harvest moon, crisp morning walks, birds flying south for the winter . . . Thanksgiving Day, Christmas . . .

I shivered, thinking of Chelsea living out the lonely days or months ahead. There had to be something I could do.

A small-scale investigation might turn up some leads. That's what Chelsea needed: someone to help her poke around a bit. Someone to help her solve the heartbreaking mystery.

I couldn't wait to phone her.

Running toward my house, I darted in through the back door, eager to use the phone. I nearly stumbled over my cats—Shadrach, Meshach, and Abednego—and one ivory kitten named Lily White, bright as a lily.

All four cats were lined up comically beside two empty bowls near the back door—my cue.

"Oh, I'm sorry." I squatted down beside the foursome. "You're waiting for snack time, aren't you, babies? You know I'd never forget you guys on purpose, don'tcha?" I marched to the fridge. "It's just that I got stuck at school. That's why there's no milk."

Mom joined me inside, car keys jangling. "Oops, guess I overlooked something." She smiled knowingly, spying the hungry anticipation on the furry faces.

"It's not your fault, Mom," I said. "I'm the one who missed the bus, remember?"

We laughed about how spoiled the cats had become. "Thanks to their doting mama," chortled Mom.

It was true. I *had* spoiled my cats rotten. But wasn't it the sensible, loving thing to do with felines? Programming them to expect fresh, rich cow's milk every day after school was part of being a pampering pet owner. Or as Mom said, a doting mama.

"You'll have to forgive me this time," I said, pouring the raw, cream-rich milk into two medium-sized bowls. Abednego, being the oldest and fattest, had his own opinion about pecking order. He allowed only his next-in-line brother, Shadrach, to share his bowl.

I grinned and brushed my hand over their backs. "Mama's so sorry about the late snack."

Sitting there on the floor hearing the gentle lapping sounds of healthy, contented cats, I thought again of my friend Chelsea. She needed a phone call. Now.

Without another word to my furry friends, I scanned our country kitchen. Mom had evidently gone upstairs.

Quickly, I crossed the room to the phone, picked it up, and listened for the dial tone. I knew Chelsea might not be able to talk openly if her dad was within earshot, but at least she could hear me out.

"Hi, Chels," I said when she answered. "It's Merry and I've got a genius idea."

"You say that about all your ideas." She wasn't laughing.

I was smart enough to know it wasn't a compliment. "Can you talk now?" I asked.

"I'm talking, aren't I?" She sounded depressed.

"But is your dad around?"

"Daddy's still at work. Someone has to work around here."

"Yeah."

"So what is it—your genius plan?" she asked.

"Well, I've been thinking. We oughta go over your place with a fine-tooth comb. You know, search for clues."

"I thought of that, too." Her voice sounded small. "Do you wanna come over?"

"Sure."

"Tomorrow after school?"

"Okay, good. Have you heard anything more about your mom?" As soon as I voiced the words, I wished I'd kept quiet.

"No, but there was an urgent message from the bank on Dad's computer when I got home," she said. "It seems that some money is missing from my parents' joint account." Her voice was hollow.

"You're kidding?"

"Not one word to anyone, you hear?" She was silent. Then— "I can't believe Mom would do this. She'd *never* do anything like this if . . ." Chelsea stopped, and I heard her breath coming into the phone in short little puffs.

"It's okay, Chels," I said. "You can trust me."

"Oh, I don't know. I keep wondering if someone's brain-washed Mom—taken control of her somehow. Have you ever read about stuff like that?"

"Brainwashed? Why do you think that?"

Chelsea whimpered into the phone. "I have a weird feeling about that guy and his wife."

"Any idea who they are?"

She exhaled. "Maybe Dad remembers their names. I sure don't."

"Why don't you ask him when he gets home?" It was just a suggestion. We didn't have much else to go on.

"I'll wait and see how he feels tonight."

I wanted so badly to tell her not to worry, that I was trusting God to work things out. But that was exactly the sort of talk that often disconnected Chelsea from me. So I said, "Hey, call me anytime, okay? Even in the middle of the night if you want. I'll put Skip's portable phone in my bedroom, and no one'll ever know the difference."

"Won't the ringing wake up your parents?" she asked. "If you give me the number, I could call your cell instead."

"No, the cell phone's just for calling my parents. And don't worry about bothering anyone here. Dad's working the late shift at the hospital, so he won't be home tonight, and Mom's a heavy sleeper. She'll never hear it ring."

"And you *will*?"

I chuckled. "I'll stick the phone under my pillow if that makes you feel better."

"It's a deal." Her voice was stronger. "Well, I've gotta figure out something for supper. Dad likes big meals."

I remembered that Chelsea had said they'd been eating meatless meals for the past week. "Surprise your dad and make something gourmet," I suggested.

"Yeah, right. I'll talk to you tomorrow, if not before."

"Okay. Good-bye." I hung up the phone, concerned about the latest information. The message about the bank business didn't sound good. Could someone actually be coerced to pull money out of their bank account?

When Mom came downstairs, I wanted to ask her about it, but I'd promised not to tell anyone. So I held it all in—every single heart-wrenching detail.

"When's Skip coming home?" I asked Mom.

She straightened up from putting a frozen casserole in the oven. "He should arrive by suppertime tomorrow."

"So . . . he's really homesick, huh?" I hoped Mom would give some other reason for his coming to spend the weekend. I was downright worried he might move back.

"Adjusting to college life is harder for some students than others," she explained. "I think Skip may be having a little difficulty. Sometimes I wish we'd found a Christian college for him to attend."

I reached for two dinner plates; it was going to be just Mom and me tonight. "Well, *I* sure don't want to go off to some heathen college campus."

Mom scowled. "Your brother is *not* attending a heathen college. There are several wonderful Christian organizations right there on campus. In fact, one group meets in Skip's science lab after hours. He said something about being invited to one of the meetings last week."

"Oh." That's all I said. There was no arguing with Mom.

Later that night while working through a pile of homework, I found a slip of paper wedged down in one of the pockets of my three-ring binder. I pulled it out.

A photography contest notice! How could I have over-looked this? My heart leaped up as I thought about the annual event. As a tenth-grader, I would have oodles of opportunities to display my talents at Buchanan High School, starting this year! The competition would be stiff, but I could hardly wait.

One of my passions in life was photography, followed by a close second—poetry. Especially romantic sonnets. Not writing them but *reading* them and occasionally agonizing over them. And if I were completely open about my hobbies, I'd also admit that I loved word games—and Jon Klein included . . . probably.

Jon hadn't yet reached the level of maturity required to acknowledge such profound things as love. *Give him another year*, I figured. *Maybe then he'll start seeing me for what I am. Girlfriend material.*

The biggest roadblock was our new pastor's daughter. Ashley Horton was the kind of girl people—especially guys—noticed when she walked into a room.

Ashley wasn't beautiful only on the outside; she did have some depth of soul. She was kind to animals and never spoke out of turn in Sunday school class. Ashley wasn't a typical preacher's kid, and people knew it the first time they met her. She didn't seem interested in pushing the limits like some ministers' daughters. In other words, she wasn't wild. She was genuinely nice. A little dense, but nice.

One other thing: Ashley had developed a huge crush on Jon. Just plain couldn't keep her eyes off him. Everyone knew it. Everyone except Jon.

It started to rain. In spite of intermittent lightning flashes, I settled into working two pages of algebra, sailing right through—thanks to getting help from Dad last school year. Everything about solving unknown factors made complete sense to me now. If only there was a way to solve the unknowns in Chelsea's life.

Where *could* her mom have gone? And why?

Questions haunted me all evening. By the time I finished my homework, the phone was ringing. I scooted my desk chair back and hurried to stand in the doorway, listening.

Mom's voice floated upstairs. Ashley Horton was on the line. "Take the call in Skip's room if you'd like," she suggested.

I hurried down the hall to my brother's vacant bedroom. "Hello?" I said as I picked up the portable phone and sat on his bed.

"Hi, Merry. I was wondering about that photography contest at school. I suppose you're going to enter." It was almost a question, but not quite.

"Well, yes. I plan to."

"I thought maybe you could give me some ideas for subject matter—you know, the types of scenery or things that took first place other years."

Was this girl for real?

"Well, I suppose there are lots of things you could do," I said, trying not to patronize or give away any of my own genius ideas.

"Could you give me some examples of shots that *might* be winning photos?" she asked.

"Oh, sure . . . things like windmills and Amish settings. White dairy barns might be a good choice, or rustic tobacco sheds. Let your imagination go. But watch your lighting, depth perception, things like that. Since photos taken with digital cameras aren't allowed, you won't know what you've got until after you've developed your film."

"Oh, Merry, those are such good ideas!" she gushed. "Thank you so much."

"It was nothing." Then remembering about an important taboo, I warned, "Be careful around the Amish. They don't want to be photographed, so I wouldn't advise flaunting a camera in front of them."

"Aw, but they're so adorable in those cute long dresses and aprons. Those black felt hats the men wear . . . and their long beards."

Oh please, I thought. *I don't believe this!*

"Whatever you do, Ashley, if you care anything about the Amish people, you won't sneak shots of them."

"So you really think taking pictures of Plain people is a problem?" She sounded as if she was speaking alliteration-eze.

I wanted to make her promise not to offend the Amish that way. "Please, don't do it, Ashley. I'm serious."

That seemed to subdue her. "All right," she said. "But I guess I don't understand."

Ashley and her family had moved here last year from somewhere north of Denver, Colorado. Naturally, they wouldn't know much about Amish tradition.

I explained. "If you want to know the reason why they don't approve of having their pictures taken, read the Ten Commandments—Exodus twenty, verse four. They take the verse literally. We'll talk more tomorrow at school."

"Okay. And thanks again very much. You've been a big help."

"See ya." I hung up.

I could imagine Ashley rushing off to her father's study at their parsonage to look up the Bible verse this very instant. That was Ashley.

I hoped I'd convinced her to keep her camera lens away from the Amish. It's strange how people often want to do the very thing they're told *not* to do. Must be human nature.

Anyway, as I headed back to my own room, I decided to make a list of my top-five favorite scenes to photograph in SummerHill by tomorrow.

Tomorrow . . .

Chelsea and I would search for clues at her house tomorrow. I hoped that if there were any, they'd lead us to her mother.

And tomorrow evening Skip was coming home.

I hurried downstairs to gather up my brood of cats for the night. Skip despised my pets. "Maybe if they weren't ordinary alley cats, I'd feel differently," he'd told me once.

But I knew better. The real reason he resented my precious, purry critters was his snobbish mentality. Skip wished I'd be more selective about my pets. Stray cats—stray anything—disgusted him. For a person studying to become a medical doctor, his nose-in-the-air approach to life didn't fit. Not in my opinion.

Downstairs, I picked up Lily White and cuddled her as I opened the back door. "Come to beddy-bye, little boys," I called out into the night.

Shadrach and Meshach came running. They were only slightly damp because they'd been hiding in their favorite place— under the gazebo. Abednego, true to form, was missing.

"Where's your big brother?" I asked them.

Meow.

"Well, wherever he is, we can't wait up for him." I headed for the back stairway, hoping Abednego wouldn't come inside all muddy. That wouldn't set well with Mom.

After a warm bath, I snuggled into bed with my Bible and teen devotional. I slid the cordless phone under my pillow as promised. Just in case Chelsea called.

Abednego, surprisingly clean, decided to grace us with his presence at last. He took his sweet time getting situated on top of my comforter. Now all four of my cats were safe and snug.

I reread the selection for the day, thinking about the poem that accompanied the devotional prayer. Feeling drowsy, I turned out the light. "Sweet dreams," I whispered into the darkness as the sounds of soft purring mingled with the gentle *tinkle-pat-pat* of rain on the roof.

In the stillness, I prayed—first for Chelsea, then for her mother. "And, Lord," I added a short PS, "will you please help us find something tomorrow that'll point us in the right direction? I'm trusting you. Amen."

To say that I was trusting my heavenly Father was all well and good. Now I had to hang on to those words and live by them. For Chelsea's sake. And mine.

House of Secrets **Five**

The halls of Buchanan High were clogged with students, some trying to get to lockers, others milling around.

Jon Klein seemed unruffled, however, his arms loaded with textbooks and binders for his morning classes. In fact, he appeared to be rejoicing at having sneaked up on me. "What's the weird word, Merry?" he babbled.

I chuckled. "Isn't it 'what's the *good* word'?"

"Good won't work with *w* words," he replied, alliterating almost without thinking. That's how it seemed, anyway.

I looked up at him, trying to secure a soon-to-be avalanche of books in my locker. "You know something? I think you're getting too good at this word game of ours."

"Here, help's on high." He reached over my head and grabbed my precarious pile of books off the top shelf with his free hand. "Being barraged by books is . . ." He paused, searching for a *b* word.

"Bad," I said, filling in the blank.

"Boom!"

"Bane," I shot back.

"Barely believable."

The Alliteration Wizard had won again. Or had he? I felt a surge of words coming.

"Being barraged by books is basically a bumpy battle." A triumph for me!

Jon's brown eyes blinked in surprise. "But . . . but . . . bested I be."

"Yes—I won!"

He grinned and nodded. "Not bad for a gir—" He stopped.

"Don't you dare say it!"

"Okay, you win. *This* time."

After I reorganized my books, I grabbed a notebook and was ready for the first bell.

"See ya later," he called, catching up with some guys heading for his homeroom.

" 'Bye." I walked alone to mine, wondering where Chelsea was hiding out. I stopped by her locker and noticed Belita Sanchez, the girl whose locker was next to my friend's. "Have you seen Chelsea today?"

"Maybe she's running late," Belita commented.

"Well, if you see her, please tell Chelsea I'm looking for her. Okay?"

"That's cool." Belita started to turn away, and then she reached out to touch my arm. "Merry, is something wrong with Chelsea?" Her dark eyes searched mine.

"What do you mean?"

"Oh, she seemed tense and really stressed yesterday."

I didn't want to lie. "Chelsea's . . . uh, she's . . ."

Belita raised one eyebrow in a quizzical slant, waiting for my faltering response.

Then—"Hey, Merry!" came a familiar voice.

I turned to see our auburn-haired friend dashing down the hall toward us. Breathing a sigh, I was more than glad to see her. "Oh, good, you're here."

"Dad drove me," she said, indicating with her sea-green eyes that something was up.

"Hi, Belita. How's it going?" she said as I hung around. The girls exchanged small talk, then Chelsea and I hurried off to homeroom as the first bell rang.

"You look exhausted," I said. "Did you sleep at all?"

"Not much." Her eyes lacked their usual brightness.

I felt sick with concern. Chelsea seemed even more depressed than yesterday. "More bad news?" I asked.

"Uh-huh. But I can't talk about it until we're absolutely alone."

I followed her into our homeroom, where Mrs. Fields, who was also our English teacher, greeted us. "Morning, girls." She stood up as we skittered to our desks. "Several of you have been asking about the photography contest."

I leaned forward, listening intently.

Chelsea whispered to me, "You look too eager."

Our mutual friend, Lissa Vyner, two desks away, turned around. "I heard that," she mouthed, curling her fingers in a delicate wave.

I waved back as the teacher continued. "This contest is one of the most important extracurricular events of the year here at Buchanan High. The judging is strict, and the photography exhibit is always very professional. Last year two students tied for first place initially, but the panel of judges agreed to go back to the table and choose a definite winner."

Amazing! I wondered who'd ended up with the coveted trophy. Quickly, I made a mental note to ask Mrs. Fields after class. I *had* to know.

"For interested students," she continued, "the forms, as well as additional information, will be here on my desk. You may pick them up before leaving for first-period class."

Lissa raised her hand. "What's the deadline for the contest?"

Mrs. Fields glanced at the information sheet. "Here we are. The deadline for all applicants is November fourth." She looked at the wall calendar. "Exactly one month from today."

I wrote the date on my assignment tablet with the words: *Remember to do something truly amazing!*

Mrs. Fields took roll, and then the principal's voice came over the intercom. "Good morning, students. Today is Friday, October fourth. We will have schedule A today. Faculty and students, please make a note of this."

I folded my arms and tuned him out. Why did Mr. Eastman recite the same boring things *every* morning? I'm not sure why the monotony of it bothered me so much. Maybe because we were now in high school. Wouldn't it make better sense to encourage students to figure out what the day's schedule was on their own? Thinking for yourself was part of growing up.

"And now . . . our national anthem," the intercom boomed.

I stood up, joining the other students. The taped rendition warbled in places, and I wondered if it was wearing out—like Mr. Eastman.

My mom had shown me his yearbook picture from twenty-two years earlier when *she* was in high school. I thought he looked almost elderly back then.

"Mr. Eastman always had a heart for kids," Mom told me when I'd first asked about him. "Times have changed, and he probably should retire. But it's a free country, and the dear old fellow's hanging in there."

"Barely," I said. "You should hear what he does every morning for opening exercises—at least that's what he calls it."

I told her.

Mom smiled in recognition. "That's precisely how he always started the day. Just be thankful he doesn't personally sing 'The Star-Spangled Banner' anymore."

I gasped. "Are you serious?"

"Mr. Eastman warbled it every morning all through my high school years." Mom burst out laughing. "Except when he was ill. Then the secretary would invite the whole school to sing in unison."

"That's incredible. What was his voice like?"

"Oh, your average Joe's—nothing special."

"So it wasn't too obnoxious?" I asked.

"Not really. I think it was simply the idea of having the principal croon the national anthem on the PA system."

"The what?"

"The public address system," she explained.

"Oh yeah—back in the *olden* days." I smiled. So did Mom. She was a good sport.

Hearing Mom talk about her high school days and Mr. Eastman made me curious about other things. The age of our school building, for instance. James Buchanan High was a picture postcard building of dark red brick—two stories high—partly covered with ivy. The exterior windows jutted out with white sash bars below. Inside, there were hinged transom windows that actually opened high above each classroom door.

The vine-covered brick structure smelled old, almost musty on rainy days when the windows had to be kept closed. I could see why Mom loved the place. She adored antiques, old buildings included. It was one of the reasons we lived in a drafty hundred-plus-year-old farmhouse. One of the reasons why Mom had furnished our house with beautiful, gleaming heirlooms. Even *my* room, where a massive antique white-pine desk graced one entire wall.

The bell for first period jolted me out of my musing. I hurried to Mrs. Fields's desk and stood in line behind Lissa and two other girls waiting for the information sheets and application forms for the photography contest.

On the way toward the door, I asked Mrs. Fields about last year's winner.

"Oh yes," she said. "It was really quite something. The winner turned out to be Mr. Eastman's grandnephew."

"Really? I don't think I know him. Did he graduate last year?" I moved aside to let students pass.

"Why, no, I believe Randall's a senior this year."

Randall Eastman. The name didn't click. Yet I was mighty curious.

"Well, thanks," I said. "I'd really like to meet him."

"He's not much into athletics," Mrs. Fields said. "You can usually find him in the library, in the reference section."

"Okay, thanks." I hurried to catch up with Chelsea and Lissa.

Later, in algebra, Ashley Horton passed me a note.

Hi, Merry,

I read the fourth commandment last night—the one about not making any graven image. I really want to thank you for pointing this out to me. You can be sure I WON'T be taking pictures of any Amish people.

—A.H.

I smiled at her across a row of desks, feeling a bit relieved. One less thing to worry about.

Leaning back in my seat, I listened as the teacher introduced the next chapter and took good notes so I'd understand how to do the algebra problems at home. I glanced over at Chelsea. Her eyes were glazed over, and she seemed to be staring into midair.

Oh, Chelsea . . . Chelsea. What horrible things have happened since yesterday? I wondered.

The blood had drained from her face. Even as fair-skinned as she was, it seemed she'd turned a chalky white.

Without warning, she keeled over. Fainted right on the spot!

My heart pounded ninety miles an hour as I leaped out of my seat.

Kids gasped as Chelsea's limp body slipped off her chair and onto the floor. The teacher asked one of the girls to get the school nurse.

I made a beeline to my friend, knelt down, and checked her breathing and pulse. Reaching for some paper off Chelsea's desk, I began to fan her, pushing the thick covering of hair away from her face. *Dear Lord, please help!*

The nurse arrived almost immediately. I moved back to make room, watching as she placed her hand gently behind Chelsea's neck. She opened a small bottle of spirits of ammonia and waved it under Chelsea's nose.

The harsh, irritating odor did the trick. Chelsea wrinkled her nose, her eyes fluttered, and she sat up.

The smell took my breath away.

"Whoa, smells like week-old underwear," one of the boys said, scrunching up his face.

"Worse!" remarked another, holding his nose.

Guys, I thought. *Will they ever grow up?*

Chelsea sat up and looked around, blinking her long lashes.

"Let's see if you can get up, hon," the nurse said. She and I helped Chelsea stand up. Everyone else went back to their desks, the excitement over.

Chelsea leaned on both the nurse and me as we assisted her out of the room and down the hall.

"You okay?" I asked as we headed toward the nurse's office.

"I don't know what happened," she mumbled. "One minute I was sitting in my seat listening to the algebra assignment, and the next, I was on the floor."

"It's called fainting," I said, hoping to humor her. She still looked ghastly pale.

The nurse's room was a square cubicle where a cot and chair took up most of the space on one wall. A small desk and a second chair filled the opposite side of the room.

Kindly, the nurse got Chelsea settled into the chair.

"Now"—she surveyed my friend—"tell me about breakfast. Did you have any?"

Chelsea shook her head.

"Your first mistake." The nurse gave a nervous chuckle.

I could see Chelsea wasn't interested in an interrogation. She stared into space almost defiantly.

"Are you having your period?" the nurse inquired.

"Not quite yet," Chelsea answered.

"Well, you're certainly welcome to lie down and rest here until you feel stronger. Or," she said, glancing at me briefly, "would you rather call your parents?"

I cringed inwardly. The fainting episode was probably due to the fact that *both* of her parents weren't around. Stress can do weird things.

Chelsea looked at me with pleading eyes. I shook my head to let her know I wouldn't break my promise. The nurse didn't need to know that her mom was missing. Not now. Maybe not ever.

Chelsea opted to stay at school. At lunchtime, I encouraged her to eat even though she said she wasn't hungry. "You don't wanna go falling off any more chairs, do you?"

"I know, I know," she said as we found a table in the cafeteria.

Ashley and Lissa came over and joined us. "How are you feeling?" Ashley inquired. "Did you hit your head?"

"I don't think so." Chelsea felt the back of her head. "Guess I was just so relaxed, I slithered to the floor like a rag doll."

Lissa nodded. "You sure looked like one. I felt so sorry for you. Are you sure you're okay?"

Chelsea muttered something about still not feeling well.

"You look awfully white," Ashley pointed out.

I spoke up, eager to put an end to this worrisome talk. "After a person faints, it takes a while to recuperate." I asked for the ketchup. But Ashley and Lissa kept fussing over Chelsea. Finally, I blurted out, "Does anyone know who Randall Eastman is?"

"Who?" Lissa said.

"Randall Eastman," I repeated. "I heard he's the principal's grandnephew—the student who won first place in the photography contest last year."

Ashley sat up a bit straighter. "*I'd* be interested in meeting him, too. In fact, I'd like to see his award-winning photograph. Do you think maybe we could?"

We?

I sputtered. "Well . . . I don't know. I guess one of us has to track him down first." I felt foolish in spite of the obvious competitive undertow. "Mrs. Fields says he's a senior this year. Anyone know any upperclassmen?"

"Not really," Lissa said. "Maybe some of the guys in the youth group might know him."

Ashley's eyes lit up. "Oh, what a wonderful idea! That's easy enough. We can ask around on Sunday."

"What about asking Nikki Klein?" Chelsea suggested. "Nikki's a senior this year, I think."

"Hey, your brother oughta know," Lissa said. "Skip took Nikki out several times last school year."

I sighed. "Skip's coming home for the weekend. Maybe I'll ask *him* about Randall Eastman." I turned to look at Chelsea. The color was returning to her cheeks. "Hey, you're starting to look—and sound—more like yourself."

She didn't exactly smile at my observation but tilted her head modestly my way. "After school I think I'm going to go home and take a long nap."

I wondered about that. "Do you still want me to come over?"

"Sure, why not?"

I couldn't discuss or rehash our sleuthing plans in front of Ashley and Lissa. Still, I wondered if Chelsea was backing out, maybe getting cold feet about gathering clues to find her mom.

Fortunately, I didn't have to wonder long. When Ashley and Lissa finished eating, they excused themselves. At last, Chelsea and I were alone.

"Is it safe to talk now?" I glanced around.

She leaned close, whispering, "I found something in my parents' bedroom this morning."

I was all ears. "Something important?"

"My mom's diary," she said. "I'll show you when you come over."

"That's terrific! Any leads?"

She kept her voice low. "It's hard to say. There's so much repetitious writing in it."

"What do you mean?"

She explained. "The same sentences are written over and over."

"Like what?"

"Things like, *I will turn off my mind and let things float.*"

"Uh-oh." My heart sank.

"What?" Chelsea frowned. "What do you think it means?"

"I really can't be sure, but it sounds almost hypnotic."

"Really?" Chelsea was wide-eyed. "Why would my mom want to hypnotize herself? That's stupid."

"How many times did she write it?"

"Over a hundred, I think."

I shook my head. This was truly frightening. "What about your dad? Does he know what you found?"

"Dad had to leave early this morning to get to the bank. He's frantic about the missing money. I hated to ask him anything about that strange couple that kept inviting Mom to go places."

"I understand." I sighed as helpless feelings swept over me. "So you must've been snooping around this morning?"

Chelsea nodded. "*That's* why I didn't have time to eat breakfast. I was upstairs in my parents' bedroom, turning the place upside down. I found the diary between the mattresses on Mom's side of the bed." Her eyes glistened. "None of this makes any sense. I'm scared to death."

I wished I could tell her I was trusting God for her, that I was praying, but "Everything's going to be all right" was the only thing I managed to say.

She pushed her long, thick locks off her shoulder. "I sure hope you're right."

I gathered up my trash and stuffed it into my empty cup. "We can't give up. We're just getting started, you know."

She slid her chair back and stood up with her tray. "I know, Mer. Thanks for being there for me."

"Any time."

Together we headed for the kitchen and deposited our trays. Even though Chelsea appeared to be feeling better physically, I knew deep inside she was carrying a sorrowful burden.

I sighed, praying and hoping and counting on God to take away her burden—and to bring Chelsea's mom back home. The sooner, the better!

After school, the long yellow bus automatically stopped near the willow grove on SummerHill Lane.

I called to Mr. Tom, the driver, that I wasn't getting off. "I'm going over to Chelsea's today."

He waved his hand. "No problem!"

When we arrived at the Davises, I spotted a car in the driveway. "Hey, look! Someone's home."

Chelsea groaned. "It's my dad's car. This can't be good news—he's home way too early."

We made our way down the narrow aisle toward the front. The bus door screeched opened and we got off.

"Why do you think your dad's home so early?" I asked as we moved toward the bricked walkway.

Chelsea didn't speak. Her eyes scanned the front of the house.

"I hope it's not about . . ." I didn't finish. No need to heap worry on top of whatever else was flitting through her mind.

"C'mon, Mer." She pulled me around to the side of the house where a massive white ash tree stood sentinel. "We're not going inside yet. I have an idea."

For a second, I grinned. Chelsea was starting to sound like me. "What's up?" I asked.

She pointed to a slight clearing in the woods behind their house. "Remember the old hut back there? The one that nearly scared us silly when we were kids?"

I strained to see past the thick underbrush, but I knew very well what she was talking about. My childhood memories of the ancient place were clear enough. "What about it?" I said, trying to hide my apprehension.

"Something in Mom's diary makes me think that maybe, just maybe, we might find something important back there in the woods."

"Something important? Like what?" A creepy shiver crept down my spine.

Chelsea turned, heading toward the arbor gate. "Are you coming or not?" Her eyes dared me.

"Look, if we're gonna do some real sleuthing, I oughta have my camera, don't you think?" The thought had literally popped into my head—a clever way to postpone the inevitable moment, perhaps. I kept talking. "That way if we *do* discover something, we'll have proof to show the police or a private investigator."

Chelsea stared at me like I was wacko. "Who said anything about cops? And a private eye—hey, they cost big bucks. Right now, according to my dad, we're broke."

I refused to back down. I wanted a camera—now. "Still, I think it would be smart to take pictures."

We stood under the giant ash, its purple leaves covering us, having our first major standoff. After a few more desperate pleas, Chelsea came to her senses. Maybe she realized I wasn't going to budge. Best of all, she didn't appear to have sensed my uneasiness.

"Why don't you ride my bike down to your house?" she offered, going around to the overhang under the back porch. Her bike was in perfect shape, as though she never, ever rode it.

"You sure?" I asked, noting the fancy leather seat and other expensive touches.

"Go ahead." She parked her books on the patio table nearby before helping secure my schoolbag on the bike.

"Thanks. I'll be back in a jiffy," I called to her as I pushed off and headed for the driveway.

The distance to my house was all downhill. Coming back, I'd have to pedal hard to make it.

Mom was cooking something wonderful when I dashed into the house and through the kitchen. "Mm-m, smells great!" I said. "Special dinner for Skip?"

"He should be home soon," she called up the back steps. "What's your hurry?"

"I came home to get my camera," I said. "Never know when I'll stumble onto a glorious shot."

Mom didn't respond. Either she hadn't heard, or she was already lost in her culinary dreams and schemes. Skip was her one and only son. Naturally, she'd want to knock herself out to make his first homecoming extra-special.

Upstairs, I deposited my schoolbag on the bed. Then I filled my camera pouch with film and both my 35-millimeter camera and the smaller digital one. I wanted to be fully prepared. No stones left unturned and all that detective-sounding stuff.

Mom's eyebrows arched when I rushed through the kitchen again, telling her I'd see her later. "Chelsea's expecting me back at her house. We're doing some investigating, I guess you could say."

"Nothing too serious, I hope."

She had me. "Well, maybe. But I won't be long. 'Bye!"

Mom called after me, "Be careful."

"I will," I shouted back. "I promise."

"And be back in time for supper!"

"Okay, Mom."

I made a run for it on the steep hill, but eventually slowed to a steady pumping. My latest mystery—*our* latest mystery—

could possibly be wrapped up and solved in one afternoon. That is if Chelsea and I were brave enough to go where the solid leads might be lurking.

I should've been jumping for joy about the prospect of finding Chelsea's mom, but something about the mission made my mouth go dry. It was the old shack. The eerie place out there on the edge of the dark forest.

I licked my lips as I pedaled for all I was worth. If only we didn't have to deal with the mysterious woods and that hut.

The feverish dryness in my mouth persisted even after I arrived back at Chelsea's house and gulped down a full glass of water in her kitchen.

I gazed through the window at the trees beyond the rickety wooden arbor gate. In the foreground, the arbor was cloaked in rambling grapevines now brittle and brown.

The gateway beckoned.

Goose prickles popped out on the back of my neck. I poured more water and drank. The cool water helped—but only for a moment.

Looking out through the kitchen window, I surveyed the fairy-tale entrance to the dark, foreboding forest. The arbor gate seemed to summon me. White stepping-stones, bordered on both sides by a stone foundation wall, scattered away from the arbor, creating a mysterious pathway.

I shivered, thankful for daylight.

Chelsea noticed. "Are you afraid?"

In all the years Chelsea and I had known each other, neither of us had ever set foot in the vine-covered shack. The first time I'd ever gotten close enough to investigate, I'd promptly decided it was too far back in the woods for a kid's hideaway. Too far from the safety of the house.

Chelsea, being a timid sort of girl back then, had wholeheartedly agreed.

Better to use it for storing tools and the lawn mower, I'd thought at the time. But the place hadn't been used that way. As far as I knew, the vine-tangled shanty had stood empty all these years.

"So . . . are you afraid?" Chelsea repeated, eyeing my camera bag.

I stood tall, ignoring the question. "Ready?"

"I've got the diary." She held it against her chest. "Now, if I can just find the right page." She glanced toward the living room. "Dad's in there making phone calls, so we'll have to keep our voices down."

"Does he know I'm here?" I leaned around the fridge to peek at him.

"Not really. But if we're quiet . . ." Her voice trailed off, and I struggled to push away creepy thoughts.

Chelsea held the diary open. "Right here." She pointed to a four-line passage that looked like poetry. "I'm pretty sure my mom is referring to the hut out back." She pushed the diary into my hands. "Read it for yourself."

Carefully, I studied the cryptic words.

Approach a labyrinth of snarls and tendrils,
Follow the white-stone way.
Spirit-dew, rain on they who here reflect.
House of secrets bids you stay.

"It's a poem—it rhymes." My lips quivered. "When did your mom start writing poetry?"

"Beats me. Mom's never written any before, at least not that I know of."

Her answer concerned me even more. "Chelsea"—I turned to her, pressing the diary pages shut—"what on earth *is* this writing? These words . . . that spooky stuff . . . it doesn't feel right to me. I think it might be coming from an evil influence."

She pouted. "You're only saying that so we won't have to go out there and look around."

The tension, the urgency of the situation, made me forget about her dad. "No!" I shouted. "No, that's not it."

"Sh-h! Merry!"

Suddenly, I heard footsteps. "What's all the noise?" Mr. Davis came through the doorway to the kitchen. "Hey, you two having a party without me?" He smiled casually.

"Oh, sorry, Daddy," Chelsea said.

I kept the diary hidden behind my back. "Hello, Mr. Davis. I didn't mean to be so loud."

He ran a hand through his thick graying hair, grunted something, and left the kitchen.

Chelsea motioned me outside on the back porch. "Dad'll probably want to eat supper soon, so we'd better get started. That is, if you're ready."

I nearly choked. Truthfully, I was glad for the momentary encounter with her dad. Anything to take the edge off what I'd been feeling.

The word *occult* drifted through my thoughts, and although I didn't plan on telling Chelsea about it, I knew I'd have to pray extra-hard tonight. If her mother's mind was being controlled by someone or something outside herself, we were in big trouble—in way over our heads.

Then unexpectedly—like the swift flutter of wings—a Scripture verse I'd learned as a little girl came to me. *For he will command his angels concerning you to guard you in all your ways . . .*

Over and over, the verse echoed in my mind.

He will command his angels . . . to guard you. His angels will guard you. . . . Angels . . .

Adjusting my camera case straps, I moved forward. I glanced around me, wondering, *Are they here? Are God's angels with us now?*

Chelsea followed close behind me, clutching her mother's diary. Together we passed beneath the tall, rectangular arbor gate to get to the white stone pathway.

They will lift you up in their hands, so that you will not strike your foot against a stone.

I looked down at the stony passage leading us to the dark woods, then ahead to the deserted shanty. God had promised to send His angels. They were here.

I wish I weren't, I thought.

Closer, closer we came to the edge of the forest. Dense and foreboding, it loomed ahead like a giant monster waiting to devour us. The sinister-looking hovel came into view as we entered the black woodland, leaving the light of day behind us.

Chelsea's face muscles twitched nervously. "Let's stay together, okay?"

"I'm here" was all I could say. My throat was so dry I could hardly swallow.

Suddenly, she stopped. "Listen!" Her hand trembled—the one holding her mom's diary.

"What is it?" I whispered. "What do you hear?"

Chelsea inched forward. "That sound. . . . What's that weird sound?"

I strained to hear, my knees quaking. "I don't hear anything."

Chelsea turned to me. "Didn't you hear that?"

I listened. Then in the distance, I heard the *snap-a-crack* of a dry twig. I wanted to drop to my knees. "I don't know about you, but I'm going to pray."

"Right here?" Her eyes bugged out.

I nodded.

"But—"

"I'm not going to ask if you mind," I interrupted. "You say you don't believe in God, but I know He's here with us. I also know He wants to help your mom."

She didn't argue this time. I bowed my head and folded my hands with Chelsea's hand stuck between mine. "Lord, we don't know what we're going to find inside this spooky place, but you do. Please keep us safe. And thanks for your angels, who protect us. Amen."

Chelsea didn't say a word about the prayer—or the angels. In fact, she was trying to act real cool. But I knew the prayer had touched her. Her eyes were brimming with tears.

Quickly, she turned away. "Okay, let's go," she said.

Help us to do the right thing, Lord, I prayed silently as we moved forward, taking one white stepping-stone at a time.

Hesitantly, I reached through the vines to unlatch the narrow door. Chelsea held back the thick branches, hands trembling.

"Anyone home?" I called.

We listened.

Nothing except the whispery sound of wind high in the trees.

"We're coming in!" I shouted, feeling more confident at the sound of my voice. With a shove, I opened the door.

There, piled up on the wood floor, were candles—some half burned—two black-and-gold incense containers, and several empty wine bottles.

"What on earth?" I muttered.

Chelsea sniffed the air. "Hey! That's my mom's favorite incense." She picked up one of the round incense holders and held it to her nose. "Weird," she whispered, almost to herself. "I wonder if she's been coming here to meditate."

"Your mom meditates?"

Chelsea was quick to set me straight. "It's *not* what you think, Merry," she said. "My mom's been interested in getting in touch with her inner consciousness for a long time. She likes to spend time concentrating and stuff like that, usually in a quiet place."

"We won't know more unless we keep searching." I spied a long black box high atop a potting shelf in the corner. "Look up there," I said, pointing. "What's in that box?"

"Let's check it out."

I dragged a chair under the shelf. Reaching up, I encountered a thick spider web. "Yee-ikes! There are cobwebs all over this place."

Chelsea steadied the rickety chair as she stared up at me. I jumped down, holding the black box, and opened the lid. Inside, we discovered a strange array of items. More candles—mostly black ones—and matches, incense, and several large, black square cloths. And a book with a frightening title: *Taking the Oath*.

A sickening wave of terror welled up in me. "Oh, Chelsea, I think your mom's hooked up with something truly dangerous!"

"Why?" She picked up the book and flipped through the pages. "Because of this?"

The hair on the back of my neck prickled, and I wanted to run. Anything to escape the oppressive sensation that seemed to hover around us.

I noticed some strange markings on the inside of the box but said nothing. By the looks of things, Chelsea's mom had been using the abandoned shack as a hideaway—a place to practice her occult exercises in privacy.

Quickly, I replaced the lid on the box and returned it to its original place, deliberately avoiding annoying spider webs.

Leaping down off the chair, I glanced around at the inside of the hut—about the size of a large bedroom. Fighting off nightmarish feelings, I aimed my digital camera, taking several shots of the bizarre surroundings before closing the door and latching it.

"Is this building on your property?" I asked as we hurried away.

"It's been here as long as we have," Chelsea replied, "so it must be."

"You're sure it's not on your neighbor's land?"

"Positive."

I wanted to make sure we weren't trespassing. There was a strong possibility I'd want to return.

"Let me see that poem your mom wrote again," I said.

Chelsea handed the diary to me, and I thumbed through the pages till I found the peculiar poem.

> *Approach a labyrinth of snarls and tendrils,*
> *Follow the white-stone way.*
> *Spirit-dew, rain on they who here reflect.*
> *House of secrets bids you stay.*

I stared at the diary entry. "That's it! The hut has to be the house of secrets," I blurted. "Look, Chels, it's right here." I pointed to the page.

She stopped cold, and I reread the words to her.

"Do you think . . . ? Could it be?" Her voice became hysterical. "Do you think my mom's lost her mind or something?"

"I hope not." What else could I say? The signs pointed to . . . what? I didn't know. But whatever was in that place and in that black box surely wasn't meant for the praise and worship of God.

We quickened our pace, not looking back. I stuffed the diary into my back pocket.

Chelsea's wheezy breathing worried me as our feet flew over the white stones, through the opening in the arbor gate, and back to the safety of her yard.

"Whew." She collapsed on one of the patio chairs on the back porch. "I can see why we avoided that wretched place as kids." She was totally freaked.

"I'll get you something to drink," I offered, heading for the kitchen door.

Chelsea looked too pale to get up. "I'll be right there."

"Just take it easy," I called over my shoulder.

Inside, I let the water run so it would be cool without ice. Sometimes Chelsea had asthma flare-ups, and I knew better than to give her ice water. I wandered over to the cupboard, searching for a clean glass, when I heard startling words coming from the living room.

"What do you mean, you're not coming home?" Mr. Davis was saying.

I held my breath, listening as I hugged the doorframe.

"Where are you now? Where is our money?"

A long pause.

"But that money belonged to me, too," he insisted. "We had plans for that account, you and I—we . . ."

My heart ached for Chelsea's dad. Evidently, Mrs. Davis was on the line. Would she tell him where she was? Why she'd left?

"Please come home, Berta Jean. This is craziness, every last bit of it. Those people, they're nuts and you know it. Why, those crazy mixed-up notions about making the world a better place—and that hocus-pocus nonsense, c'mon!"

Silence again.

Then—"But how can you up and leave Chelsea and me for a bunch of crackpots?" Mr. Davis was weeping now.

Another long pause.

His voice came softly. "I love you, Berta, don't you see? I want you here, to live with our daughter and me. . . ."

I backed into the kitchen, hurrying to turn off the water. Once again, I felt helpless and frightened for my friend and her father. The pleading continued, but I stood in the kitchen wrapping my arms around myself—trying desperately to block out the frantic words.

"What's that?" Mr. Davis howled. "Me, come and join that weird bunch? Why, Berta Jean, that's ridiculous. I wouldn't think of leaving my life behind for that oath-taking baloney. How can *you*?"

I fought back tears and hurried outdoors with the glass of water. By the time Chelsea was ready to come indoors, the phone conversation had come to an abrupt end. It wasn't up to me to fill her in. I shouldn't have heard any of it in the first place.

"You okay?" I asked, watching my friend closely.

She steadied herself against the kitchen counter. "I'm so mad I can hardly stand up," she admitted. "All the weird stuff. Mom's totally flipped—hiding out in that shed, so close to our house."

"It's not *that* close." I glanced out the window. "You can hardly see it from here."

She came over and stood beside me, still wheezing slightly. "I guess you're right, but . . ." She stared out the window, wearing a troubled look. "You don't think . . . my mom's not living out there, is she?"

"There's no evidence of a bed or anything." I thought about the phone conversation I'd partially overheard. "No, Chelsea, I don't think your mom's staying there."

"I sure hope not," she whispered, forcing her gaze away from the window.

I gave her a quick hug good-bye. "I think it's time you talked to your dad, though. Just the two of you."

Her father came into the kitchen looking dejected, and Chelsea rushed over, crying. They scarcely noticed as I slipped out the back door.

The sun was slipping fast over the horizon as I ran down the dirt lane toward home. I held on to my camera case, keeping it from flopping.

Lights twinkled in the downstairs windows of my house just ahead. How I welcomed their golden glow!

At the intersection of Strawberry Lane and SummerHill, I ran across the street, then darted up the long, sloping lawn, past the grand white gazebo centered in our backyard, and onto the back steps. For once I didn't check to see if any of my feline friends still lingered outdoors.

It wasn't until I was washing my hands for supper that I realized I hadn't returned the diary. The hard, fat lump protruded out of my back pocket.

Chelsea's mom had been writing bizarre things in her daily entries, that was true. I could only hope that by snooping a little, perhaps I'd find additional clues.

Where *was* Chelsea's mom?

Supper by candlelight meant one of two things at our house: Either we were entertaining company, or it was a holiday.

Mom had a funny way of connecting with holidays—even the insignificant ones. They were her excuse to show off culinary skills, not to mention her fine hostess abilities.

But a linen-and-lace tablecloth and napkins on the first Friday in October by no means represented a holiday, significant or otherwise.

Still, it *was* a special event—Skip's first weekend home since we'd bid him farewell on that sweltering day in August.

"How's college treating you?" Dad asked, slapping Skip's shoulder playfully as the two of them wandered into the dining room.

"I like it just fine," Skip said, his face shiny and hair still damp from his shower. Mom always liked it when we freshened up before mealtime. Besides, Skip probably needed freshening up—he'd driven many miles in order to put his feet under her table.

We sat opposite each other, Skip and I. Dad's easygoing grin stretched from ear to ear as he settled into his usual spot at the head of the table. Mom sat at the far end across from Dad, nearest the kitchen. Dad prayed, thanking the Lord for

Skip's safe return, then the food was passed. Prime rib, mashed potatoes and gravy, dried-corn casserole, sweet baby peas, homemade biscuits and butter—the works. Once again, Mom had knocked herself out for us. For Skip, really.

Halfway through supper, I asked Skip if he knew who Randall Eastman was. "Supposedly he won first place in the photography contest last year."

Skip glanced at the ceiling, thinking. "Oh yeah, I remember hearing something about that. Isn't he the principal's nephew or something?"

"Something like that." I couldn't believe he hadn't paid attention to last year's contest. Having a sister who was a photography fanatic ought to have tuned him in at least a little. "So do you know him?" I persisted.

"Barely." He pulled on his open shirt collar. "Seems to me the guy's a loner. A little nerdy, too."

"That figures," I sneered. "Most artists are misunderstood."

He shot back, "Well, you oughta know." Skip was taunting me. I wished he'd stayed at college.

Mom leaned forward, reaching for my hand. "Oh, honey, that's not how we think of *you*." She'd always been quick to qualify off-the-wall statements by her firstborn. Especially those directed at me. Or Faithie. Except that my twin sister hadn't lived long enough to experience the unrelenting nature of our big brother's flapping tongue. I was almost positive if Faithie were alive today, she would be even less tolerant of Skip's constant condemnation.

"You just have to have someone to pick on," I muttered.

Mom eyeballed me. "Your brother's been home less than an hour, and here you are—"

"Hon," Dad intervened as usual. "It's okay. We're all a little tense from the long week. The kids, too."

"Yeah," Skip said, hopping on Dad's bandwagon. "Let's cool it, okay?"

I wanted to bop him good. How was it that he could get by with derogatory comments? This was firstborn ballyhoo at its best!

Mom and I cleared the table, letting the men in the family sit around and twiddle their thumbs. The way I saw it, if Dad truly had a say in serious table etiquette, he would've been up helping us by now. He didn't strike me as the kind of guy who insisted on being served by females. Never had.

But Skip? My brother simply adored being waited on. Hand, foot, *and* mouth. I, despising the submissive younger-sister role, had made a point of sidestepping the issue as much as possible. With him at least.

The festive dinner tapers had burned down about an inch when Mom and I brought in her cream cake. Made with sweet milk from the Zooks' dairy, the dessert was unbelievably rich. The cream filling alone was outrageous. Dad's cousin Hazel had once called the sumptuous dessert sinful due to its extravagant, fattening ingredients.

"Well," Dad said, eyes shining in anticipation, "shall we ask the blessing once again?"

Mom giggled like a schoolgirl. "You may, if you like."

"Oh, Dad, please," I groaned.

Skip joined Dad in rubbing his stomach and, in general, hammed it up.

Dad was on his second cup of coffee when Skip started telling about some of the extracurricular activities on campus. "You name it, we've got it," he said with pride. "Several Bible study groups meet after hours. One in particular is kinda cool."

Dad's cup clinked as he placed it back on the saucer. "Let's hear about it, son."

I knew I'd be required to stay put and listen, even though Skip's idea of captivating conversation was about as interesting as a car mechanics manual.

After another ten minutes of college talk, I excused myself. "I'll start loading the dishwasher."

Mom nodded silently.

Unfortunately, I could still hear Skip's voice even as I made the usual kitchen clean-up noises. I drew the hot water for the silverware. Never in a million years would Mom allow the dishwasher to clean her good stuff. So I washed the flatware by hand, beginning with the spoons.

Dad's comments floated into the kitchen. "Sounds like a simple case of first-semester blues," he was telling Skip. "You'll survive it, son. Give it a few more months."

Without help from Mom, I finished off the work in the kitchen, even the pots and pans. I was on my way upstairs, heading to my room to tackle homework, when I thought of Chelsea. I said a prayer for her and her family and then worked on history questions until I got stuck. Quickly, I went back downstairs to ask Dad about it.

In fifteen minutes, I had my answer and was scurrying to my room when I nearly collided with my brother. He was coming down the hall, waving his portable phone. "Was my little Merry hiding the phone?" he taunted.

I lunged at him. "Were you in my room? You know better! And don't call me your little Merry!"

Playfully, he pushed me away. "Hey, relax, cat breath." He shoved the phone into his back pocket. "Don't freak out."

"Stay out of my room, you hear?" I shouted, turning on my heel and slamming my bedroom door.

Mom came up in a few minutes, inquiring about the racket. "I want the two of you to stay away from each other," she said as we stood in the hallway.

I glanced at Skip. "For the whole weekend?" I hoped she meant it.

"We'll have to wait and see." Before she said more, Skip, sporting a smirk, disappeared into his room. "Now, Merry," Mom continued, "your brother's home for a reason. He's tired and was severely homesick, so I want you to ease up on him. Please?"

"Tell *him* that!"

"Merry? What's bothering you?" She looked concerned.

I fought my anger over Skip's coming home and barging back into my life. I struggled with feelings of helplessness over Chelsea's mother. Where was she? How could she leave her family? I hated the lump in my throat.

Then I did an impulsive thing. I threw myself into Mom's arms.

"Merry, honey, what's wrong?" She held me close.

I cried as though my heart would break. Actually, it *was* breaking. Breaking for my friend Chelsea and the horrible thing she was going through.

Before too many more seconds passed, I broke free of Mom's embrace without a word and made a beeline to my room. There, I finished crying my eyes out in private.

Eleven *House of Secrets*

Thank goodness Mom didn't hound me about being upset. She was smart that way. She'd learned not to push things with me when I was off-kilter. And it was a good thing, too, because there was no getting around it—I wouldn't break my promise to Chelsea.

Later, when I settled down a bit and my voice didn't sound all crackly from crying, I called Chelsea. "I've been thinking about you," I said, curled up in Dad's comfortable desk chair downstairs. The study was quiet—no chance of being disturbed here.

"I'm glad you called," she said. "My dad and I talked for a long time after you left. And I told him that you knew everything."

"Even about the missing money?"

"That too."

"Is it a problem . . . my knowing?" I asked hesitantly.

"Not really. Dad's so bummed out he couldn't care less who knows anymore. But I'm not just gonna sit around and wait for him to wake up. I'd like to jolt him good."

"What do you mean?"

She sighed. "Oh, Dad's so into himself these days—won't talk much. Withdrawn, I guess you'd say."

"He's mad, probably." *I would be, too*, I thought.

"I've been thinking, Mer. What if we called the cops and reported a missing person?"

"That's a jolt, all right."

"So . . . what do you suggest? Got a better idea?" I could tell she was desperate.

"There *is* something," I said, thinking about the phone call from Chelsea's mom. "You know about your mom's call to your dad today, right?"

"Uh-huh. Dad told me, and he's mighty sick about her attitude."

"Well, what if there'd been a tap on your line when she called? Then the phone company could've traced the call, and we might know where your mom is hiding out."

"Hey, a genius idea, Mer! When could we get it done?"

"The sooner the better," I suggested.

"But . . . wait a minute. Don't we need to call the police about something like this?"

I gripped the phone. "I don't know. Probably."

"Okay," she said, trying to sound more confident. "I'll call the police department tomorrow morning."

"What about now?" It was a test. I wanted to see how serious she really was.

"Now?" came the raspy reply.

"Sure. Why not?"

There was an unusually long pause. "Well . . . okay, I guess."

"Call me after you talk to the cops," I said.

"Man, Dad's gonna kill me," she whispered.

"Wait till he goes to bed—then call."

"Good idea." She paused for a second. "Could you put the portable phone under your pillow again tonight?"

"I'll see. I'll have to smuggle it out of Skip's room, you know. He's home now and being a bear about it."

"Try really hard. Please?"

"Okay, I'll give it a shot, but knowing Skip, I can't promise anything." I sighed. "Oh, before I hang up, I'd better tell you that I accidentally brought your mom's diary home with me."

"Just bring it over tomorrow."

"I will . . . and Chelsea?"

"Yeah?"

"I wanna go back to the hut again."

"You do? Why?" There was fear in her voice.

"I wanna have another look around."

"Didn't you get enough pictures?" she asked.

"We'll talk about it tomorrow."

"Okay. Thanks for calling, Merry."

"Take care. 'Bye." I hung up feeling closer to Chelsea than ever. Something was different between us. I couldn't put my finger on it, but I sensed it strongly. I was pretty sure when things had begun to change—after the prayer on the stone walkway today. That was it! Chelsea actually seemed different after my prayer.

⸺

I fooled around, watching TV for a while. Skip kept to himself in his room the rest of the evening. Dad and Mom were kind of out of it, too. I didn't blame them for hanging out upstairs in their master bedroom. They had a sitting area in one corner, and I could imagine Mom curled up with a book in her favorite overstuffed chair. Dad was probably already snoozing. He fit the old adage, "Early to bed, early to rise, makes a man healthy, wealthy, and wise."

Around nine-thirty, I felt restless. Nothing good on TV, as usual. I retreated to my room, calling for my cats to follow but keeping my voice down. Skip was cat queasy, and the last thing I wanted to deal with tonight was a tongue-lashing about my precious babies.

Once inside my room, the cat quartet knew where to go. My blue comforter was their favorite indoor place to be.

I undressed for bed, looking forward to sleeping in. No school tomorrow—Saturday. I knew I'd have to get up at a fairly decent hour, though. I wanted to start scouting out the possibilities for good photography subjects. The contest deadline was one month away, but the way I liked to work, I needed every bit of that time to choose a subject, take various angles, have the film developed, and then select my best work.

All comfy in my long pajamas, I slipped into bed and pulled up the blanket and comforter. My Bible was within reach on the nightstand, but when I stretched out my arm, my fingers touched something else: Mrs. Davis's diary.

I picked it up. *Do I dare read it?* I wondered.

Feeling a twinge of guilt, I opened to the first page. The name *Berta Jean Davis* was scrawled across the top. I looked for a phone number or an address but found nothing.

I studied the writing. Since I had no idea how Chelsea's mother usually signed her name, I had no method of comparison. But looking at it now, her signature seemed hurried, almost frantic.

Mrs. Davis had never impressed me as someone in a hurry. She was the epitome of neatness and order. She was a nurse after all, and must've been a very good one to reach administrative levels.

I was about to close the diary and quit my snooping when a tiny set of symbols caught my eye. It was quite difficult to see them—if a person hadn't been searching out clues as I was, there'd be no spotting them.

Anyway, there in the lower left-hand corner, I noticed the same mysterious marks as I'd seen on the long black box in the shanty hut. Only these had been written upside down.

I stared at them, fighting the urge to record the strange marks on a piece of paper. Hesitating, I wondered if they might be some sort of curse. I cringed at the thought of having the diary inside my house. At night, no less! I abandoned the idea of copying the marks and placed the diary back on my lamp table.

Stress had always triggered hunger pangs in me, so I got up and went to my walk-in closet. There, in several shoe boxes, I had stashed snack food. My own private food pantry. Although Mom thought it was downright silly, she didn't mind. I found some apple-flavored fruit leather to munch on. After brushing my teeth the second time in less than an hour, I reached for my Bible and devotional book, allowing the Scriptures and thoughts for the day to wash over me.

I kept waiting for Chelsea to call. After all, I'd gone to great lengths to get back the portable phone—waiting until Skip was asleep to make my move. Into his room I'd crept, tiptoeing through enemy territory. Silently, I'd snatched the phone off the dresser and padded down the hallway, quiet as a cloud.

Now the phone lay innocently under my pillow. But it hadn't rung yet, and I seriously doubted if Chelsea had called the police like she'd said she would.

Sleep played tag with me—I was 'it' and couldn't catch her. I turned on my side, thinking of Chelsea Davis and the eerie feeling I'd had as my friend and I stepped gingerly toward the hut. Worse, I remembered Chelsea's dad's persistent pleadings when his wife had called.

The day's images floated over me. I flipped on my back, staring up at the dark ceiling. "Oh, Lord, please do something," I prayed. "Don't let Mrs. Davis get sucked into this . . . this evil hole."

More images. This time, the memory of Chelsea's eyes darting away from mine, tears glistening after my prayer. I felt dizzy. Lying here in my own bed, I felt faint! Yet the more I pushed the images and words away, the more they persisted. *True light . . . resisting the true light. The woods . . . dark, snarling vines . . . the old hut. Black candles . . . incense . . . wine bottles . . . the possibly satanic book . . .*

I rolled over onto my other side as the sights and the sounds of the day poured over me without stopping. At last, I got up and sat on the edge of my bed, longing for peace.

"Dear Jesus, I need your help. I can't sleep because of what's happened," I prayed.

In the darkness, I slipped to my knees. "Please, Lord, take care of the Davis family. I can't help them the way you can."

I stopped pleading long enough to thank my heavenly Father. In turn, I was reminded of Psalm ninety-one—the one about the angels. *He will command his angels concerning you to guard you in all your ways. . . .*

I don't know how or when it happened, but I must've crawled back into bed and fallen asleep. Either that or my guardian angels tucked me in. Anyway, I woke up the next morning in bed, having slept soundly, eager to see Chelsea again.

Maybe *today* we'd find her mother!

During Saturday brunch with my family, a phone call came from Ashley Horton. "Merry, guess what I found out?" she said almost before I could say hi. "The guy who won the photography contest last year—you know, that Randall Eastman? Well, he's in Nikki Klein's homeroom."

I was flabbergasted. "You called *her* about this?"

"Last night," she admitted, "after I talked to Jon."

Why'd she have to talk to him? I wondered.

She continued. "But the thing is, this guy Randall, he doesn't go by his real name. He has a nickname, and it's really different. Kind of odd."

I wished she'd get to the point. "Yeah, so what's his nickname?"

"Stiggy. His name's Stiggy. Isn't it corny?"

Nobody says corny anymore, I thought, trying to smother my sarcastic thoughts.

"From what Nikki said, I guess Randall's younger brother couldn't pronounce his name when they were growing up." She laughed. "It doesn't figure—I mean, how do you get Stiggy out of Randall?"

"Maybe Randall was stingy growing up," I offered. "Or stinky."

She actually giggled at my remark. It made me wonder why she was acting like this. So jubilant. Unless . . .

"Oh, so you must've *called* Randall . . . er, Stiggy. Right?"

"How'd you guess?" Ashley asked. "Yes, I talked to him, and he says he'll show me his trophy-winning photo sometime next week." She was going way overboard with her enthusiasm.

"That's nice," I said, remembering that it originally had been my idea to meet him. But, not willing to get into a fuss with our pastor's daughter, I let it drop. Who knows, maybe I'd run into Stiggy in the library on the same day he brought his work. And I would certainly know which day that would be. Ashley wasn't very good at keeping things to herself.

"Well, Merry," she was saying, "have you decided what you're going to do for the contest? Or is it a big secret?"

From you it is, I thought, wishing she'd quit asking.

"I have no idea what I'll be photographing. What about you?" I felt I had to show *some* interest.

"Well, I'm torn between several subjects," she explained.

Torn? When was Ashley ever going to come down to earth?

"You don't have to take this so seriously," I advised. "It's only a contest."

"Only?"

"Well, you know." I was antsy to get going. I had a mystery to solve, a life to save . . . and who knows what else might pop up today.

"Only?" she repeated. "How can you possibly say that?"

"Okay, the contest is a big deal," I said. "It only happens once a year." *Now maybe she'll get off my back.*

Mom motioned for me to return to the table.

"I've gotta go, Ashley," I said politely. "See you tomorrow at church."

"Save me a place in Sunday school," she added before saying good-bye. It wasn't actually a command—still, her request bothered me. Was Ashley taking advantage of our one common interest? Make that *interests*—Jonathan Klein was mighty interesting, too.

I went back to my family, who was enjoying a very late breakfast. Mom liked to refer to a meal at this hour as brunch. It had nothing to do with whether or not we were eating breakfast and lunch-type food combined, just the lateness of the hour.

"Well, what are your plans today?" Dad asked Skip.

"I think I might ride around and see some of my old high school buddies." He leaned back in his chair.

"While you're at it, don't forget Nikki," I teased.

A smile spread across his face. Evidently, there were still strong emotions connected to Jon's sister.

"It's okay if you ask her out while you're here." I grinned. "I'll let you."

"Thanks for your permission, little girl."

Mom's eyes darted between Skip and me. But I didn't retaliate and turn our playful banter into something Mom needed to referee.

"What about you, Merry?" Dad asked. "What are you doing today?" He delighted in asking questions like this, especially on weekends. For his kids to have definite plans seemed terribly important to Dad.

"I'm going over to Chelsea's, if that's okay."

"How are the Davises doing these days?" Mom asked, picking up several dishes and carrying them to the sink.

"Oh, busy." Vague words.

I thought of the risky prospect of my family hearing about Mrs. Davis on the news or in the papers—especially if Chelsea really *had* gotten the nerve to call the cops.

Yee-ikes, I thought. *Maybe I should change my tune.*

But the more I contemplated the matter, the more confused I became. I could easily bring up the possibility of Chelsea's mom having been engaged in occult practices—meditating in an old, run-down shed strewn with empty wine bottles.

But what if Dad kept me from spending time with Chelsea today because of it? What if I didn't get another chance to investigate the hut?

Skip and I cleared the table for Mom, which came as a surprise to both her and me. He seemed more like his old self. Maybe he simply needed to come home and get a good night's sleep for a change. Maybe his sickness was cured, and he could go back to college—out of my hair!

The sun was already high when I parked my bike in Chelsea's front yard. She was coming around the side of the house. "Hi," she said, obviously glad to see me. "Did you remember to bring my mom's diary?"

"It's right here." I pulled it out of my back pants pocket. "Did you call the cops?"

She nodded. "This morning—after Daddy left the house. One of the cops I talked to asked if my mom kept a diary." The dark circles under her eyes suggested that she'd slept fitfully or not at all. "They want to look at it." She took the diary from me, fanning through its pages again.

I followed her around to the back porch. "How can the diary help?"

"The police'll compare some of Mom's repetitious writing with that of other known cult members."

"You must've told them about her diary, then."

"Sure did."

"So . . . they probably think she's involved in a cult, right?"

"Maybe." Chelsea pulled on her long, thick ponytail.

"What about the phone tap?"

"An adult has to request it," she said glumly.

"Did you tell the police that your mom has already called and that she could very well call back?"

"It's no use. Daddy has to be involved, or the phone company won't do it."

"Definitely a problem," I muttered.

Chelsea squinted toward the woods behind their house. "The cops want to get a statement from my dad about Mom's disappearance, but I doubt he'll even talk to them."

"I hope he will," I replied. "When are they coming?"

"In an hour or two." She frowned, leaning back in the patio chair. "Daddy's not gonna like it one bit."

I snapped open my camera case. "Well, it's the only thing you could do. I mean, we're only teenagers—we can't stay on the trail of a missing person forever."

Chelsea pushed her bangs off her forehead. "Remember how you wanted to go back and have another look at the hut?" Her eyes widened. "Let's go now."

"Okay!" I was eager for this second chance to snoop.

Chelsea put her mom's diary in the house before we headed for the arbor gate, down the white stepping-stone path to the mysterious shanty. Cautiously, we approached the old place, surrounded by towering trees.

Chelsea waited behind the trunk of a tree several yards back. Glancing around, she called in a whispery voice, "It's awfully dark in here. Let's hurry!"

I took two steps forward, staring into the darkness around me. Then I stopped, captured by the shanty's haunting image just ahead. I groped for my camera bag and took out the 35 millimeter.

"This is genius," I muttered to myself. Instantly, I targeted my subject matter for the photography contest. Now, if I could just get the correct lighting—what there was of it. In the dim and shadowy underbrush, I fussed with my camera, setting the lens and the aperture. "Hold on, Chels." I stepped back, steadying myself with my left foot. "I've found a shot too incredible to pass up."

The shack was covered on one side with a tangled maze of ivy dappled by a single shaft of sunlight. I'd seen paintings similar to this—depicting lavish light and contrasting shadow—but never anything like this in real life!

My heart pounded as I steadied my camera. It was truly marvelous the way the sun cast its brilliant luster over the place. *House of secrets*, Chelsea's mom had called it in her strange poem. The occult-ridden structure, now bathed in light, stood for something else in my mind—something other than witchcraft and hocus-pocus. The white light above the roof of the hut represented overcoming evil with good. I laughed out loud, dispelling my fears.

"I think I've found a winning photograph!" I called to Chelsea, considering various angles. Then, stepping closer, I turned the camera on its side for several vertical shots, taking one picture after another.

She shouted back, "C'mon, Mer. What are you doing?" Her voice sounded frantic.

"I'm finished now. Honest." I slipped my camera back inside its case and turned to see her crouched near the base of the giant tree. "You okay?"

"I hate it here." She gazed nervously into the shadows. "I'm . . . I'm really scared."

"Come with me," I insisted.

"No, you go. I'm staying right here."

"I'll hurry, I promise. You stand guard, okay?" I called over my shoulder. "If you see something . . . or someone, just whistle. I'll come running."

That settled, I moved forward, fighting off yesterday's tormenting visions. As I came within inches of the narrow door, I noticed a frightening thing.

The latch. It was hanging open!

Firmly, I placed my hand flat against the door and pushed. It was hard to see inside. There were no lights, not even a lantern.

Within seconds, my eyes began to adjust to the dim surroundings, and the first thing I noticed was the vacant spot where the candles and incense holders had been yesterday. I searched the area around me. My eyes scanned the old potting shelf high on the wall.

Empty.

The black box?

Gone!

My hands turned clammy. "Someone's been here. Maybe someone saw us yesterday." I spun around, heart in my throat, leaving the shanty door gaping open. "Chelsea, let's get out of here!" I called. "Hurry!"

We scrambled out of the forest and into the sunlight. My knees shook as we ran toward the safety of Chelsea's house.

A few solemn moments passed before either Chelsea or I could speak.

"Oh, Chelsea," I cried as we dashed toward her backyard. "Do you think your mom saw us snooping yesterday? Do you think we scared her away?"

Chelsea's mouth twitched. "I . . . I hope not."

"What can we do now?" I groaned. "We were getting so close, and now this!" I remembered that the police were supposed to be showing up soon. "Do you want me to wait here with you for the cops?"

We collapsed into a matching pair of cedar patio chairs. Chelsea pulled out a tissue from her pants pocket and blew her nose. "Mom might've been nearby. Maybe she even saw us go into the hut. She could have called my dad from a cell phone yesterday. Oh, Merry!" She began to sob.

I got up and went over to her, touching her shoulders. "I'm so sorry. I'm truly sorry."

Suddenly, she looked up through her tears. "You know what I wish? I wish your prayers were actually going somewhere. I guess I . . ." She stopped for a second. "I wish there really was a God."

I studied my friend as I sat on the arm of the other patio chair. The physical similarities were strong between Chelsea and her father. She had his straight nose and rounded chin. Other striking resemblances were evident—the way her left eyebrow arched slightly upward and the rich color of her auburn hair.

"Have you ever heard of people being made in God's image?" I asked.

Her eyebrows arched even more. "Not really. Why?"

"The Bible says we are. I guess if you believe God's written words, it's easier to believe His unwritten ones."

She frowned. "I don't get it."

"Look around you, Chels. See the autumn hues on every tree, the flecks of white in the blue sky, the way those grapevines wrap themselves around that old arbor gate?" I hoped I was making sense. "The way I see it, these are God's unwritten words to us. It's like a photographer with a good camera telling a picture essay. You know the old saying, 'a picture is worth a thousand words'?" I played with the camera strap on my case.

Chelsea leaned forward. "So you're saying that nature points us to something or someone who created all this?"

"I'm *sure* it does. Nothing else makes sense."

She turned to me and smiled thoughtfully. "I don't understand half of what you just said, but it sounds nice. I wish it were true."

I didn't have a chance to respond. A squad car was pulling into the driveway. We could see the front end of the hood.

"Come on," Chelsea said. "We have some fast talking to do."

"Yeah. I sure hope the police help us find your mom."

We hurried around the side of the house just as Lissa Vyner's dad was getting out of the car.

"Officer Vyner!" I called to him. "Boy, are we glad to see you."

Chelsea looked confused but somewhat relieved. "I thought . . . uh, I mean, how'd *you* find out about this?"

Officer Vyner explained. "When I heard about your call and what was going on over here, well, I decided I wanted to be the one to handle the report."

"Thanks," I said softly. "It means a lot."

Chelsea nodded soberly. "Thanks for taking this whole thing seriously." And she began to pour out every last detail.

Soon, it was my turn to talk. I told about what Chelsea and I had seen in the old shack yesterday and offered him prints of the shots I'd gotten before everything was taken away.

Officer Vyner sat on the back porch step, filling out an official report, writing down exactly what we said. I'd never felt so shook-up in my life, but by the time we finished, I was relieved to have shared the secret burden with someone who could truly help.

"Anything else?" he asked, his pen poised in midair. "Is there anything we've overlooked?"

"Well, there *was* something scratched into the bottom of that black box we found," I said. "I didn't get a picture of it, but I saw the exact same thing on the front page of Mrs. Davis's diary."

"Can you describe the markings for me?" Officer Vyner asked as he prepared to take additional notes.

"Would you like to see the diary?" Chelsea asked, looking a bit hesitant.

I nodded, offering moral support. "Good idea."

She went inside and came out quickly.

When the marks were found and scrutinized, I heard Officer Vyner mention the words "satanic cult." The implications made me shiver, and while he continued to talk to Chelsea, I went indoors to call my parents. Dad answered on the first ring.

"Could you please come get me?" I asked, now on the verge of tears. "I'm at Chelsea's, and there's something I should've told you . . . uh, before today."

"Honey, are you all right? You sound—"

"Please, just come," I pleaded.

Again he asked. "Merry, honey, are you all right?"

"I'm fine, but hurry."

He said he'd be on his way, and it was comforting to know that there'd be another adult in the house. And soon.

"Thanks, Dad." I shuddered to think how he would feel when he got here and saw the police car and heard the horrifying story of Chelsea's missing mother.

Dad arrived a few minutes later looking relaxed and fit in his black sweats—nothing even remotely close to the way he dressed to work at the hospital. Today was one of the few days he'd had off all month. Being the head of the ER trauma team at Lancaster General and on call most of the time made it difficult for Dad to have leisure time.

"What's going on?" he asked as he came up the front steps. He'd arrived before Chelsea's dad, and it was truly a good thing because it gave me a chance—with some help from Chelsea and Officer Vyner—to fill Dad in on exactly what had been going on.

After Dad heard the story, he offered his medical assistance. "I'd be more than happy to help the department in any way," he said.

"Well, for starters, we'll have the phone line tapped," Officer Vyner informed us.

Chelsea brightened a bit. "You mean, you can do that without my dad requesting it?"

"I'll be talking with your dad soon enough," he said, sliding the clasp on his pen over his shirt pocket.

We heard the sound of tires on the dirt road out front.

"Daddy's home!" Chelsea shouted and ran out to meet him. I was close on her heels, with Dad trailing a few inches behind.

Mr. Davis was clearly surprised to see Officer Vyner and my dad hanging around his house. He eyed Chelsea nervously. "What's going on here?" he grumbled.

Officer Vyner spoke up. "I understand your wife's missing?"

Mr. Davis ignored him and kept walking toward the house.

"Daddy!" Chelsea called. "Please talk to him."

Her father stood still and erect, not moving for a moment as he faced the screen door, perhaps contemplating a response. Then he opened the door and went inside.

"Now what'll we do?" I said, worried for Chelsea.

She scuffed her foot against the dirt near one of the many flower beds her mom had tended through the years. "Daddy's been like this ever since . . ." She stopped and pulled out her tissue. "What's *wrong* with him?"

Officer Vyner tried to explain. "Your father's hurting, Chelsea. He may be in denial, but no matter what, you must give him your support . . . your love. He needs you now more than ever."

She dried her tears. "What exactly is the occult?" she asked. "Is it the same thing as a cult group?"

Dad was quick to answer her questions. "The words do sound similar, but the occult is most often linked with astrology, psychic prediction, and sometimes magic or witchcraft. The word *cult* simply means a group of people whose leader persuades them to believe he deserves unquestioned loyalty and obedience. Some cult groups may employ occult practices, as well."

Dad's gentle eyes studied Chelsea as she stared down at her mother's flower bed, now hard and dry.

"Thanks for coming, Doctor Hanson," she said, turning to face Dad. "And for explaining things."

"We'll be praying that your mother is found soon," Dad told Chelsea as we headed for the car. "Please keep us informed. I know Merry will be in touch."

"Thanks again," she said. "And don't worry about me, Merry. I'll be fine."

I waved to my friend. "I know you will."

Dad opened the car door for me and hurried to get in on the driver's side after stowing my bike in the trunk. Nothing was said about hanging out with the wrong company—none of that. Dad was sweet. He reached over and squeezed my hand. "I'm glad you're all right, dumpling."

He started the car and drove down SummerHill Lane to our house.

"Do you think they'll find Mrs. Davis?" I asked.

Dad glanced at me. "Chelsea and you did the best thing for Mrs. Davis by getting the authorities involved." He explained that there was a special forces unit at the police department. "They have a number of highly trained dogs who can follow car-exhaust fumes and pick up many other kinds of scents."

"Wow, that's incredible. So you think it's possible Mrs. Davis might be coming home soon?"

Dad shook his head, wearing a gloomy expression. "I didn't say that. You have to realize that members of cult groups lose their ability to reason clearly. Their minds become prisoners, controlled by a leader who is often power crazed."

"Is that what you call brainwashing?" I asked, remembering the repeated sentences in the diary.

"People adhering to mind-controlling practices—and, in this case, mystical formulas—often don't realize what's happening until it's too late. Their minds can be trapped in a short time frame." He steered the car into our driveway.

"Do you really think Chelsea's mom could fall for something like that?" I asked, afraid to hear his answer.

"Didn't Chelsea say that her mom has always been intrigued by the mystical?"

I grimaced, remembering how Mrs. Davis was obsessed by astrology—especially reading her horoscope and forecasting her future. "I'll pray she comes to her senses." I got out of the car, heading for the kitchen door. I hoped Chelsea's mom would be found soon.

My cats were waiting inside. "Hello, babies," I cooed, scooping up Lily White. Then I turned to Dad as he came in. "Thanks for helping Chelsea and me today."

He nodded. "I only wish you had told your mother and me right away, when you first heard about Mrs. Davis." He lifted the lid on the strawberry-shaped cookie jar and reached in, pulling out two homemade chocolate chip cookies.

I truly hoped getting Dad and Officer Vyner involved might speed up the process of locating Chelsea's mom. I hoped it with everything in me.

"Want some Kitty Kisses?" I asked my feline foursome. Abednego, the self-appointed spokescat for the group, licked his chops.

"Okay, that settles it—liver and tuna crunchies coming up." I pinched my nose shut with one hand and reached into the box with the other. "Chow time!" I divvied up the smelly, heart-shaped cat snacks.

That done, I washed my hands and headed out front to get the mail. There was a fat pile waiting, and without glancing through any of it, I hurried into the house.

"Mail call," I said, putting the stack of letters and bills on the corner table in the wide entryway.

Mom emerged from her sewing room looking dazed. She often appeared rather intense when she was designing a pattern for a new outfit. I told her briefly about Chelsea's nightmare and what had transpired in the last several days.

"Merry, honey," she said, pulling on her hair. "You should've told us. Something like this . . . you shouldn't have carried the burden all alone."

I knew she would say something like that. "It's okay, I guess. I usually learn the hard way."

She was relieved to know Dad had been up to see the Davis family. "We certainly must follow up on them. Chelsea and her father will need all the emotional support they can get. Plenty of prayer, too."

We talked for a while longer, and then I excused myself to go to my room.

I was approaching the top of the long front staircase when Mom called to me. "Merry! I think you'll be very interested in this." She waved a white envelope.

"Is it from Levi?" I asked.

There was a surprising smile on her face. "Looks as though he wrote a scripture on the back of the envelope."

I flew back down the steps. "Levi loves studying the Bible. He'll make a great preacher someday." I snatched up the letter and darted up the steps, taking two at a time.

Shadrach and Meshach must've taken my galloping as an invitation to follow. Here they came, tearing up the stairs and down the hallway.

"Hurry up, little boys," I said, waiting for them before closing my door.

Ah, privacy. After the hectic, emotional events of yesterday and today, I was more than happy to pack away my camera and settle down with a long letter from Levi Zook. Four hand-written pages!

My dear Merry,

For such a long time, I have been wanting to write to you. Many wonderful-gut things are happening to me here in Virginia. I am excited to be learning how to write and spell better. My English is improving, too, which I am thankful for. Also, the way I am understanding the Scriptures more and more urges me to get out and preach the Gospel as soon as possible.

How are you doing, Merry? Do you enjoy your new position this year at your high school?

I chuckled as I read the last sentence. Levi hadn't remembered to call me a sophomore. Since Amish young people only attended school through the eighth grade, they didn't have to bother with class names like we English did in public school.

I eagerly read on.

> Receiving your letters has been very much enjoyed by me, and I must say that they have helped me learn about writing my own thoughts more expressively.
>
> I miss your laughter, Merry, and your bright eyes. If it is not too much to ask, would you mind sending me a photo of you? You see, now that I am not going to join the Amish church, I feel it would do me no harm to carry your picture in my wallet.

I reread the last paragraph. He wanted my picture for his wallet!

Suddenly, an overwhelming sense of loss came over me. I don't know if the sadness was triggered by a delayed reaction to the dire situation with Chelsea's mother or what. But a hard, dry lump sprang up in my throat. My vision blurred, and I reached for the blue-and-white striped tissue box on the nightstand.

Why was I crying over Levi's letter? This was the boy I'd grown up with. His Amish culture was as familiar to me as the palm of my hand. When he had struggled with his decision to leave the Amish church, I'd tried to be patient and listen to his reasons. I'd worried about the consequences. But Levi wanted God's will above all things, so who was I to regret his leaving SummerHill?

Of course, my loss was nothing compared with that of Levi's parents, Abe and Esther. They'd always had high hopes for their next-to-oldest son. Like any faithful Old Order Amish mother and father, they longed to see each one of their children follow in their footsteps.

But Levi had sometimes been rebellious as a child, pushing the limits. He loved learning and books and constantly asked questions, too. None of that set well with traditional Amish society. Being obedient and submissive to the rules laid out by the *Ordnung*—the agreed-upon blueprint for Amish life—was the top priority in the Plain community.

And here I was, missing Levi Zook. Missing him and wishing he were home. Drying my eyes, I continued to read his letter.

I hope you will not be very disappointed to know that I am planning to go overseas to help build a church. Because I have not been assigned to a country yet, I cannot tell you where I will be working. I suppose all those years of raising barns in a single day will help me assist other Christian carpenters.

My eyes drifted away from the letter. Building a church overseas? This meant that Levi would not be coming home at the end of the first quarter as planned. I wondered when I'd see him again. Thanksgiving? Christmas, maybe?

I was eager to know.

You must please forgive me, Merry, if this news comes as a surprise. We will have many other happy times together, I trust.

But when? If Levi went overseas and got involved in building projects, maybe he'd *never* want to return home.

I finished reading the letter, hoping against hope that he might explain further his decision not to come home in two weeks. But there was no additional explanation.

Feeling empty, I put the letter in my desk drawer and headed over to the Zooks' dairy farm. Maybe Rachel, Levi's younger sister, could explain things. Besides, a visit to my Amish neighbors was sure to do me good.

Through the willow grove and past the white picket fence, I flew. The sun cast angular shadows over the meadows as it played peekaboo through a fleeting cloud.

Rachel was outside beating rugs with her sisters, Nancy and Ella Mae, and they stopped to wave to me. "Hullo," they called in unison as I sprinted across the meadow toward the old white farmhouse.

The girls wore long brown work dresses with buttonless gray aprons over the top, fastened in the back with straight pins. The strings on their white-netting prayer *Kapps* flapped in the breeze.

"Looks like someone's having house church tomorrow," I said, running up to the long front porch.

"*Jah*, it's our turn," Rachel said. "Wanna help?"

"Sure." I picked up a multicolored rag rug and beat it against the porch railing. "Have you heard from Levi lately?"

"Only that he's not comin' home fer a bit." They'd heard about the overseas project, all right.

I sighed. "He must like his new college life."

Rachel nodded, careful not to say too much in front of her younger sisters. "We miss him around here. 'Specially *Dat*. He's not as young as he used to be, ya know, and farmin's gettin' to be harder for him."

Especially hard the way they do it, I thought. Mules instead of tractors, and kerosene or gas lamps instead of electricity. The inconveniences and hardships of Old Order Amish life were mind-boggling.

"I'm thinkin' that Levi's gonna get spoiled," Rachel said. "There's no chance he'll ever come back to farmin'.

"You're probably right," I said, helping the girls carry the rugs inside. I stayed around awhile, mostly to visit with Rachel. She and I hadn't seen each other as much as we liked because of my homework load this semester. Rachel, too, seemed busier now that her younger siblings were back in school for the year. Sometimes Rachel had to help with the more strenuous outdoor chores, filling in for Levi in his absence.

I wanted to ask her about Matthew Yoder, the Amish carpenter's son down the lane, but no opportunity presented itself. There was simply no discussing such things as guys in front of the rest of her family.

"Let's show Merry our puppies," little Susie said, coming into the kitchen. Her eyes sparkled as she pulled on my hand, leading me out the back door and across the wide yard to the barn.

Rachel, Nancy, and Ella Mae followed exuberantly. Inside the hayloft, on a warm bed of hay, Levi's silky gold cocker spaniel lay sleeping next to her pups.

"Oh, they're beautiful." I crouched down for a closer look at the four golden-haired darlings.

"Wanna take one home?" Susie offered. "Pick out the puppy ya want."

I shook my head reluctantly. "Mom would never stand for it," I confessed. "It would be a waste of time to even try to talk her into it."

Rachel leaned down and picked up one with a hint of a wave in his coat. "This one's my favorite," she said, "but Dat says we hafta give them all away."

Susie poked out her bottom lip. "I wish we could raise puppies. Levi and I were gonna have us a fine pup ranch. But he went away."

Rachel put her hand on Susie's head. "Don't fuss over what might've been. We'll find good homes for the pups like Dat says. That's all ya need to think about now."

Soon it was time for the afternoon milking. Since I was already here, I decided to don Levi's old work boots and help out. It felt mighty strange clumping around in the mud and manure wearing my former boyfriend's boots. Memories of last summer filled my mind with warm, cheerful thoughts as I washed down the cows' udders in preparation for milking. Funny, but it was a job I used to dislike.

Levi and I had pretty much turned things upside down this past summer. My own parents had more than raised an eyebrow when I'd consented to spend time with an Amish boy. Mom's concern was that Plain folk often marry young. *"Next thing, Levi will be looking for a wife,"* Mom had said.

Dad, on the other hand, was more nonchalant about Levi's interest in me. *"It's not like Merry's going out with some stranger,"* he'd said, laughing.

Dad was right. Levi and I were family in a very distant sort of way. One of my great-great grandfathers was one of Levi's ancestors, too.

After nearly two hours of rolling the metal milk cans back and forth to the milk house, I was quite exhausted. The Zook kids set high standards for themselves, however, and kept going. They were used to it, though, up at four-thirty each morning milking and hauling the fresh milk out to the end of their lane for the milk truck.

"I'll come see you again soon," I called to Rachel as her father shuffled into the barn. Now was a good time to exit since Abe would help finish up. I removed the familiar work boots and waved good-bye, wondering how long before Levi would miss the old home place. Or if he would at all.

Right before supper, Chelsea called. I was in no mood for more bad news, so I took the phone somewhat reluctantly. "Hi, Chelsea," I said. "What's up?"

"You'll never believe this," she began. "The police have already found evidence to prove there are other members of a satanic group in the area. It is a definite cult group—could be the one my mom's hooked up with."

"Wow, fast work. Now, if they can just find your mom and get her out of there."

"I know," she said. "Hey, my dad's coming around—finally! He's been talking to the police. Officer Vyner's been incredible. He told Daddy that they were able to track down several information files in the Lancaster newspapers. The media might be able to help us, too."

Chelsea sounded upbeat and excited. "I guess sometimes bad stuff can turn out to be good—in a way," she added.

"You're right," I replied, hoping this was one of those good times.

"And, Merry, I think you might be the reason for it."

"Me?"

"Your prayer that day, remember?" She said it softly. "You got me thinking about God—angels too—especially when I was scared spitless out there in the woods."

I hardly knew what to say. Chelsea had never shown any interest in God or His angels.

She changed the subject and chattered about school and boys, and even her algebra homework. Eventually, we said good-bye and hung up.

I dashed back into the kitchen with the phone cord dancing behind me. "Things are looking up for Chelsea and her family," I informed everyone.

"Prayer makes a difference," Dad was quick to say.

"Sure does," Skip said.

My head jerked up as I looked at him across the table. "You're praying, too?" I asked Skip, who'd heard about Chelsea's mom in only the past few hours.

"Mrs. Davis can't begin to know what she's up against with all of us praying," Skip said. It was the one serious comment he'd made all weekend.

Odd, but my brother didn't pick a single fight at this meal. Not one.

I didn't purposely save a seat for Ashley Horton in Sunday school the next day. At least, I didn't go out of my way to. But there it was, a vacant seat next to me just the same, and she spied it when she arrived.

Ashley made quite a production out of getting from the doorway to her seat. "Oh, Merry, you remembered," she acknowledged, prancing over to me. "Thank you so much." She sat beside me, smoothing out her dress and looking down at her nylons—I don't know why—maybe to make sure there were no runs, heaven forbid.

She certainly accomplished what she'd set out to do. There wasn't a single set of male eyeballs in the classroom that had missed her entrance. Jon Klein's included.

"I heard about Chelsea's mom on the news last night," she said.

By now, several other kids had come over to discuss the horrendous situation. Lissa too.

"What was all that about Chelsea's mom being involved in a cult?" Lissa asked.

"It's a frightening thing," I said, trying to explain everything quickly before the teacher arrived. "But I believe God will take care of Mrs. Davis."

Jon came over and sat in front of us. Ashley nearly died on the spot. I, however, remained cool and calm. Collected? Not on the inside!

Fortunately, the Alliteration Wizard didn't spring something on me right there in front of everyone. I probably wouldn't have been able to think fast enough. Besides, I loved the fact he was keeping our word game hush-hush.

After all the talk about Chelsea's mom and her disappearance tapered off, Ashley asked me quietly about the photography contest. Again.

"So . . . have you decided anything yet?" she asked.

Jon had turned around in his seat and was grinning at me. I smiled back. "Oh, that . . . the contest."

"Well," she huffed, "isn't it about time to make some sort of decision?"

"Probably." I was being evasive and she knew it, but I didn't dare share my photography idea with anyone. Especially not with Ashley Horton. Next thing, she'd be out tramping around in the woods near Chelsea's house, searching for an old shanty with a beam of light pouring down on it from out of the sky.

Jon turned around, and I opened my Bible, looking for my notes. I'd actually written some on the lesson for today. Not something I often did, but the trauma of the weekend had served to put my mind on the things of God. Tragedy has a way of doing that. Besides, today's lesson was about angels.

Mr. Burg showed up right on time. His blond hair was accentuated by his gold and blue paisley tie. "Good morning, class." He smiled warmly. "Today we're going to discuss God's unseen protectors."

I opened my Sunday school lesson book so I could follow along. Mr. Burg started the class with prayer and then recited various documented stories about intervention by angels. I was fascinated, remembering how the Lord had dropped the verse from Psalm ninety-one into my heart last Friday. In that chilling moment, I'd prayed on my knees—in front of Chelsea, the self-declared atheist.

What made me do such a thing? Thinking back, I knew I'd done a wise thing.

Ashley's Sunday school lesson slid off her lap, startling me back to the discussion at hand. The book conveniently landed under Jon's chair. Not surprisingly, he leaned over and reached back to pick it up. Ashley literally gushed her whispered thanks, and I felt embarrassed to be sitting next to her. The girl was obviously determined to get Jon's attention. No matter what.

I could only hope he would remember who his equal was in the world of words. Merry, mistress of mirth, made the maddening maiden Ashley seem meaningless by a major margin. Or so I hoped.

Monday morning before school, I dropped off my precious roll of film at the photo lab. Skip had decided to stay an extra day before heading back to college, and I was shocked when he offered to drive me to school. I was ages from having a car of my own, and it was nice having him behave so brotherly.

I knew he would be gone by the time I arrived home that afternoon. "I hope things go okay for you at school," I ventured, tiptoeing around the fact of his former homesickness.

His smile reassured me. "Dad talked to me—said I could come home any old weekend I wanted." He waited for the red light two blocks from Buchanan High, turning in the driver's seat to look at me. "I'll be praying for your girl friend's mother," he said softly.

"Sounds to me like she needs all the prayers she can get," I replied.

Skip continued. "Well, I'm glad Chelsea has a friend like my little Merry."

He'd called me that ever since I could remember. At least today he'd abandoned "cat breath"—the nerdy nickname he often called me.

Grinning, Skip pulled up to the curb. "Well, here you are."

"Thanks for the ride."

He poked my arm playfully. "See ya at Thanksgiving."

"Yeah, see ya. 'Bye!" I jumped out of the car and watched him drive away. Thank goodness he'd begun to show signs of actual reform. Could it be that my brother and I might someday enjoy a decent sibling relationship?

I hurried up the steps to the school, anxious to turn in my application for the photography contest. Even before stopping at my locker, I dashed down the hall to Mrs. Fields's homeroom. No one was there, but I noticed that someone had already returned an application. I leaned over, studying the paper on the desk. Lissa Vyner's name was at the top. I wondered if Ashley Horton would be turning in her application early, too. Since she was in another homeroom, I had no way of knowing.

Later, right before Mr. Eastman came over the intercom with his usual boring remarks about the day, I passed a note to Lissa.

Hey!

I see you turned in your photo contest stuff early—just like me. Any idea what Ashley's up to?

—Mer

Lissa wrote right back during the long verses of the national anthem. I remembered what Mom had said about Mr. Eastman, our principal and hers, crooning "The Star-Spangled Banner" way back when.

Mer,

You've been snooping on me, huh? Personally, I don't know what's with Ashley these days. I suspect she's planning to get some ideas from Stiggy Eastman—you know, last year's winner?

Let's eat lunch with her today and check it out.

Later,
Lissa

It didn't take long to figure out Ashley's next move. She spelled it right out for us over hamburgers.

"Stiggy's been so helpful," she announced to Lissa, Chelsea, and me. "You should hear him talk about things like the composition of the shot, and—oh yes, the most striking element of a scene. I'm really impressed, though I won't be viewing the winning photograph until Wednesday."

Wednesday!

Even though Ashley didn't bother to invite either Lissa or me to tag along, we weren't going to pass up the chance to have a look. We'd just have to concoct our own plan.

"By the way, have the police followed up any more on your mom and that cult she's in?" Ashley asked Chelsea.

"They're getting close." Chelsea cast a meaningful glance my way. "And my mom called late last night."

I gasped. "Did they trace the call?"

"She was phoning from a fitness gym somewhere west of town" came the disappointing words. "At least we know she's still in the area."

"Maybe she'll call again," I offered, hoping to comfort my friend.

Ashley's eyes widened. "Well, I certainly hope so. Everyone at church is praying that she'll come home soon."

I wanted to say, *Be careful how much you tell her* but spooned up some applesauce instead. Only God knew whether Mrs. Davis would come home soon or not. And He certainly wasn't to be underestimated. Not in the least!

The next day, Tuesday, Lissa and I sat together in study hall. We ended up passing notes, working out a plan for gracefully bumping into Stiggy Eastman and his wonderful award-winning photography. Tomorrow!

For me, it really didn't matter much; mainly because I was fairly certain my own subject matter was superb. The beam of light hovering over the old hut was both dramatic and unique, but I wouldn't know how well I'd captured it until I picked my photos up after school.

Lissa was mighty charged about seeing the kind of competition we were up against. She whispered to me when the teacher wasn't looking. "If Stiggy's work was really incredible, you know the judges will be looking for more of the same quality this year."

She was right. "Don't worry, just do your best," I advised, deciding to cool it and get to work. The study hall teacher was beginning to scowl; her eyes glared a warning.

I mumbled a barely audible sound, and Lissa knew that, for now, our conversation was history.

The time passed quickly, and soon the dismissal bell rang. I walked with Lissa to her locker in the middle of an ocean of kids.

"Mind if I tag along to the photo lab with you?" she asked, twirling her combination lock.

I smirked. "You're kidding, right?"

"I'm serious. I wanna see my competition."

"It's probably not a good idea," I said, stalling—hoping she'd drop the subject. "You know how I am about this. If I show you, then Chelsea and Ashley . . . *everyone* will want to be in on it."

Lissa's eyelids fluttered upward in disgust. "C'mon, Mer, no one else has to see."

I shook my head. "Can't."

"Why, 'cause you think your pictures are so good?" There was a touch of sarcasm in her voice.

"Actually, you never know," I replied. "My lighting could be all wrong." It was true—the lighting had been tricky that day—the one thing that most concerned me.

"Well, have it your way." She reached for her books and slammed her locker.

Chelsea came over with several other girls. "Riding the bus home?" she asked me.

"I plan to if I get back from the photo lab in time."

Chelsea's face lit up. "Oh yeah, I wanna see your pictures."

I was afraid of this. Chelsea was the only person who knew about my subject matter for the contest—that is, *if* she'd paid attention that day in the forest. I couldn't be totally certain, though. Chelsea had been literally freaking out behind the tree trunk.

Lissa leaned against her locker, her arms crossed, waiting for my reply. She would be hurt if I gave in to Chelsea's request, ignoring hers.

"Tell you what," I said. "I'd better pick up my prints all by my lonesome. That way no one'll feel left out." I shot a sympathetic smile at Lissa, who pinched up her face in response.

"Aw, Mer!" Chelsea wailed.

Lissa leaned forward. "It's okay—we'll get to see Merry's incredible work soon enough."

Lissa and Chelsea were still yakking when I excused myself and slipped away to the photo lab down the street.

———

The white-haired man behind the counter seemed confused. "How many rolls of film did you say?"

"Only one—twenty-four exposures."

He searched through the alphabetized packages for the second time, humming off-key as he did. I could see that he was coming to the end of the stack, and my throat felt tight.

"Excuse me," I ventured. "Is the woman here, the one who took my film yesterday?"

The old gentleman shook his head. "I'm sorry, young lady, but that was the manager's wife, and she and her hubby are off to New York City on a business trip."

"I see."

What experience does this guy have running the place? I wondered.

"But not to worry," he added. "I'm fairly certain your pictures will turn up."

Fairly certain? Yee-ikes!

He opened a drawer and pulled out a pad and pencil. "Let's have your address and phone number."

"Uh . . . sir, you don't understand," I said, willing the panic out of my throat. "I *have* to get those pictures back. It's important . . . for a school photography contest."

His watery blue eyes seemed to register my concern. "I'll call you the minute I locate them."

"Where else might they be?" I persisted, trying to sound mature about this despite the knot in my stomach.

"Wait right here." He turned and shuffled off toward the back room.

Peering over the counter, I read the upside-down names on the packages. I was clear up to the *d*'s when he returned. Stepping away from the counter, I noticed his hands were empty.

"No such luck." He tilted his head to the side, and his hands flew up in front of his face. "I did all I know to do, but—" and here he sighed—"I'll keep tracking them for you."

"Please, will you call me the minute you know something?" I pleaded.

"I certainly will."

He waved as I left. I didn't.

The sun cast intermittent splotches of light along the sidewalk as I hurried back to the school. "I can't believe this," I muttered as the frustration mounted inside me. I took the steps to the high school two at a time.

Chelsea was coming out one of the front doors as I pushed on the metal bar opposite her. "Oh, Mer, there you are," she greeted me, eyes searching. "How'd your pictures turn out?"

"Don't ask." I shrugged. "They're lost."

"They're *what*?" She started to follow me inside.

I put up a hand. "Hold the bus for me. I have to pick up my English notebook and some other stuff."

"You got it." She turned and headed back outside.

The semi-empty building seemed almost hollow, reminding me of the afternoon Chelsea had first told me the startling news about her mom.

Dashing through the hallways toward my locker, I took note of the muted sounds my tennies made in the hushed corridor. Quickly, I passed the many narrow rows where the upperclassmen had been assigned lockers earlier in the year.

Someone down the hall was saying. "Oh, Jonathan, how funny!" A tight little laugh followed.

I rotated my combination lock. *Click.* Cautiously, I glanced over my shoulder and pulled down on the lock at the same time.

Two people, way at the end of the hall, were talking. One was laughing. I heard Jon's name again, and then Jon himself said something. The echo distorted the sound of his voice, so I couldn't make out exactly what the Alliteration Wizard was saying. But there were a few words I did catch—something about helping to set up a photo shoot Friday after school.

I slammed my locker door, the sound reverberating through the vacant hallway. As fast as I could, I ran for the front doors and down the steps.

Chelsea leaned out one of the bus windows, calling to me. "Hurry, Merry!"

Rushing into the bus and up the steps, I stopped to thank the driver before sliding in next to Chelsea.

"Never a problem," Mr. Tom said, reaching for the lever to pull the bus doors closed.

When I looked out the window on Chelsea's right, I noticed Jon Klein strolling out of the building. His eyes spotted the bus, but he turned to speak to a girl—probably the same one who'd been laughing while they talked in the deserted hallway.

Fuming, I called to the driver. "Better wait. Here come two more stragglers."

Mr. Tom reached for the lever, and the doors screeched open wide. I fumbled for my English notebook, pretending to read as Jon hopped on the bus, followed by none other than Miss Ashley Horton.

"What happened to your pictures?" Chelsea asked.

I stared down at my English notebook, trying to block out the vision of Jon and Ashley boarding the bus. For all I knew, they were sitting together!

"The pictures," Chelsea repeated. "Where are they?"

"No one seems to know," I muttered, not looking up.

"But how could this happen?"

My eyes bored a hole in my notebook.

Chelsea nudged me. "Mer?"

"Never mind," I said through clenched teeth. "And don't turn around if you know what's good for you."

She controlled herself—didn't careen her neck like a giraffe and scope out the situation the way I thought she would. "What's going on?" she whispered.

"Tell you later. Get off with me at my house, okay?" I sounded mechanical through stationary lips.

"Deal," she replied, lips clamped.

We burst out laughing at our robotic antics. I did my best to keep my eyes forward.

Next thing I knew, Lissa showed up and scrunched her petite body in next to mine.

"Hey, *three* don't exactly fit here," I said, squirming.

"Listen, I've got some really good stuff." Lissa bent low, and Chelsea and I matched our heads to hers. "Ashley meets Stiggy Eastman at the sandwich shop tomorrow. Twelve sharp. Be there!" Almost as quickly as she came, she disappeared.

"Oh-ho," I shouted. "I love you, Lissa!"

Chelsea grinned. "What do you care about Stiggy and his work? That's last year's stuff. You've got a fantastic setup for *this* year," she encouraged me.

"Yeah, if the photo lab ever finds it."

"Maybe you should call them again when we get to your house."

I nodded. "Genius."

That's what we did. The minute Chelsea and I walked in the back door, we slipped past the expectant faces of four felines and headed for Dad's study.

After finding the number in the phone book, I dialed the lab. The old man answered. "Photo lab, may I help you?"

"I hope you can. This is Merry Hanson calling. I wonder if you've been able to find my single roll of developed film."

"*Who* did you say?"

I went through the whole rigmarole again, reminding him who I was, what I wanted, and why I was concerned.

Finally, he said, "Ah yes. I've been trying to phone you, but there's been no answer."

"Well, I just got home," I explained. "So . . . you must've found my pictures." I tingled with excitement.

"Yes, yes, they're here."

"Oh, thank you, sir. I'll pick them up first thing tomorrow." I paused, grinning at Chelsea. Then, turning my attention to the voice on the phone, I said, "You'll hang on to them for me, won't you?"

"I certainly will, young lady. Glad to be of service."

Actually, when it came right down to it, I couldn't wait to see the photos. The minute Mom arrived, I pleaded with her to drive with me down to the photo lab. She had other things on her mind.

"Evidently, you girls haven't heard the latest," Mom was saying.

"About what?" I asked, peering wide-eyed at Chelsea.

"It seems that someone has discovered a page of repetitious writing—something similar to what's in your mother's diary, Chelsea." Mom looked at her, then me.

"Where?" Chelsea asked.

Mom's eyes shone. "In a gas station somewhere in the area of Mt. Pisgah."

"Really?" I couldn't believe it.

Mom said, "The news report I just heard indicated that a cult group has been located and certain members identified."

"This is so-o incredible!" Chelsea exclaimed.

I gave her a squeeze. "Your dad's probably beside himself, don't you think?"

Chelsea nodded. "I'd really like to go home. Do you mind, Mer?"

"Of course not—you're outta here!" I was delighted.

———

Mom let me drive the short distance up the steep grade to drop Chelsea off at her house.

"Do you think this could be the end of the ordeal?" I glanced over at Mom as we headed toward town.

Her eyes were thoughtful. "Keep praying. These situations are never open-and-shut cases, as you might think. Chelsea's mother won't come home unless *she* chooses to do so, which is highly unlikely. And that probably won't happen for a long, long time."

I thought about that for a moment. "Wouldn't Mrs. Davis have to be totally brainwashed if she doesn't want to come home? I can't understand it!"

"People—normal, intelligent people—fall prey to cult recruiting every day, Merry." She reached over, resting her hand on my shoulder.

"I sure hope someone can help Mrs. Davis." I bit my lower lip.

Mom sighed. "Your father doesn't offer much hope for her return, at least not of her own free will."

"What are you saying?" My throat felt as if a lump was lodged in it.

"This is absolutely *not* to get out." When I looked over at Mom, her eyes were serious. "You must not breathe a word to Chelsea or to anyone else. Do you understand?"

Eyes back on the road, I nodded, wondering what she would say.

She sighed audibly. "Mr. Davis has been talking with Dad about the possibility of kidnapping his wife and having her deprogrammed."

I gasped. "Chelsea's dad would kidnap his own wife to get her back?"

"Desperate family members do it all the time."

This was unbelievable. "When will it happen?" I asked.

"I don't know for sure, but I think it will be soon. The longer he waits, the longer her rehabilitation could be."

"But it's only been five days since she left," I said.

"Five days of living with a power-crazed leader who orders everything his followers do and sometimes say—from their bedtimes to the amount of hours they're permitted to sleep, to the way they interact with each other, to what they eat. . . . "

I got the picture. Besides that, I remembered Chelsea hinting that the mind-controlling techniques had probably started weeks before her mom ever left. And there was Mrs. Davis's long-standing fascination with the occult.

The photo lab was within view now. I thought about the things Mom had told me as I pulled up to the curb and parked. "I'll wait for you here," Mom said.

I hopped out, feeling a bit numb. Yet I was eager to lay eyes on my options for the photo contest. Quickly, I closed the car door and headed toward the shop.

Inside, no one was tending the register. I waited impatiently for several minutes before I rang the bell on the counter.

The old man peeked around the corner, smiled a grin of recognition, and lumbered across the room. "Yes, yes," he said. "You're the young lady who called."

I nodded, dying to get my hands on the photos.

He thumbed through the alphabetized packages, half humming, half muttering to himself. "Ah, here we are. Merry Hanson of SummerHill Lane." He handed the package to me and proceeded to ring up the amount.

Anxiously, I tore open the package and carefully slid out the five-by-seven color glossies. I held up the first photo—a picture of a tall, stand-up antique radio.

"These aren't my pictures." I looked at the next and the next. "None of these photos are mine." My voice quivered.

The old man lowered his spectacles and peered over the top of them. "What did you say?"

I held up the prints, showing him. "These aren't my pictures. I didn't take pictures of antique furniture."

A frown furrowed his brow. "Well, let's have a look." He checked the film size and the special instruction section on the package. Bewildered, he glanced up at me. "Must be some sort of mix-up."

No kidding, I thought.

I inhaled deeply. "How could this possibly happen?"

He shrugged. "I've never seen anything like this. Not here."

"What do you mean, sir?" Worry clutched my throat. "Did someone get my pictures by mistake?"

"Well, it certainly seems that way, but it was a simple oversight," he said, pausing to scratch his chin. "Let's see. You brought your film in yesterday morning."

"That's right, yesterday—Monday." I was in the process of making a mental note to boycott this photo shop forever— never, ever to darken the door again!

Someone came in the door behind me. It was Mom.

"Is everything all right?" she asked cheerfully.

I explained the problem, and Mom reacted kindly to the old man. Certainly more compassionately than *I* had.

"My daughter's very talented," she was saying. "The school photography event means everything to her."

He nodded, fumbling around in his pocket for a stick of gum. "We'll just have to sit tight and wait it out and hope the other customer opens the package and discovers the mistake."

I cleared my throat, attempting to speak without shouting and without chewing him out—which is definitely what I thought the wrinkled-faced guy deserved. "Sit tight?" I was losing it, plain and simple. "I can't do any such thing! I need those pictures immediately."

For a split second, I wished my dad was an attorney instead of an ER doctor. Thoughts of a lawsuit zipped around in my mind.

Mom wrapped up things politely and ushered me out of the store. I fussed and fumed all the way home, desperately trying to push thoughts of Ashley Horton and Stiggy Eastman out of my head.

House of Secrets Twenty

Supper lasted longer than usual with Mom lecturing me about my horrid behavior at the photo lab. I tried to explain why the pictures were so important.

"They weren't just any shots, Mom. You should've seen the lighting that day—I mean, it was something out of a masterpiece painting. Honest."

She wasn't impressed. "Terrific or not, you mustn't ever lose your temper like that. The man was only trying to do his job and cover for the owners. You heard him."

I'd heard him all right, and the timing for a New York trip couldn't have been worse.

Dad showed up when we were half finished with supper. He avoided my questions about the kidnapping and subsequent deprogramming of Mrs. Davis. He and Mom wanted to discuss things alone—I wasn't dense—so I excused myself and went to the family room to watch TV.

Within minutes, a news bulletin about Mrs. Davis came on. "Mom, Dad!" I called. "Come quick!"

They came in and stood watching as the reporter linked the strange repetitious writing to a commune of cult members hidden away in a remote hilly area several miles west of Lancaster.

"This is similar to the report I heard on the radio earlier," Mom mentioned.

"I wonder if Chelsea and her dad are watching," I said.

Dad nodded with an air of certainty. "They're doing more than watching. They're probably recording this right now." That's all he would say.

I fidgeted, eyeing my parents more than the TV screen. Annoyed and frustrated, I finally got up and left the room. They weren't going to clue me in, that was one-hundred-percent-amen clear!

So . . . not only had Chelsea and I kept secrets from the world, now it seemed my parents had secrets of their own.

I phoned Chelsea from Dad's study, out of earshot. "Did you see the news report just now?" I asked when she answered.

"Did I ever! Wow, it looks like another one of your prayers was answered. You've been praying, haven't you, Mer?" I heard her sigh.

"I said I would, didn't I?"

She ignored my comment. "I can only hope Mom's okay . . . *if* they find her!"

"Me too." Then I got up the nerve, after former repeated rejections, to invite her to church this Sunday. "You'll never guess what we're studying in the high school class." I told her about the angel stories Mr. Burg had shared with us last week.

"Really? Angels?" She paused for a moment. Then—"Sure, I'll come."

I nearly swallowed my tonsils. "Great, we'll pick you up."

Joy, oh joy! I completely forgot the mistake at the photo lab. My woes had vanished, just like my pictures.

Unfortunately, Chelsea asked about them. "Did you get your photos back?"

"Oh, that. Well . . ." And I began to fill her in, leaving out the part about feeling hostile and angry. Mom was right. My behavior had been mighty pitiful. Coming on the heels of this good news from Chelsea—that she was coming with me to church—well, I wanted to alter my attitude problem right then and there. Photo lab flub or not.

⁓

The next day at high noon, Chelsea, Lissa, and I showed up at the sandwich shop. We sat in the booth right behind Ashley and Stiggy. They didn't seem to mind, probably because we pretended not to be interested.

Chelsea hammed it up a bit much, though, calling it a coincidence that all of us had shown up for lunch at the same place. "Who would've thought!" She laughed to herself as she scooted past their table.

Later, when the right moment presented itself, Lissa got up and went to the ladies' room. Chelsea and I talked about everything under the sun, except the latest report about the commune. I kept my promise to Mom and didn't say a word about her dad's plans to kidnap-rescue her mother.

On the way back from the rest room, Lissa just happened to saunter up to Stiggy's side of the table, where he was showing off his art portfolio. "Wow," she said, staring at the picture. "Is this a winning photograph or what?"

It was our cue to get out of our seats and rush over. And we did. All three of us girls leaned over the award-winning picture, gawking.

The photo was a city scene—the square in downtown Lancaster. The street glistened with a covering of rain.

I looked more closely. Brightly colored umbrellas, Central Market in the background, and people scurrying by—the whole offering lent itself to award status. The subtle play of light and shadow on the pavement made for a delightful picture.

"Did you take the shot right after sunup?" I asked.

"Excellent perception," Stiggy replied. "You must be a photographer, too."

"Man, is she ever," Lissa piped up, even though I tried to get her to hush. "You should see her gallery of pictures."

"Right," I said.

"Oh, Merry, don't be so modest," Chelsea said. "You're so good my grandmother wants to pay you to take pictures of her for her Christmas card this year." She turned to Stiggy. "Trust me, Merry's good!"

I smiled. "Thanks, but this guy's photography is truly amazing." I turned the group's attention back to Stiggy's work.

He seemed flattered by our oohing and ahhing, and Ashley really didn't know what to make of it. She never said a word to distract us, but I wondered if she wasn't feeling a bit ticked off despite not showing it.

Finally, she got around to introducing all of us to Stiggy. He forced a half smile and soaked in the recognition while twiddling his thumbs. He sat tall in the booth, shifting his dark brown eyes from one girl to another. It seemed as though he'd never had to deal with accolades before. Reluctantly, we headed back to our table to finish lunch.

It wasn't until Friday after school that I began to freak out over Ashley. She followed me as I headed for the school bus. "What's *your* subject matter going to be?" And before I could reply, she added, "Surely you've decided by now."

I didn't tell her my subject matter had been swallowed up at the photo lab down the street. And still no word from the old man running the place. Not even a phone call to apologize!

I griped to Dad at supper. "How on earth could something like this happen? You'd think after all this time someone would be wondering where his pictures are and want to trade the wrong ones for his own."

Dad nodded rather apathetically between bites.

With my fork, I poked at the carrots on my plate. "The photos of ancient furniture were probably taken by some antique dealer. I wonder if I should call around to all the dealers in town and see if they've lost some pictures."

Mom zeroed in on the word *antique*. It defined her main interest in life. "It does seem strange that someone would take pictures of antique furniture unless they were recording them for an inventory of some kind," she suggested.

"But why the enlargements—full-color glossies?" I asked, noting that Mom seemed as perplexed as I.

Dad offered no help, and I was really beginning to wonder about his preoccupied state. Was the Davis kidnapping attempt coming up? Maybe this weekend?

Mom had little to say on the Davis subject when I pumped her for answers as we cleared the kitchen table. Both my parents were keeping a tight lid on things. "I wish you'd never told me anything about rescuing Mrs. Davis," I finally blurted out in sheer frustration.

"I only told you about it so you would pray" came the terse reply. There was no messing with Mom.

Tired of inquiring, I dropped the subject. When the kitchen was cleaned to Mom's satisfaction, I went upstairs and pulled out Levi Zook's letter. I reread it straight through; then I found some floral stationery and began to write.

An hour later, Ashley Horton called.

"Merry, hi," she said. "I hope I'm not calling you at a bad time."

Now what? I wondered.

"This is fine," I said.

"Well, I'm beginning to wonder if I should even bother to enter the photo contest," Ashley whined.

"Really?"

"Oh, I don't know, I guess I'm getting cold feet after hearing how astounding Stiggy's entry is supposed to be this year."

"*This* year's photo?"

"Uh-huh."

"Have you seen it?" I asked.

"Well, no."

"Then how can you possibly know if it's any good?"

She was silent.

"I sure haven't heard anything wonderful about his latest entry—except from you. Maybe Stiggy's trying to scare off his competition."

"Why would he want to do that?" she asked.

"Who knows? Maybe his picture isn't really all that great, and he's just saying it is."

"Oh, Merry," she gushed, "I wish I'd called you earlier about this. I've worried too much."

I sighed. "Just do your best. That's all any of us can do."

"That's what Jonathan keeps telling me."

My heart flipped hearing his name. "Well, he's right, you know."

She sighed into the phone. "I think he must be right about everything."

I thought I'd die or drop the phone. Or both. She was talking about *my* Jon. Again!

"Merry? You still there?"

"I'm here." I wished I weren't!

"What do you think of Jonathan Klein?"

Who is she kidding? I thought. I wondered if steam was spouting out my ears yet.

"I've known Jon for a very long time," I found myself bragging. "He and I go way back."

"Oh really? How far?"

I wanted so badly to start alliterating to see if she could do it, too. Wanted to show her up any way I could, but I gripped the phone with my left hand and pulled on my shirt with my right.

"Why don't you ask Jon?" I blurted.

"About you and him?"

"Sure, if you want."

"Okay," she sounded a bit reluctant. "He's coming over in a few minutes."

Now I felt really foolish. What if she asked him about me like I was fishing to find out how he felt? That secondhand girl-asks-boy stuff was so junior high, and it certainly wasn't what I'd had in mind!

"Jon's going to help me with my photo shoot," she explained. "In fact, that might be him at the door now. I'd better get going. Well, 'bye, Merry. See you Sunday."

My heart was pounding ninety miles an hour as I hung up. This girl was driving me bazookas!

It was a good thing I'd nearly finished writing my letter to Levi *before* Ashley called. My mind was so clogged up with the phone conversation that I simply put the letter away. I did remember, however, to cut out one of my wallet-sized school pictures and slip it into the envelope.

Standing at the window, I surveyed the cornfield across SummerHill Lane. I recounted Ashley's words and decided that she'd actually called me to flaunt Jon. He was coming to her house—that's why she'd called. All that baloney about Stiggy and his wonderful work . . . it had nothing to do with anything.

I ran downstairs and grabbed a Windbreaker from the hall closet. "I'm going for a walk, Mom," I called.

"Don't be long. It's getting dark."

"I know." But I wanted it to be dark. I wanted the night to close in around me. I'd been through all this before—only with Lissa last spring. Why was it that right when Jon and I were really clicking, someone else had to step in and spoil things?

Quickening my pace, I headed for the steep grade that led to Chelsea's house. The dusk chirped and buzzed as tiny insects and other small animals prepared for night.

Several cars were parked in the driveway at the Davis residence when I arrived. One of them was a squad car. Probably Officer Vyner's.

Chelsea came to the door carrying a golden-haired puppy. "Oh, Mer," she cooed, hugging me with her free arm, "look what Rachel Zook brought over."

I touched the cocker spaniel's neck gently. "For keeps?"

"He's all mine." Chelsea's eyes were shining as she led me upstairs to her room. "I'm going to call him Secrets."

"When did Rachel come?" I asked, settling down on her window seat.

"A little while ago." Her eyes searched mine. "Somehow or other, she heard about my mom. You never told her, did you?"

"No, but one of their Mennonite cousins may have heard about it on the news. Or—" I stopped, realizing who the true informer might've been—"maybe it was Levi!" My smile gave me away.

Chelsea noticed. "Good old Levi. You've always liked him, haven't you?"

"We're friends, but that's all there is to it. He's off in Virginia at a Mennonite college."

She grinned, holding the puppy up for me to see. "Isn't he adorable?"

I noted the slight wave in his silky coat. Rachel had chosen Chelsea for the caretaker of her favorite pup. "Better not bring him around my cats," I warned. "They'd scratch his pretty nose right off."

We joked about our taste in pets and then got to discussing church and what she could expect on Sunday morning. She was especially interested in the discussion on angels. "Are you sure they'll be talking more about it?" she asked, her eyes bright with anticipation.

"Positive," I said. "And since you're interested, I have to tell you something. You know the day we first went snooping in the woods?"

She nodded.

"Well, the strangest thing happened. This Bible verse I learned when I was a kid popped into my head out of nowhere. It was so unusual."

"Really? What was the verse?"

I was hoping she'd ask. "It goes like this: 'For he will command his angels concerning you to guard you in all your ways; they will lift you up in their hands, so that you will not strike your foot against a stone.' "

"That's in the Bible?" she said, eyebrows at attention.

"Sure is."

"Where?" She stood up as though she were going to get one and bring it to me.

"Do you have a Bible in the house?" I asked, surprised at this turn of events.

"Daddy does," she admitted. "It's a family book. We never read it, though."

"Well, go get it, and I'll show you the verse." This was truly incredible!

"Here, take care of Secrets." She handed the pup to me.

I caressed his tiny head and back as I often did my cats. Then in a moment, Chelsea was back, lugging the heavy book. *Thunk*, she put it to rest on the window seat.

"There. Bet you never thought you'd see the day," she announced, grinning.

I was careful not to say anything to distract from the moment. Gently, I opened the enormous Bible, locating the passage in Psalm ninety-one.

She knelt down and read verses eleven and twelve out loud. "Hey, what a cool thing," she said. "It looks to me like the angels from heaven take their orders from . . . from God."

She'd never mentioned the heavenly Father that way. My heart leaped.

There was a catch in her voice as she read the verse again out loud. Looking up, she whispered, "Can you believe it, Mer—a God who sends angels, His very own angels, to guard us on earth?"

I smiled through tears, and poor little Secrets caught a few drops on his nose. It was best that I didn't say a word. Chelsea was the one who needed to talk—to express her true inner feelings.

The sound of tires on the dirt lane caught our attention. Reluctantly, I turned to look out the window and was surprised to see my father pull up in the driveway. "What's my dad doing here?" I asked.

Chelsea peered out into the darkness. "Half the community is over here."

I didn't say anything, but I wondered about it. Rescue by kidnapping—it seemed so drastic. But love sometimes demands extreme measures.

Chelsea sat down opposite me on the window seat. "I'm glad you're my friend, Merry," she said. "Yet I've given you a hard time about God and the Bible all these years."

I shrugged, playing it down. "We're still friends, though, right?"

"But I think things are going to be different. I won't put you down about God anymore. I promise."

Chelsea's change of heart was a major breakthrough. One I'd been praying for. Levi and Lissa had been praying for her, too, since last spring.

She got up and switched on her matching dresser lamps. The room was filled with brilliant light, and after having sat there in the fading light of dusk, my eyes had to grow accustomed to it. I knew it would be the same for Chelsea. Just because she'd begun to recognize God as a living spirit didn't mean she was necessarily ready to accept the Good News of Jesus. It would take some getting accustomed to. And Sunday was another day.

Chelsea told me to stay put. She went downstairs and soon returned carrying two cans of soda. "You know, I heard something today at school."

"What?"

"Some kid told me that Stiggy Eastman has photographed an amazing shot for this year's contest."

I snickered. "I heard it, too. From Ashley."

Chelsea stared at me. "Hey, you never told me how your photos came out."

"Well, when Mom and I went into town to pick them up, I found someone else's pictures in my package."

"Oh, Merry . . . no. What'll you do?"

"What *can* I do?" I sighed, twisting my hair. I hated discussing this topic. "If you wanna know the truth, I think the photo lab flat-out lost them."

"That's despicable."

"Maybe I'm just not supposed to enter the contest this year."

"How can you say that?"

"Look, nothing can be done except a lot of praying," I admitted.

"Well, then you better keep praying," she said, surprising me.

Something was truly changing in her. She'd never, ever said such a thing to me.

"In my opinion," she said, "the old shanty was the perfect choice, even though I was kind of ticked at you for snapping pictures when I was so freaked."

"I know, and I'm sorry." I looked at her beautiful bedroom with its white French-provincial furniture and thick throw rugs. "I don't think I ever apologized for turning my back on you in the woods when you were so frightened."

"It's okay—no big deal. Besides, we oughta look on the bright side. I think my mom's coming home."

"When . . . how?"

She beamed, her eyes dancing. "That's why all those people are downstairs," she informed me. "Daddy's got a plan, and I know you won't believe this, but it's true: He's going to kidnap my mom because he loves her."

I nodded, reaching for her hand. "I heard about it, I just didn't know when it would be."

She shook her head. "Mom's gonna be so bummed out over it," she went on. "But in time, when everything's behind her, she'll be coming home."

We talked for a while longer, and she explained that her dad didn't want her involved in planning the kidnapping. "That's why I'm glad you came over. With all the talk going on down-stairs . . . well, I'm really glad you're here, Mer."

I glanced at my watch. "I better call my mom. She'll worry if I don't let her know where I am."

"Good idea," she said. "Maybe if all of us did that—let people know exactly where we are—the world would be a better place."

I must admit, I wasn't totally sure what Chelsea was referring to, but I had a sneaking suspicion it had something to do with her new view of life and love. And God.

Sunday was a glorious autumn day in more ways than one. Chelsea went to Sunday school and church with us and actually raised her hand to ask questions in class.

It was strange dealing with my emotions, however. On one side of me sat exuberant Chelsea, so eager to be here, and on the opposite side was flirtatious Ashley, trying her best to get Jon's attention.

I didn't want a single thing to spoil my day with Chelsea, so I honed my concentration skills and did my best to block out all distractions.

In the hallway after class, Ashley cornered me and shared the events of her Friday evening with Jon and their cozy photo session. She reviewed every detail for my benefit.

"Sounds like things went well," I said, refusing to show a smidgen of jealousy and keeping an eye on Chelsea, who'd gone back into the classroom to talk to Mr. Burg.

"Oh, did they ever!" Ashley carried on.

"Well, if I were you, I'd steer clear of that photo lab near the school."

Her eyes burst open. "Really? That's the place Stiggy recommended to me. He said he's always gone there."

"Well, do what you want," I said, going to find Chelsea. "But don't say I didn't warn you."

Ashley cocked her head suspiciously. "Did something happen?"

I wasn't going to tell her my photographs were missing. Not in a million-trazillion years!

"Excuse me," I said, flouncing off to get Chelsea.

Mr. Burg was showing her a scripture, and she asked to write it down. Tickled at her genuine interest, I waited patiently.

It was after the morning worship service, when people were milling around, that I ran into Jon. Actually, he ran into me. Not literally, but he was there in the lobby, smiling his wonderful grin.

I included Chelsea in our conversation, never regretting for one minute that Jon and I wouldn't be speaking alliteration-eze this time around. There were more important things in life than silly word games.

"Everyone's talking about the photography contest," Jon said with a quizzical expression on his handsome face.

I didn't volunteer any information about my lost photos, and I knew I could trust Chelsea not to mention anything, either.

Jon started to alliterate a couple of times, probably out of habit. Chelsea brought up the angel discussion from Sunday school, and Jon listened, apparently pleased to see Chelsea taking interest in such things.

Monday morning, Mr. Eastman missed his daily date with the intercom. Mrs. Fields, my homeroom teacher, explained that our principal had seemed mighty upset about a roll of film. "Evidently, some prized pictures he took have become misplaced," she said before the opening announcements.

Had Mr. Eastman taken his film to the same photo lab as I had? I decided to stop by his office later—maybe during lunch.

The school secretary ended up doing his beloved duty. "Good morning, students," her sweet voice rang through the classrooms—a delightful change. "Today is Monday, October fourteenth. We will have schedule A. Faculty and students, please make a note of this."

Next came the national anthem. I leaped out of my seat, the first student standing as the warbled tape began to play. I felt truly terrific.

The past eleven days had brought traumatic ups and downs for all of us on SummerHill Lane. But the worst was behind us. Mr. Davis, with the help of my dad and several other men, was able to snatch Chelsea's mom away from the cult group after her evening workout at a fitness center. From what Dad says, Chelsea was right—her mom did resist the "rescue." The good news is that Berta Jean Davis will be coming home someday. Not soon, but someday.

Levi Zook? He'll be getting a letter with my picture enclosed sometime this week. I mailed it off this morning before catching the school bus. I'm glad he's listening to God's call. Still, things are going to be very different on SummerHill with Levi off at college—and overseas, too.

As for Jon Klein, he's starting to wake up and realize I'm a girl, not just a buddy—at least I think so. We don't have many classes together this semester, but today he wandered over and sat with Chelsea, Lissa, and me during lunch. Ashley scrutinized the situation from three tables away. If I had my wish, she'd back off entirely. We'll see. . . .

Miracle of miracles! My photographs were finally located. It seems that the owner's wife took them with her to New York by pure accident. And Mr. Eastman found his, too. They were

127

the photos of antique furnishings—some that had been in his family for several generations.

Meanwhile, I guess it doesn't matter much who wins first prize in the photography contest this year. I suppose it would if that's all a girl had to look forward to. But things like hoping to lead a friend to Jesus; writing and receiving letters from a young, handsome preacher-to-be; and oh yes . . . working to improve a sagging relationship with a big brother, now those are higher goals.

The photos of the shed *are* truly incredible, however. Not because of any genius photography on my part. Serene—almost heavenly—are probably the best words to describe the one I'm going to submit for the contest. It's uncanny the way an ethereal white mist showers down over the dark house of secrets.

When I showed it to Chelsea, she got all charged up about it. "I'm telling you, Mer," she declared, "if you stare just right at the shaft of light, you'd think there was a very tall angel hovering over the place."

"A what?" I studied the photo.

"Right there. See that?" She pointed, tracing the outline. "Check out that long, flowing gown. And there . . . I see wings. I do!"

"But it doesn't make sense," I argued. "Why would God's messenger be *there*?"

"Merry," she said, looking at me as if thoroughly aghast. "You prayed, don't you remember?"

I nodded, a smile bursting across my face.

Chelsea was right. I'd asked God to send His angels to watch over us. Maybe there *was* an angel in the photo, but maybe there wasn't. Someday in heaven, I would know for sure.

I thought of my twin sister. "Hey, Faithie already knows," I said, perched on Chelsea's window seat, facing out toward the dusk.

Chelsea sat cross-legged next to me. We gazed at the first star of the evening. Its light shown against the navy blue darkness, topping off our day. "Are you sure she knows?" she asked softly.

I leaned back against the wall and smiled at my friend. "One-hundred-percent-amen sure."

Echoes in the Wind

For Christine Dennis,
my young writer/friend,
who has much in common
with Merry Hanson.

And . . .

for Becky Byler,
my little Amish friend,
who has more in common
with Rachel Zook.

Friendships multiply joys. . . .

—HANDBOOK OF PROVERBS, 1855

"If I die before my mom gets to come home," Chelsea Davis said one wintry afternoon, "will you tell her how much I loved her?"

I stopped playing with my kitten, Lily White, and stared at my longtime friend. "You're *not* dying, and your mom'll be home soon. You'll see."

"But it's taking forever to get her well again." She scooted over the living room floor, going to sit cross-legged in front of our stone fireplace. Her auburn hair fell halfway down her back as she stared into the flames. Turning, she motioned for me to join her.

I abandoned Lily White, who had succumbed to a catnap, and went to sit on the rug next to Chelsea. The warmth from the fire made my face all warm and rosy.

We fell silent, becoming almost drowsy as the blaze crackled and snapped before us. It was the coldest December day in twenty years, or so the noon weatherman had just announced. And I was absolutely thrilled that my friend had come to stay for the weekend. Because, for more than one reason, I was worried about her.

Recently, Chelsea and I had become close friends. Probably because we'd lived through a real-life trauma—the nightmarish event of her mother's running away to join a cult group.

Back in October, Mrs. Davis had made friends with an outgoing couple and, unknowingly, had fallen under their spell and that of their leader. She'd even taken some sort of oath and gone away to live at a compound, leaving Chelsea and her dad alone—and terribly hurt and confused. Now Mrs. Davis was being rehabilitated, and the family hoped she'd be released in time for the holidays.

"When was the last time you heard from your mom?" I asked.

"Last week." Her eyes grew serious. "But she didn't wanna talk much. I don't think she likes the phone—one of her new phobias, maybe."

"So why don't you tell her how you feel in a letter?"

"That I love her?" She seemed surprised.

"Or send a card that says it for you."

Chelsea turned back to watch the fire. "I don't know."

"It's only a suggestion."

Nodding, she continued. "How would *you* feel if your mom went off and lost her mind?"

I took a deep breath. "I really don't know."

Truth was, Chelsea's mom was as sane as anyone in the Lancaster County area. She'd been brainwashed, though, and as my doctor dad had explained to me, *sometimes these things take a long time.*

Not wanting to stir up more sorrow in my friend, I steered the conversation to other things. "Did I tell you? Levi Zook is coming home."

"For Christmas?" Her sea-green eyes brightened. "Since when?"

"Well, he's back from his overseas mission. I know that much."

"Hey, I think you've been holding out on me," she insisted. "Did he write or something?"

I tried not to grin.

"Well, what are we waiting for? Let's have a look at the letter." She was getting pushy now. First morbid . . . now bossy. Which was worse?

"You don't *really* want to read it, do you?" I said.

But she saw through me. "Okay, Mer, if that's the way you wanna play it, fine." And with that, she got up and ran for the stairs.

Of course I was trailing close behind. I didn't want Chelsea to actually find Levi's letter—let alone read what the former Amish boy had written.

Levi Zook was probably the most sincere and loyal seventeen-year-old guy I'd ever known. But then, I hadn't really known many guys his age, except for my brother, Skip, who was a year older than Levi and also in his first year of college.

Actually, Levi and I—and the other Zook children—had grown up together. Our properties shared the same boundary—a thick grove of willow trees. Having grown up in an Old Order Amish family, Levi was fun loving and hardworking. He was also very persistent. Seemed to know exactly what he wanted out of life.

"So where's the letter?" Chelsea demanded, sporting a grin.

I closed the door to my bedroom. "How about if I just summarize it for you?"

"Forget it! I want details—the latest in the ongoing romantic saga between—"

"Romantic? Levi and I aren't . . . uh, together or anything."

"Could've fooled me." She sat at my desk, flashing a sneaky smile as, slowly, she pulled out the narrow drawer. "Is this it? Is this your hiding place?"

I folded my arms and watched, refusing her a single clue. Leaning against the door, I waited.

Naturally, she wasn't anywhere near the spot where I kept private letters and things. But I was surprised to see that she had found something. Something I'd completely forgotten about.

"Well, what do we have here?" She held up a note from Jonathan Klein. It was the one he'd passed to me during math class on Thursday, two days ago.

I knew if I didn't respond, Chelsea would think she'd discovered a gold mine. "Oh that." I pushed my hair back over my shoulder nonchalantly. "Go ahead, have a look."

She moved her lips, probably trying to decipher his alliterated words, then frowned, apparently puzzled. "Does he always write like this?"

I wasn't about to divulge Jon's and my big secret—our ongoing word game. Frequently, we talked to each other in what we called alliteration-eze, trying to see who could think faster off the top of the head. Usually, it was Jon, and for that, I'd secretly named him the Alliteration Wizard.

"Oh, you know Jon," I said, hoping she'd drop the subject.

She glanced at the note again and then waved it in a mocking manner. "Seems to me the next few weeks could be *very* interesting around here."

I didn't have to think twice to know what she meant. The fact was, both Levi and Jon would be breathing the same brisk Pennsylvania air this Christmas.

My one and only hope was that they wouldn't show up at my house on the exact same day.

Echoes in the Wind Two

After supper, Chelsea did some more poking around. "C'mon, Mer, won'tcha give me at least one little hint?" She opened the door to my walk-in closet, then glanced over her shoulder at me. "Well . . . am I hot or cold?"

Honestly, she was very warm; in fact, she was close to stepping into forbidden territory. "Let's just say you're downright nosy!"

We burst out laughing, and much to my relief, she closed the closet door and came to sit on the bed beside me. "You really don't want me to read it, do you, Merry?"

I ignored the question, wandering over to the bookcase to search through volumes of old poetry. "Here," I said, thumbing through Longfellow. "Now, this is truly cool."

Hearing her exhale, I knew she was restless about my being so evasive. "What's this got to do with Levi Zook?" she insisted.

"Just wait. You'll see." I planted myself in the middle of the room and cleared my throat. "I want you to hear a beautiful passage from *Evangeline*."

"Oh, real sweet, Mer," she retorted, folding her arms. "How boring can you get?"

"No . . . listen. It's incredible, really." I glanced at her, waiting for the fake scowl to fade. "Are you ready?"

"Do I have a choice?"

I held the book open and began to read, " 'And, when the echoes had ceased, like a sense of pain was the silence.' "

She gazed up at me incredulously. "Who wrote that?"

"Henry Wadsworth Longfellow."

"Read it again," she said softly.

I did and, by the serene look on her face, knew Chelsea had actually enjoyed it.

"What's it mean?" she asked.

Returning the book to the shelf, I gave her my two cents' worth. "I suppose you could read into it whatever you want to. But for me, it's about Levi. I mean, there are many happy echoes in my mind from our friendship."

"Last summer?"

I nodded. "And before that, because Levi and I are friends from childhood. But they—the echoes—are starting to fade."

Do I dare express something so personal?

Levi had told me, without mincing words, that I was the girl for him. Trouble was, even though we were only a year apart, he was off at a Mennonite college in Virginia these days, and I was a sophomore at James Buchanan High. For now, we'd agreed to remain friends; nothing more. And since I had my heart set on the Alliteration Wizard, that was ideal.

"Are you saying you're suffering because of Levi's silence?" Chelsea asked.

"Well, he hasn't written for weeks. But then, he's been down in South America building a church."

She stretched her arms high over her head. "Whoa, I'm totally confused. I mean, the way you look at Jon Klein sometimes . . . what's that about?"

"What?"

She giggled. "C'mon, Mer, you know what I'm talking about."

"No, I don't. And I think it's time you spill it out!"

She jumped off the bed and started pulling on my arm. "Come sit down and stop showing off, and maybe I will."

I probably *was* overdoing the dramatics—reading high-brow poetry and all, especially to a down-home girl like Chelsea. Actually, we were both country girls. "Okay, I'm sitting. So talk."

She told me what she'd been observing every morning in the hallways of James Buchanan High. "Jon's always hanging out at your locker. And you . . . you're always soaking it up."

"What do you mean, soaking? Aren't friends supposed to pay attention to each other?" It was a pitiful comeback.

"But this thing you two are always doing," she added. "It looks so . . . so weird."

"What? What's weird?"

She pulled on a strand of her hair, pausing for a moment before going on. "Oh, I don't know, you always end up staring at him, Mer, not saying a word—like you're love-struck or something."

"Oh that. I know exactly what you're saying. But it's not what you think!"

Her eyes bore into me. "So, what *is* it?"

I fell over onto the bed in a torrent of giggles. What Chelsea didn't know was that each morning before school, Jon would show up at my locker with some sort of clever greeting. Always alliterated, actually.

He expected me to fire back something similar in response. So what Chelsea had termed pining over Jon was nothing more than mere concentration on my part.

"What's so funny?" she demanded. "Are you nuts over two guys? Is that it?"

This was a curious comment, and one I certainly didn't want to explore further. Not with Chelsea. Probably not with anyone.

I grabbed one of my sham pillows and playfully began flinging it at her. "You ask way too many questions."

Unexpectedly, she followed suit, walloping me good with the other bed pillow. "I must be right!" she hollered gleefully. And the first pillow fight of the weekend had begun.

But Chelsea was *not* right. Not even close. I have to admit that it was I who liked Jon—liked him a lot. But it was Levi who liked me.

During family devotions, Chelsea listened as Dad read the Bible. She surprised me by being attentive. This was the formerly atheist girl friend who'd resisted everything I'd ever said about God or the Bible up until a few months ago. Tomorrow she was going to attend Sunday school and church with me and my family. Not for the first time, either.

Later, when we changed into our pajamas upstairs, Chelsea asked me to pray with her. "You know, about my mom," she said with trusting eyes. "More than anything, I want her back home for Christmas."

"Sure, I'll pray." We knelt beside my bed, surrounded by Shadrach, Meshach, Abednego, and Lily White, my four wonderful cats. Folding my hands, I began. "Dear Lord, thank you for being with Chelsea's mom and—"

"And for getting her this far safely," Chelsea cut in.

I smiled, my eyes still closed. "We know you have a plan for her . . . and for the whole Davis family," I continued. "We're counting on you to work things out."

She was quick to add, "And if you don't mind, could you please bring my mom home in time for . . . for your birthday?"

I was so delighted, I could hardly end the prayer. Instead, Chelsea jumped right in and finished for me. "Amen, and thanks for hearing Merry's and my prayer."

Turning, I gave her a hug. "Hey, you're good. Is this a first?"

She dipped her head, looking sheepish. "First time praying out loud, yeah."

"So . . . you've been talking to God silently sometimes?"

"At home in my room."

Getting up, I arranged the cat quartet toward the foot of the bed on top of my blue-striped comforter. "I'm glad you told me, Chels." I was going to let her have my bed for the night. The floor and my sleeping bag were just fine for me.

"Now that you know one of *my* secrets, how about if you tell me about that letter of yours?" She was steadfast and persistent. Almost as determined as Levi!

Before going to the closet, I swept my hair back into a loose ponytail, securing it with a band. Then I located the pinkish shoe box nestled on the middle shelf of my closet near my camera collection and pulled it down. "Okay. You wanna know about Levi . . . here goes." I felt surprisingly comfortable with what I'd decided to do.

Sifting through the small box, I found his latest letter and handed it to my friend. By the eager look on Chelsea's face, she was itching to have a peek. Maybe if she read it for herself she would see that *I* was not the one pushing to be more than friends! Not in the least.

Three *Echoes in the Wind*

"Okay with you if I read out loud?" Chelsea wore a triumphant look.

"Don't be too loud." I glanced at the door. "You know how a mother can be sometimes." Suddenly, I realized how foolish my comment was. From what Chelsea had been saying, she'd give anything to have *her* mother around.

Chelsea began reading: " 'My dear Merry,' " Stopping for a second, she hinted a smile. "Is this how he always starts?"

I shrugged. "Read it. Don't analyze it."

She went on. " 'I realize it may seem like a long time since you've gotten a letter from me, and it has been. But all this time I've been helping build a church in Bolivia with other Mennonite students.

" 'Please, Merry, don't be thinking that I haven't thought of you every day, though, since leaving SummerHill.' "

She paused momentarily, gazing at me with quizzical eyes. "This guy's crazy about you!"

"Shh! Keep your voice down," I reminded her.

"Yeah, yeah . . . because your mom's gonna think Levi's coming home to propose if she gets wind of it, right?"

"There's no chance of a proposal. I'm one-hundred-percent-amen sure about that."

Chelsea chuckled at my pet phrase. "Sounds like you're mighty positive."

"I'm *only* sixteen. Levi's got better sense."

"Well," she shot back, "everyone knows the Amish marry young."

"But he's not Amish anymore." I motioned for her to continue the letter. "He's Mennonite, remember?"

She smiled a taunting smile, then found her place and continued. " 'The Lord willing, I'll be coming home December 20th to spend Christmas with my family. I want to see you, Merry. Will that suit you?' "

By now, Chelsea was bouncing up and down on my bed, reacting to the quaint, folksy sound of his letter, no doubt.

"Calm down," I said. "It's no big deal."

But she was beside herself with glee, waving the letter around. "I can't believe you're not freaked out about this. I mean, this Levi person is definitely in love with you, Merry Hanson!"

I dashed over and snatched the letter out of her hand. "Let me see that!" Scanning through it, I especially scrutinized the remainder.

Remember, if it won't work out for us to visit together before or during Christmas, we'll have plenty of time to talk afterward. I'll be in the Lancaster area well into the New Year. God bless you always, Merry.

With greatest affection,
Levi Zook

It was out of the question. No one was going to read the ending of this letter! Quickly, I returned it to the safety of the envelope. "I think you've had enough for one night," I stated.

"Hey!" Chelsea wailed. "Don't do this to me!"

The noise brought an almost instant knock on my bed-room door. "Girls, girls, it's getting late," Mom's voice crept through.

"Sorry," I called. "We were just going to bed."

"Don't you wish," Chelsea whispered, eyeing me.

"We *are*," I insisted after the sound of footsteps faded away.

"Aw, don't be such a party pooper," she whined.

"This isn't a party. Besides, I'm tired." And I was ticked, too. Chelsea was being a real pain. I turned out the light and wiggled down into my sleeping bag. " 'Night."

"Don't be so sensitive" came her reply.

I huffed a bit. "Well, I am, so get over it."

A few moments passed, and my eyes began to adjust to the dark room. I wondered if I'd been too short with her.

Then Chelsea's voice broke the silence. "Hey, I'm sorry. Okay?"

"Sure. See you in the morning."

———

Sunday breakfast was served promptly at eight-thirty. Dad—not Mom—expected us to be at the table without delay. Which meant both Chelsea and I were rushing around taking turns in the shower.

Dad had always been a stickler for promptness, especially on Sundays. To him, it was better to show up for church half an hour early than to be ten minutes late.

When Chelsea and I made our entrance into the kitchen, he peered over his newspaper briefly, sporting a stubby growth of whiskers as he sat at the head of the table. "Good morning, girls."

"Morning," we said in unison.

Mom served up her best blueberry muffins, along with scrambled eggs, bacon, and a side dish of cantaloupe. Chelsea gave me a sideways glance, eyes wide.

"Mom doesn't mess around at mealtime," I said, loud enough for Mom to hear.

She smiled, coming over to the table with fresh butter from the Zooks' farm and a dish of whipped cream for the muffins. "Merry's right," she said, serving Dad first. "Always remember: Good eaters make good citizens."

To that, Dad closed his paper, clucking as Mom sat across from him. "I don't know about the 'good citizens' part," he said. "But it never hurts to eat heartily now and then."

Chelsea bowed her head along with the rest of us when Dad said the table blessing. Having her in the house like this—seeing her eager to join in with our family routine—encouraged me. I couldn't wait to tell Levi about the changes happening in her. Maybe it was the one thing we would feel comfortable talking about while he was home. Back last spring, he'd agreed to pray for Chelsea, as had Jon Klein and several other of my church friends.

Truly amazing things had begun to take place. In fact, the girl was a walking, breathing turnaround. And now, sitting beside her at our family table, I was beginning to feel sorry about the way I'd cut her off last night.

After the prayer and a quick morning devotional, Mom poured orange juice for everyone. "I almost forgot, Merry," she said. "Rachel Zook stopped by earlier."

"She did?"

"She wants you to visit her sometime this afternoon."

I glanced at Chelsea. "Wanna see an authentic Amish dairy farm?"

"Cool," she replied.

"Good. Then we'll go right after dinner."

Dad stirred sugar into his coffee and mentioned a recent rumor he'd heard. "Is it true that Levi is coming home for Christmas?"

He was asking *me*!

Chelsea smirked, no doubt dying to see how I handled myself.

"Levi's coming home, all right." I was unable to control my smile.

"Oh?" Now it was Mom's turn to perk up her ears.

I flashed a warning to Chelsea. Now wasn't the time for her to blurt something out about the guy's "sweet" letter.

After a gulp of juice, I explained, "Rachel's probably planning something special for him. Who knows? A welcome-home party *would* be nice." It was an attempt to divert the focus of the conversation, even though I knew well and good the Amish weren't much for throwing parties.

Dad resumed his coffee drinking and—thank goodness—seemed to be losing interest.

Mom wasn't as easy to sidetrack. "How is it that you know all this?" she asked.

Chelsea was anything but discreet in her reaction to Mom's pointed question. She coughed and nearly choked! And if I hadn't been in complete control of *my* wits, I'd have sent her a fiery dart with my eyes.

Or worse.

That afternoon, we bundled up in the warmest clothing we could find. Chelsea, who hadn't anticipated the snowy trek to our neighbors' farmhouse when she'd packed, borrowed a scarf and heavy mittens from Mom. We were so heavily wrapped in layers, we moved like lunar astronauts. Laughing, we lumbered down the long front walk, then on toward SummerHill Lane.

I didn't even think of taking the shortcut to Rachel's house this time. But I told Chelsea about the secret place deep in the willow grove, now buried in snow, far back from the road.

"Really? There's a secret place in there?" She shielded her eyes from the sun, looking.

"It's impossible to see from here."

"Does Levi know about it?" she teased.

I shook my head, breathing hard as we turned into Zooks' long, private lane. "The willow grove has always been Rachel's and my place, I guess you could say."

"I can't wait to see where she lives up close."

"Rachel might sound a little different—I mean, the way she talks and stuff," I explained.

"I remember." Then Chelsea reminded me that she'd already met Rachel. "She came to my house with the cocker spaniel puppy in October . . . after Mom left us."

"Oh, that's right." I breathed in the icy, damp air. "So . . . what did you think of her?"

"Well, for starters, I think she needs some help choosing her wardrobe." She snickered. "Other than that, she's okay."

"All Amishwomen dress that way," I said. "You know that."

Chelsea hurried to keep up with me. "What's she gonna think, your bringing a stranger over?"

"Oh, you just wait," I said, shivering. "Rachel and her family are the most hospitable folk you could ever want to meet."

"Wow, that's hard to believe. Seems to me that *your* family's the most neighborly around here."

"We try, but the Amish have us beat all to pieces." I turned and headed up the freshly shoveled walk.

Almost immediately, Rachel appeared at the back door, greeting us as she opened it. She was wearing her usual long, dark dress and apron, as well as a white head covering. "*Wilkom!*" she said. "Come on in and get warm." She helped Chelsea with her coat and scarf, smiling broadly when I introduced my friend. "It's real nice to see ya again," Rachel replied. "How's that new puppy of yours?"

Chelsea responded eagerly. "Oh, you oughta see him. He's growing fast now. And so cute!"

I stood beside the old woodstove, rubbing my hands together and taking in the enormous kitchen, sparkling clean as usual. "Did I ever tell you what Chelsea named the pup?"

Rachel shook her head. "I don't recall."

"She named him Secrets," I volunteered. "Isn't that dear?"

At the mention of the pup's name, little Susie came over from the kitchen table, where she'd been coloring. "I heard ya talkin' about that puppy dog," she said, still holding a crayon.

I gave her a quick hug. "Maybe Secrets can come for a visit sometime. Would you like that?"

Her eyes were bright. "*Jah*. Then he can see his mama again!"

Abe and Esther Zook glanced up, smiling from their rocking chairs, where they were both reading. It was evident that Sunday—the Lord's Day—particularly a cold, snowy one, was meant to be shared together as a family at the Zooks' farmhouse.

The other children, Nancy, Ella Mae, and Aaron, continued to play their games quietly at the table. Susie, however, had to show off her coloring book before Chelsea and I followed Rachel toward the hallway stairs.

"Make it snappy," her father said. I knew he wanted all his children gathered around the warm stove in the kitchen.

Soon, I understood why. Rachel's bedroom was practically a deep freeze. Wishing for my coat, I hugged myself. Chelsea did the same.

Almost as soon as the bedroom door shut, Rachel started jabbering up a storm. "Oh, Merry, didja hear? Our Levi's comin' home for Christmas!"

I nodded, determined not to look at Chelsea. She'd be getting too big a kick out of this.

"Matthew Yoder—my friend down the lane—and I wanna have a skating party on the pond. You know . . . for couples. Wouldja come and be Levi's partner?"

"Uh . . . maybe Levi should have a say in it. You know."

"No, no, it's all a surprise for him," she insisted.

I paused briefly, thinking things over. Chelsea nudged me from behind, and I knew there was no begging off.

"Oh, do come, won'tcha Merry?" Rachel pleaded. "Do it for Levi?" Her heart was set on this. I could see the excitement in her shining eyes.

"Okay," I said. "Sounds like fun. When?"

"How 'bout the day after he arrives?" She studied me hard. "That's Saturday, I'm a-thinkin'. And please, keep it a secret from him, won'tcha now?"

Chelsea started to giggle slightly, but my eyes sent a dart of disapproval her way.

"Don't worry. I'll keep it quiet," I promised.

"*Gut*, then it's set." Rachel touched her *Kapp*, the white devotional head covering Amishwomen and girls wore.

Silently, we headed downstairs to the toasty kitchen—a welcome relief in more ways than one.

"So . . . the Amish don't throw parties, huh?" Chelsea taunted as we trudged home over the encrusted snow.

"The adults aren't real big on it," I said.

We walked a ways farther before Chelsea said, "Seems to me, Rachel has more than an inkling how her brother feels about you. Am I right?"

I sighed. "Rachel's got herself a boyfriend now—calls him her *beau*. She must be thinking that everyone else should be in love just 'cause she is."

"Is Rachel's boyfriend Amish?" Her breath hung white in the crisp air.

"You better believe Matthew's Amish. Rachel's bound and determined to marry in her church. In fact, last I heard, they're planning to take instruction classes late next summer to prepare for baptism."

"Hmm. I wonder what it would be like," she said.

"What?"

"Oh, being Amish."

I laughed a little. "Well, for a while there, I wondered the same thing. Even almost convinced myself that I should become Plain."

"Last summer?"

"Uh-huh."

She stared at me. "You've gotta be kidding. All that talk about Levi Zook wanting you to be his girl for the summer—was that for *real*?"

I chuckled. "Surprised even me."

Chelsea adjusted her earmuffs against the wind. "Whoa, Mer, I can almost hear your mom going on about it."

"You don't know the half of it."

"That bad?" she questioned.

"Let's just say it was one of those times in my life when we truly clashed." I left it at that.

We hurried around the side yard, past the gazebo, and toward the back door.

Chelsea seemed to want to pursue the topic, but Mom was watering her African violets in the corner of the kitchen when we walked in. "How are the Zooks?" she asked over her shoulder.

"Oh, you know, it's Sunday, so it's pretty quiet over there," I said.

"Mighty cold, too," Chelsea offered.

Mom turned around, wearing a frown. "Something wrong with their woodstove?"

"Oh, nothing like that," I was quick to say. "But we went upstairs with Rachel for a bit—it was ice-cold up there for sure!"

Mom seemed to understand and, fortunately, didn't press for more details.

But Chelsea did. Thank goodness she waited till we were back in my room, though. "Does your mom know you still like Levi?"

"What?"

"C'mon, Mer, you heard me. You're always saying 'what' for no reason."

I shrugged and sat down at my desk across the room from her. Chelsea was right: Saying "what" was a cop-out—a bad habit. But *what* could I do about it?

My friend started to gather up her clothes and things. "You know, I have this very strong feeling," she said without looking at me.

Snorting, I went to stand at the window, staring out at the pristine white. Fresh snow covered the field across SummerHill Lane like a wide, thick blanket. "You and your feelings," I muttered.

"Yeah, well, today I was sure that you couldn't wait to go visit Rachel," she added.

Not answering, I turned from the window and went around the room finding her brush and perfume and makeup, helping pack her bag.

"You *know* I'm right, Merry." She folded her pajamas and bathrobe. "I mean, you should've seen yourself during church today. You were, uh . . . pretty distracted."

I suppose she had a point, except that I hadn't been thinking about Levi during church. And before saying anything to deny it, I piled a handful of her belongings into the overnight case. "Weren't you listening at all yesterday when I read that line from Longfellow?" I said at last.

"Longfellow, short fellow . . . Plain fella. What's the difference?" she tittered.

And that was the beginning of our second and final pillow fight of the weekend.

Monday dawned, bringing with it more subzero temperatures. A ferocious wind blew out of the east, making me shiver as I waited for the bus in the early morning light. I thought of a poetic phrase by Dickens. *I am always conscious of an uncomfortable sensation now and then when the wind is blowing in the east.*

The old school bus poked its way up SummerHill Lane, puffing white exhaust smoke out the back. The day seemed colder than I ever remembered a Pennsylvania winter, even though, according to the calendar, winter wasn't officially scheduled for nearly two weeks.

Two more weeks. . . .

Levi would be home soon. How would I act when I saw him again? What would I say? An awkward feeling followed as I thought about seeing him face-to-face.

Then I spotted Abe Zook turning out of his private lane, driving an open sleigh piled with his younger children—all but Rachel, who had already completed the eight grades of school required by the Amish.

One-room Amish schools never had to close for bad weather around Lancaster. Plain folk were well behind modern technology, but they sure knew how to put ingenuity to good use.

Abe Zook whistled to Apple, one of his three Belgian horses, and made the turn onto the road. The children waved and called their cheerful "hullos" to me.

Grinning, I was sure Chelsea—if she'd been here to witness it—would have enjoyed this down-home touch of Plain life.

My teeth were chattering by the time the bus creaked to a stop. Half frozen, I stumbled up the steps and into the bus. Chelsea motioned to me, and I slid in next to her.

"Did you see the Zooks' one-horse open sleigh?" I pointed to it through the windshield.

"Hey, cool." Chelsea started singing "Jingle Bells"; then she told some of the kids behind us about my Amish neighbors. "They're the nicest people, really," she said.

Jon Klein sat several rows ahead of us—nose buried in a book. I tried to recall if he'd looked up about the time I got on. But I knew if he had, I would've remembered.

I stared at the back of his head—his light brown hair was always well-groomed. Jon was the picture of perfection.

Say that with all p*'s*, I told myself, wondering how I'd fare if he ever decided not to stop at my locker for our session of silliness. What then?

I shot a desperate look at Chelsea. She shook her head and shrugged. "Why waste your time on a guy who hardly knows you exist?"

This was a brand-new approach. "Really?" I said. "Sounds to me like you think I oughta welcome Levi home with open arms."

She twisted her thick auburn locks, worn straight today. "At least if you ended up with Levi, you wouldn't have to hire a translator to read his letters," she said, referring back to Jon's note.

"No, but I think I oughta have a genuine call from God first."

She frowned. "What are you saying?"

"Truth is, Levi Zook is studying to be a preacher. He really shouldn't be hanging around with just any girl."

"So . . . you think you're a lousy choice. Is that it?"

"Don't be sarcastic. I *mean* it. Levi should be spending time with girls who feel inclined to become a preacher's wife."

She leaned her elbow on her books and looked straight at me. "You know, Mer, now that I've actually started paying attention to all your God-talk, I think I better tell you something. Not to be mean, but I get the strong feeling you aren't very trusting these days, at least not toward your heavenly Father."

This comment seemed strange coming from Chelsea Davis, a former self-proclaimed atheist turned almost believer.

"You're kidding," I heard myself say. "You actually think that?"

"Let's put it this way: Maybe if you spent less time reading that absurd poetry of yours . . ."

She didn't have to finish; I knew what Chelsea meant. Reading the Bible was far more helpful—and important—in the long run.

"Well, if this isn't a switch—you preaching to *me*." I laughed, and wonder of wonders, the Alliteration Wizard turned around and smiled!

Jon began spouting alliteration-eze after his usual "Morning, Mistress Merry" greeting. "Whether wind be wintry or wild, we'll wile away the wait for warmer weather."

"What?" I said, prolonging closing my locker. With its door gaping wide and Jonathan standing near me, I felt sheltered from the world of school and students. It was only an illusion, of course. "*W*'s, huh? Well, if you ask me, your sentence doesn't make much sense," I was glad to inform him.

His heart-stopping grin caught me off guard. "Better not boast 'bout brilliant comebacks," he replied.

Man, was he good!

"We'll see about that," I said. "Pick a letter. Any letter!"

He thought for a moment, but as he was about to speak, Ashley Horton, our pastor's daughter and probably the prettiest girl in the entire school, came trotting by with Stiggy Eastman, winner of this year's coveted photography contest honors.

"Hello-o, Merry. Hi, Jon," she cooed, waving.

"Ashley!" The Alliteration Wizard turned suddenly. "You're exactly the person I need to see." And with that, he dashed off after her, completely forgetting our word game. Forgetting something else, too—a proper good-bye.

All day long, the east wind blew. And with it came echoes—memories of my past days and years as Levi's friend. Was I worrying too much about my next encounter with him? Or was something else bothering me? Anyway, I was truly miserable and told Lissa Vyner, another one of my church friends, about it during P.E.

"You know what's discouraging?" I said. "Every time I think Jon and I might actually have a chance, Ashley comes flouncing along and interferes. It's so-o frustrating."

Lissa pushed her wispy blond hair away from her delicate face, looking at me with wide blue eyes. "Are you praying about this?"

"No," I reluctantly admitted. "I know I should be. It just seems like some of us get all the breaks."

I remembered that Jon had been interested in her for a while last spring.

Lissa didn't say anything, and we hurried out of the gym locker room wearing our white shorts and tops, ready for a rousing volleyball game. "How about if I call you tonight?" she said, hurrying off to take her position near the net.

I spotted Ashley Horton on my team. *Oh great*, I thought. How was I going to play a decent game with my competition hurling her smile around the court?

Off and on during the match, my mind seemed to play tricks on me. I actually started second-guessing my friendship with Jon. Maybe he was using me . . . could that be all it was? Was I simply someone to play his word game? I knew I was truly good as his partner in phrases. And I also knew for a fact that none of the other girls he'd ever liked had been introduced to the Alliteration Game.

What did it mean?

"Heads up!" The P.E. instructor blew her whistle.

I ducked.

But . . . too late.

The ball slammed into my head. I fell backward, stumbling onto the floor.

"Merry!" I heard Lissa call out.

But in nothing flat, I was sitting up, a goose egg on the back of my head.

I'd hit the floor hard, and the teacher was worried. "We better have the nurse check you out, Merry," she said.

So with Lissa and Ashley on either side of me, I limped dizzily down the hall to the nurse's room.

Served me right, I suppose. Men were a menace to the mind. Hey, I liked that!

And I made a mental note to communicate it to Jon after school.

Six *Echoes in the Wind*

The knot on my head turned into a sickening headache by suppertime. Of course my dad made a big deal about checking the pupils of my eyes. "Have to make sure they're dilating normally."

"Do I have a concussion?" I asked, letting Mom baby me by bringing meat loaf, mashed potatoes, and green beans up to my room on a tray.

Flicking on his penlight, Dad shined it in my right eye, then away. "Looks to me like you'll be just fine, honey."

"Why didn't my head hurt earlier?"

Mom pulled up a chair and sat down, watching me eat. "Could be a delayed reaction."

"Perhaps," Dad was saying. "Often the body will kick in enough adrenaline to carry through the moment of injury and awhile beyond."

"But then, look out—whammy!" I joked but avoided laughing. My head was throbbing too much for that.

When the phone rang, Mom rushed out of the room and down the hall.

Dad winked. "I believe she's expecting a call from your brother."

"Is Skip doing okay now?" I asked. He'd found the adjustment to college life tougher than expected.

"If you're referring to his homesickness, yes, I think that may have run its course."

I sipped some hot tea. "Like my headache will, right?"

Dad rubbed his chin thoughtfully. "How did it happen—the volleyball hitting you in the head?"

To tell the truth, I felt uncomfortable spilling out the details to Dad. I mean, he wasn't one to come down hard on stupidity or anything. But I couldn't bring myself to talk about the state I'd been in during P.E.—contemplating the Alliteration Wizard during a fast-paced volleyball game. C'mon!

"I guess I wasn't paying much attention," I mumbled. Picking up my fork, I proceeded to fill my mouth with mashed potatoes and gravy. That way if he asked additional questions, I'd have plenty of time to think of a genius response while chewing.

"Merry," Mom called from the hallway. "Do you feel up to talking to Lissa Vyner?"

I nodded my answer to Dad, who passed it on to Mom. Soon enough, she brought the cordless phone to me, and my parents made a reluctant exit.

"Hi, Lissa," I said.

"How are you feeling now?"

"Okay, except for a monstrous headache."

"You really got whacked today. What do you expect?"

"I'll live, I guess," I replied.

"Aw, Mer, don't say that." She paused. "Oh, before I forget, Ashley wants you to know she's worried about you."

"That's nice."

Silence came and went. "Uh . . . you two still aren't—"

"It's nothing to worry about, really," I was quick to say. True, Ashley and I still experienced some friction between us, off and on. Probably because both of us had our hearts set on Jon Klein.

Lissa went on. "Will you let me know if there's anything I can do?"

"Thanks, Liss, but I'll be fine."

"Well, if you need homework assignments or anything, have your mom call the school secretary and let me know."

"I really can't miss school tomorrow," I assured her. "But thanks anyway." We said good-bye and hung up, and I resumed eating my supper.

Later, when the pain medication finally took hold, I opened my Bible to the mini-concordance in the back. I searched for the word *echo*, curious to see if it was represented anywhere in the Scriptures. It wasn't.

Then, silly me, I even thought of calling Ashley to ask if she might borrow her father's big concordance to look up the word. Instead, I decided to try a synonym. I looked up the word *answer* in my Bible.

Sure enough, oodles of references. Actually thirty or more. I didn't take time to locate all of them, but I did read Psalm ninety-one, enjoying it for its rhythm and flow—much the way an excellent poem is written in free verse. The part about the angels in verses eleven and twelve always excited me. To think that there were heavenly messengers in charge of protecting us here on earth!

Then I came to the next to the last verse. The one with the word I was looking for: *answer*.

God's Word prompted me to pray for Chelsea's mother once again. When I finished, I wondered if it was too late to call Chelsea herself.

I checked the clock in my room. Eight-thirty. She'd still be up. Swiftly, I dialed her number.

"Davis residence." It was Chelsea's father.

"Hello, Mr. Davis. This is Merry Hanson. May I please speak to Chelsea?"

"Hold on." *Clunk.* He set the phone down hard.

I waited for a moment, feeling uneasy, then Chelsea answered.

"Is everything all right?" I inquired.

She sounded hesitant. "I'm not sure if Daddy wants me telling you this, but my mom just called."

"She did? That's great."

"Well, I don't know. We got the feeling she doesn't wanna come home quite yet."

My heart sank. "Oh, Chelsea, I'm so sorry."

"Me too." She sounded as if she might cry. "What if this rehabilitation stuff doesn't work out, Mer? What if she never gets back to her normal self?"

I tried to comfort her. "My dad says it takes longer for some patients. But, please, don't give up. We're praying, remember?"

She was silent for a few seconds. Then—"I really think your prayers are the only thing keeping us going."

I felt a lump in my throat. Dear, dear Chelsea. What she'd gone through! How could I help her now?

"You said something today that was absolutely correct," I added, remembering our conversation on the bus. "About my obsession for poetry. Well, I looked up some verses in the Bible on the word *answer*, and guess what? I found a bunch of truly terrific Psalms."

"Why that word?"

"Remember how we were talking about echoes—from that poem by Longfellow?"

"Yeah?"

"Well, I decided to check out some verses using a similar word. And 'answer' was it."

"The book of Psalms does seem a little like poetry," she remarked.

"You're right."

Soon we were talking about her worries and fears over her absentee mother. "Sometimes I get the feeling she doesn't love me anymore," Chelsea said.

"You're her own flesh and blood—the only child she's ever had. Of course she loves you."

I heard her sigh. "I wish none of this had ever happened, Merry. I really do!" She paused for a moment. "Will you read one of those verses you found?" she asked unexpectedly.

"Sure." I reached for my Bible. "Here's Psalm ninety-one, verse fifteen. It goes like this: 'He will call upon me, and I will answer him; I will be with him in trouble, I will deliver him and honor him.' "

"Wow," she whispered. "That 'he' in the verse could be anyone, right?"

"Yep."

She paused, then said, "Knowing that makes me feel a whole lot better."

"It's a comfort," I admitted. "We can count on those words, you know."

"Hey, I'm gonna look it up in our big, old family Bible."

"Good idea," I said.

It was getting late by the time we said our good-byes. I was anxious to sleep away my headache—praying, too, that an end was soon to come to the Davis family's nightmare.

Almost two weeks later, the lump on my head was completely gone. And—oh glory—it was the last day of school before Christmas break! It was also the day Levi Zook was scheduled to arrive home.

Getting off the bus after school, I glanced around almost sheepishly. In the distance, beyond the long grove of willow trees between my house and the Zooks' farm, I surveyed the area for clues of Levi's return.

"What's with you?" Chelsea cast a sideways stare.

I shrugged, not wanting to let on how nervous I was.

She laughed. "Levi's nowhere in sight. Honest, Mer."

I said nothing and scurried toward the white-columned front porch. Chelsea and I headed inside by way of the front door—the quickest way to warmth. Smells of hot cocoa, mingled with freshly baked chocolate chip cookies, greeted us.

I hung up my coat, scarf, and gloves in the hall closet. "In case you didn't already know it, my mom's a genius in the kitchen," I told Chelsea.

"You don't have to convince me." She yanked off her snow boots and tossed her jacket onto the coatrack. Then the two of us, as if pulled by a magnet, hurried to the kitchen.

My mom, being the hostess she is, sat us down and brought steaming hot cocoa and a plateful of cookies to the table. "Did you girls have a good last day of school for the year?"

"Hey, that's right!" Chelsea said.

"No school till after New Year's, right?" I chimed in.

"Two incredible weeks away from school!" Gleefully, my friend reached for a cookie.

"Be sure to take some cookies home with you." Mom removed the red-and-green plaid apron she'd been wearing.

My friend's face seemed to radiate at the offer. "Thanks, Mrs. Hanson. My dad absolutely adores chocolate chip cookies. In fact, my mom used to make . . ." Her voice trailed off, and I felt a lump push up in my throat.

But leave it to my mother—a true master at steering conversation in a happier direction. And she certainly did that, maneuvering it clear away from Chelsea and right over to me. "Oh, Merry, you'll never guess who I saw today." There was mischief in her smile.

"Let me guess," I said, wrinkling my face. "Levi Zook?"

Mom blew lightly on her hot drink, then looked back at me. "Merry? What's the matter?"

"Nothing, really." Quickly, I got up to check on my cats. They seemed to be having a heyday with their own milky snack.

My abrupt reaction may have been a bit too obvious—giving myself away. But I certainly did not want to discuss Levi. At least not in front of both my mom *and* my girl friend.

Chelsea shot me a sympathetic look, and I leaned over to pet my furry friends, calling each one by name.

Later, Chelsea and I were secluded away in my room. "Are you upset?" she probed.

"Not really."

"Does your mom know about Levi's letters?"

"She's not dense. Anyone in this house can see that his letters are coming less often, if that's what you mean. But as far as ever reading them, no, Mom really doesn't know what he writes to me."

Chelsea sat on the floor and leaned back on the side of my bed. "What would she think if she knew he was in love with you?"

I laughed it off. "Levi's too young to know that."

"Meaning?"

"C'mon, you know what I'm saying." I joined her on the floor, sitting cross-legged, too. "After all his years growing up Amish, Levi's only now having a chance to experience the outside, modern world."

"So?"

I sighed. Why was she making me spell this out? "So I guess I really don't know how I feel about him anymore. Maybe he's feeling the same way." There, I'd said it. Straight and clear.

"Aw, Mer, you've gotta be kidding me" was her reply. "You gave up a chance with Jon last summer so you could hang out with Levi. Now you're telling me you don't care about him?"

The confusion in her eyes was evident. And the longer we sat there, the more I realized that if I were to be honest with myself, I'd have to admit I didn't quite understand it, either.

Only time would tell. Unfortunately, time was against me. Tomorrow was the skating party on Zooks' pond. Rachel had talked of nothing else for the past few days. Among other things, the party was to be an opportunity for me to meet Matthew Yoder, the boy who'd been taking her home from Saturday night singings for several months now. The boy she was sure would shine his flashlight onto her bedroom window someday—a time-honored signal among the Old Order Amish indicating a marriage proposal.

"Echoes . . . only echoes of the past," I said. "That's all Levi and I have now."

She waved my comment into the air. "Merry, when will you ever come down out of that cloud of yours?"

I bobbed my head, looking around, pretending to see what she was talking about. "Hey, something *is* missing," I teased. "We need some music in here. How about some cloud music?"

She laughed but seemed to agree. So I turned on the radio and found my favorite contemporary Christian station. Maybe the music would drown out our conversation if there were curious ears nearby.

Then I had a flash of an idea. "I think it's high time for a photo update," I said, heading for my walk-in closet. "When was the last time you had your picture taken?"

She grinned. "September, for school pictures."

"That's much too long ago," I said, removing my digital camera from its case. "It's nearly Christmas. Let's have a photo shoot and send some pics to your mom. Okay with you?"

Her face turned serious for a moment, then brightened. "Hey, maybe this is the answer—the very thing to encourage my mom to hurry and get better."

I took off the lens cap and stopped in my tracks. "Wait a minute. Are you saying she doesn't have any pictures of you?"

"Nothing from the present, only the past." Her words came out sounding choked and dry.

"Maybe your *future* will rest on this." I motioned for her to lift her head a bit. "I'll get prints made right away, and you can send the pictures off to her."

Click.

"And she'll have them before Christmas." She sighed audibly. "Only thing is, I wish Mom would come home to SummerHill instead."

"How about this," I continued. "Can you smile real big—you know, kinda make your eyes plead into the camera? Good. Now hold that pose right there."

Click.

Another nice shot. Chelsea was actually getting into the spirit of things.

In the end, I had seven or eight truly great poses. Even Chelsea seemed impressed.

"Okay, first thing tomorrow, I'll have my dad get prints."

"Great, Mer. Thanks."

I returned the camera to its leather case, making a mental note to back up the files later on the downstairs computer. "You might be able to mail the pictures to your mom by the time the postman comes tomorrow afternoon."

My plan seemed to please her, and she wore her happy face awhile longer.

When Mr. Davis stopped by for her around suppertime, Chelsea was loaded down with two boxes of home-baked goodies. "Thanks for everything," she called to Mom and me.

"Anytime." Mom waved to her.

We stood in the doorway, watching them pull away. I was delighted at having thought of the photo shoot. Chelsea had seemed almost cheerful when she left.

And I was thankful, too, for Mom's mouthwatering cookies, which had seemingly worked a healing all their own.

Eight Echoes in the Wind

Just as I figured, the hours before the skating party were stressful ones. Honestly, I kept thinking Levi might show up on my back doorstep—plumb out of the blue—wanting to see me. But remarkably, and much to my relief, he didn't come.

I couldn't begin to count the times I went rushing down the hall to Skip's bedroom, though, to gaze out the window. Once, I even caught a glimpse of Levi hitching a horse to the family carriage, probably so his mother could ride to one of the many quilting frolics going on this time of year. Seeing Levi from this distance, I felt nothing at all. No heart-pumping surges . . . nothing.

I knew I wouldn't be able to keep barging into Skip's room once he arrived home for the holidays, so I took every advantage to do so this morning.

Then it happened. While leaning on the windowsill and gazing in the direction of Zooks' farm, Mom strolled into the room.

Hearing her, I spun around. "Oh . . . hi, Mom."

"Merry?" She eyed me suspiciously. "What are you doing?"

"Oh, nothing really." And with that, I dashed from the room, feeling really silly. Embarrassed too.

My mother had caught me gawking at the farmhouse next door. She was probably thinking that I simply couldn't wait to meet Levi for the skating party. She never would have guessed the truth.

Sunlight glinted off the snowy surface of fields and pastureland, creating a dazzling brightness as I walked the plowed road to the Zooks' later in the afternoon.

Old Man Winter had parceled out plenty of ice and snow from the first weekend in December until now. In fact, in some peculiar way, it almost seemed as though the frigid temperatures and foul weather were somehow related to the arrival of Levi's last letter—the one saying he was coming home.

Anyway, I was dressed for the occasion: earmuffs, fur-lined gloves, long johns under my jeans, and my down-filled jacket. As I turned onto Zooks' private drive, I saw in the distance Levi, Rachel, and Matthew Yoder heading for the pond, their skates slung over their shoulders.

It almost startled me, how shy I felt. I even thought of turning back and going home. Why hadn't they waited for me? Was I late?

Over a week ago, Rachel had mentioned something about having Levi come to my house to pick me up for the occasion. It had sounded too much like a date, though, and I had been determined that he not do such a thing. "Levi and I are really just good friends," I'd reminded her.

Most likely that was the reason the three of them were now approaching the wide pond ahead of me, and I was clear back here. By myself.

Nearing the farmhouse, I glanced at the window and spied Rachel's mother working in the kitchen. The dark green window shades had been pulled up all the way, making it easy for me to see inside. Nancy and Ella Mae flitted about, helping their mother bake bread and probably some spice cookies—Levi's favorite.

Big brother had returned. The prodigal had come home for Christmas. But it wasn't as if Levi were returning to the Amish church; he'd never joined, which, in many ways, was a good thing for him, especially since he'd up and left the Amish community of SummerHill. Old Order Amish church members put their wayward members through a strict excommunication and shunning if they ever took a step away from their baptismal vow.

I kept going, following the barnyard and on over into the snowy meadow, stepping in the deep boot prints already made by the threesome ahead of me. The wintry path would lead me to the pond, which spanned half the width of Zooks' property and a portion of ours, as well.

Sections of the pond, especially out toward the east, were known to have deep, almost bottomless holes. All us kids knew about them because in the summer we loved to go diving in those spots. Sometimes, we'd even found treasures in the pond's "cellar," as we called the deepest places.

I heard a sound behind me and thought it was Aaron, the youngest Zook boy. Turning, I investigated.

"Merry, wait up!" the voice called.

When I stopped and looked, I saw that Jon Klein was running toward me!

What on earth is he doing here? I wondered.

I waited while he caught up, and in my mind I pretended he was running in slow motion, only it was springtime and the daisies were a sea of yellow as he called my name.

"Hi, Jon," I said, bringing my short-lived fantasy to a close.

He halted to catch his breath, the gold flecks glinting in his brown eyes. "Surprised to see silent me?"

"Silent?"

174

He nodded. "I've been following you since you made the turn into your neighbors' yard."

"Really?" I asked, surprised I hadn't heard him before.

He pointed toward my house on the other side of the willow grove, just up the hill. "I doubt you can see it, but my dad's Jeep is parked in your yard. He came out to talk to your dad about something. Said I could come along and keep him company."

He began to alliterate without thinking, it seemed.

Meanwhile, my heart had sped up. I was caught between ecstasy at Jon's being here and worry over how to involve him in Rachel's private pond party.

I certainly wouldn't be rude and send him away. Not the guy I'd secretly had my eye on for as long as I could remember.

But what could I do? Invite him to go skating with us? What would Rachel say if I spoiled her "couples" event? And Levi? How would *he* react to Jon?

"Looks like you've got some plans," Jon said, offering to carry my skates.

"Uh . . . yeah." I relinquished my skates, thrilled at his thoughtful gesture. "A group of us from around here are going skating on Zooks' pond." I pointed to it, struggling with how to tell him that Levi was one of the group.

"Sounds great. Mind if I watch?" he said.

"Me . . . mind?"

He laughed his warm, deep laugh, and we made our way through the snow together. "Wanna work the word game?" he asked.

I glanced toward the pond, where the others were already beginning to lace up. "Maybe later," I said.

Something sank in me, and I felt helpless. Torn in half, in a strange sort of way.

Without warning, Jon stopped walking. "Listen, I really don't have to hang around here," he said quickly.

"No . . . no, I didn't mean you should go. Nothing like that." Truth was, I wanted him to stay. More than anything in the world!

He stood there, looking down at me with his inquisitive eyes. Little streams of breath floated around his mouth and nose. "I don't wanna intrude."

"Don't worry, Jon, you're not," I insisted. "C'mon!"

Running ahead, I felt the exhilaration. Jon was here—he was right here with me! The thought spurred me on, and I actually outran him.

"Merry, hullo!" Rachel called from the ice. She sped over to Jon and me. "I want ya to meet Matthew."

The stocky teenage Amish boy skated over and stuck out his hand. "Gut to know ya, Merry." He smiled broadly, showing his teeth. "Rachel here, she's been talkin' a lot about ya."

"Well, it's nice to meet you, too," I said, conscious that Levi was observing me as he glided across the pond toward us. Politely, I turned to Jon. "This is Jonathan Klein, a friend of mine from school." Then I introduced my Plain friends by their first names.

Before I could explain the reason why Jon was here, he spoke up. "My father's over visiting Merry's dad." He glanced at me almost shyly. "Merry had no idea I was coming."

Levi grinned at us. "Well, s'good to see ya again, Jonathan," he said. Then he looked straight at me. "How are *you*, Merry?"

"Fine, thanks. Are you glad to be home?" I replied, feeling worse than awkward.

Levi nodded. "I'd forgotten how much I missed this old place." Looking out over the expanse of pond and meadow, he added, "I do believe there's plenty of room for the five of us. That is if Jonathan wants to slide around on the ice in his shoes."

We laughed, and then it hit me. Levi had remembered meeting Jon last summer. A short encounter, for sure, but another uncomfortable meeting—just outside the mall entrance in Lancaster.

Matthew Yoder came to the rescue. "How 'bout if ya wear my skates after a bit? See if they fit."

Rachel clapped her hands. "Oh, that's a wonderful-gut solution. You fellows'll take turns."

And that's what Matthew and Jon did—took turns.

Someone else took turns, too. Levi. He had to share his skating partner with the Alliteration Wizard. Although it didn't seem to bother Jon much, I saw the initial disappointment in Levi's eyes.

Still, we played everything from Fox and Geese to Crack the Whip. After an hour or more, Levi and Matthew built a bonfire on the south bank, and we began to warm ourselves.

While we did, Rachel tried her best to teach Jon and me how to sing "What a Friend We Have in Jesus" in German. We did pretty well, I suppose, considering that neither of us had ever studied the language.

Jon seemed to be enjoying himself. And to be truthful, that was really all that mattered. At least to me.

After a time, Levi ran to the house and brought back a bag of marshmallows. While we toasted the gooey treats, we listened as he told of his church-building experiences in Bolivia. Matthew entered into the conversation, telling about his new workplace—the cabinet-making shop he now shared with his father. Rachel listened silently, eyes shining.

I remembered to tell Levi about Chelsea's interest in spiritual things. "She's been going to church with me lately," I said. "I hope you'll keep her in your prayers."

"I sure will," Levi said, offering me another marshmallow.

"Is her mom doing any better?" Jon asked.

"Chelsea and her dad are hoping she'll be home soon. Maybe in time for Christmas."

When Matthew asked about Jon's interests, the Alliteration Wizard said he enjoyed books. "Lots of them." He smiled at me. "Sometimes I even read poetry."

Poetry? Had he ever told me this? It was one more thing Jon and I had in common!

In a short while, we were all back on the ice. Except Matthew. He handed over his skates to Jon and kept the bonfire going as we played another round of Crack the Whip.

"Who wants to be the tail this time?" Rachel asked, grinning at me.

"Okay, I guess I will," I volunteered. "But only if you don't go too fast."

"Aw, the faster the better," Matthew called from the pond side, laughing heartily.

I shrugged. "Maybe for you."

Joking around, the four of us joined hands. Levi at the center, followed by Rachel, then Jonathan. I was at the end. The tail.

Soon we were zooming around and around. Faster and faster, speeding across the ice in a giant circle. A group of jubilant young people enjoying a sunny winter day.

Suddenly, quite unexpectedly, Jonathan stumbled over his skate. My grip broke free from his gloved hand as he tumbled forward.

I was airborne, flying across the pond's glassy surface. An outline of bare trees against the sky jeered at me in the distance.

I heard myself scream, "Help!"

Rachel was shouting at the top of her lungs. "*Ach*, Merry, no! There's thin ice!"

Hers were the last words I heard. The next sound was a terrifying *crack* as I plunged through the frozen surface—into the icy black hole below.

Numbing cold, raw and biting . . . rushed in on all sides. My body responded with violent spasms. I'd fallen into liquid ice. This deep, deep hole . . . was sucking me down.

Call upon me, and I will answer. . . .

I attempted to touch bottom with my feet, still aware of my heavy figure skates tied tightly around my ankles. But in spite of repeated efforts to find the depth, it was no use—the pond bed gave way to nothingness. I'd fallen into the "cellar."

Holding my breath, I tried to swim back to the opening above. Grappling with my hands and arms, I searched.

Where is it?

I made several attempts, aware that if I succumbed to having to see my way back and opened my eyes, they might freeze in their sockets. I grasped for something . . . anything to pull me up.

The pond rumbled in my ears, mocking me. Desperately, I thrashed about, my lungs aching for air.

Then as I fought to find the surface, my head bumped against something hard. I pushed on it, daring to open one eye.

Light burst all around me. I'd hit the pond's surface!

In one last frantic struggle, I pounded on the icy ceiling above me, praying. *Dear Lord Jesus, please help me!*

Ears throbbing, I broke through the opening, pulling hard for life-giving air, only to be pushed back into the frigid water by an unexpected body. Someone was trying to rescue me. . . .

But the chasm beneath wrenched at me, inhaling me. Down, down the pond's cellar drew me into the arctic abyss. I was lost again. And in my stony confusion, something told me that one of two things was going to happen. I would either freeze to death . . . or drown. Four days before Christmas.

Was this how it had been for Levi at age nine? Had he sensed how close he was to drowning in this very pond, even as he struggled to yank his foot away from the willow root?

I had saved him that day eight years ago.

Who would save *me*?

Precious seconds ticked by, merging with the frozen underwater blackness. My lungs screamed for breath; my body stiffened, paralyzed.

An eternity later, a hazy form began to emerge out of the murky darkness. When I looked more closely, I knew that it was Faithie, my little twin, swimming toward me.

It did not occur to me to question how or why my dear, dead sister was here with me now. Yet I could feel her loving arms encircle me, guiding me. "You must not breathe yet, Merry," she warned. "Wait . . . wait. . . . "

***

The heaviness in my chest was the first sensation I felt when I regained consciousness. Slowly, painstakingly, I forced the sounds and smells of this new place to separate themselves in my mind.

Then my mother's face, distorted and wavy, began to sharpen—coming into focus. "Is this heaven?" I asked. "Did I die?"

"No, darling, you're very much alive." She squeezed my hand.

If I was alive, why did I feel so dead?

Within seconds, I felt my body yielding to sleep again. But in my drifting, I felt my mother's hand still holding mine, and a thousand questions faded away.

———

The next face I recognized was Daddy's. A whole twenty-four hours later, one of the nurses remarked. He looked downright exhausted, probably because he'd gone without sleep for a very long time.

"It hurts to breathe," I told him.

"Try not to talk, honeybunch," he said as another doctor examined me.

I didn't feel up to talking. Especially later when several strangers came in to visit. Two boys and a girl.

Levi and Jonathan were the boys' names. The girl was very sweet—someone by the name of Rachel. She said she was Levi's sister and cried when I didn't remember them.

All of this seemed very confusing. Why were they so happy to see me when I didn't even know who they were?

When I asked my mom about it later, her face turned pale. And hours later, in the privacy of my hospital room, she and Dad told me that I'd lost certain portions of my memory.

"Is it serious?" I asked. "Will my memory come back?"

Dad smiled slightly, stroking my hair. "You had a horrible accident. We almost lost you, baby." And he began to explain what had happened yesterday afternoon on the pond.

"Why can't I remember?" I put my hand to my forehead, trying to think, but it only made my head hurt worse. "Who did you say rescued me?"

He sighed. "Well, your friend from church and school, Jonathan Klein, literally jumped into the pond, trying to bring you up to the surface for air."

Mom chimed in. "But you sank back down, and he couldn't find you."

"Which pond?" I asked.

"Our Amish neighbors'—out behind our property and the Zooks.'"

"Zooks?" The name sounded foreign to me, but Mom and Dad were talking as though these people—the Zooks—were longtime friends.

"Tell her what happened next," Mom prompted Dad.

A smile burst across his face. "Your childhood friend Levi Zook risked his life to save both you and Jon."

"Levi?"

"He's the one who saved you and your school friend," Dad explained.

"Well, whoever these boys are, I want to thank them—both of them. Levi . . . and Jim?"

"*Jon*," Mom said. "Short for Jonathan."

The nurse came in to take my blood pressure, and while she did, she asked if I remembered her name. I fooled her and read it off her name badge. But she patted my arm as though I'd said the wrong thing, then left.

When my brother came in, my parents started introducing him. "This is your big brother, Skip," my dad said. "He's home for Christmas from his freshman year in college."

"You don't have to tell me who my own brother is," I said, which made Skip and everyone smile. "So when's Christmas?" I asked.

"In three days," Mom said, glancing away. She took a tissue out of her purse and dabbed at her eyes. I had an empty feeling. Something was terribly wrong.

That is until Chelsea Davis, my spunky girl friend, showed up and I recognized her, too. "Hey, Mer, whatcha doin' in the hospital? It's almost Christmas, for pete's sake!"

Mom assured me that Chelsea had already heard the details of my skating accident. "But she's curious to know what happened to the pictures you took of her. She was going to send them to her mother."

"Oh yeah," I said, remembering. "Ask Dad . . . he was supposed to get them printed. I forget the exact day, though."

My parents and Skip—Chelsea, too—started clapping. "Way to go, Merry," my redheaded friend declared.

"Come here, you." I motioned to her. "Is your mom better?"

"About the same."

"So you've heard from her again?"

"Just a few minutes on the phone."

"But you'll be able to get the pictures to her, won't you?" I asked. "In time for Christmas?"

Chelsea nodded, glancing at my dad. He gave us a thumbs-up gesture. "Don't worry about a thing," she said. "I'm planning to deliver them to Mom in person. Daddy and I are going for a surprise visit."

"When?"

Her eyes shone. "Christmas Eve."

"But I thought—"

"No, Mom won't be home for Christmas this year," she interrupted. "It's not the right time for her, I guess."

"I'm sorry, Chels."

"Me too, but hey, it's better than nothing, right?"

We talked awhile longer about the recent snowstorm—one I'd missed while cooped up at Lancaster General—as well as Chelsea's Christmas list. "Mom's homecoming is at the top of my list," she said.

"I don't blame you. It's the best wish of all." I started to cough.

Almost on cue, the therapist came in and massaged my lungs—front and back. When she was gone, I wiggled my finger, indicating that I wanted Chelsea to lean over so I could whisper something. "That guy—the one who pulled me out of the pond—do you think he's cute?"

She chuckled. "Levi's a college man," she whispered back to me, "studying to be a minister."

"How old?"

"Only seventeen, I think."

I decided right then and there that this Levi fellow sounded pretty good to me. A real hero, too!

"But," she added, "the other guy, the one who jumped into the pond after you, now *he's* the one you always liked best, even though he's a bit of a bookworm."

"Jim?"

"Jon, short for Jonathan. Remember?"

"Not really, but what a nice name."

She shrugged. "Nice enough, I guess."

Her answer made me curious. Who *was* this Jon fellow, and why did I like him so much?

The college boy, the one studying to be a minister, came for a visit with his sister the next morning. She was wearing a long green dress with a black apron and a white head covering. I wondered where she'd gotten such an unusual outfit, but I was polite enough not to ask.

"Hullo, Merry," Levi said, hovering near the hospital bed. "Rachel and I have been worried about ya."

"Worried?" I said.

Rachel spoke up softly. "Because you don't remember who we are. It's not like ya at all." She looked down at me with gentle eyes. "You're our dear friend, Merry. And our cousin, too."

I glanced at Levi, feeling suddenly strange about having asked Chelsea if he was cute. "We're related?"

"Jah, but only distantly," Rachel said, her dimples showing.

"I'm very sorry that I don't know you . . . er, remember you," I volunteered quickly, "but hopefully, my memory will return soon. For now, though, I want to say thank you, Levi, for saving my life."

"The way I see it," he replied, "it was the right and gut thing to do, savin' ya thataway, Merry."

I studied his short brown hair and blue eyes. He was tall and lanky—quite handsome, really. And there was such a kind-hearted manner about him.

"You see," he continued, "back when you and I were young-sters, you saved *me* from drownin' once."

"I did?"

How very strange that I could've saved him, I thought. He looked so strong.

He nodded, a twinkle in his eye. "Jah, Merry. You did."

The soft, gentle way he said my name made me want to get well instantly. Maybe then I'd have a chance at getting better acquainted with this soft-spoken boy.

"Well, I really wish I could remember that day," I said, studying his sister.

Rachel, eyes cast down, went to sit by the window, leaving Levi and me somewhat alone in the room. I was a bit surprised when her brother touched my hand. He held it lightly as he told me about the summer I was eight and he was nine. "We'd all gone swimmin' in the pond out behind the barn—same one where ya fell through the ice. Anyways, we kept on divin' into them 'cellar' holes out over near the east side of the pond. And wouldn'tcha know it, my big brother, Curly John, pulled himself up a scrap piece of metal deep down."

"Did you say a cellar . . . in the pond?" I was thoroughly confused.

Smiling, Levi showed his teeth. "That's what we always called the deepest part," he explained.

A flicker of a memory danced in my mind, then faded. "Oh," I said, catching my breath.

He leaned over, gazing down at me. "Merry, are ya all right?"

"I think so . . . it was . . . something I thought I was about to remember."

With that comment, Rachel rushed over, and Levi let go of my hand. "What was my brother just now sayin' to ya? Somethin' about the cellar hole out there in the pond?"

"Jah, that's right." Levi nodded. "Do ya remember the summer Curly John found himself a souvenir at the bottom of the pond?"

"Ach, sure do," she said.

"Well, I wasn't gonna be outdone, so I dove in headfirst," Levi continued. "As far down as I could go with one breath, I went, searchin' for something to bring back up."

"And 'pride goeth before a fall'—ain't it so?" Rachel teased. "You went and got yer foot caught in that willow root and near drowned."

"Sure would've, if it hadn't been for Merry here." He looked at me with dancing eyes. And for one silly minute, I thought I might be falling in love.

───────

Chelsea came for a visit about an hour after Rachel and Levi left. She brought the pictures I'd taken of her posing in my room. "I wanted you to see how the prints turned out," she said. "They're really good. Even better than they looked to me on your camera."

I'd always been very critical of my work, so I studied each of the photos carefully. Though Chelsea thought they were good, only four of the shots were tops in my opinion.

She handed me two five-dollar bills. "This'll pay for the prints."

"Oh, keep your money, really."

"But I want to give you something." Chelsea plopped the money down on the table beside my bed. "You can't imagine how glad my mom'll be to get these."

"She'll probably be happier to see *you* in person," I quipped. "How long has it been?"

"She left on October third, over two and a half months ago."

I was wheezing heavily now and propped myself up with more pillows. "I'll keep praying for you and your dad. For your mom, too."

"Thanks." She pulled up a chair. "Hey, has Jon Klein come to see you again?"

"I'm not really sure," I said. "You could ask my mom, though. There were several visitors here when I was out of it."

"You were zonked, all right. But you're doing better, aren't you, Mer?"

I smiled back at her. "The docs are saying I might get to go home for Christmas Eve. That is if I promise to take my antibiotics and let Mom give me my lung massages."

"Hey, cool. That's tomorrow."

We chitchatted some more, but Chelsea seemed most interested in discussing Jon—the boy who'd so bravely jumped into the icy pond water, attempting to save me. Or so my father had told me.

"Mind if I give you a little background on this guy?" She reached into her jacket pocket and pulled out a folded paper. "I found this in your desk drawer . . . at your house. But don't freak out, your mom gave me permission, okay?"

I leaned forward to see. "What is it?"

"It's a note from Jon. But since you're in a fog zone right now, you'll just have to trust me when I say that you like him, Mer. Anyway, he passed this to you in math class. You told me yourself." She handed the note to me. "Take a look."

I began to read it—very unusual the way most words in a sentence began with the same letter of the alphabet. "This is some weird writing."

She agreed. "That's what I thought last week when I first read it. But the thing I can't let you overlook is that you . . . *you* are crazy about this guy. Before you nearly drowned, you and he would always meet every day at school at—"

A faint image sprang up. "At our lockers?"

"Hey, that's right! What else?"

I sank back onto my pillows. The impression had fizzled. "I don't know now. It's gone."

"Tell me . . . what did you remember?"

I stared at the many get-well baskets and vases of flowers lining the shelf along the windowsill, thinking back to the past few seconds. I tried squeezing the recollection out of my brain, forcing it into my consciousness. "Something about lockers at school. I could almost see my combination lock dangling."

Chelsea was hopping happy. "This is truly terrific."

"Hey, isn't 'truly' *my* word?" I said, laughing now. Laughing so hard, I began to cough.

For some reason, she ran out of the room, bringing my mom back with her. "I think it's happening," Chelsea exclaimed. "I think her memory's kicking in!"

———

Jon Klein was my very last visitor of the day. "Finally," he said, "I timed things to a tee."

"Was I sleeping when you came before?"

He nodded. "Snoozing so soundly, very still, silent . . . such sleep."

"Oh . . ." Another image shot past. "What's that you're doing? All the *s*'s?"

He grinned, standing tall next to my hospital bed. "It's our word game, Merry, Mistress of Mirth. Can you still talk alliteration-eze?"

I shrugged. "Whatever *that* is."

He began to explain, stopping to run his hand through his hair. He seemed a bit frustrated. "C'mon, Mistress Merry. Think through it."

I shook my head. "I have no idea what you're talking about—a word game? And what's with the nickname?"

His face drooped at my response.

"Look, I'm real sorry," I said, "but I don't know what to say about the strange language you speak."

"Hey, you're doing it." His face brightened. "You're starting to alliterate!"

"I am? What do you mean, Jim?"

He looked hurt just then, and I wondered if I'd forgotten something. Like maybe calling him the wrong name.

Again.

Echoes in the Wind **Eleven**

I was thrilled when the doctor said I'd be going home for sure. Being stuck in the hospital at Christmastime was anything but fun!

Our one-hundred-year-old farmhouse had never looked so good as it did when I first spied it from a quarter-mile away. The idyllic words from Longfellow's "Song" boosted my spirits.

> *Stay, stay at home, my heart, and rest;*
> *Home-keeping hearts are happiest,*
> *For those that wander they know not where*
> *Are full of trouble and full of care;*
> *To stay at home is best.*

My white figure skates were lying on the floor near the radiator in my room when I arrived. They felt like soaked cardboard—coerced to dry out. There they were, greeting me home, ugly as all get out. I decided I never wanted to wear them again. In fact, I didn't even want to look at them. So when Mom came upstairs to serve some sort of soup, I decided to ask her to throw them away.

"Something bothering you, honey?" She eyed me curiously.

"It's the skates. I don't like looking at them. They remind me of . . ." I didn't know for sure.

She didn't argue, just put them in an old shoe box and closed my closet door. "How's that? Out of sight, out of mind."

"Much better."

She came over and felt my forehead. "I'm so glad to have you back home. We all are."

"Me too. I hate hospitals. They're a hassle. Home's a haven, a much happier place."

Mom looked at me funny. "Merry, why are you talking that way?"

"What way?"

"Everything's . . . uh, kind of alliterated."

"It is?"

She scratched her head and smiled. "You know, there are some people who would love to be able to do that naturally."

"Jim?"

"Who?"

"The boy who tried to save me but fell in the pond instead?"

"Oh, you mean Jon Klein?" She frowned a little. "Why? Does *he* talk that way?"

"He did at the hospital yesterday."

Mom paused to make a fuss over my cats, who were beginning to crowd me on my bed. Then she left the room.

Why did I keep forgetting that guy's name? Sure, he was cute, but what on earth had been so wonderful about him? I struggled to remember who he was—and what it was that he and I liked to do at our lockers every day.

Was Chelsea just giving me a hard time? Why would I go gaga over a guy with a hang-up for head rhyme?

Deciding to get to the bottom of this, I pulled out my yearbook from last year. Then, so Mom wouldn't worry that I'd have a setback, I slipped back into bed and began to browse.

There were plenty of pictures of Jon Klein—no sports shots, though. Jon was on student council and did all kinds of other academic stuff. From the looks of things, he was super smart. Even made the honor roll both semesters!

I closed the book and let my cats creep closer to me on my comforter. What had attracted me to the guy? Besides his attending my school and church, what else did we have in common?

Chelsea might know, I decided. When she called to tell me about her Christmas Eve visit with her mother, I'd ask her more about Jon.

I must admit, I could hardly wait.

Dad arrived home earlier than usual from his duties at the ER. He came right upstairs to see me. "How's my girl doing?" He kissed me on the top of my head and sat on the edge of my bed.

"I'm feeling better, I think. Ready to tackle the Christmas tree—what's *under* the tree, that is."

He smiled, looking far less tired than he had in the past two days. "Would you like to go downstairs? There's a rip-roaring fire in the fireplace. It's the place to be on Christmas Eve."

"I'll do anything to get closer to the presents," I teased.

Nearly grown as I was, he scooped me up in his arms and carried me downstairs, planting me on the living room sofa in front of a crackling fire.

In the corner stood a nine-foot tree, showering the room with twinkling white light. The tree filled the expanse of space between the hardwood floor and the high ceiling—typical of the old Pennsylvania farmhouses. Mom had carefully trimmed its thick branches with clusters of cream-colored grapes, baby's breath, pearl hearts, dried hydrangeas, ivory angels, and snowy-white poinsettias. Definitely a white theme this year, and by the looks of so many winged messengers, an angelic one, too.

Soon Mom came running with afghans, and Skip brought cushions for my back. My family fluttered about me, plumping up pillows and making sure every inch of me was covered in warmth. Except my head, of course.

"Better watch it," I warned. "You'll have me spoiled in no time."

"Too late," Skip said, laughing.

Dad pulled his easy chair closer to the sofa. "So, tell me, did you remember anything new today?"

I stared at the tree. "Well, for no reason at all, I sorta remembered the deep snow on the day I nearly drowned. The wind, too."

He nodded. "We did have quite a lot of snow prior to your accident. And again afterward," he said softly. "Anything else?"

"Echoes. There were echoes in the wind. In my ears . . . I could hear whispering in my ears as I—yes, that's it, I remember skating now. I really do!"

"Who was with you, Merry?" Dad seemed terribly excited, leaning forward as he anticipated my answer.

I strained to recall. But not a single face came to mind, even though I'd been told Jon and Levi were there.

The phone jangled me out of my reverie, and a few minutes later, Mom appeared in the doorway. "Are you up to a phone call, Merry?"

"Who is it?"

"Lissa Vyner. She said it'll just be a minute."

"Sure, I'll talk to her."

Dad picked up the evening paper and began to read. I waited patiently for Mom to bring in the cordless phone. She came smiling, bringing it along with a cup of herbal tea for me. Carefully, she set the teacup and saucer on the coffee table. "The tea's very hot, so don't burn your tongue," she whispered as I took the phone from her.

"Hello?" I said.

"How *are* you, Merry?" My friend's voice cheered me immediately. "Everyone's been asking about you."

I wondered who *everyone* was. "Well, I'm home from the hospital, that's the best thing. That place tends to smell a little offensive, know what I mean?"

"The antiseptic, probably."

"Yeah, that and other icky stuff."

We talked about her grandmother, who she said was scheduled to arrive any minute. "Grammy Vyner's still bragging about the pictures you took of me in my junior bridesmaid's dress. On your porch last July . . . remember?"

"Of course I do. Just because I've blocked out random chunks of my life doesn't mean I've gone completely senile."

"I didn't mean that, really." She apologized all over the place. "Oh, Merry, there's something I have to tell you before we hang up. It's about Jon Klein."

"What about him?"

"He called last night and started talking in some sort of bizarre code or something."

"What do you mean?"

"I'm not sure I can describe it. I guess you could call it alliteration, except doesn't that usually show up in poetry?"

"Other places, too. I've seen it in some prose."

"Is he into some new author, or what?" she asked.

I glanced at Dad, whose head was bobbing while he tried to read the paper. I was determined not to snicker, but it was very hard to keep a straight face.

"Merry?" she said, calling me back to the conversation at hand.

"Oh, sorry, Liss, it's just that you should see my dad. He's trying to read the paper, and he keeps falling asleep."

She didn't seem to care what my father was doing at the moment. "I just thought maybe you could give me some idea about Jon's latest craze. That's all."

"Me?" I sighed. "I wish I could help you, but I have no idea who the guy really is. Everyone keeps telling me how attached I was to him before . . . " I stopped for a moment.

Lissa jumped in. "Oh, it's true, Merry. I think you really *did* like Jon before you nearly drowned."

"But why was he skating with me that day? What was that all about?"

"Well, did you ever think that maybe Jon likes you?" she said. "Maybe *that's* why he was there."

An awkward silence fell between us before she continued. "I really hope you have a great Christmas, and I'm so sorry about your accident. Who knows what horrible thing might've happened if Levi Zook hadn't saved you."

"He's a mighty special guy, that Levi. At least you can understand *him* when he talks," I joked.

We giggled a little and then hung up.

"Dad?" I whispered to my dozing parent, putting the phone on the coffee table. "It's almost suppertime."

He snorted awake, blinking his eyes. "Uh . . . sorry. What did I miss?"

"Oh, some girl talk. Nothing earthshaking."

He sat up and straightened himself. "I guess the past few days have left me more tired than I thought." He smiled at me. "I don't think I've mentioned this to you since your accident, but Jon Klein's father came to see me on Saturday afternoon. That's why Jon was over at the Zooks' farm when you fell through the ice."

I listened, wondering what he was about to tell me.

"Seems that your friend is interested in photography, same as you. I gave his dad some pointers on what kind of camera and lens equipment to get. But it's supposed to be kept top secret, so don't say anything."

"Jon wants a camera for Christmas?" It seemed that maybe Chelsea hadn't been pulling my leg about all we had in common after all.

"Yesiree, Jonathan's getting a big surprise come tomorrow," Dad announced.

"So you're saying he's into photography?"

"Absolutely."

Just then Mom came to serve me a hearty bowl of home-made vegetable barley soup for my Christmas Eve supper. Dad got up and headed for the dining room, two rooms away. I could hear him getting settled at the elegant holiday table that Mom had no doubt set for the rest of the family. But it was their hearty laughter that caught me off guard, if only for a second.

The sounds of their chuckling reminded me of something. Laughter . . . on the ice. Echoes of fun—all the wintry games. Echoes began to wing the events back to me.

Slowly they came, little by little. . . .

An Amish boy stood near a bonfire. He was calling to me. *The faster the better*, he said.

Those of us on the ice began to play a game of Crack the Whip. Faster and faster we flew.

Someone tripped and fell, breaking the chain of hands.

Then someone screamed. Who? Was it Rachel? Was it my own frightened scream?

With all my might, I tried to think what came next, wondering hard why Chelsea had insisted that I surely must've been delighted to be skating with Jon that day.

In spite of myself, no such information or emotion emerged from my scattered memory. It was as if someone had closed the door on it. Tight.

Twelve *Echoes in the Wind*

I was beginning to resent the constant questioning from my family. Chelsea and Lissa, too. Everyone seemed more interested in helping me remember than anything else. People were more concerned about my temporary loss of memory than they were about my upper-respiratory infection, which had come from aspirating icy pond water.

All during that Christmas Day, I was barraged with one reminder after another that I'd forgotten a whopping twenty-four hours . . . and much more. Not to mention a few key people, too.

Levi Zook, however, had a totally different approach to things. He came with a gift for me early Christmas afternoon, after our family gift opening and a splendid dinner of prime rib and scrumptious trimmings.

I was resting in the living room, staring into the fire, trying my best to boost my brain.

"Merry, you have company," Mom said softly, showing Levi into the room and arranging the chairs so he and I could enjoy both the fireplace and the Christmas tree.

Slender and fit, Levi seemed content to sit in Mom's big Boston rocker, holding the rectangular-shaped gift box in his lap. For the longest time, he sat very still, not allowing the chair to move. He looked very handsome in his light blue sweater. "How are ya feelin' today, Merry?" he asked in a soft voice.

"Getting stronger every day, thanks."

He glanced down at the present in his hands. "I brought a little something for ya." Handing it to me, he beamed an innocent yet charming smile. "God bless ya, Merry. Happy Christmas."

"Thank you, Levi," I said, feeling a bit giddy.

I opened the gift—a box of assorted chocolates. "Enjoy the sweets when you're all well, jah?"

I assured him that I'd wait. "It was so nice of you to think of me."

He leaned toward me slightly. "Oh, Merry, I'm always thinking of ya. Always."

My heart skipped a beat, and I have to admit, I was a bit relieved when he turned to admire Mom's large antique nativity figurines displayed on the hearth.

"God's been so good," he was saying. "To think what might've happened out there on the pond . . ."

"Let's not talk about that," I said.

Then he began to reminisce about our childhood days—riding in the Zooks' pony cart, pitching hay with the grown-ups, swinging on the rope in the hayloft, sampling his mother's jams and jellies.

Slowly, deliberately, he worked his way through the years, to the recent past. "Last summer was a real special time for us, Merry," he remarked. "We even had a nice buggy ride in the rain one Sunday afternoon."

He didn't ask me if I remembered, and I listened, telling my brain to relax for a change.

"Miss Spindler, our neighbor, raced right past us in her sports car. Ach, you were so worried that she'd spread it around SummerHill that you and I were seein' each other."

"And she did, too, didn't she?" I spoke up.

Levi grinned. "That's right! The busybody told your daddy that she'd seen us together. And you got the willies, thinkin' I'd be gettin' myself in trouble for taking a pretty 'English' girl for a ride in my open carriage."

I felt myself blush at his comment, remembering vaguely what he was talking about. But the more Levi spoke, the more I knew for sure that I liked him.

"How're your college studies?" I asked, relying on the information Chelsea had given me.

"Well, to be honest with ya, it's the best thing I ever did for myself. So much of what I always wanted to do is happening now. The Lord's work is all around me, Merry. I'm excited about preachin' the Gospel—and very soon."

The joy in his heart was evident in his eyes. They sparkled as he spoke, matching the bright surroundings of tree and tinsel.

But something else was happening. Levi was behaving as if I'd never forgotten who he was—or the affectionate ties we'd once had. Truly exciting.

Things were not as comfortable, though, between Jon Klein and me when he called a little later. "Merry Christmas, Merry, maiden of misery," he said, then laughed apologetically. "It's jovial Jon, or at least that's what you used to call me."

"Before I fell through thin ice?" I said, not sure he was joking.

He ignored my remark. "How was your holy holiday?"

"Okay, I guess." I noticed his use of *h*'s but didn't say anything. My mind was on something else—wondering if I should inquire about the surprise present from his parents.

Before I could get the words out, he brought it up. "You'll never guess what my folks gave me for Christmas."

I didn't blurt out the answer in case he hadn't received the camera equipment yet. "I really hate guessing games," I said, still feeling strange talking to this guy who seemed to know me so well.

"I'll give you a hint." Unfortunately, the hint he was talking about had much more to do with his eagerness for me to remember the past. Specifically, for me to recall who *he* was . . . and that ridiculous word game he kept referring to.

I resented his style of prompting my defunct gray matter. Couldn't he simply accept me as I was—the way Levi did?

Jon kept talking, though, now about my love of nature—the desire I'd expressed to capture God's beauty in photographs. I had a feeling he was working up to telling me about the grand surprise he'd received from his parents, probably trying to spark memories along the way.

"Hey, do you remember the cool shot you took behind Chelsea's house?" he asked.

"The one in the woods?"

"Right—the picture you entered in the annual school contest back in October."

I laughed. "You mean the one that placed second?"

"That's it." He began to backtrack, discussing in detail the isolated shanty I'd selected as a subject.

"Look, Jon," I said at last, "you don't have to help me remember any of that. I haven't blocked out *everything*—only certain events . . . and people."

"So what's causing it—your memory loss?" He seemed restless about my condition. Not worried, but almost impatient.

"My dad says amnesia can occur for several reasons. The trauma of my accident for one. Even a slight concussion, which I had a couple of weeks ago, can bring it on."

"But it's only your short-term memory, right?" he probed.

"And some scattered memories—random memory, I guess you'd say."

"When will it all come back?" he asked.

His attitude frustrated me. "Do you have to be so antsy about this?"

"Aw, Merry, don't go getting upset."

"Well, since you put it that way, I *am* angry. I mean, all you've done since we got reacquainted or whatever is to try to force me to remember you." I sighed. "You and that weird word game . . . well—"

"Hey, that's good, Merry. Keep going!"

I had no idea what on earth he was saying, but at this point in the conversation, I wanted to bail out. "Thanks, Jon. It was nice of you to phone—but I've gotta get going."

He was whooping it up. "Merry, did you just hear yourself? You're doing it—you're alliterating!"

"I'm sorry," I said. "It's not intentional. Good-bye."

I didn't actually slam the phone down or hang up on him, but it was definitely an abrupt farewell. Funny thing was, I felt no guilt for my actions. After all, I didn't really know him. Not anymore.

Clicking the Off button on the phone, I leaned back, taking in the dazzling decorations around me. Mom had outdone herself this year. Above each window dressing, white satin bows, crisscrossed with grapevines, served as folksy ornaments. Centered on the mantel, a spray of white long-stemmed tulips framed the broad fireplace. And an array of ivory candles—some round, others tall, all of differing heights—on both sides of the centerpiece created a truly ethereal effect.

Gazing at the flickering lights, I began again to recall fragments of the bonfire at the ice-skating party.

Levi had gone back to the house to get marshmallows, and we roasted them on the ends of coat hangers. It was one of those never-to-be-forgotten moments, full of nostalgia and wistful rememberings—something I'd want to tell my grandchildren about someday. Not so much because of the people involved. It had more to do with the setting, the tingly feeling of expectation in the air—the wintry delight that had pervaded the atmosphere around us.

Both Levi and Jon had offered to help me with the simple chore of poking my marshmallows through with a hanger wire, even though I was entirely capable of cooking up my own treat. That much of the significant day I *did* remember. I was surprised how easily it wafted back to my present consciousness.

Now if only I could get a grasp on my relationships with Levi and Jon. Especially Jon. It was the one thing that truly bugged me this Christmas.

Thirteen *Echoes in the Wind*

Miss Spindler, also known as Old Hawk Eyes—the neighbor lady who lived in the nearest house behind ours—breezed in for a visit late Christmas afternoon.

I was still hacking away, trying not to cough all over everyone, even though the doctors said I wasn't contagious. Mom, bless her heart, gently massaged my lungs at various intervals—doctor's orders. But I was up and about for short periods and had even sat at the table for Christmas dinner. According to my medical genius father, I was making solid progress.

Being cooped up in the house, no matter how beautifully decorated, was a pain for some people. I, being one of those prone to cabin fever, had to resort to other things for my entertainment. I'd never been much of a television watcher and was limited in other activities, so I was actually delighted when I heard Miss Spindler's old voice crackle in our kitchen.

I sprang from my solitary post on the living room couch—surrounded by the new poetry and photography books Mom and Dad had given me for Christmas—and tiptoed toward the kitchen.

Miss Spindler had come bearing gifts: two pumpkin pies and three-dozen snickerdoodle cookies. "How's every little thing?" she asked when I peeked around the corner. Her blue-gray hair was done up in a bouffant style; it looked as if she'd swept much of it from the lower section of her head to cover the meager patches at the crown.

Quickly, Mom spoke up on my behalf. "Merry's recovering quite nicely." She didn't go on to mention my memory lapses, thank goodness.

Miss Spindler smiled at me, nodding her head. "I can see the dear girl's improving. Her smeller's a-workin', ain't it?"

I had to chuckle. Leave it to Old Hawk Eyes to make an on-the-spot assessment of my physical condition based on my response to a couple of spicy pumpkin pies.

Being careful not to go near our drafty back door, I pulled out a kitchen chair close to the radiator and sat down, enjoying the warmth as it drifted around me.

"Talk has it that our little darlin's suffering from amnesia these days," Miss Spindler continued.

I wondered how Mom would go about explaining things.

She began by setting down mugs of hot apple cider on the table for the three of us. "Merry doesn't have full-blown amnesia. Her type of traumatic memory loss can last anywhere from a few hours to several weeks."

Our nosy neighbor kept sending persistent glances my way, but I remained quiet.

Mom gave me a reassuring smile. "We're doing everything the doctors said to do for our girl."

The way my mother put things sometimes gave me reason to smile. She was quite the lady, my mom, even when making semi-small talk with SummerHill's biggest gossip.

"Well, what on earth is causin' Merry's brain to fuzz up?" Miss Spindler asked, looking for all the world as though she was genuinely interested in my present mental state.

Mom took her time sipping the cider, looking at me with a twinkle in her eye. "You may have heard about Merry's mishap on the ice Saturday?"

"Oh, dear me, yes indeedy, I did!" There was no telling what sort of spin on the actual facts she'd heard and possibly reconcocted by now!

"Well, sometimes trauma can trigger a short-term memory loss," Mom replied. "But we're not worried about it, so please, Miss Spindler, don't you be, either."

The woman sighed and held her bony hand up to her chest. I could see her breathing heavily, like she was near ready for a fit or stroke or who knows what. Anyway, after a few moments, Miss Spindler settled down and moved on to other topics.

But the most interesting aspect of the discussion came as Old Hawk Eyes was about to say good-bye. "You do know, Merry, that your Amish friend Levi Zook is responsible for yer bein' alive this very minute."

I was surprised to hear this from her lips.

"Yes, indeedy," she said. "That there Levi done pulled ya out, Merry—that other fella tried to, too."

Mom's mouth actually dropped open. "How do you know all this?" she asked.

A curious expression snuck up on Miss Spindler's face, and suddenly she clammed up. It was as if she'd been caught telling on herself. "Oh, bless my soul, I guess I best be headin' home now." She glanced over her shoulder at the kitchen window. "Well, I'll be, lookee there. It's a-comin' down mighty good again. I tell ya, this is the most snow we's seen around here for many a winter."

Miss Spindler was right about that. The snows had come hard and lay good and heavy for most of December. Thing was, she wasn't about to fess up to any spying tactics or reveal whatever made it possible for her to see all the way to Zooks' pond and beyond.

Still, I couldn't help but push for some answers. From what she'd already said, I figured she'd secretly observed what had happened on the ice from her attic window or somewhere else.

"Any idea how Levi went about saving me, Miss Spindler?" I asked.

A smile passed over her face, and for an instant, she honestly looked like one of the angels on our Christmas tree. "Ever heard tell of a human rope?" she said softly.

"Are you saying Levi had some help?" I said.

Unexpectedly, Miss Spindler eagerly spilled out her information, though not the method by which she'd acquired it. "Three other young people were there. They all got themselves right down on the ice—down close to the thinnest part—and I tell ya, they held on to one another and pulled for dear life."

From the sound of this, it seemed that Old Hawk Eyes had witnessed my rescue—Jon's, too!

"Thanks for telling me," I found myself saying. "You don't know how much it means to me, knowing this, Miss Spindler."

The old woman got up and walked to the back door with Mom accompanying her. "Happy New Year, Mrs. Hanson, Missy Merry," Ruby Spindler said with a crooked smile.

"Oh, do be careful on the snow," Mom cautioned.

In the still of dusk, the crackly voice came back, "Oh, don'tcha be worryin' none."

Two of my cats, Shadrach and Meshach, raised their eyelids as a gust of cold wind blew through the kitchen.

"Can you imagine?" Mom said, shaking her head. "She saw it all happen . . . your accident. Somehow Miss Spindler saw you fall through the ice."

"It's truly amazing" was all I could say.

Mom's eyes were on the ceiling as if reliving the frightful day. "Well *that* explains how the paramedics arrived so quickly." She seemed dazed. "Do you realize that Ruby Spindler may have played a role in saving your life, Merry?"

I appreciated Mom's sentiments toward Old Hawk Eyes. But my mind was twirling. What device had our elderly neighbor used to spy on us? How did she manage to survey the Sum-merHill area?

Mom's voice disrupted my thoughts. "Isn't it something? In spite of herself, our nosy neighbor probably had a big part in coming to your aid, Merry." She began to clear the table, carrying teaspoons and Christmasy mugs to the sink.

"Who knows," I said. "Maybe Miss Spindler could help me solve some of the mysteries that keep cropping up around here."

Mom eyed me more seriously. "Better wait till you're com-pletely back to normal before you try cracking another case."

I had to chuckle. "Don't worry, Mom, I'm not physically ready for sleuthing just yet." But in the heart and soul of me, I was. Plenty of forgotten parts of my own life awaited discovery.

"Good, because I, for one, have had more than my share of excitement. Enough to last a lifetime."

I agreed and went back to the living room, where Abed-nego and Lily White—my oldest and youngest cats—joined me a few minutes later. In their own unique way, the felines kept watch over me with an occasional shift of an eyelid at half-mast. It was the cutest thing I'd seen either of them do in a long time.

"Hey, what's with the wily watch guard?" I teased them, not realizing Mom had followed me into the room.

"There you go again, Merry. You're talking that way again— alliteration style."

I thought back to what I'd just said. "Hey, you're right. I wonder why."

Her eyebrows flew up at the additional *w*'s. This weird way of conversing reminded me of Jon Klein. For some strange reason, he kept trying to get me to speak like him, too. It had something to do with a word game, he'd said.

Although I pondered the situation, it was impossible to come up with a solution. Unless . . .

"Mom, can nearly drowning or a trauma like that alter someone's speech patterns?"

She sat across from me on a chair beside the hearth. Turning to face me, she frowned for a second. "Are you worried about it, Merry?"

I shrugged. "It seems so odd that I would alliterate almost without thinking."

She got up and came over to sit in her prized Boston rocker, handcrafted in the late eighteenth century. "Honey, the human brain is a complex and wondrous creation of God. I honestly don't think you have anything to be worried about. The doctors checked you out thoroughly in the hospital—neurologists, you name it. Your father saw to it that you had the very best doctors in all of Lancaster County."

"So you don't think I'll be alliterating like this the rest of my life?"

She reached for my hand. "We'll pray, if you'd like."

"I've already been talking to the Lord about it," I said. "Told God all about my accident and the awful, aimless aggravation—"

"Merry?" Mom had stopped me on purpose. "Take a deep breath and start again."

I groaned. "What'll I do? I mean, what if I keep this up? Alliteration isn't addicting at all, is it?"

The look on my mother's face spelled apprehension. Sure as anything, she must've thought I'd lost it.

There was only one thing left to do: I would simply have to make myself remember everything I could about Jonathan Klein and his wacky word game.

Fourteen *Echoes in the Wind*

It was dark by five-fifteen on Christmas Day evening. Mom went around lighting all the candles on the main level of the house. The fireplace mantel was aglow with soft, golden light.

After insisting that I bundle up in an afghan and my furriest slippers, Mom was finally satisfied that I was cozy and warm enough to be abandoned briefly while she went to make a simple supper.

I thought about Chelsea. Poor girl. Alone this Christmas season without her mom. She'd promised to call and fill me in on the first visit to the rehabilitation center.

But when my friend hadn't called by the time we finished eating the main course, which was mostly leftovers from noon, I began to fret. "It's not like Chelsea," I said as Dad and Skip cleared the table. "She said she'd let me know how things went with her mom last night."

Dad stood behind his chair, pausing to reflect. "Well, I certainly hope there was a counselor on hand when Chelsea and her father visited. The initial face-to-face encounter is often upsetting . . . for all concerned."

I thought for a moment. "Well, I hope everything went okay." Then I remembered the Christmas gift Chelsea had planned to give her mother. "Do you think the pictures I took might've upset Mrs. Davis?"

Dad pulled out his chair and sat down. "You wouldn't think such a thing would be troubling, but in brainwashing cases—especially those involving a cult—it's often difficult to say what may trigger emotional problems."

Now I was really worried and decided I couldn't wait any longer to talk to Chelsea. As soon as dessert was finished, I'd give her a call.

Mom brought over a tray of coffee for Dad and hot chocolate for Skip and me. She sliced one of the pumpkin pies. "Do you feel up to having sweets?" she asked me, picking up the whipped cream.

Dad grinned and reached across the table, squeezing my elbow. "Bring on the goodies, dear. Our girl is recuperating quickly." He looked at both Skip and me. "We have so much to celebrate this year!"

Skip nodded—one of the first times I'd ever seen him remotely acknowledge that his "little Merry" was worth her salt. My brother's genuine smile warmed me to my croupy soul.

Once again, I was excused from kitchen cleanup. Hurrying to Dad's study, I closed the door and phoned Chelsea, hoping and praying things were all right with her.

"Hello, Davis residence" came a stiff response.

"Mr. Davis," I said, "this is Merry Hanson calling. May I speak to Chelsea, please?"

"Well, I believe she left to go caroling with some friends. But I'll sure have her return your call."

"Thanks," I said, getting ready to hang up.

"Uh . . . wait just a minute, Merry." He coughed a little. "I heard you took quite a spill on Zooks' pond last weekend. Just wanted to say that I'm mighty glad you're feeling better now."

"Why, thank you, Mr. Davis. That's very kind."

He sighed a bit. "Well, I'll give Chelsea your message when she comes in."

"Okay, and thanks again. Good-bye."

We hung up, and I was surprised at how friendly Mr. Davis had seemed this phone call.

"Everything all right?" Dad asked as I passed him in the hall.

I stopped to tell him what Mr. Davis had said. "But I didn't get any new info on Chelsea's mom. I guess Chelsea's out caroling somewhere."

"Well, don't worry. I'm sure you'll hear something soon." Dad headed for his study, and I went back to enjoy my Christmas gifts in the living room—specifically the new photography books.

While I thumbed through them, I thought about Jon Klein. What was it about him that made me so curious? From what I'd learned of him in the days since my accident, he and I shared a whole slew of common interests. But what about *before* my memory lapse? What had gone on between us then?

Speaking in alliterated sentences seemed terribly important to him for some reason—almost a preoccupation. The more I thought about it, the more baffled I became. I was more anxious that ever to interrogate Chelsea, getting her to tell me everything she knew about Jon.

My mind wandered back to the conversation with Chelsea's father. Mr. Davis had said she was out caroling with friends. But my friends were her friends, so why hadn't I heard about this?

The answer came swiftly, almost on wings. The doorbell rang, and when Dad opened it, I heard singing. "Joy to the world, the Lord is come!"

I listened for a moment. The clear sound of Chelsea's soprano voice was evident. So *that's* why I was kept in the dark! Maybe it was intended as a surprise.

Dad called from the foyer. "Merry, some friends of yours are here."

Mom got out of her chair and scurried to the front door to greet them. "Come in, come in," I heard her say. "Merry Christmas to all of you!"

Chelsea and a group of our mutual friends from church came into the living room, greeted me and then went over to stand by the hearth to warm themselves. Soon they were sipping hot chocolate, compliments of Mom, of course.

"We came to cheer you up," Chelsea said, grinning first at me, then at Lissa Vyner, Ashley Horton, Jon Klein, and his sister Nikki, along with three other teens.

I tossed the afghan aside. Having carolers come indoors on a freezing-cold night, especially when they were dear friends, brightened everything. Especially my outlook. "Happy to have a houseful," I said. "Sing some more songs."

Jon smiled broadly, and I noticed that he turned to Ashley and poked her. "See, that's what I mean. Merry's supreme," he said.

I felt uncomfortable. But Jon's comment didn't seem to bother anyone else. Soon they were singing again—"Angels We Have Heard on High."

Chelsea came over to sit on the throw rug next to the couch. "How are you doing?" she asked as the group continued to sing.

"I'm okay, but what's with Jon?" I whispered.

"Don't freak out," she said, keeping her voice low. "Ashley'll never catch on to his ridiculous game. He thinks you're tops."

I didn't exactly understand what had just happened, but I assumed she'd explain later. What I really wanted to know was how the visit with her mom had been. I was resigned to wait to bring it up, though, until she and I could talk privately.

The angel song came to a lilting climax. Dad started the applause. Mom, Skip, and I followed suit.

"What's your favorite carol?" Lissa asked. "Maybe we could sing it for you."

"If all of us know it," Ashley piped up, smiling at Jon.

"Oh, it's an easy one," I said. "Do you know 'I Heard the Bells on Christmas Day'?"

Jon and two other boys were nodding that they knew it and began testing their baritone and tenor ranges just for fun. Someone said it was getting too toasty by the fire, so they all sat down on the floor while Mom went to find an old hymnal. Ashley and Lissa ended up finding the right pitch for the group, and they began to sing, sharing the hymnal as best they could.

Sonorous but sweet sounds filled the room. They sang mostly in harmony, four part on certain phrases. During the last verse, Mom disappeared from the room again, only to return with two large serving plates of cookies—the snickerdoodles from Miss Spindler and Mom's own specialty, rich chocolate chip.

Chelsea stayed close to me throughout the visit. In between cookie munching and sips of hot chocolate, the casual choir of carolers entertained us with a cappella music.

Skip even joined in on several choruses, clowning around with his old girlfriend, Nikki Klein, who seemed mighty happy about seeing him again.

All in all, the evening was entirely too short.

"It's getting late," Ashley said, glancing at her watch.

They got up and were milling around, some of them going over to ooh and ahh at Mom's splendid angel decorations on the tree.

When Dad offered to drive them back to Chelsea's house, she graciously declined. "Thanks anyway, but we want to make a quick stop at Miss Spindler's."

"Oh, how thoughtful," Mom said, getting up to collect the empty mugs.

"After Old Hawk Eyes' place, where are you headed?" Skip asked.

Mom looked startled at Miss Spindler's nickname, but Skip wiggled his head comically, grinning back at her. "It's okay, Mom. Really."

Nikki giggled. "You should come along," she invited him.

The twinkle in Skip's eyes gave him away. Going off to college hadn't wiped away his memories of Jon's pixie-faced sister.

"We'll probably end up at the Zooks' house last," Chelsea said. "I want to personally thank Levi for saving Merry's life." She smiled sweetly at me.

When I glanced back at the group, astonishment was written all over Jon's face. He began to rub his chin, looking puzzled. "No one said anything about singing for the Amish," he muttered.

"Oh, you don't have a thing to worry about," my brother said. "The Zooks are some of the nicest people you'll ever meet. Right, Merry?"

Jon glanced at me again at that juncture, as well as Skip. The big question marks in Jon's eyes made me nervous.

Ashley—the dear girl—corralled Jon into the hallway just then, where Dad's voice could be heard assisting the carolers with the location of jackets and other personal things.

Chelsea got up and leaned down to speak to me. "Hope you liked the surprise, Mer. Happy Christmas."

"Thanks. It was really great," I said, gazing over my shoulder. "And it was especially fun watching Jon and Ashley together."

"I think he's got an alliteration agenda. Something about that word game of his."

"Really? How do you know?" I said, wondering why I should even care.

She straightened her thick sweater. "I overheard Jon saying it was time to teach more of his friends how to speak alliteration-eze."

"Meaning Ashley?" I said. "Think she can do it?"

Chelsea frowned. "Do you remember disliking her . . . from before?"

"I never disliked Ashley. *Never.*" I studied my friend. "Did I?"

Chelsea was nodding her head and making groaning sounds.

"Well, I can't imagine why. I mean, Ashley's got a lot going for her."

Chelsea grabbed my hand. "If you don't get your memory back pretty soon, Mer, she's going to have a lot more going for her!"

I didn't ask her to spell things out. I was sick with a lousy cough and a faulty memory, but I wasn't ignorant. Anyone could see how Ashley felt about Jon.

"Call me the minute you get home," I pleaded. "We have to talk—tonight!"

"I'll call, but don't hold your breath about Ashley. She may not be Jon's intellectual equal, but she likes him. And I mean a lot!"

I almost told her that it didn't matter, that *I* liked Levi Zook a lot. But knowing Chelsea, she'd only remind me that Levi wasn't the one for me. Or something like that.

"I really don't know what to tell you about Jon," Chelsea said later when she called. "But I know one thing—before your accident you really liked him. And that's the honest truth."

"What about Levi?" I asked hesitantly.

"I don't think you were all that excited about seeing him this Christmas. I tried my best to read the end of his last letter, but you snatched it away, like it was private or something."

"There's a letter from Levi? Where?"

"You hid it. Probably with all the others."

I could hardly believe this. "You mean Levi's been writing me? Oh, Chelsea, this is such wonderful news!"

She was groaning now. "Listen, Mer, this entire conversation is hopeless. I mean, you really can't decide anything about either guy until you get your memory back. Don't you see?"

I didn't want to talk logic. Not now. "So you want me to move slowly because you think I had a crush on Jon, is that it?"

"Think? Girl, I *know* you were nuts about Jon. But why, I couldn't begin to tell you. Most of the time his head's buried in some book. Grades have always been more important to the guy than girls."

"Hey, have you been practicing Jon's word game?"

She laughed. "Not on your life. That alliteration stuff is for ingenious people."

"Like me?" I laughed. Somehow it relieved the stress.

She didn't answer, though, and I felt very sympathetic toward her when she changed the subject to her mother and the visit last night. "It was a disaster."

"Oh, Chelsea. I wondered why you didn't call."

"Well, Mom couldn't exactly handle the emotion of seeing either Daddy or me."

"And the pictures? What did she think of them?"

"They made her cry. She could hardly talk to either of us. Like I said, it was awful."

I remembered what my dad had said about a counselor. "Was a professional with you during the visit? Someone to help deal with the transition?"

Chelsea breathed hard into the phone. "There were two advisors present, but none of it seemed to help much. I guess it was too soon for Mom."

"I'm sorry," I blurted. "We'd all hoped—"

"Please, don't give up, Merry. I'm not."

"That's good, because your mom needs you. I hope you know that."

"It's just so depressing, especially when I had my heart set on something special happening . . . for Christmas."

I could feel her pain, even though I didn't fully understand what she was experiencing. "I'll keep praying, okay?"

"Thanks," she said with tears in her voice.

"I wish you'd told me sooner," I said.

"It wasn't the easiest thing, holding it inside, but I was worried about *you*, Merry. I nearly lost you. I wouldn't want to say or do anything to make you worse."

"Thanks to Levi, I'm still here."

She laughed a little. "I wish you could've seen him tonight when we caroled over there. Levi kept asking your brother about you after almost every song!"

"You're kidding! In front of everyone?" My neck grew warm envisioning the scene.

"Levi's very unique," she said. "But he's not Jon."

I moaned. "Oh, what'll I do? My feelings are all so jumbled up since I fell into the pond."

Chelsea promised to do what she could to help me regain my memory. "But only when you're ready."

"I'm ready now. Honest!"

She was giggling. "You name the time, and I'll be there."

"We can't do anything about it tomorrow," I said. "My grandparents are coming from New Jersey. They spent the first part of the holidays with my aunt and uncle."

"I bet they loved seeing your twin baby cousins. How old are they now?"

"Becky and Ben will be seven months old tomorrow. Grandpa and Grandma Landis—my mom's parents—always divide the holidays between Aunt Teri and Uncle Pete, and us."

"Well, I won't push you, Mer, but time's running against us, if you know what I mean."

"We have to keep Jon from falling for Ashley."

"We have some work to do," she said.

"Whatever you say." I smiled into the phone. "But what makes you think you can cure me?"

"For starters, we can always pray about it, right?"

"Always," I said.

"And there's the matter of your poetry books."

"So?"

"You'll see what I mean." Chelsea seemed so confident. I hoped she was right. Because for once in my life, I realized I was *not* the one being counted on. Miss Fix-It was the one in most need of repair.

Even though I always thoroughly enjoyed time spent with my grandparents, having them come to stay with us now was a bit distracting. I needed time to focus on what Chelsea had said—that she wasn't kidding when she declared right down the line that I'd liked Jon and not so much Levi.

Trust was the key. What else could I do?

I searched high and low for Levi's letters the day after Christmas, hoping they might give me some insight into my former feelings.

I started with my desk drawers, searching through school assignments, old address books, and an occasional note from Jon Klein. Funny, on one of them, I'd penned the nickname *The Alliteration Wizard*.

Somehow, though, the title didn't do anything for me—not as far as bringing back the memory I'd lost. And I knew that even if Chelsea had been here, I wouldn't have given the nickname more than a passing glance.

The shelves of my walk-in closet were next on my list. Scouring the colorful shoe boxes and scrapbooks on the first shelf, I found only odds and ends. Nothing pertinent to either Levi or Jonathan.

It was late in the day when I discovered the pinkish box on the middle shelf. I'd come upstairs to get my digital camera because Mom wanted some close-up shots of Grandpa and Grandma beside the nativity scene in the dining room. That's how I happened onto Levi's letters. Almost half a shoe box full.

Of course, I couldn't just sit there and sift through them with relatives waiting to be photographed. So I set the box on my desk and told my cats to guard it with one of their nine lives.

Grandma was fussing over Grandpa's shirt collar, trying to get it perfectly aligned with his tie, when I arrived. He grumbled about it, glancing over at me every so often until the collar was exactly to Grandma's liking. "Don't you want to look nice for your granddaughter's picture?" she coaxed.

He mumphed and garrumphed, and finally the two of them were posing with broad smiles.

"Don't wear out your smiles yet." I walked backward around the long table, checking for exactly the right angle. Leaning on the buffet, I steadied my hand. "Okay, one . . . two . . . three." *Click*.

"Now, hold it right there," I said. But I coughed unexpectedly and had to retake.

Mom went to the kitchen to get my evening dose of antibiotics and cough syrup. Then it was time to try for several more shots.

Grandpa was in a bad way by the time I was completely satisfied. In fact, he was pushing his tie loose and unbuttoning the top button on his dress shirt as I put my camera in its case.

Trying not to think about Chelsea, who was probably waiting for a phone call, I joined my family for home videos featuring Ben and Becky. The tiny twins were adorable.

"Looks like Becky might be a little bigger than her brother," Mom observed.

"Well, you know how it is with girls," Grandma offered. "They fill out quickly."

Grandpa laughed outright. "They're only babies, for cryin' out loud. Give the little fella some slack."

We chuckled at his comment, and the next time I looked over at Grandpa, he was sound asleep in his chair.

By the time I dressed for bed, I was too exhausted to bother with all of Levi's letters. My respiratory infection and the worry over my fickle amnesia had worn me out.

But I took time to pray, beginning with Chelsea's mom. "Dear Lord, it would be terribly hard for me to be in my friend's shoes, but you know what to do to ease her disappointment and pain. And I pray for Mrs. Davis. Please, will you help her adjust to the idea of coming home . . . and soon? Chelsea and her father really need her. They want her with them."

I continued on, praying that in God's perfect time and way I would remember the things I needed to know about my life. "Not just because there might be some cute boy involved, Lord. I ask this because I'm your child and I know you love me. Amen."

Maybe tomorrow things would clear up for me. If not, I'd keep trusting. It was the only way.

First thing, even before I showered, I read Levi's letters. Every last one of them. Wow, what an expressive guy! From reading them, I could tell that he was determined and directed. Knew what he wanted. Maybe *that's* what I liked so much about him.

Chelsea had been absolutely right—Levi had his sights set on me. Oh glory! But if what she'd said about my former feelings was accurate, I wasn't supposed to be overjoyed about it. Not anymore. I had to keep telling myself that Jon was the boy the pre-accident me had liked. *He* was the guy of my dreams.

Such a mix-up, not to understand your own feelings.

I got out of bed, sweet-talking my cats into coming downstairs with me for their breakfast. Mom and Grandma were already up scrambling eggs and making Belgian waffles on the new waffle iron Mom had received for Christmas.

"Hope you're hungry," she said, coming over to see for herself how I was doing today.

"I hardly coughed all night," I told her. "The medicine must be working."

I caught her studying me. "Something else is working, too." Mom smirked a bit. "You're not alliterating."

"I'm not?"

She nodded. "I think it may be a good sign."

"Maybe my memory's mending."

She grinned. "Meaning?"

I laughed. "Mom, you're amazing. Wait'll I tell Jon Klein about you."

She waved her hand with a smile and went to help Grandma with breakfast.

―――――――

Chelsea and I had the most remarkable fun together that next afternoon. Actually, what she had in mind proved quite revealing.

She stood comically in the center of my large bedroom, just the way I had almost three weeks ago when I'd read out of my poetry book. "Okay, here's what we're going to do," she said, sitting me down on my desk chair, facing her. "Don't say anything, Mer, just listen." She pulled out a piece of paper, turning it so that I could see the long list of things she'd written.

"I'm listening." I snuggled with Lily White.

"This is a list of memory starters," Chelsea began.

Squelching a snicker, I pretended to be impressed. "Go ahead—trigger my brain."

"C'mon, this is serious stuff." She put one hand on her hip and began. "Three weeks ago, when you and I visited Rachel Zook—that's Levi's sister, in case you forgot—she invited you to her surprise skating party when we were upstairs in her bedroom. She wanted you to come and be Levi's partner, and you said, 'Maybe he should have a say about it,' or some such thing. Anyway, for a little while, I thought you were going to say no, but then Rachel spoke up. 'Do it for Levi,' she said."

"*You* must have a good memory," I said. "Thanks for doing this, Chelsea. I'm enjoying myself."

She shrugged, apparently not too pleased that the first thing on her list hadn't worked an immediate miracle. "Okay, moving on. How about this? Way back as long as I can remember, you've watched out the school bus window, probably watching for Levi when we rode past the Zooks' cornfield. And most every time I'd tease you with something like, 'You must want to hand sew all your clothes or go without electricity all your life.' " She paused, waiting for a reaction from me. "Does that do anything for you, Mer?"

"Nope." I sat very still, trying not to giggle.

She surveyed her long list. "Here's one that might stir up something: number three. This one's about Jon. You and I discussed him right here in this very room three weeks ago. Anyway, I told you that it looked like you were soaking up whatever he was saying each day at your locker. And you said—and I quote—'Aren't friends supposed to pay attention to each other?' End of quote."

I couldn't help it; I let out a giggle. "This is so weird listening to you document my every movement—everything I said. It's like you're a walking diary—of *my* life!"

Chelsea flopped down on my bed, obviously not because things were funny. Clearly, she was discouraged. "What are we gonna do, Mer? Don't you see I'm doing all this for you? So you won't freak out when you regain your faculties but have lost your . . . your . . ."

"My boyfriend?" I asked.

She sat up abruptly. "Oh, I don't know, maybe we're not supposed to force things like this."

"No, wait a minute." I thought of something I'd written about Jon Klein. "Here, let me show you this." Pulling out my desk drawer, I found the note from Jon, where I'd written the nickname for him on the back.

Peering over my shoulder, she read *The Alliteration Wizard*. "Hey, we might be on to something. I mean, if you thought enough of his . . . uh, abilities to alliterate or whatever, and— well, you know—had him on some kind of pedestal about it . . . maybe the crush you had on him has something to do with the word game." She eyed me. "Maybe *that's* what you two were always doing at your locker—talking in your bizarre language."

Then, before I could reply, she started getting all hyped up about it. "Yes! I think we're getting closer to the truth, Mer." She snatched up her list from the bed and scanned it. "Here we go. This is another item about Jon. Now, listen carefully."

"What else can I do?" I teased. "I'm stuck in my own house. I can't go anywhere, right?"

She started reading off something about Jon's sudden interest in photography. "If it's any consolation to you, you'd be flying high if you were in your . . . uh, right mind, I guess you could say. Don't you see? This must be a major breakthrough—Jon wanting a camera like yours. Could be things are changing, about to become more serious."

Chelsea got up and went to the window. She stood there, staring out at the snow and ice. "You know, I haven't forgotten that verse by Longfellow—the one you read to me when I stayed overnight."

I got up and went to the corner bookcase and started pulling classic poetry books out. Piling them up, I set them down in front of Chelsea on my bed. "Here you go. Which one?"

"So you don't remember reading about the echoes?"

"Oh, *that* one," I said. "I almost know it by heart." Quickly, I found the page. "Want me to read it to you?"

"Sure, go ahead."

" 'And, when the echoes had ceased, like a sense of pain was the silence.' " I handed her the open book.

A car horn sounded out front. Chelsea got a queer look on her face, and she ran to the window. "It's Daddy," she said. "What's he doing here so soon?"

"Better go see," I said, joining her at the window. "It might be about your mother."

She turned to me. "You might be right. Oh . . . I hope it's not more bad news." And with that, she scurried out of the room and down the steps.

I lingered at the window, watching as Chelsea ran to her father's waiting car. She stopped momentarily to look up and wave, and I waved back.

Curious about my friend's situation, yet feeling quite tired and a bit overwhelmed, I pulled my blue-striped comforter back and crawled into bed for a nap.

In the distance, I heard a midday train whistle twice, echoing across hundreds of acres of slumbering farmland. Straining, I listened as its mournful wail died away.

He will call upon me, and I will answer him. . . .

I imagined the train, going who knows where, rumbling over hills and through valleys. Speeding toward the horizon and beyond. Who was riding today? Where were the people going? Where had they been?

I will be with him in trouble. . . .

I felt as if I would fall asleep any minute. Maybe I already was.

I will deliver him and honor him. . . .

In the heaviness before sleep actually takes place, I thought I heard the creaking sound of the windmill behind Zooks' barn and saw the outline of bare trees toward the east. Far, far across the frozen pond, where "cellar" holes gobble up lost girls.

And for the first time since my fall through the ice, my past blended with the present.

I remembered.

Seventeen *Echoes in the Wind*

When I awoke, I pulled the comforter off my bed and wrapped it around me. I sat quietly near the window, letting two of my cats rub against my ankles.

"Jon Klein's hung up on having an alliteration partner, whether it's me or someone else," I said to the cats. I felt a little sad realizing the truth.

But there was hope, I decided. After all, Jon probably hadn't wanted the same kind of camera equipment as mine for nothing. Time would tell about that.

Meanwhile, I'd let him know next time he called that alliteration-eze didn't have to be an exclusive thing between us. That way I'd let him off the hook. In fact, if I were to admit it, it would be kind of fun to get everyone in our youth group talking that way, sort of a community-wide inside joke.

Even Ashley Horton, bless her heart. Given the opportunity and training, of course, she might become very adept at the word game. Depending on her teacher.

I went down the hall to Skip's room, my comforter dragging like a royal train behind me. He was out, probably with Nikki again, but that was all right. Life was too short not to be with your friends whenever possible.

I reached for the phone on my brother's desk.

When Ashley answered the phone, she seemed quite surprised to hear from me. "Hi, Merry. It seems like forever since we really talked."

"Since the photography contest at school," I volunteered.

"How're you doing?"

"Well, I wish I could tell you just how truly terrific I'm feeling, especially now."

"Oh? Something happen?" She sounded excited and eager.

"You're the very first person to hear about this. I've regained my memory."

"That's great, Merry. Did it happen today?"

"Just a little while ago. I was resting, and the Lord brought everything back to me. Clear as . . . as ice."

She laughed. "I'm sure Jon and the others will be thrilled. I know I am."

I inhaled quickly. "Would you mind letting Jon know about it—that is, if you happen to talk to him before I do?"

"I'd be happy to tell him. In fact, I'll probably see him on New Year's Eve at the church. I hope you'll feel up to coming."

I knew what she was talking about. Every year the youth pastor put together a special "Farewell Service," which included a Bible study, prayer time, and lots of special music. We usually finished up the old year on our knees in prayer.

"Well, I'll have to see what my parents think, but maybe it'll work out for me to come."

"Great," she said. She paused before going on. "Uh . . . Merry, could I ask you a question? It's about Jon's word game— alliteration-eze, I believe he calls it."

"Sure. What do you want to know?" I said, not feeling the least bit intimidated.

"How hard is it to talk that way?"

"To be honest, Ashley, if you practice, you should be able to catch on pretty fast."

"Really?"

"Sounds like it's important to you." *Like it is to Jon,* I thought.

She laughed softly. "It's a challenge—that's all, really. Most people think I'm a little dense. Maybe if I can do this, like Jon and you do, maybe it'll stretch my mind. You know what I mean?"

Now I was the one chuckling. "Sure, Ashley, I know exactly what you mean. And I know just the person to help you get the hang of it."

"Really? Are you saying *you'll* help me?"

I reached down to stroke Lily White. "Won't Jon be surprised?"

"Maybe we can outdo him someday," Ashley said.

I switched the phone to my left ear. "That's exactly what I had in mind."

She laughed, and I knew this was a genius idea!

Chelsea called right after supper. "You'll never guess what," she said the minute I answered the phone.

"I hope this has something to do with your mom."

"She's home, Merry! My mom's sitting right here in our living room."

"You're kidding! This is fantastic. What happened to make her change her mind?"

Chelsea was chuckling. "Your pictures, Mer. She kept looking at them after we left on Christmas Eve. Something started working on her heart, and she really began to miss Daddy and me. She missed us so much that she convinced her therapist and doctors to allow us to come for another visit."

"And that's where you were going when your dad stopped by this afternoon?"

"Oh, I can't believe this is happening," she said. "It's absolutely the best possible New Year's gift."

"I'm truly happy for you, Chelsea." Then after we discussed all the details of her mother's return, I told her *my* news.

"I remember everything!" I announced.

She couldn't stop talking about it. "Do you think maybe all that reminiscing we did together—you know, my list and everything—do you think it might've helped?"

"Oh, I'm sure it did. So did your prayers."

"It's really special when friends can do something like this for each other," she said. "Your idea about taking pictures of me for my mom sparked something deep in her and . . . well, you know what I'm trying to say, don't you?"

I knew. We'd touched each other's lives in a powerful, meaningful way. Thanks to friendship—and prayers.

As it turned out, I did get to go for a short time to the New Year's Eve service at church. Mom made sure I was bundled up, and Dad drove me into town with the car heater going full blast.

Jon, Lissa, Ashley, and all the others congratulated me on being well enough to show up.

"Lookin' like lots of lively links to our language." Jon glanced around at the group. "Everyone's eager to exercise energy and—"

"You just wait," I interrupted, referring to Ashley's and my secret plan to outwit him. Boy, was the Alliteration Wizard in for it!

"Aha, do I detect a duel, dear Merry?"

My heart didn't do a single somersault. I stood tall and said, friend to friend, "We'll have a contest very soon."

Grinning with delight, Jon motioned for me to sit with him for the devotional, which I did.

The next day, the first of the New Year, I spent part of the afternoon with Rachel Zook and her younger brother and sisters—Levi too. He took me for a short ride in his car, and while we rode we communicated.

It wasn't akin to alliteration-eze, but a language that has been universal since the beginning of time. We sang—in two-part harmony—mostly Christmas carols. It seemed like a fun thing to do, especially since I'd missed out on the caroling around SummerHill. And Levi had missed out on singing in harmony most of his life because of his Amish upbringing.

"It's wonderful-gut seein' ya all smiles again, Merry," he said, turning into their long lane.

"And I'm very glad you came home for Christmas, Levi," I said, returning his smile.

There was no reaching for my hand or anything else romantic. Levi stopped the car and turned to look at me. "You and I must go ice skating before I go back to Virginia to school. Jah?"

I gasped. "Oh, I don't think so."

He nodded thoughtfully. "That's what people often say after a car wreck, too. But ya can't be waitin' much longer, Merry. You need to get back on your skates."

I had all sorts of excuses, though. "My skates are completely ruined."

"Aw, such a shame," he joked. "We'll just hafta see 'bout that."

Like I always said, Levi was persistent. Never gave up. And because he was stubborn this time, I got my courage back. And much more.

———

The winter sun was high a week later when Levi knelt to lace up my brand-new skates. "Let's just say they're a gift from an old friend." He grinned up at me.

The first few steps on the ice frightened me nearly to death, but Levi reached for my hand. Then, supporting my back, he pushed forward, sending the two of us gliding across the pond. Together.

The wind was gentle and kind on my face this day. And far away were the echoes of fear, growing more distant with each stroke of our skates.

⁓

When Levi left for his Mennonite college, I said good-bye with only a touch of sadness. It won't be long—he'll be back for spring break. And there'll be letters . . . plenty of them from each of us.

Chelsea remembered to take her puppy, Secrets, for a visit to his cocker spaniel mama. Little Susie Zook was tickled to see the beautiful gold-haired pup again.

Mrs. Davis is acclimating to her own home and surroundings surprisingly well. According to Chelsea, she hopes to plant an extra-large flower garden come spring.

As for Jon, the way I view him has begun to change. A brush with death often alters things between friends. For the better, I believe. He's asked me to show him some of the features on my 35-millimeter camera—the same as his. He could probably figure it out if he read the instruction booklet, but maybe this is the start of a new kind of bond between us.

And Ashley Horton? She and I are planning a big sleepover on Valentine's Day with Chelsea and Lissa—complete with a lesson in alliteration-eze. It's about time the women of SummerHill unite.

Speaking of the neighborhood, Miss Spindler might be pleased to know that I'm offering my services to house-sit the next time she leaves town. The way I see it, someone's got to get to the bottom of things over there. I mean, how *does* she do it—keeping track of everything and everyone?

Chelsea's offered to help me snoop around—that is, if I ever get inside Old Hawk Eyes' house. Meanwhile, I may have to be content with my imagination. Not an easy task. Especially for a girl who hears echoes in the wind.

Hide Behind the Moon

For Larissa
with love.

*"There's all the difference in the world, you know,
between being inside looking out and
outside looking in."*

—FROM *ANNE OF WINDY POPLARS*

BY L. M. MONTGOMERY

"Shh! We daresn't be heard," whispered Rachel Zook, my Amish girl friend. Silently, she leaned over the old attic trunk and pulled open the heavy lid. Her eyes were filled with glee.

"I can't believe I let you talk me into this," I said, looking around at our creepy surroundings. "Cobwebs aren't exactly my cup of tea."

She stifled a giggle. "*Ach*, leave it to you, Merry Hanson. You ain't scared, now, are ya?"

The musty darkness stretched all the way under the attic eaves in both directions. Rachel's kerosene lantern swayed back and forth from the rafters, casting lively shadows over wooden crates and old canning jars.

"So *this* is what an Amish attic's supposed to look like," I teased. "Thought it'd be more organized."

"It's about as *ret* up as it can be. Besides, lookee here, I think I might've found somethin'. " She stood up, brushing the dust off the sleeves of her purple dress and long black apron, staring at the dilapidated-looking stationery box in her hand.

I inched closer, very curious. "You sure it's such a good idea to snoop like this?"

Rachel's blue eyes were serious, determined. "I'm getting warmer," she said. "I can feel it in my bones."

"Well, *I'm* cold. It's freezing up here." I waited for her to take the hint, but she kept rummaging through the box, searching for what, I didn't know exactly.

"I'm almost positive there're some old poems up here," she muttered to herself.

"Well, they can wait, right? Till summer, maybe?"

"But we're here now . . . and *Dat* and *Mam* are gone for a bit. *Jah*, I think we best go ahead and keep lookin'. "

Rachel motioned for me to come over to help, so I did. After all, besides being sixteen like me, she was one of my dearest friends in all of Lancaster County. SummerHill, to be exact.

Oh, she'd gotten this hare-brained notion that there was a strain of writing talent in her family somewhere, and she just had to prove it to her English friend, namely me. *English* meaning I wasn't Amish. Or as Rachel often said, "You're my English cousin."

Technically, I *was* related to her. My Swiss ancestors and Rachel's had arrived in America back in 1737 on the same boat—*The Charming Nancy*. We shared a common relative— Joseph Lapp, one of my great-great grandfathers—which made us distant cousins.

"Here's another big box," I said, pulling it out of a hodge- podge of quilts and linens and things. "Looks like a diary."

"Let's have a look-see," she said.

I sat on another dusty trunk near the lantern's eerie circle of light, observing as she opened the oblong wooden box.

She rummaged through some loose papers inside, but nothing seemed to catch her interest. "Nah, nothin' much here."

Growing impatient, I asked, "Isn't it about time to be mak- ing doughnuts again?" I wanted to get her mind off her pres- ent pursuit and start her contemplating sweets, one of her weaknesses.

"Jah, this Saturday we'll be making some," she replied, still nosing around in the trunk.

"Well, am I invited?"

She stopped her searching, glancing over at me. "Of course you're invited. What'sa matter with ya, askin' something so foolish?"

I just smiled, watching her bend over and remove several more boxes from the seemingly bottomless trunk.

"Better put everything back the way you found it," I told her.

"Ach, as if I ain't smart enough to know that."

I sat there a few minutes longer, itching to get back to the warmth of the Zooks' kitchen, just below us.

Then without warning, she jerked up. Stood right up and stared at something small and square in her hands. "*Himmel,* what's this?" she sputtered.

I hurried over to see what great treasure she'd uncovered. "Looks like . . . is it a *picture*?" I asked, amazed.

"Well, goodness me, I don't rightly know." She rushed over to the lantern, and I followed.

There under the light, she held up a photograph of an Amishman. It was old and tattered. Where it had come from, I had no idea, because Amish folk don't believe in such things as taking pictures of themselves. Especially the Old Order Amish, which Rachel's family certainly was.

"Who *is* this?" she whispered, eyes wide with wonder.

"Maybe your parents could tell you."

She turned to look at me, worry creasing her brow. "Now, don'tcha breathe a word of this to Dat or Mam, ya hear?"

I was startled. This was one of the few times she'd ever spoken so frankly to me.

"Okay," I replied. "We'll keep it secret."

She nodded, lowering the picture. "We hafta zip up our lips about this, honest we do. 'Cause I think I've stumbled onto someone. Someone who ain't too fondly remembered in these parts." I knew by the scowl on her face she meant business about not spilling the beans.

Still, I was dying to know. "Who do you think it is?"

"I think this here's Joseph Lapp . . . perty sure 'tis."

I inhaled sharply. "Our ancestor? The man who got himself shunned for marrying outside the Amish church?"

"It's beyond me why he thought he had to go off and marry his English sweetheart" was all she said.

"Count on me to keep it quiet," I said. "Nobody'll hear it from *my* lips."

So it was settled. We had a secret between us. A big, juicy one.

"Why do you think your parents kept this photo all these years?"

Rachel shrugged her shoulders. "Dat probably knows nothing of it. Mam must've hid it, I'd guess." She shook her head, puzzled. "Looks to me like it's been passed down for generations. Really odd, though."

It *was* peculiar, to say the least. But even more intriguing was the inquisitive look on Rachel's face. Why her sudden interest in a shunned man, one who'd left the Amish church?

Esther Zook, Rachel's mother, was a devout and energetic woman who derived great satisfaction from the simple things: cooking, baking, caring for her children, and cleaning house.

Nearly every year, long as I could remember, she would throw a doughnut-making party, usually in mid-February. After all, it was the dullest, bleakest time of year, smack-dab in the dead of winter. Of course, Esther would never admit to calling it a party. Amish folk didn't engage in such "fancy" things. Still, it was a major event all the same.

Often on Valentine's Day—an icy Saturday morning *this* year—she liked to fill up her kitchen with close friends and her married sisters. Rachel and her younger sisters—Nancy, Ella Mae, and little Susie—were the ones most encouraged to join in the fun. And today was the annual doughnut-making day at the Zooks' old farmhouse, just across the meadow from my house.

This time of year, it was fairly easy to see the Zooks' place through the bare branches of the willow grove. The trees ran along the dividing line between our property and theirs. Only an occasional dried-up leaf clung to the wispy limbs.

I made my way down snow-packed SummerHill Lane, glad for fur-lined boots and gloves and my warm earmuffs.

Pennsylvania winters weren't anything to scoff at. The sting in the wind was enough to turn my cheeks numb by the time I made the turn onto our neighbor's private lane.

Gray carriages galore were already parked in the side yard, their tops glistening with a hint of snow. The horses had been led to the barn for warmth and watering by Rachel's father, Abe, and her younger brother, Aaron.

"Come in, come in," my friend greeted me as the back door swung wide.

"Br-r, it's cold," I said, closing the door quickly and slapping my gloved hands together.

"Warm yourself by the stove," she offered.

"Thanks," I said, hurrying over to the large black wood-stove, where Rachel's mother was keeping a watchful eye on the fryer.

"Glad you could come over and help." A dimple appeared in her cheek as she smiled.

"Nice to be here," I said, grinning back.

The kitchen smelled heavenly, of yeast and dough. My mouth watered at the aroma. "Mm-m, I can't wait for a bite," I told Rachel.

"Me neither." She took her mother's place at the stove, monitoring the oil in the fryer, making sure that it did not exceed the temperature needed to begin cooking the doughnuts.

Nancy, Rachel's thirteen-year-old sister, scurried about taking my coat and hanging it on one of the wooden pegs in the outer utility room, just off the kitchen. "Now we hafta find you a spot to work," she said.

"Ready when you are," I said, tying on the long Amish apron handed to me by one of the women.

"There," Nancy said, stepping back to have a look at me. "Don't you look perty . . . and Amish."

I curtsied comically, and she laughed. Glancing around, I looked for Susie, the youngest Zook.

"If it's Susie ya want, she's kneading dough over there." Nancy motioned for me to follow her to the long wooden table.

Little Susie, now seven but still quite petite, was squeezing and punching at a big mound of dough. "Come and take a poke, Merry," she said, eyes sparkling.

I noticed her pretty blond hair, wound around her head in braids, and her long rose-colored dress and white smock-style apron. She was the cutest young Amish girl in all of Lancaster County!

I rolled up my sweater sleeves and folded Susie's piece of dough over and over. "How am I doing?"

She giggled sweetly. "Ya must've remembered from last year."

"Guess you're right," I said, looking up.

Across the enormous kitchen, Rachel was chattering in Pennsylvania Dutch. When she caught my eye, she waved at me, wiggling her fingers in midair.

"Have ya heard anything from Levi lately?" Susie asked.

I didn't respond immediately, thinking what I should say about her big brother's most recent letters. "He's been writing me every now and then. You have to remember, your brother keeps very busy with his classes during the semester."

She nodded. "I miss him around here. Wish he'd come home for *gut.*"

"I know you do."

"Maybe if ya say you'll marry him someday . . . maybe then he'll come back to SummerHill and stay put."

I had to chuckle. What she didn't know was that no amount of pleading from me or anyone could bring Levi Zook back to SummerHill. He was right where he believed God wanted him to be—in Virginia, attending a Mennonite Bible college.

Besides, Levi and I had sort of come to an agreement about our friendship. That didn't mean he wasn't still "sweet" on me, as he would say, but we knew where we stood as far as dating.

At sixteen, I was in no way ready to be thinking of settling on a steady boyfriend. Especially one who was bound and determined to be either a preacher or a missionary.

Sure, someday that could change if I received a "call" to be a minister's wife. I was open to it. That is, if the Lord had something like that planned for my future. Still, I had all the time in the world—one of my mother's all-time favorite expressions when it came to guys and romance. None of that kept me from answering Levi's wonderful letters.

"When's my brother coming home for a visit next?" Susie asked.

"He hasn't said," I replied. "Honestly, I think you'll hear about that long before I do."

I sighed, thankful that Rachel was heading our way in time to interrupt this awkward conversation.

She and her sisters and the other women began shaping the dough for frying, but nobody felt the need to stop talking. No, the chatter and the work seemed to flow effortlessly, as smooth and easy as the feel of the dough beneath my fingers.

In a matter of minutes, the deep-frying stage was complete. The youngest Zook girls were called on to create the creamy, rich frosting that would fill up the doughnut holes.

Susie and Ella Mae squealed with delight. They'd been given the honor of having the first taste test. I watched them smack their lips and lick their fingers.

"It's Merry's turn," Susie said. The adorable little girl stood in the middle of the kitchen, waiting for me to have a sample.

"Oh, it melts in your mouth," I said after my initial bite. And it did, literally. The deep-fried doughy treat and the gooey filling dissolved on my tongue.

Rachel came up behind me and whispered in my ear. "Still keeping our secret?"

"My lips are sealed," I replied.

"Gut, then. If ya keep that secret, there's another one forthcoming."

I turned to face her. "About you-know-who?" I was referring to Joseph Lapp.

"No." She shook her head. "I'll tell ya later."

Her eyes shone, not so much with excitement as with a hint of apprehension. About what, I had no idea.

Three *Hide Behind the Moon*

I was still wondering about Rachel's comment as I hurried home around noon, arms laden with a box of delicious home-made doughnuts. "You won't believe how truly amazing these are," I boasted to my mother.

"I'll be the judge of that," she said with a grin, opening the box lid.

I watched her munch on the first bite, her brown eyes popping. "What do you think?"

"Mm-m. Out of this world!"

"How'd we get them down here?" I teased, parroting one of the fun-loving phrases my father liked to say.

She went to rinse her sticky fingers at the sink while I placed the box of doughnuts on the kitchen counter. "Save some for Dad, okay?" I said.

"If we don't, we'll never hear the end of it," Mom said with a twinkle in her eyes. She reminded me that Dad had already been informed of today's Amish get-together. "He'll be think-ing 'doughnut heaven' all day long, most likely."

"You're right," I said, pitying the poor emergency-room patients who might have to put up with his distraction.

Mom went to tend her African violets in the sunny corner of the kitchen. She pinched off an occasional leaf, commenting on the special plans I had for the afternoon and evening. "What time are your girl friends coming for the Valentine's sleepover?" she asked.

"Around four. But don't worry, we won't need a meal or entertainment."

"No supper?" She looked startled. "How can that possibly be?"

"Oh, we'll eat later on, for sure. It's just that Ashley and I have an agenda."

"I see," she said, without inquiring as to our plans.

Relieved, I picked up Lily White, my smallest cat, and carried her upstairs to my bedroom. As usual, Shadrach, Meshach, and Abednego followed on my heels.

"What have you been doing all morning, little boys?" I asked as the male cat trio made themselves at home on my bed.

Abednego had something to say. His eyes did the talking, and it seemed to me that he wasn't one bit pleased. Disgruntled was more like it.

"Okay, okay, I confess I enjoyed myself over at the Zooks' making doughnuts, but you know you're not supposed to be eating fattening, icky sweet things. S'not good for your health."

That didn't cut it. Shadrach got up and went over, plopping himself down next to Abednego. As if to say, *We're united on this sweets thing.*

"What can I say?" I shot back. "Cats as fat and sassy as you have to cut back somewhere."

Nobody was listening. Especially not Abednego, the fattest of the group.

Lily White, petite and demure, seemed to agree with me, however. But that was par for the course—she was always taking my side when it came to ganging up on the masculine animals in the Hanson household.

"Okay, if that's all there is to it, I've got work to do." I told them about the sleepover. "There'll be four young ladies here in this room tonight, so it will be a bit cramped with all of you hanging out. I want everyone on his best behavior. Hear?"

Abednego, the feistiest cat God ever made, closed his eyes slowly, deliberately. *We'll see about that,* I could almost hear him say.

"Better get a grip on your attitude," I shot back. To which he merely snoozed.

I set about cleaning my room, dusting and vacuuming. I wanted the floor especially spotless because we were going to roll out all of our sleeping bags so we could be together. It was time for the women of SummerHill to unite.

The English ones, that is. I honestly couldn't see inviting the Zook girls over here. No chance they'd be allowed to come, anyway. Abe Zook was a very strict father, following Amish church rules to a tee.

Ashley Horton, our pastor's daughter, and I had been planning this overnight event since right around New Year's. Thank goodness Lissa Vyner and Chelsea Davis had agreed to come, too.

There was only one slight concern—Jonathan Klein—the reigning Alliteration Wizard. The boy I'd had a crush on forever and ever. He'd decided now that it didn't really matter *who* he partnered with for his word games. Not anymore. So my idea to teach my girl friends how to speak alliteration-eze was a way to show him that our game didn't matter much to me, either. Besides, I wouldn't have to let Jon in on our secret plans. He'd find out soon enough. . . .

⁓

Four o'clock, on the dot, the girls arrived.

"Listen to this," Chelsea said as we settled in to my bedroom. "Like lions, lizards lick their lips."

Ashley frowned. "Is that true? Do lizards have lips?"

All of us burst out laughing.

"That's not the point," I explained. "Chelsea just used mostly *l* words in her sentence. That's what alliteration-eze is all about."

Ashley nodded, her eyes wide with embarrassment. I could see that getting through to her might be a chore.

"Does Jon have any idea that we're meeting like this?" Lissa asked. She'd perched herself on my bed, cross-legged as usual.

"I sure hope not," I said. "But so what if he does?"

"Yeah, I'm with Mer," said Ashley. "What's it matter if he finds out?"

"He thinks he's so good at his little word game," Chelsea remarked. "Better than anyone around."

The girls looked at me. "Maybe Merry's the only marvelous mind," said Chelsea.

"Hey, you're getting the hang of it. Been practicing?" I asked.

She nodded. "My mother and I have been talking in alliterated sentences for fun around the house."

I was thrilled to hear it. Chelsea's mom was coming around, it seemed, and it was about time, too. She'd recently been through excruciating experiences after being brainwashed by a bunch of weirdos—a cult group, to be exact. The nightmare had left her disoriented and shattered emotionally and spiritually.

"Good," I said. "Sounds like your mom's having fun again."

"Finally," Chelsea said.

We settled down to the task at hand. I gave out index cards and sharpened pencils to each girl. "Let's write ten words, either adjectives or nouns, using the first letter of your first name." I glanced at my watch.

"No time limit, please," Chelsea pleaded. "This isn't school."

Lissa nodded in agreement, her blond hair brushing against her chin. "You've been doing this lots longer than any of us, Mer," she said softly. "We need time to catch up."

I figured they'd need plenty of practice. Guess this sort of thing came easy to some and hard to others.

Abednego and his brothers nosed their way either into my lap or close by. Lily White snoozed high on my desk top.

Good, I thought. *They're on their best behavior.*

Watching the girls scribble down their word lists, I wondered if I was doing the right thing, letting them in on *my* thing with Jon. For the first time since Ashley and I had dreamed up this secret study session, I felt a twinge of regret. Was I really ready to kiss this game between Jon and me good-bye? Of course, he was the one who'd nudged that door open—to Ashley, at least.

Chelsea's hand was in the air. "Oh . . . oh, teacher," she joked. "I'm ready."

I leaned back against the bed, pulling my knees up to my chin. "Read away."

She glanced around almost sheepishly. "Here goes. 'Charming, cheery, chief, chicken, chime, chop, cheese, church, chum, chasten.' "

"It's genius," I said.

Ashley was nodding her head, eyes wide with near terror. "I can't do that . . . not so quickly."

"Okay, just keep working," I said, and we listened to Lissa's list next.

"Do I have to?" she asked, almost in a whisper.

I leaned forward. "Only if you want to."

She took in our circle of four. "Okay, but nobody laugh, promise?"

We promised, and she read, " 'Light, long, laugh, limit, lash, Lord, lavender, loss, lanky, life.' "

Everyone clapped. "Truly terrific," I said.

She blushed pink. "Thank you."

Just then Lily White rolled off my desk, landing—*kerplop*—in Lissa's lap.

"Oh!" she shouted.

Quickly, amidst loud giggling, I ran to rescue my too-relaxed kitty. "Say sorry," I said in her ear.

Lissa grinned. "Don't worry, I'm fine."

"It's the cat Mer's worried about," Chelsea joked.

I placed Lily White on my bed. "That's not even close to being true," I reprimanded Chelsea. All three of the girls giggled gleefully.

Now . . . for the biggest challenge. Ashley Horton's word list. I was worried sick for her—about what she would or wouldn't come up with.

"Are you ready?" I asked her.

"I'll give it a shot." She touched her hair, laughing nervously. "I've got 'ashen, azure, alphabet, amazing, animal, accordion . . .' "

She stopped.

"Good start," I told her.

"That's all for now," she said, covering her index card with her hands.

I knew she was struggling. "Okay, the next thing we'll do is create sentences out of the words on your list."

"You've gotta be kidding," Ashley said.

Chelsea, on the other hand, went right to work. Lissa thought for a moment and then began to write.

"I'll help you," I said, sliding over next to Ashley.

"Thanks," she said, offering a smile. "You're a lifesaver."

In no time, Chelsea seemed to be dying to read her sentence aloud. Like it or not, she was inhibiting Lissa and Ashley with her ability, but I couldn't stop her. Besides, it was fun to see someone blossoming under my tutelage.

"It sounds ridiculous, but here's what I have," she said. " 'A charming and cheery chief chopped a piece of cheese, chastened his chum the chicken, and headed for church when he heard the chimes.' "

Her sentence brought hooting and hollering. "She's better than Jon!" declared Ashley.

Chelsea beamed. "Thanks, but I still need practice."

"We *all* do," Lissa said, crumpling up her list.

"Time for tea," I said jokingly. It was time for a change of scenery, that was certain. Couldn't have my other students getting discouraged so soon. This was supposed to be light-hearted fun, after all.

I went to the door and opened it, calling down the steps. "Mom? Got any snacks?"

"Come on down, girls," she said. "There's plenty of whatever you like."

Thank goodness for food, I thought. And friends and family.

The next day, Ashley, Chelsea, Lissa, and I sat together in Mr. Burg's Sunday school class. Chelsea and Lissa paid close attention. I was thrilled. Neither of them had grown up in church; both were new to the Gospel, Chelsea having declared herself an atheist years ago. Her heart had recently softened toward the Lord since the heartbreaking circumstances with her mother. Best as I could remember, she hadn't skipped a single Sunday morning service since her mother's return home.

After class, when Jon Klein came over to greet us, he pulled out all the stops. "Goodness, it's great to get God's gift going . . . and going."

"Sharing salvation's story?" I asked.

"Ah! Most moving, Merry, Mistress of Mirth," he said, flashing his big smile and brown eyes.

"*Must* you?" I said, teasing. Would he assign me a letter of the alphabet—*m* for instance?—in front of my girl friends?

Mentally, I got ready for a montage of *m*'s while he showed off, alliterating left and right. But nothing was said about my joining in, and I realized we weren't even close to challenging him to an alliteration match as a group. He was way too good.

"Finally figured out fun stuff on my fantastic camera," Jon said, directing his comment to me at last.

"A fine thing for the faces of family and friends." I chuckled.

Ashley was watching me now. Had to be careful. I couldn't let on to her how important this alliteration thing was to me. She was just so . . . so *terrible* at it.

Anyway, Jon told us about the cool camera he'd received for Christmas, complete with telephoto lens—the works. Since I had a very similar camera in my collection, I understood his enthusiasm.

"In fact," he said, "I'd like to focus on the four of you, maybe in the foyer later?"

"I don't mind," Chelsea spoke up. "Just do something creative."

"Yeah, like have us hug hymnals," I suggested.

His eyes lit up. "I have an idea. . . . " That faraway look seemed to take over.

"It's time for church to start," I said, cooling it with the alliteration. "I can't believe you brought your camera along."

He shrugged off my comment. "Let's meet in the coat room right after church," Jon said.

"It's a deal," Chelsea said, grinning.

Ashley and Lissa seemed hesitant.

"What's the matter?" I asked later. "It's just a couple of poses? So what?"

"We're hobnobbing with the enemy," Lissa said.

Chelsea was nodding her head. "Yeah, I thought we were supposed to produce puns and provoke a parade of phrases, not *pose* for the pal."

"Great! You're getting good," I said, congratulating her and secretly wondering if she might not dethrone the Alliteration Wizard. Soon!

"So?" said Chelsea. "What about it?"

"Don't you see?" I told them. "By hanging around the Wizard, you'll pick up a lot. Just keep your ears open."

We walked down the aisle and sat in the pew right behind my parents. Mom and Dad turned around and greeted us politely. "You're welcome to have dinner with us," my mother told the girls.

They thanked her quietly for the invitation because the music was beginning to swell.

"We'll talk about it after church," I said, settling back into the comfortably cushioned pew. Mom was always interested in hostessing—*my* friends, *her* friends, and Dad's friends from the hospital. Leave it to my mother to assemble a group of people for the sole purpose of feeding them. She didn't live to eat—she lived to feed others!

I noticed how beautifully the church was decorated, with several bouquets of red and white roses. When I read the bulletin, I saw that three different families had donated flowers in memory of loved ones who'd passed on.

Briefly, I thought of Faithie, my own deceased twin, and wondered if she might've had the gift of alliterating had she lived past age seven.

I reached for the hymnal, eager to sing the songs with my friends—the old, inspired hymns of the church.

By the close of the service, I was curious about Jon's invitation to us to pose for pictures.

Why *had* he asked us?

Ashley was all bubbly about the picture-posing session, and I assumed it was because she still had a crush on Jon. Not that I blamed her. He was a cute guy. Though only our age, he seemed older, more studious.

Anyway, we met in the coat room. "Do you mind wearing coats?" he asked rather shyly. "We should go outdoors."

The boy was learning fast. Although it was high noon, the sun had been hiding behind clouds most of the morning, so Jon was wise. He'd probably been reading up on the best light, which was typically just after sunrise or just before sunset. That's when the low sun casts a golden glow over everything—people, animals, and landscape.

We were all bundled up now, standing on the front steps. Ashley wore her new outfit, a red wool coat—very stylish—with a hat and gloves to match.

Lissa, on the other hand, wore a camel-colored hand-me-down coat I'd given her—clean and neat. Looking at her, I realized the full-length coat fit her far better than it had ever fit me.

Chelsea was wearing a big grin. "I didn't dress up much today," she said, eyeballing the rest of us. Hers was a cute down-filled ski jacket of blue and green.

"You're fine," I said, picking lint off my own steel blue dress coat. "Where do you want us, Jon?"

He had us line up on the church steps, single file. Lissa, being the shortest, stood on the bottom step. Next came Ashley, me, and on the very top step, Chelsea.

"Okay, let's have a serious pose," he said.

"Like we're proper, eighteenth-century ladies?" Chelsea asked, turning this way and that.

"Why not?" Jon replied. "Think *Little Women*."

Trying to be serious when you're told to be isn't the easiest thing in the world. So we attempted somber faces, but what followed were waves of hilarity. We sincerely tried to keep a straight face, just never quite succeeded.

Jon started snapping, whether we were ready or not. "Beautiful, ladies," he said, crouching down to get unique angles. His actions reminded me of the way I always liked to lean into my own picture taking.

When Mr. and Mrs. Klein came out of the church, Jon's father expressed momentary astonishment and then motioned to his son.

"Uh . . . thanks, girls," Jon said, running to catch up with them.

"We're finished?" Ashley said. "Just like that?"

"And Jon didn't even alliterate once," Lissa moaned.

"That's okay," I whispered, "because we have lots of work to do before we'll ever get as good as he is at alliteration-eze."

"You're right," Ashley muttered.

I drew them into a huddle. "Who's coming to my house for dinner?"

Maybe the girls were afraid I'd make them recite alliterated phrases all afternoon. I don't know, but they all said they couldn't come.

"Thanks for a super sleepover, though," Ashley said.

I gasped. "Hey, you did it!"

"What?" she asked, wide-eyed.

"You used two *s*'s in a row. And without thinking." I gave her a big hug.

"I guess all that brain strain is paying off," she said.

"Alliteration Wizard, move over!" Chelsea laughed.

We waved and went our separate ways, scattering across the parking lot of the church. Mom was disappointed that my friends weren't joining us for another meal.

"Maybe I'll invite Rachel Zook over for dessert," I told her as we rode the short distance to SummerHill Lane.

"Oh, *would* you, Merry?" she pleaded. "It's been a long time since I've seen your Plain friend."

So it was settled. After dinner, I would go to the Zooks' and fetch our neighbor. Maybe Rachel and I would have time to talk privately. Then she could share her additional secret. The one she was so fired up about yesterday.

Five Hide Behind the Moon

By the time Mom's four-course dinner was served and eaten, it was beginning to snow again. Donning my warmest clothes, I headed out into the blustery air.

I plodded along the footpath that led from our back porch to the main road out front. Anticipation began to build in me, and I played guessing games with my imagination. What secret did Rachel have "forthcoming," as she'd said so evasively?

Pausing along the side of the road, where the ditch had filled up with snow, I tried to remember how the grassy slope looked in the summertime. "Warm days have flown," I said to the ground, lamenting the cold. My breath turned into instant ice crystals in the frosty Pennsylvania air.

Hurrying on, I breathed through my nose, wrapping the warm, woolen scarf around the lower portion of my face. I almost laughed out loud, suddenly realizing to what extent I was willing to go to satisfy my mother's need to be hospitable.

What if Rachel decided she didn't want to brave the elements and return with me for pie and ice cream?

Br-r. The thought of anything cold to eat made me shiver.

Surely she'd come, though. I was close to one-hundred-percent-amen sure she would. The Sundays without a Preaching service were a visiting day for the Amish. Today was one such day.

Unexpectedly, I spied Rachel's big brother Curly John up ahead. He was helping Sarah, his wife, out of their parked carriage. I had no idea how they'd arrived without my seeing them. They must've pulled into the Zooks' lane while I'd dawdled on the side of the road, daydreaming over summer, long gone.

Sarah handed a long, blanketed bundle to Curly John. Realizing that this must be the former "baby Charity," the abandoned baby I'd found in our gazebo last July, I called to them. "Sarah! Curly John! Wait up." I scurried over the snowy lane to catch up.

They greeted me with warm "Hullos" and "Howdy-dos" as we hustled into the old farmhouse, where the Zook family was enjoying the afternoon in their toasty kitchen. Abe and Esther sipped hot coffee, while their children played games at the table and on the floor near the woodstove.

"*Wilkom*, Merry," Abe said, waving one of the children over to hang up my coat and scarf.

Almost instantly, the family gathered around the baby. They were drawn to her like bees to honey.

"How's our first grandbaby?" Esther cooed, taking Mary right out of Curly John's arms.

"She's really grown," I said, squeezing into the circle with Rachel on my right.

The children took turns kissing the little one's hand and touching her button nose ever so lightly. Even Aaron, the only boy there, stroked her rosy cheeks.

Sarah turned to me and smiled. "Our little Mary's such a blessing. We thank God every day that you found her and took such good care of her for us."

I hadn't seen Mary since I'd baby-sat for her at the end of last summer, before school started. "What is she now—nine months old?" I asked.

"Jah, you're right." Sarah helped her mother-in-law untangle the baby blankets, then asked, "Wanna hold her?"

Did I ever! I took one look at that adorable face and nearly cried as Esther placed her in my arms. "Oh, she's so beautiful," I whispered.

Mary tried to babble sweet baby words, probably some simple Dutch, raising her chubby hand up to my face to be kissed. The gesture took me back to that first night we'd spent together, this precious baby and I, when she'd curled her infant fist around my finger and squeezed with all her might.

Rachel's father was begging for equal time. "Come see your *Dawdi* Abe a bit," he said, slapping his knee.

I kissed her baby ear. Gently, I set Mary on her grandpa's lap, relinquishing her to his strong, loving arms.

Before I could blink an eye, someone had slipped a plate of warm apple pie and a hearty dip of ice cream into my empty hands. "Oh, uh . . . thanks, but—"

"Don'tcha want none?" Rachel asked, a quizzical look on her face.

"Well, I came to invite you for dessert at *my* house." We burst into laughter, standing near the rocking chair where Abe Zook played with his adopted granddaughter.

"'Tis hard to fellowship with friends and not be feeding one's face, 'least not in an Amish household," Rachel said.

She was right about that.

"What'll I tell my mother?" I said. "You know how she loves to cook and entertain."

She nodded, eyes shining. "My mam and yours could do right fine together—opening up a restaurant somewheres," she admitted.

"That would never do."

"Why not?" she asked.

"Because *two* cooks in a kitchen are always one too many!"

We giggled about that, taking turns making over the baby. "Wouldn't Miss Spindler be surprised at how quick Mary's a-growing?" said Rachel.

"That's the truth," I said. "But you know how Old Hawk Eyes is . . . she probably saw Curly John's horse and buggy pull into your barnyard long before you ever did!"

"Probably so." Then Rachel's eyes softened, and she took my hand, leading me into the front room. "When you're done with your dessert, Merry, we hafta disappear for a bit, if ya know what I mean."

I must admit, I was thrilled. At long last, she was going to reveal her secret. Whatever it was.

"Wanna come to my house?" I whispered, glancing over my shoulder.

She nodded. "In a bit, we'll go."

My curiosity had been piqued. Still, it would take some doing to tear myself away from Rachel's darling baby niece.

To my surprise, Sarah Zook asked if I could help her out with Mary. "Occasionally, on Saturdays, just during quiltin' season mostly."

"I'd love to!" I said, putting on my coat and scarf.

"If you could come over to our place, that would help me an awful lot." She stepped into the utility room, where Rachel was struggling with her snow boots.

"Maybe Mom will let me borrow her car," I told her.

"Well, ask your mama, and just let Rachel know, jah?"

I said I would, yet I wondered why she hadn't chosen someone Amish to baby-sit for her.

Rachel pulled on her boots with a grunt and then located her long, gray woolen shawl on a crowded coat hook. "Ya noticed, didn'tcha, that my own sister-in-law didn't ask *me* to help with Mary," teased Rachel.

Sarah's cheeks blushed bright pink. "Oh, forgive me, Rachel. I would've asked, but—"

"I's just foolin' ya," Rachel replied. "How on earth can I hold a baby and do my best handstitchin', all at the same time?"

"Gut, then, you're not mad." Sarah offered a pleasant smile. "God be with ya," she bid us.

" 'Bye!" I called to her and now to Esther, who'd come to see us off.

Before I could turn around, here came Nancy and Ella Mae, then little Susie, pushing her way against the storm door. "Where's Rachel goin'?" Susie hollered out.

"Oh, just over to Merry's for a bit," Rachel called back, a stream of her breath floating over our heads.

"She won't be gone long," I promised.

That is, if she spills the beans on her secret right off, I thought.

My mother was overjoyed to see Rachel. "Oh, here, let me take your wraps," she said, playing the ultimate hostess.

"*Denki*," Rachel said softly, removing her black outer bonnet and shawl. She glanced down at her feet nervously.

"Forget something?" I asked.

"Shoulda brought warm socks along," she whispered.

"Don't worry. I'll loan you a pair." And I proceeded to help her pull off her high snow boots.

Mom served up pumpkin pie a la mode, and Rachel and I ate it as if we'd never had any sweets at the Zooks'. After all, we'd just had some wintry exercise, and our eagerness pleased my mother to no end. Upstairs, we had my big bedroom all to ourselves. I'd straightened things up earlier from the sleepover last night. Even spent a few minutes smoothing out my comforter and reorganizing my books and knickknacks while Mom put finishing touches on our dinner.

"Ach, your cats have about taken over the place!" Rachel remarked, looking around at the four of them as I closed the door.

I knew it was hard for her to accept mouse catchers living the pampered life inside the house. She'd always insisted that where they were *really* needed was outside, in a barn somewhere.

"I think you and my mother must have a conspiracy going about my pets," I told her, finding a pair of knee-length socks in my dresser drawer.

"Oh? What makes ya say such a thing?"

"Well, my mom put her foot down about taking in any more strays." I picked up Lily White and cradled her in my arms.

Rachel, watching me, smiled. "Maybe it's 'cause you treat 'em like they're babies."

I laughed. "Oh, but they *are* babies. Kitty-cat babies."

She shook her head, puzzled, then pulled out the chair beside my desk and sat down. "I hafta tell ya something, Merry, but ya must promise never to tell a soul."

I felt my forehead crease to a frown. "What do you mean?"

"Better sit down," she advised.

With Lily White in my arms and Abednego creeping closer, vying for his position as "top dog" cat, I sat down on my bed and leaned against the bed pillows. "I'm listening."

"Gut, 'cause I need your help."

"*My* help?" Who was she kidding? Rachel was one of the most resourceful teenagers around. Like most Amish girls, she could can peas and carrots to beat the band. She sowed the straightest rows of lettuce and tomatoes you ever did see and knew all about how to spring clean a house up and down and inside out.

Not only that, she had a hope chest already bursting with all sorts of essential linens and household items, ready to settle into keeping house and raising a family, which is what young Amishwomen did early on—when the right Amish fellow came along. That was probably the case; she'd probably said "yes" to Matthew Yoder, her one and only beau. Even though Amish wedding season was months away, Rachel probably wanted me to know before anyone else. . . .

Still, I dared not mention any of what I was thinking, only studied her solemn face and her hands, folded as if she were about to pray.

"Well . . . do ya promise me, Merry Hanson?"

I took a deep breath before I answered. "I think you better say why you need my help. Then maybe I can make a promise."

Her eyes darted to the windows. SummerHill Lane could be easily seen from my bedroom, and right across from the road were acres and acres of field, now dormant.

I spoke up quickly. "I didn't mean to offend you, honest."

She looked my way again, making a few quick nods with her head. "Been ponderin' this for the longest time. I hope ya won't think I've up and gone berserk."

Now I was really confused. "How could that be? You're smart as a whip, Rachel. Don't worry what I think, anyway. We're friends, right?"

"The best of friends," she said, looking truly inspired. She reached into her dress pocket and pulled out the old picture. The one of Joseph Lapp. I knew even before seeing the front that it was the same photo, because the edges were yellowed and uneven.

Rachel stared at the picture in her hand. "I've been keeping a secret—a forbidden ambition—for ever so long, really. The People would be shocked and befuddled, especially my parents." She was almost whispering, and my heart went out to her, not knowing what she was thinking or feeling.

"Are you all right?" I asked.

"Don't rightly know" came the haunting reply. "I feel I may be ready to put some of my upbringing to the test."

I was worried. What could she be thinking?

"Oh, Merry . . . I wanna have *my* picture taken," she said suddenly, almost breathlessly. "It is the most vain, wicked thing I could possibly think of doin', yet I want it more than words can say."

"What about your Amish beliefs?" I asked.

"The People's opinions are not mine just yet. I must cast aside the Old Order rules for now," she said, alluding to her *Rumschpringe*—the Amish term for the running-around years before baptism into the church and marriage.

Beginning at sixteen, Lancaster Amish young people are allowed to experiment with the outside world—try on the various aspects of modern life and decide if Plain living is right for them. Most of them, in the end, choose to remain Amish and take the life oath at the time of their baptism.

"Are you completely sure about having your picture taken?"

"Never more so," she replied. "Now . . . ya must be wonderin' how you could be helping me."

I'd already assumed she wanted me to be the one to take her photograph. And I was right.

"Dat and Mam are going out to Ohio to visit some relatives next weekend. I thought it might be a gut time."

I listened—didn't even nod my head to give consent.

"The moon'll be on the wane come Friday night," she informed me. "We'll hide behind it, ya know."

I had to chuckle. She'd considered every possible angle.

"Then ya'll do it? Ya'll get out your camera and take my picture?"

"How can I?" I protested. "Knowing what your family believes . . . what your church teaches?"

"Making graven images?" she said. "Is that the problem?"

I moved my cats off my lap carefully and stood up. "Rachel, have you thought about the shame this could bring to your parents?"

"Ach, we've been through all this before," she answered. "A thousand times."

I realized she was talking about Levi now, her big brother. He'd gone off and embraced higher education, a no-no for Amish offspring. Of course, he'd nearly broken his father's heart by not joining the church at the appropriate age, instead leaving SummerHill and heading to Virginia to college, of all things.

"Why put your parents through it?" I argued.

She looked at me, her eyes pleading. "You sound so Amish, Merry. You sure ya ain't?"

I laughed, which was probably a good thing. Our discussion was getting entirely too serious.

"Let's think about it. Don't rush into something you might regret later," I suggested.

She shook her head. "This could be my only chance, Merry. The only chance I'll ever have to see myself in a picture."

I leaned down and looked into the face of Joseph Lapp. "Guess my great-great grandfather got something started, didn't he?"

She stood up, not looking out the window but at my wall gallery of framed photographs, some I'd taken of my twin sister long ago. "Please be thinkin' long and hard about this, Cousin Merry," she said.

I simply couldn't let her push me into this. And at the moment, I wasn't too receptive to being called her cousin, either. I had to admit, her obsession with vanity irked me.

"What about 'Children, obey your parents in the Lord'?" I said, picking up my Bible. "Does that count for anything?"

She whirled around. " 'Course it does! I've been following the *Ordnung* my whole life. Never once strayed from it, neither. But having my picture taken won't be disobedient to Dat and Mam . . . not really."

"Why not?" I asked, amazed at her logic.

"Because my *parents* never said not to."

"But the bishop and Preacher Yoder, what about them?" I had her. She couldn't shy away from the truth.

"Oh, Merry . . . please don't go makin' me feel worse than I already do."

"Okay, then. How about if I let you know what I decide in a couple of days?" I said at last.

"Gut," she replied, turning toward me. "We'll have my first and only picture taken in the barn."

"What?"

"You heard me," she said. "In the haymow."

Hadn't she listened to a word I'd said? I was flabbergasted, plain and simple.

Unfortunately, it wasn't as easy for me to stand my ground on Monday. Rachel showed up at the bus stop, first thing. She came running up the lane, waving at me like there was some emergency.

"Hullo, Merry," she said, out of breath.

"What're you doing here?" I glanced up the road for the bus.

"Didja think about it yet?" she asked, her cheeks red with the cold.

"Oh that . . ."

"Jah, 'cause we need to start making plans."

"Well, I still don't think it's such a good idea."

"But you're my only chance, Merry," she said, eyes pleading, hands rubbing together.

"You could go into town and have your picture taken," I suggested. "That's easy enough."

"What . . . in one of them little booths with the black curtains?"

"Sure, why not?"

The bus was coming now. I could hear it rumbling before I actually saw it. I was positive she wouldn't want to be stared at by the public school crowd—I read it in the frenzied look on her face.

Darting her eyes back and forth between me and the crest of the hill, Rachel seemed nearly frantic. "Aw, Merry . . ."

"Better relax," I warned. "Go home, and we'll talk after school."

"I'll come right over then." She dashed off, her long skirt and apron flying under her woolen shawl.

"See you later!" I called to her, hoping I hadn't offended my friend.

"Jah, see ya," she replied.

———

At lunch, Chelsea showed up with Lissa. I was already getting seated at a table with Ashley.

"Well, here we are, together again," Chelsea said, salting her fries. "Has anyone seen the wizard today?"

"Not me," Ashley said.

"Not *I*," I echoed, correcting her English.

Ashley grimaced. "Where do you think he's hiding?"

I shrugged. "Jon never misses school—doesn't seem to catch colds much."

"True," Lissa said. "Wish I knew his health secret."

I laughed. "I think *I* know. He scares the germs away. As simple as that."

Ashley gasped. "You can't mean that, Mer. Jon's drop-dead gorgeous."

"Of course she didn't mean he was homely. Everybody knows Jon's cute," Lissa said. "*Very* cute."

"Ah, gotcha! Somebody's got a crush on the Wizard," I said. But my heart sank.

The four of us leaned on our elbows into the table, whispering comments about some of the other guys in our class. And that's the way we spent our time—eating and sharing girl talk.

When the first bell rang, Chelsea groaned. "Aw, we didn't practice our you-know-what."

"Oh well," said Ashley. "If Jon's out sick with the flu or whatever, he's lost a whole day of alliterating, too."

"What do you mean, *too*?" I reached for a napkin. "We haven't lost any time. Let's practice on other students—locker partners, teachers—you get the picture."

"Oh! Wait a minute," Chelsea blurted. "You just said something that reminded me of where Jon might be."

I frowned, thinking back. "What did I say?"

"You said, 'Get the picture' . . . and I *do* know where the Alliteration Wizard is." She went on to explain that the basketball all-stars were having group shots made for the school yearbook. "Betcha Jon's taking pictures right now!"

"Let's check it out," I said. My girl friends picked up their trays and followed me right up to the cafeteria window to deposit our empty trays and trash, then down the hall to the gymnasium. I felt like the Pied Piper of James Buchanan High.

"Sure enough," I said as we peered through the door to the gymnasium.

"There's our man," Ashley sighed, her hair falling down over her shoulder.

I didn't exactly know what to think of her comment. But I realized anew that my commitment to teach these girls how to speak alliteration-eze was actually spilling over into my formerly private territory.

"Why are we spying?" I said at last, stepping back from the door.

"That's what I wanna know," Ashley spoke up. "We oughta be working on our secret language."

The final bell rang.

"Yee-ikes! We have three minutes to get to class!"

It must've looked mighty strange, four girls scrambling off in opposite directions. But we did exactly that, and I didn't see Jon in any of the usual spots—not even at his locker—for the rest of the day.

⁓

I did encounter Rachel Zook, however. She'd kept her promise and was waiting on my front porch, all bundled up in her Plain attire.

"Goodness, girl, what're you doing sitting out here in the cold?" I said, running up the steps.

"Waiting for my English cousin."

"C'mon." I grinned at her, and the two of us headed inside, arm in arm.

For once in a blue moon, Mom wasn't waiting with hot cocoa, freshly baked cookies, and a big smile as we entered the house. But my cat quartet was snug at home, and they came bounding down the main hall toward Rachel and me.

"Well, look at all of you," I said, bending down to pet each one.

Rachel put up with my fussing over the cats, though she seemed antsy to get on with what she wanted to discuss.

"Want something hot? A snack, maybe?" I asked.

"Hot chocolate's nice." She followed me down the hallway to the kitchen. There on the counter, I discovered a scribbled note.

Merry—

I mixed up some cocoa for you to warm . . . there's a new batch of cookies in the pantry.

You mustn't worry when you read this. Daddy wasn't feeling too well this morning, so I'm heading to town to be with him.

Love you, honey,
Mom

I almost laughed—sarcastically, that is. "Don't worry, she says." How was *that* possible?

"What'sa matter?" Rachel asked.

Her voice startled me. "Uh . . . I . . . my dad got sick, I guess," I told her.

"How sick?"

Suddenly, I was no longer interested in heating a chocolate drink for either Rachel or myself. "Excuse me for a second," I said, heading to my father's study down the hall.

"I could come back another time," Rachel was calling to me from the kitchen.

"Just wait. I want to call the hospital." I hurried into the study and picked up the phone.

Something's weird about this, I thought as I punched the numbers. When the hospital information person came on the line, I asked if Doctor Hanson had been admitted.

"Yes, he's in room 127. One moment, please." I thought she'd never connect me.

"Hello?" my mother answered, and I was truly relieved to hear her voice.

"Mom, what's going on?"

She sighed. "Oh, honey, it's been a frightening day, but Daddy's going to be all right."

"What do you mean? What happened?"

"I don't want you to worry about this, Merry," she said. "Your father's ulcer flared up again, but he's going to be fine."

"He'd *better* be," I mumbled, tears welling up. "Can I see him?"

"Not tonight, but soon. He's going to spend the night here . . . they'll be doing additional testing first thing in the morning." She sounded tired, and I knew I was pushing my luck to keep asking questions.

"Tell Daddy I love him," I said. "And you, too."

"I'll be home later, after supper sometime," she said. "There's plenty of food in the fridge. You won't starve."

"No problem, Mom, I'll warm up something. Count on me."

"Thanks, Merry. I'll see you soon."

I hung up, strangely aware of steam whistling lightly in the radiator under the window next to me.

Pulling the curtain back, I looked out. The sky was trying to show its icy-blue face, but low clouds kept interfering, skimming across like white, wooly lambs chasing each other in the springtime.

"Oh, Lord Jesus, help my dad," I whispered to the heavenlies. "Please . . ."

Quickly, I headed back to the kitchen and filled Rachel in as I set about getting something to soothe us.

She played with the strings that hung down from her *Kapp*, staring at the table. "Ya know, I think about things like this, Cousin Merry. That is, if something unexpected would happen to me, ya know."

"You're too young to worry like that! You're not going anywhere, Rachel—I'm telling you right now."

She looked up at me, her voice shaky as she spoke. "I've actually worried what would happen if I died before—"

"Before what, Rachel? What on earth are you talking about?" I asked her sharply.

"There are certain things I wanna do. *Hafta* do. Not because I wish to hurt my parents or disobey the bishop. It goes deeper in me than any of that."

I suspected where she was going with this. "You're talking about the picture you want taken. Am I right?"

"Jah." She nodded her head.

"Well, if it means that much to you."

She stood up suddenly. "Ya'll do it for me? Honest, ya will?"

I stirred her hot chocolate and placed it down on the mat in front of her. "I'm your very own personal photographer."

I must've been out of my mind to agree to her wishes, but those no-nonsense blue eyes were far too serious to ignore. We were distant cousins, for pete's sake!

Eight Hide Behind the Moon

My mother still hadn't returned home as I headed for bed. I'd finished all my homework, even chatted on the phone with Chelsea and Lissa for a while—filling up the emptiness in the house.

I never mentioned a thing about Dad spending the night in the hospital. Just wasn't in the mood to talk to them about it, especially because I didn't really know what was wrong.

Welcoming the dark, I slipped into bed and pulled the sheets up around my head. Turning on my side, I held Lily White close. The freshly laundered smell of my pillow slip reminded me that most likely Mom was the one bearing the brunt of the day's trauma.

In many ways, she and I were alike. She took charge when there was a crisis, automatically it seemed. I was the same way. "Miss Fix-It," I'd called myself in the past. But I felt as if I might be mellowing a bit when it came to being such a rescuer.

Still, in rethinking my answer to Rachel's request for a photograph, I should've refused. The "old" Merry might've. But I was feeling more adventuresome these days, and I felt it was time to change things about myself. Not that I'd be one-hundred-percent-amen successful.

Thankfully, it wasn't going to be a stormy night. It's hard to feel confident during a storm—makes you feel helpless, almost childlike. With my older brother, Skip, away at college and Mom becoming more involved in collecting antiques, which involved some travel, I had to be at home alone at least occasionally.

So tonight I was thankful for a moon and a starlit sky. Feeling cozy under my comforter, I talked to God, expressing my concern for Dad. "Please let him know you're there with him, and bring my mother home safely. In Jesus' name, Amen."

I don't know why I didn't pray about Levi Zook, as I often did. Nor did I ask the Lord to make it clear to me if and when I might also receive a divine "call" like his. The main thing on my mind tonight was the idea of being alone in this big, one-hundred-year-old house. Without Dad. And with Mom somewhere between SummerHill and downtown Lancaster.

About the time my eyes were too heavy to keep them open, I heard the car pull into our driveway. Good. Mom was home. It was okay to give in to the sandman.

The next morning at breakfast, Mom was full of talk. "It was like pulling teeth to convince your father to spend the night in the hospital."

"But the docs wanted to check him out, right?"

She nodded, looking perky for the early hour. "You know how he is."

I knew. In fact, I'd gotten some of my own stubborn streak from him. "Will he have to be more careful about what he eats again?" I asked, staring at the mountain of scrambled eggs and two pieces of toast on my plate.

"I wouldn't be surprised," she said, sitting down.

"Guess he'll have to start doing the cooking around here, then," I teased her.

"Meaning what?"

"Dad's just . . . uh . . . not as hung up on food, I guess." I almost added, *like you are*. But I was smart and kept my mouth shut.

"Well, along with adhering to a stricter diet, he's going to have to get out and exercise. I've been telling him for years, a brisk twenty-minute walk can make a big difference."

Mom oughta know. She was religious about her daily walks. Couldn't talk her out of walking even if a tornado was heading this direction.

It turned out that Dad was given nearly a week off. But did he follow doctor's orders and rest? My father chose this period of time to get overly involved in my homework assignments. *All* of them. Meaning he stood over me as I worked. I should've been mighty glad about the academic help, I guess, but by Thursday it was beginning to annoy me.

"Don't you have something else to do?" I teased, hoping he'd catch on. But he stayed right there in the kitchen, watching me work algebra problems, offering unsolicited assistance every few minutes.

"Dad, I'm fine. I *know* how to do this." This was my second year studying the subject.

He blinked and frowned. Before I could stop him, he stood up and left the room.

"This is truly horrible," I muttered, getting up to go to find him.

He was in the living room, reclining on the sofa, eyes half-mast. I sat down across from him, wondering what to say, wishing I could unravel the last few minutes.

"I'm sorry," I whispered.

He looked up at me and smiled. "Don't worry, sweets. I'm just an old man twiddling his thumbs, anxious to get back to work."

"Better take care of yourself, though, don't you think?"

He nodded. "Can't do much else around here."

"Yeah, well, we wanna keep you kicking for a bunch more years."

He chuckled. "Don't you worry about that. The Lord's got plenty of work for me to do before He puts me out to pasture."

"Oh, Daddy, don't talk that way. You're not a cow, and you're not old."

"Fifty years . . ."

I could tell he was struggling with his latest birthday. A milestone event. I couldn't even begin to imagine having that many candles on my cake. Still, I needed to cheer him up.

"Think about this," I said, pulling something out of the air. "What would it be like never having had your picture taken?"

"My whole life?" he said. "Well . . . sounds to me like you've been talking to some Amishman. Now, am I right?"

I couldn't blow Rachel's secret. Best be careful what I said from here on out. "Is it a sin for them to pose for a camera?"

"All depends how you look at it." He laughed at his pun and then went on to explain the reason for their belief. "Many Plain folk believe that it is sinning against God to have pictures made of themselves. It's included in their view of 'the graven image' in the Ten Commandments."

"But is it *really* a sin? Or just thought to be?"

He shook his head. "To my way of thinking, the only way it would be a sin would be to worship the photograph—let the picture come between the person and God."

"Makes sense."

"So . . . whose picture are you thinking about taking?" he asked, grinning.

I couldn't believe it. He knew me too well.

"Guess that's all I'd better say for now." I got up and stood beside the chair. "Need anything before I get back to my math problems?"

He waved me on, smiling as if he'd seen through something top secret. Which, of course, he had.

Rachel would clobber me good if she knew!

By the time Friday evening rolled around, I was actually looking forward to sneaking off to Zooks' hayloft with Rachel. I
needed a break from my dad, and he from me.

I'd never participated in a picture-taking session like this
before, and I wondered how things would play out. Originally,
Rachel had said she wanted only one picture of herself, but
when I explained that most photographers try several poses
in order to get one *good* shot, she quickly agreed.

Silly girl! I was turning her into a debutante.

The moon was only half full as we approached the barn
door. A few stars shone through stark tree branches to the east.
If I hadn't known better, I might've thought the night was a
bit spooky, but Rachel wouldn't be thinking such a thing. She
urged me on, lantern in hand, eyes wide with anticipation.

"This is your big night." I made small talk, conscious of
the shoulder strap on my camera case as we hurried up the
ramp of the two-story barn.

The wide wooden door creaked open as we pulled on it.
Then, silently, we stepped into the sweetest-smelling place in
all the world. The haymow.

"I'm glad you picked this setting," I told her.

"Oh? Why's that?" she asked.

"It's beautiful, that's why." I looked at her all dressed up in her Sunday-best Amish dress and shawl, her winter bonnet nestled over the top of her devotional Kapp. "And tonight, you look pretty as a picture."

A flicker of a smile crossed her face. Then she looked more serious again. "I wanna let my hair down in one of the pictures," she announced.

"You what?"

"It's all right. Nobody'll ever know."

I shook my head. "People will know. *I'll* know . . . and so will the person who develops this roll of film." I studied her, my eyes beginning to squint. "Are you absolutely sure about this, Rachel?"

She didn't answer, just went over and stood next to a bale of hay, leaning on it. "Here's a gut place for the first one," she said, a hint of stubbornness in her voice.

"Sit down right there, why don't you." I pulled my camera out of its case. "And smile, okay?"

She posed and smiled, all right. I, on the other hand, felt somewhat sad as I clicked away. Not because she was doing anything truly horrible, as far as I could tell. No, I was down in the dumps because she seemed to be changing—my longtime friend had definitely been different the past few days. She was changing into a young woman with thoughts and ideas; plans that nobody in her entire household would ever agree with. Maybe not even Levi, her so-called wayward brother.

After many shots and numerous poses, I watched, stunned, as she removed her outer head covering and then the white veiling beneath. She didn't ask me to hold the sacred symbol, and for that, I was grateful. Rather, she placed it inside her dress pocket before quickly taking the bobby pins out of her bun.

Like a waterfall, the light brown hair cascaded over her shoulders, past her waist. She stood there smiling as though she'd already accomplished something mighty important. "There, now," she said. "I'm ready for the last picture."

"I hope we're doing the right thing," I muttered.

"Don't be questioning this, Merry." The sharp way she said it sounded as if she were reprimanding me.

I aimed and focused, recalling the days when I was fascinated with taking before-and-after pictures of people and things. Hoping this new look of Rachel's wasn't an indication of things to come, I finished up the final shot.

"Done," I said, packing up my camera equipment.

"Denki." She wound up her hair and put the veiling back on her head. "It's getting cold."

"It's *been* cold," I replied, wondering what delicious thoughts and ambitions had kept her warm during the rather lengthy picture-taking session.

"Now what?" she asked.

I looked at her, trying to see the real Rachel, my dear Amish friend. "What do you mean?"

"Wanna come to the house?" she asked.

We made our way over the particles of hay that dusted the wooden floor. I helped her close the barn door before answering. "What'll I do with my camera?" I reminded her.

"Jah, that's a problem."

"So I guess we oughta say good-night," I suggested, feeling a bit reticent with her now. As though I didn't know what to say next.

"Supposin' you're right."

It was an awkward moment, and even more so because I spied little Susie leaning out the back door. "Looks like somebody's missing you."

"I best go in." She reached for my hand and squeezed it. "I'll never forget this, Merry." And she was gone, running across the yard to the house.

I stood there watching from the moonlit shadows, listening as the two of them chattered away in their Amish tongue—Pennsylvania Dutch.

Soon, though, the storm door slammed shut and the animated talk faded. I was glad for the flashlight in my pocket. Amish barnyards were such dark places at night. Except for the pale light of the February half moon.

My parents would be waiting. I'd told them I was going to visit Rachel. Dad, bless his heart, had had the most comical look on his face. Of course, Mom had no way of knowing what the cheesy grin was all about. But I suspected he'd shared the unspoken secret with her while I was gone.

Hurrying up the drive toward SummerHill Lane, I glanced back at the barn, now dark. We'd hid behind the moon, all right, just as Rachel had said. And no one—no one in her Amish community, at least—was ever to be the wiser.

I expected a prick at my own conscience but felt no guilt. Dad was right, I supposed. Wasn't a sin at all to have your picture made.

The next day was Saturday, and I'd agreed to baby-sit Mary while Sarah Zook hosted a work frolic—a quilting bee—in her home.

I arrived early, before the many horses and carriages I knew would be making their way to the Amish farmhouse. Sarah seemed delighted to have me come so soon and opened the door with a warm greeting and a bright smile. "Ach, Merry, gut to see ya," she said. "Come in and get yourself warmed up."

I followed her inside to the front room, which was sparsely furnished: two matching hickory rockers similar to the ones in the Zooks' farmhouse, brightly colored handmade rag rugs and throw rugs adorning the floor, and a tall, pine corner cupboard, displaying Sarah's wedding china set—typical for Old Order Amish homes.

But the thing that captured my attention was the large quilting frame set up in the middle of the front room.

Sarah must've noticed me eyeing the frame and the chairs set up around it. "We'll be making a quilt for Rachel today," she explained.

"Really? For Rachel?" I wondered if the womenfolk who were coming to piece the quilt together might suspect that Matthew Yoder was courting my friend.

I thought back to last night and the many pictures I'd taken of Rachel. I hoped I hadn't thrown things off-kilter by agreeing to photograph her, because this quilting bee seemed ripe with purpose. Was the soon-to-be-made quilt intended for Rachel's hope chest? Was this church district holding its collective breath for another wedding come next fall . . . or the next?

Thankful that Rachel was still young, though not too young to consider marriage, I wondered if she was feeling pressured. Was this the reason she wanted to "sow wild oats"?

Sounds in the kitchen—baby babblings—brought me back to my responsibilities at hand. "Mary must need some company," I said, anxious to see the little dumpling.

Quickly, Sarah led the way, calling to her baby daughter as we hurried to her. "Ya know it's your English friend, now, don'tcha? Do ya know your favorite sitter is here?" She leaned over and lifted Mary up, handing her to me.

"Well, hello again, sweetie," I cooed into her big blue eyes. What fun I was going to have!

Almost on cue, she nestled her head against my shoulder. "Ah, she's a bit droopy," Sarah said, offering a blanket and a bottle. "Thank goodness, she ain't cranky. It's 'bout time for her mornin' nap, but ya just never know. Mary doesn't like to nap all that much anymore. Likes to be up and about, watchin' what everybody's doin'. 'Specially at a quilting."

I kissed the soft cheek. "We'll just rock a little, then. How's that?" I suggested to my precious bundle, heading for the rocker in the corner of the kitchen.

"Ya'll see what I mean," Sarah said, grinning. "She's a live wire, that one."

I hugged Mary, wondering what I was in for today. She didn't seem restless now, but I smiled to myself, thinking that maybe, just maybe, this baby felt comfortable with me, the girl who'd first found her.

Choosing to believe that, I sat down to rock the doll of a baby in my arms. A beautiful, live baby doll, dressed in light blue homespun linen.

One by one, and sometimes in groups of twos and threes, the quilters began to arrive. Rachel Zook and her two grandmothers came in together.

When Rachel spied me, she hurried over. "Whatever ya do, don'tcha leave till we have a chance to talk." Her eyes looked as if she hadn't slept much.

"You okay?" I asked.

"Jah, fine . . . fine. But it'll hafta wait" was all she said.

Now I was really curious. Was she having second thoughts about last night?

She scurried back to greet the women as they came into the kitchen. Most of them stood near the fire, warming their hands.

I watched Rachel, wondering why she hadn't even glanced at her little niece, now almost asleep in my arms. What could be so important that she'd ignore baby Mary?

Snatches of gossip filled the room. One group of women was discussing the weather in Dutch. I was pretty sure I was right because I recognized the word *Winderwedder*, meaning winter weather.

Closer to me, Dutch was mixed freely with English. An elderly woman was estimating the gallons of apple butter left over from one of the last work frolics. At least, I *assumed* that's what she was saying.

Without being noticed, I got up and put Mary in her playpen to nap, covering her with one of several beautifully hand-stitched baby quilts. Standing there, looking down at her pretty hair, I wondered how on earth she could sleep through the din of kitchen chatter.

But she did—twenty-five minutes longer than Sarah said she would. By the time Mary was awake again and ready to play with wooden blocks, I had gotten quite an earful of Amish hearsay.

So-and-so's cousin was found to have a portable radio in his courting buggy, and what was the preacher gonna do about it?

And would Naomi's Jake ever get himself baptized and join the church? Foolish boy . . .

I had to be careful not to chuckle. The air was thick with conversation, and soon I had the notion that the faster these women talked, the faster their stitching needles worked the fabric.

Mary was drooling and giggling now as she knocked down the tower of blocks I'd made. I reached over and tickled her under the arm. She burst into more cute chortles.

"I think you need a constant playmate," I said to her, re-building the blocks.

Unexpectedly, there was a break for the ladies, and everyone got up and had a snack of hot black coffee and sticky buns.

Rachel came over and sat down on the floor next to me, watching the block-building process only briefly before she spoke. "I've been thinking," she said softly.

"That'll get you in trouble," I snickered.

She placed her hand on my arm. "No, listen . . . I ain't jokin.'"

I turned to her. "What is it?"

"Last night . . . remember?"

I nodded, glancing at the women milling about the kitchen. "Aren't you afraid you'll be overheard?"

"Nobody's payin' attention just now," she replied. She steadied one of the baby's blocks, pausing before she continued. "I wanna take things a step further."

I knew better than to respond, so I kept quiet, listening.

"Don't say no yet, Merry. I wanna come to your house later and talk about attendin' school with ya."

"What?" I whirled around, accidentally knocking down the blocks. "Are you crazy?"

"*Monday*, that's when I wanna go to high school." Her voice was sure, but her expression was tense. My friend had lost sleep over this latest wild idea of hers.

"This Monday? Two days from now?" I squeaked out.

"Jah."

Before I could say more, she got up to pour some hot cocoa for herself.

"Yee-ikes. I think your aunt Rachel's gone ferhoodled," I whispered to tiny Mary.

And there we sat—the baby and I—mouths gaping, block tower scattered.

Eleven *Hide Behind the Moon*

After the quilting, Rachel and I continued our conversation at my house. "There's no way, Rachel. You can't do such a thing!" I insisted.

"Don't say I can't," she retorted. Her eyes were hot blue flames, her neck growing redder with each second. "What'd be so wrong with me comin' with ya to your school? I'll be your visiting cousin, just for one day."

I couldn't believe what she was asking, what she was putting me through. Shaking my head, I sat on the floor, leaning against my bed.

Rachel, on the other hand, was making a beeline for my walk-in closet. "Could I borrow something to wear?" She didn't wait for my answer, just started taking things out of the closet and holding them up for me to see.

I groaned. "Oh, now I *know* you've flipped out!"

"Jah, flipped," she muttered, turning to look at herself in my dresser mirror. "Do ya have any idea how long I've been waiting to do this? A very long time, Merry."

I watched as she rummaged through more of my winter clothes. "What's this world coming to? My Amish girl friend's losing touch with reality."

She agreed with me, smiling. "You can say that again. I'm a-tryin' on the English life, starting with *your* jeans."

"But, Rachel, do you have any idea what they feel like? They're tight, they're confining—not like the comfortable flowing skirts you're used to. And—"

"Still, I hafta know," she interrupted.

My hands flew up in surrender. "Okay, okay, try on anything you like." I hoped by my giving in, she'd give up.

The most astonishing smile swept over her face, and for the first time in a while, she looked well rested and serene.

"You mean it, Merry? You'll let me?" she asked.

"I said you could try on some clothes. That doesn't mean I'll pass you off as my English cousin come Monday."

She shrugged her shoulders, as if to say, *we'll see about that.*

One thing led to another, and in short order Rachel was putting on some light pink lipstick, then mascara, fumbling with my eyelash curler in her hand.

"No . . . no, let me show you." I took the cosmetic bag from her. "Watch me."

Her curiosity couldn't be quelled, it seemed. We spent nearly two hours making her over. Everything from curling the uneven ends of her long, long hair to brushing it straight back, attempting to hide the middle part.

Meanwhile, she did her best to persuade me. "Please, Merry, won'tcha at least *think* about takin' me to your school?" She even seemed eager to ride the school bus, for some odd reason. "I hafta see for myself what I've been missin'."

I sighed. "Oh, Rachel, what'll I do with you?"

She grinned. "You're gonna let me do this, that's what. Just this once, honest. Then I'll hush up about it."

I stared at her. She actually looked like any other teenager around Lancaster County with her makeup and long hair tastefully done. Well . . . close.

"I've turned you into a modern girl. A fancy one," I told her as she gazed into the mirror, adjusting the hand mirror to just the right angle to see the back of her hair.

"Jah."

"So what do you think?" I asked. "Like the new you?"

She went to sit on the bed, twiddling her thumbs in her lap. "I think I do." She was beaming. "Jah, I do."

I crossed the room to my closet and closed the door. "That's what I was afraid of."

"There's only one thing," she said. "I wanna wear my veiling over my new hairdo. Like a Mennonite."

"Okay with me."

"Gut, then," she said, grinning. "I'll go Plain, just not Amish."

"Better tone down the eye makeup and lipstick, then."

She groaned. "Must I?"

"Do you want to go to school with me or not?"

I had her over a barrel. She had no choice.

I couldn't tell a soul about even the tiniest part of my plan with Rachel. She'd sworn me to secrecy—not that an Amish girl would know how to do such a thing as swear, but I'd promised, at least. And that was saying a lot about the whole situation. Because I knew without question this could snowball, leading Rachel down a completely different life path—a too-modern one. But she was a mighty stubborn girl, determined to have herself a taste of English life, come what may.

My dad stayed home from church on Sunday. He wasn't feeling sick, he said, just not quite up to par. Because of that, I insisted on staying home, too. And then, because Mom was worried about Dad, she stayed home to oversee both of us.

I went around the house, upstairs and down, taking pictures of my parents. One of my mother cooking dinner, wearing her lacy apron. Another of her pouring milk into the cats' community bowl.

While Dad read his Bible silently, I took a shot of him from close up. He blinked his eyes and shook his head. "Can't you give a person fair warning?" he grumbled good-naturedly.

I laughed. "That would spoil everything, now, wouldn't it?"

He pretended to be blind for a second.

"Okay, I'm giving you advance notice this time. Don't move, just freeze," I said.

He cooperated, but it seemed that he was holding his breath, not blinking an eyelash.

I sat on the floor, angling the lens to get only his upper torso. "There," I said when I'd finished, "that's an interesting perspective."

He glanced down at me. "Not half so interesting as your photo shoot with Rachel, eh?"

"Dad, what are you talking about?"

Returning to his Bible, he smirked. "You heard me."

"Oh, you don't know . . ."

He peered over his reading glasses. "Better not lead your girl friend astray."

"How can that be?" I wailed. But I was disgusted with myself and wished I hadn't given in to Rachel's request. And I wished something else, too: that my father didn't have eyes in the back of his head!

"Let's have a devotional time," he said, calling Mom into the living room. "We'll have house church today—like the Amish do," he teased, sending a wink my way.

We took turns reading the Scripture references out loud— first Mom, then me, and last, Dad. I listened as my father read the devotional story, but the lesson didn't pertain to my dilemma with my friend. Rachel was on my mind in a very heavy way.

While my mother prayed aloud, I did so silently. *Dear Lord, what should I do about Rachel?*

It didn't take long for the answer to arrive. Although I wasn't so sure it was a divine one. Rachel herself showed up after dinner. Came right into the driveway and parked her parents' horse and carriage.

"Wanna go for a ride?" she asked as I answered the front door. "It's a right perty day for it."

I knew something was up, because I noticed a twinkle in her eyes. She was anxious to twist my arm some more about going to school.

"Come in," I said. "The kitchen's not quite cleaned up."

"I don't mind waitin'," she said, tiptoeing into the living room.

Big mistake!

Dad was sitting in his favorite chair, reading. Actually, he was closer to snoozing than anything. But he opened his eyes wide when he saw Rachel, and I hoped he wouldn't question her.

"Well, hello there, Rachel," I heard him say as I hurried off to the kitchen. The sooner I finished up the kitchen, the quicker I'd have her out of there!

Things took a strange turn, though. Just as I was wiping off the countertops, Jon Klein called. "I wanted to see if you were sick or something," he said, emphasizing the *s*'s.

"I'm not, but my dad's feeling a little out of it," I said.

"So . . . your SummerHill sisters started getting sassy. Silly too."

"Who're you talking about?"

"The tongue-twisting trio," he replied.

"Oh, Chelsea and company?" I should've known.

"None other."

I was curious to know what they'd said. "What did I miss?"

"Missed much, Mistress Merry." He was laughing. "They want a match. A meeting of the minds."

"When?"

"In a week."

"Says who?"

"Chelsea Davis got it started," he said. "She's getting good, Mer. You're a terrific teacher."

"Whatever." I was disgusted. My friends had jumped the gun. Hadn't waited for me to give the signal. They weren't even close to ready for a face-off with the Wizard.

"Hey, you sound upset. Everything okay?" His voice was sweet and mellow. Any other time—for instance, the months *before* I'd ruined things and divulged the details of the Alliteration Game to my girl friends—I might've delighted in his complimentary approach.

But now? My ability to pass on alliteration-eze was at stake.

"Fine, fabulous, fantastic," I replied.

"Yes!"

"Don't get worked up about it," I told him. "I'm not playing your game today. I'm too busy."

"Is this a bad time?"

"I'll talk to you at school tomorrow," I said.

And that was the end of it. We said good-bye and hung up. I marched into the living room.

"Well, it's good to see you're through with kitchen duty," Dad said, closing his book.

I eyed the two of them suspiciously. "Are you ready, Rachel?"

"Jah. Are you?"

"Sure am." I hurried to the hall closet to get my jacket, wondering what Dad had weaseled out of Rachel. "Let's go," I said, opening the front door.

"Your pop's awful funny," she said as we headed for the gray carriage.

"He *can* be," I said, getting in and sitting to her left.

She situated the woolen lap blanket over the two of us and then picked up the reins. "Why'dja tell him about taking my picture?"

I spun around, staring at her. "What?"

She didn't repeat herself.

"I didn't tell him, Rachel. I *didn't!*"

"Then how'd he know?"

I sighed. It was going to be a very long ride.

All the talk in the world wasn't going to convince Rachel to stay home on Monday morning.

Bright and early, she showed up at my house. "Plenty of time to change into modern clothes," she said when we were alone in my room.

"Do you honestly have to do this?" I whined.

She shook her head. "Can't talk me out of it."

Since I knew I couldn't, I started filling her in on life at public school—the teachers, the students, even the lockers.

"Lockers?" she gasped. "They have freezer lockers in a school? Whatever for?"

I couldn't help but laugh at her naiveté. "School lockers aren't for storing a side of beef or frozen vegetables, silly girl. They're for books and notebooks . . . and hanging up jackets and other things," I explained.

Eyes wide, she said, "Oh, I see."

Of course, she didn't comprehend; she couldn't possibly understand till she laid eyes on the whole setup.

I tried to prepare her for the crammed hallways, kids rushing to and fro, talking and calling to one another. "It's nothing like an Amish one-room schoolhouse," I said, brushing my hair. "There are so many kids."

"What about higher learning?" she asked, pulling on a pair of my best jeans.

"What?"

"Ya know, education past eighth-grade level. What about that?" she inquired.

"There's nothing magical about going past the eighth grade. If you're gonna be a good Amish girl, you can't be thinking about such things."

"Ya, I know. Still, it's awful tempting." Now she was standing beside me in the mirror.

"Don't tell me," I said. "You want me to do your hair like before."

"Would ya, Merry? Please?"

If I wanted her to be halfway accepted by English teenagers, I'd have to do something with her long locks. Short of cutting her hair, I had to find a more becoming style, at least for a day at James Buchanan High.

"What about a French braid?" I suggested.

She grinned, showing her gums. "Whatever that is, I don't rightly know, but it sounds mighty nice. Foreign too."

I chuckled. "It's mostly American, I guess you could say. Don't worry, nobody's gonna mistake you for a French girl."

"*Puh!*" she said, and we had a good laugh.

Thankfully, she'd already eaten breakfast at home, so we were able to bypass the kitchen on our way out the front door.

Mom was busy in her sewing room, so I put a finger to my lips, signaling Rachel to be discreet. I'd told her to meet me at the bus stop. While I went to say good-bye to my mom, Rachel crept down the hall to the entry and outside.

"What's Rachel want so early?" Mom asked as I tried to wave to her and leave.

"What?" I said.

Mom looked up, needle poised in midair. "You heard me. What's Rachel doing over here?"

I couldn't tell her the ridiculous plan. She'd put her foot down; I knew she would. As I contemplated the situation, I realized that I was actually looking forward to taking Rachel to school with me, showing her around, introducing her to "what she'd missed."

But first I had to get past my mother, who'd obviously smelled a rat, and that wasn't just a joke. She was on to something.

Standing up, she came to the doorjamb and leaned out into the hall. "Where is she?"

"Rachel left already." It was true.

"Oh, so that's the end of it."

"The end of what?" I said, wishing I hadn't taken a bite of her bait.

She frowned, looking at me with inquisitive eyes. "From what your father says, Rachel Zook is walking a tightrope between Amish and English. He—uh, *we* don't think you should be the one to assist her in this journey."

"I'm not trying to influence her in any bad way."

Mom put her hands on both my shoulders. "Oh, honey, I don't mean to accuse you. Please don't misunderstand. We want you to continue being a good friend to her."

"But the best of friends put up with weird things sometimes," I said, hoping Mom wouldn't read anything into my comment.

"You're right about that. And I know you'll do the right thing by Rachel Zook."

My heart was beating ninety miles an hour. I knew that if I didn't leave soon, I might start blurting out some of the top-secret plans Rachel and I had together in order to defend myself.

Fortunately, I heard the familiar grinding and groaning of the school bus. Rachel would be freaking out about now, wondering why I wasn't coming.

"There's the bus, Mom. Gotta run."

"Have a good day," she called after me.

"Thanks, I will."

Hopefully, it *would* be a good day.

First off, Chelsea wanted Rachel and me to sit with her on the bus. This came as no surprise. I always sat with Chelsea. Besides that, she no doubt remembered Rachel from a couple visits last fall and early winter. Rachel had even given her one of their puppy litter—a golden-haired cocker spaniel.

Still, I was curious if Chelsea would recognize my "cousin" today, all done up in fancy clothes.

"This is Rachel, my neighbor," I said.

Chelsea did a double take. She studied her and then glanced at me. "You're Rachel Zook?" she whispered.

"Jah," said my Amish friend.

"Say 'yes' instead," I advised her. "And please remember to say it all day."

Chelsea was beginning to frown, leaning forward in her seat to survey the situation. "You're not saying—"

"Yep," I interrupted. "And it'd be best if you play along. Know what I mean?"

"Hey," she laughed. "You're the boss!"

Relieved that she had agreed to cooperate and keep things under wraps, I talked softly to Rachel, hoping I'd covered everything necessary. "The main thing is not to worry about taking tests or doing homework assignments. Teachers won't expect you to participate. You're an observer, just visiting. Don't forget, okay?"

"Jah . . . I mean, yes."

She was catching on fast.

The biggest hurdle was getting past Miss Fritz, our gregarious school counselor. She was known to roam the halls, greeting students by their first names, always eager to visit with new kids and their parents. Miss Fritz especially liked to meet visitors to the school. Actually, you were required to check in with her about any student or visitor who was *not* enrolled at James Buchanan High. A standing rule.

The second snag in getting Rachel through the halls and safely into my homeroom would be Jon Klein and his usual pre-class routine.

With Miss Fritz and the Alliteration Wizard on my mind, I guided Rachel through the labyrinth of hundreds of students, pointing her in the direction of the counselor's office. "Don't ask questions, just follow me," I instructed. "I'll do all the talking."

Rachel seemed content with taking it all in. She scanned the rows of lockers, the banners on the wall, the water fountain, everything. There was a big smile on her face as we made the turn into the school office.

Miss Fritz was standing at her post near the attendance office, monitoring students with absentee slips and early dismissal permission slips. She was beaming as we came in.

"Good morning, girls," she said, glancing at Rachel and then back at me.

"Miss Fritz, I'd like you to meet my cousin Rachel. She's visiting school for the day," I said.

"Welcome to James Buchanan High School." Miss Fritz extended her hand. "Nice to have you, Rachel."

My heart pumped extra hard as they shook hands.

"How long will you be staying in Lancaster?" asked the counselor.

Rachel looked at me, obviously unsure of herself.

"Oh, she's from right here . . . out in the country, really."

"Whereabouts?" came the question I'd dreaded.

"SummerHill," I spoke up on Rachel's behalf.

I was one-hundred-percent-amen sure what the next question would be. *Well, then, Rachel, why aren't you in school?* she might ask.

Waiting for the inevitable, I realized I was holding my breath. *Relax*, I told myself.

The worst thing that could happen was for Rachel to be asked to leave, to go home. *Where she oughta be*, I thought.

But Miss Fritz didn't press for personal declarations. She winked at me and welcomed Rachel to school once more.

"Whew, we did it," I told her as we headed to my lockers. "We're almost home free."

"Home free?" she muttered. "What's that?"

"I'll tell you later." I twirled my combination lock faster than most days. Now . . . if I could just keep Rachel from spilling the beans to the Alliteration Wizard, we'd be on our way.

"Mistress of Mirth!" I heard my alliterated nickname come floating down through the ocean of humanity in the hallway all the way to my locker.

"Jovial Jon," I said, turning around.

He stopped in his tracks, glancing at Rachel. "Friend or foe?"

"This is my *cousin* Rachel."

His face lit up. "Well, any relative of Merry's is a friend of mine," he said, pouring on the charm.

"Good to meetcha," she said.

I wondered how on earth Rachel had remembered to substitute the word *good* for *gut*. Thinking that I would just reach up and grab my books from my locker and get going, I caught myself. I absorbed the interesting fact that Jon seemed taken with my thoroughly modern Amish cousin, clearly not remembering her from our Christmas skating party.

He was still gazing at her as I explained, "Rachel's here visiting today. She's my guest."

They were in the middle of a proper handshake, and I waited for a moment till the initial greetings had been exchanged.

Oddly enough, Jon seemed to have forgotten all about alliteration-eze and our before-the-first-bell word game frenzy.

Evidently, something more important was occupying the empty space in his brain.

Someone.

I watched, expecting him to back away from my locker, smile his biggest smile, and say "see ya around," but this non-Merry-focused encounter was lasting longer than usual. Awkwardly so.

"Say, that was some science assignment," I said, choosing *s* to bait him.

He looked at me momentarily, almost dazed. "You're right."

No alliteration comeback? What was going on?

I tried again. "Where's the wonderful word Wizard?"

W—one of his favorite letters, I thought.

"I'll walk you to homeroom," he said, meaning both of us. But he didn't jump on the word game.

Truly amazing!

So we walked, the three of us. I couldn't begin to set him straight about who Rachel really was, not without blowing the whistle on her temporary charade. But it was all I could do to stifle a giggle as we moved through the crush of students.

Wouldn't Jon be surprised to know that Rachel was Amish? Wouldn't he be embarrassed, too, that his alluring alliteration skills had just flown the coop?

The boy was smitten. For the first time in his life he was showing signs of truly liking a girl, and it had to be Rachel Zook. An Amish girl, of all things!

Fourteen *Hide Behind the Moon*

"You have to keep Rachel's secret *all* day," I told Chelsea outside homeroom—after Jon said good-bye to Rachel and a total of zero words to me.

"No problem," she said.

"I'm trusting you not to tell a soul," I whispered, hoping Rachel was gawking at the students running to beat the bell, not listening in on my conversation with Chelsea.

Staring at me with those sea-green eyes, Chelsea teased, "Is there an echo in here?"

"Sorry, it's just that I've stumbled onto something that might help us beat Jon at his own game." I had to keep my voice low. Rachel was inching closer, leaning against the classroom door a few feet behind us.

"You've gotta be kidding—like what?"

We put our heads together. "He's nuts about Rachel."

"No way."

"It's true." I went on to explain that he'd stopped alliterating around her. "I tried to get him going twice this morning. No response. Couldn't even get him interested."

Chelsea shifted her pile of books from one arm to the other. "How do you know he won't start again?"

"That's what I wanna check out," I said. "At lunch, let's see what happens."

"Great idea." She was grinning now. "I'll invite Jon to sit with us. We'll throw around some phrases . . . see if he plays along. Maybe he'll want to show off for her."

"It's genius!"

She nodded. "For once, Merry, you're right about that."

Genius? I thought. What a wondrous word.

Rachel was curious about everything, it seemed. She thumbed through my three-ring binder, reading all my homework assignments before each class. She was also quite taken with some of the posters of actors or music stars plastered inside various lockers. Other things, too. Like tiny vanity mirrors and shelves for hairbrushes and makeup supplies.

"A school locker's like a mini home away from home," I tried to explain. "A pit stop . . . to check your face. You know, to see how you look before rushing off to class."

"Pit stop," she mumbled, trying on the word for size, I suppose. "Tell me about home free?"

I was surprised she'd remembered to ask. I did my best to describe a baseball game, with all three bases loaded.

"Oh jah, Amish play baseball all the time," she said. "I know . . . you must be talkin' about stealing home?"

"Well, sorta, only it's a little different when you say you're 'home free.' It really means that you're almost where you want to be. You've almost accomplished what you set out to do."

"Ach yes, Merry. I think I see what you mean." Then she giggled.

I wasn't sure if she caught the connection between the ball game and the phrase. But she was having a good time here at school. A good morning, at least.

It would be entertaining to see what happened at lunch—
that is, if Jon joined us. I wanted to start thinking in terms of
alliterating most everything. Warming up in my mind, so to
speak.

I wished that Lissa and Ashley knew about lunch with Jon.
They needed the most work on speaking alliteration-eze off
the top of their heads. Still, I hoped that maybe today could be
a practice round . . . or better. Since Rachel would be eating at
our table, maybe her presence would distract Jon. Again.

Suddenly I wondered what Levi would think of all this
alliterating madness. Probably he'd find our mind-bending
game silly, though harmless enough.

Thinking about Levi, I decided to write a letter later today,
after I returned Rachel safely home. It had been several weeks
since I'd taken time to write. Besides, I owed my Mennonite
friend a letter.

Switching mental gears from Jon to Levi had nothing to
do with Rachel's coming to school today. Nothing to do with
Jon's obvious interest in her, either.

Nope. I had plenty of friends. Besides, why *should* I put
all my eggs in one fickle Klein basket?

Everything happened too fast.

Chelsea, Lissa, and Ashley had seated themselves on one side of the lunchroom table. Rachel and I sat on the other side.

I was trying to explain our word game to Rachel, who nodded and smiled, keeping her comments few and far between.

"You just use the same beginning sound in as many words in a row as you can. Sometimes, we've even put a twenty-second time limit on it . . . or less."

"Oh" was all she said. She seemed distracted by the cafeteria hubbub taking place around us.

We—Chelsea, Lissa, Ashley, and I—began warming up, getting ready to catch the Wizard off guard, when he waltzed over.

"Sorry so late," he said, carrying a lunch tray.

I didn't have to guess where he'd want to sit. Politely, he asked if Rachel would mind if he sat next to her. She blushed sweetly and scooted over, closer to me.

Jon took her response as a "yes" and proceeded to set down his tray.

Chelsea got things going. "Ever wonder what words work with all *w*'s?" she asked, looking directly at Jon.

He turned to Rachel, ignoring the bait from Chelsea. "She talks funny, doesn't she?"

Smiling, Rachel said nothing.

I spoke up. "I say we have a practice round of alliteration-eze. And while we're at it, why wait till next week for the championship?"

"Go for it," Chelsea cheered.

"And may the best woman win," offered Lissa. A little weak with only two *w*'s in a row, but she was trying.

As for Ashley, it appeared that she was more taken with trying to decide if Jon was falling for Rachel than attempting to alliterate sentences. Fine with me. From what I'd observed, Jon wasn't about to make a big verbal impression on any of us. Maybe it was because Rachel was keeping mum, following my orders. After all, how easy *was* it to converse with someone who remained silent?

Or perhaps Rachel's demure demeanor had locked up the Wizard's brain. (The silent woman appeal does it every time!)

Whatever it was about Rachel Zook, Jon couldn't—or wouldn't—attempt to alliterate. At least not today.

It was more than frustrating. It was exasperating, and Chelsea told him so. "Look, Jon, we've been preparing for this word game thing of yours. Are you gonna play or not?"

He shrugged and glanced down at his plate. For the longest time, he stared at it. Then when I was sure he was going to cut loose with a yard-long sentence of silliness, he shook his head. "I'm bored with it, I guess."

"Bored?" Ashley piped up. "How could anybody be bored?"

I clapped for her. "Three *b*'s in a row—even one inside a word. Not bad."

"Atta girl, Ashley," cheered Chelsea. But it was Jon we were bribing—tempting him to play.

The Wizard was caught up in his new interest, however. "Would you like some ice cream?" he asked Rachel.

"Thank you," she said simply. And he was up and out of his seat.

I shook my head. "A marvelous mind is such a sad thing to waste."

"Meaning?" Lissa asked, reaching for a straw.

"The Wizard went a-walking," Chelsea said, giggling.

"He's horribly hard to handle," I spouted off. "Has to have his handicap." I wanted to say he'd forfeited his chances at the championship, but it wasn't really up to me to decide these things.

When he returned with the ice cream, he asked Rachel about her Anabaptist beliefs. Probably because she was wearing her veiling.

I wondered if now was a good time to set him straight—reveal all—and say she was Amish. Surveying the situation, I noticed that Rachel was particularly enjoying the attention. It would be heartless of me to pull the plug on their budding friendship.

Still, I wondered how Matthew Yoder might feel if he could see the two of them together. I didn't have to guess, really. Watching Jon talk to Rachel with such animation—was it admiration, too?—seeing her nod or gesture bashfully, without saying much of anything, I knew exactly how Rachel's young Amish beau would feel.

Truly horrible!

"I told Jonathan Klein the truth after school," Rachel said as we hurried upstairs to my bedroom.

"About being Amish?"

"Jah." She smiled broadly. "Honestly, it feels awful gut to talk normal again."

"To say what you're used to saying? The *way* you're used to saying it?"

"For sure and for certain," said Rachel.

We scurried into my bedroom, and I closed the door. The conversation was headed in a very secretive direction.

"How did Jon react when you told him?" I had to know.

"He said he wasn't all that surprised. That I had a soft-spoken way 'bout me. Somethin' he admires in a woman."

A *woman*? Give me a break!

"And he wanted to know if he could come see me sometime."

I was as silent as if the air had been punched out of me. "Did you say he could?" I asked, reaching for a bed pillow and hugging it.

She shook her head. "I didn't know what to tell him, really. If Matthew gets wind of this . . ."

I was hesitant to ask. "Does Matthew love you, Rachel?"

"Jah, I think so." She paused for a moment before going on. "He's talking marriage someday, but I'm not for sure 'bout my feelin's for him, ya see. He's gonna be baptized come next fall, and I . . . I . . . Well, I don't know yet what I want."

"I think *I* know," I said softly.

We were quiet for a time. She, sitting across from me on my desk chair, still wearing my sweater and jeans, and I, crossing my legs under me as I sat on the bed. The silence became awkward, yet I did not burst out with any more questions.

Outside, the wind blew hard against the windows, and the crows in the field across the road called back and forth.

At last, Rachel spoke. "Today was the first I'd ever let myself look from the outside in—from outside my Plain world, all the way back to the way Mam and Dat raised me."

"I thought so," I whispered. "You wanted to experience a taste of modern life. Right?"

She sighed a long, deep breath. "I've lived a life separated from the world all these years. I guess I just hafta see it for myself."

"How does Jon Klein fit into all this?" I ventured, half scared of what she might say.

Her face burst into a radiant smile. "To be honest with ya, Levi got all this a-stirred up in me," she admitted. "I never woulda thought of such a thing as doin' what I did today—goin' to public school and all. Or becoming friends with an English boy."

"Levi's leaving SummerHill has changed things for lots of people," I said.

"Jah, it has." Again she was silent. She got up and went to stand in front of my dresser mirror, reached for the brush, and began to undo her hair, making it Plain again. "Ya know what, Merry? I'm awful glad Levi did it. It was just what I needed to get me thinkin' 'bout my own future."

"So you might decide to go modern, then?"

She turned suddenly. "What do ya think it would be like, Merry?"

"To leave your church and your family?" I couldn't even begin to comprehend what she was saying.

"No . . . to follow your heart like Joseph Lapp did."

So it was the wayward Joseph—his forbidden photograph— that was at the core of Rachel's restlessness.

"I don't know, really." I wondered what I could say to make things right for her. "Sometimes a girl has to follow her heart, as long as her desires line up with what God has planned."

"Oh, divine providence? Jah, I know what you're sayin.'"

But I wasn't so sure she did. The strict Amish view of such things didn't always jibe with basic Christian beliefs.

"Getting back to Jon," I said a bit hesitantly. "Does he know you're my neighbor?"

She nodded, smiling. "*Now* he does."

"So you must've told him everything."

"Jah, even about the pictures in the hayloft. He'd like to have one—when they're developed, that is."

I gasped. She'd fallen hard and fast. And now Jon Klein was going to be the recipient of my handiwork. Oh, what was this world coming to?

Totally stressed, I headed for my walk-in closet, where I kept snack food in several shoe boxes. Rachel's eyes widened when I offered her some raisins and other goodies.

"Denki," she said, taking some thin pretzel sticks.

"If you keep talking about your plans, I'm afraid I'll eat up my whole stash of munchies," I told her.

"Ach, how come?"

I explained that stress made me hungry. "Always has."

"Oh." She nibbled on the snacks. But it was the faraway look in her eyes that worried the socks off me.

Rachel talked me into letting her wear my best jeans home, under her Amish dress. I must've been out of my mind to let her, but she pleaded so desperately. How could I not grant her yet another wish?

After she left for home, I sat down with my best unlined stationery and penned a letter to Levi. Partway into it, I was struck with the notion that maybe he could help guide me through this thing with Rachel. Of course, I had to be cautious how I worded this section of the letter. I didn't want the guy rushing home from college to confront his sister.

> *Monday, February 23*
> *Dear Levi,*
>
> *Sorry it's been so long since I've written. Things are so hectic here, beginning with homework. Another thing: My dad's been sick this past week. His doctor ordered him to stay home, but he was so bored he tried to help me with my schoolwork nonstop. Having my fifty-year-old dad hover over my every algebra problem, well . . . it was difficult, to say the least.*
>
> *I was wondering. What would you say to an Amish young person to encourage them in their beliefs? That is, if the person seemed too eager to experience the outside world. Would you tell him or her to pray about it? To follow his or her heart? What?*

I need your advice, Levi. I'm concerned for someone. Will you pray that I'll do the right thing?

Oh, I almost forgot. Last Saturday, I baby-sat for your little niece, Mary. What a doll! I'm delighted that your brother and sister-in-law were the ones who adopted her. I can see that God definitely had His hand in Mary's future.

I continued the letter, telling him about Chelsea's mother— how she was improving each day. And that Chelsea was attending church with me regularly. I even commented on the fact a group of my girl friends and I were hoping to defeat another classmate at a wacky word game.

It's called Alliteration-eze—an outlandish but lovely language. (See, I just wrote it!) You use the same consonants (or vowels) to begin words in a sentence. Here's another example: Levi listens to lectures at lunchtime.

Get it? I guess it appeals to me because I like the mental challenge—at least where words are concerned!

Well, it's about time for supper here. Hope you're doing all right at school. Everyone here in SummerHill misses you, including me.

Your friend always,
Merry

I reread the letter, hoping and praying that my former Amish boyfriend would know how to put a quick end to his sister's wayward wanderings.

After school the next day, I deposited my film at the local drugstore a couple of blocks from the school. I didn't have to worry about catching the bus today because Mom had planned to pick me up. We were going shopping. She—browsing at an antique store; me—searching for a new pair of school shoes.

The ones I'd been wearing were beginning to show signs of fatigue. Meaning, there was no passing them on to the Salvation Army. Not *this* ratty pair!

Anyway, Mom met me in front of the drugstore, double-parking only briefly as I hurried to get in. "Where to?" she asked.

"Park City," I said. "*Somebody* oughta be having a sale on shoes, don't you think?"

She smiled, but I could tell she was preoccupied.

"Who's got a sale going on antiques?" I quizzed her.

That got her attention. "Alden's. I saw advertised in the paper a couple of highboys," she replied. "Let's synchronize our watches."

"Good idea."

"I'll be back in an hour or so. How's that?" she said.

"That's enough time for me. What about you?" I was trying not to laugh. In the not-so-distant past, Mom had been known to disappear, swallowed up by antique dealerships—sometimes not resurfacing for a half day or more.

"Well, maybe if I set my watch so it beeps," she replied, grinning. "And if that fails, you can always call my cell phone."

"Okay, then," I agreed as she pulled into the mall parking lot. "Drop me off at Penney's. You can meet me there, too, in an hour and a half. Okay?"

She promised not to forget.

"See ya later," I called to her.

⌒

Inside, I discovered a deserted mall. The corridors were vacant, and only a few people, mostly adults, were sprinkled here and there. It was Tuesday—one week after the popular Presidents' Day sales. Maybe the good stuff had already been purchased. I thought about that, wondering why I hadn't gone on the hunt for shoe sales *last* weekend.

Then I remembered. I'd had the Valentine's Day sleepover. Far more important than any shopping spree!

I removed my jacket, wishing I didn't have to lug it around—one of the worst things about wintertime shopping. You bundled up to go outside, but once indoors, a jacket, hat, scarf, and gloves were a nuisance.

Quickly, I headed for the Value Shoe Store, scanning the window displays. Surely this was the best place for something practical and affordable. I picked out three pairs. Then I bunched up my jacket and stuffed it under one of the tiny stools and began trying on shoes.

I was well into my second pair when I noticed another customer wander in. The teen girl had light brown hair and the bluest eyes. I wouldn't have given her a second look—mostly because she was so made up—but there was something about her. . . .

She seemed familiar. But why?

Another glance told me, and I nearly choked. Rachel Zook was here, looking downright hideous. Tight corduroy skirt, too short. Silk blouse, low cut. Hair in long, flowing waves about her shoulders. Actually, the hairstyle was the only good part of her new look.

I ducked my head, hoping she wouldn't find me gawking, instead paying attention to the size and fit of the shoes I was trying on. At least, I pretended to.

"Merry? Is that you?" she called to me.

What should I say? I didn't quite know, but I turned around and looked up. "Hi," I said.

"What'sa matter with ya? You look like ya've just seen a ghost."

"A ghost wouldn't be so startling," I muttered. "How'd *you* get here?"

"Hitched a buggy ride with a friend and caught the bus." She looked around, pulling boxes of shoes down off the shelves, one after another. "S'pose they've got red dancing slippers?" she asked.

"What do you want shoes like that for?" I asked.

"Oh, ya never know where you'll end up," she said in the sassiest voice.

"Rachel," I whispered to her, now standing up. "Are you nuts?"

She stepped back, shrugging my hands off her shoulders. "Listen here. I'm tired of doin' things the Old Way. This is *my* time, Merry. Do ya hear?"

I shook my head, fearing for her. "I'd hate to see you get hurt." Sighing, I continued. "Rachel, you can't go around dressed like that. It's not becoming to a lady."

She was laughing now, not the hearty, country laugh I was used to. It was a silly, fickle sort of giggling. Like she was purposely calling attention to herself. "What do ya think the 'running around' years are supposed to be for, anyhow?" she said, putting on some poppy-red high heels and wobbling around in them.

"Your mother would cry a river if she could see you," I replied. "And . . . she's not the only one."

Rachel stopped prancing around. "What do ya mean?"

"Your brother Levi. That's who I mean. Don't break his heart."

She squared her shoulders. "He broke mine. And Mam's and Dat's—all the People. What's good for the goose is good for the gander."

"Oh, Rachel. *Please*. You're not yourself. You're—"

"You said it, Merry! I'm *not* myself. I don't wanna be Rachel Zook anymore." And with that, she flounced off to pay for her new red shoes.

I wanted to run after her, keep her from buying the gawdy things—with all of my heart I wanted to. But something kept me locked up. Maybe it was fear. Was I too frightened to go after her? Afraid she'd push me away, not heed my words?

Shoving the boxes back onto the shelves, I was in no mood for trying on shoes. I'd just have to wear my old ones a few days longer.

There was only one thing to do. *Someone* could help Rachel. I was almost sure of it. Not one-hundred-percent-amen sure as usual. But my idea was worth a try, and there was no time to hesitate.

Avoiding Rachel at the cashier, I rushed past her, out of the store. I felt my heart thumping hard as I found a quiet corner and flipped open the cell phone I reserved for emergencies.

Now, if only I could get an answer.

"May I speak to Jonathan, please?" I said into the receiver.

"Certainly," his mother said. "How are you, Merry?"

I wasn't surprised that she recognized my voice. "Fine, thanks. And . . . I'm sorry to bother you, but this is sort of an emergency."

Jon came on the line quickly. "Merry, are you all right?"

"Well, I've been better." I began to fill him in on Rachel. "She's way out there somewhere in her head. First, she talked me into taking her picture. Then it was visiting school. And now this."

"Slow down," he said calmly. "How can I help?"

I was relieved. He was saying all the right things.

"Do you like Rachel? I mean, do you *care* anything about her?"

He was silent for a moment. "I liked what I saw the other day, yes. But I don't want to influence her away from her lifestyle."

"But if you could, would you persuade her to rethink where she seems to be headed?" I asked, wondering if he could hear the pleading in my heart.

The answer came softly. "What do you want me to do, Merry?" No alliteration-eze. None. He was playing straight with me.

"Here's my idea. Invite Rachel to go somewhere with you. For a soda or something. Tell her she should be herself. Forget about heavy makeup and dressing like someone she's not."

"I think I could do that." He decided on a time—tomorrow after school. "If she agrees, let her know that I'll meet her at Pinocchio's. My treat."

I thanked him and hung up. My heart sank. This was one of the hardest things I'd ever done—setting up *my* guy with a girl friend gone goofy.

Keeping my eyes peeled, I searched the mall for Rachel. In every department store and dress shop, I looked. But she was nowhere to be found.

In my despair, I headed back to Penney's, attempting to ignore the ever-growing population of disheveled-looking teenagers on every corner. It wasn't until I'd passed several gift shops, a potpourri place, and the food court that I spotted my friend.

She was talking to a boy who was sporting a black leather jacket and boots, and I wasn't sure, but it looked like he had on black fingerless gloves.

I watched as she smiled up at him, her face not nearly as innocent now as it had been yesterday at school.

Silently, I began to pray. *Dear Lord Jesus, help me to help Rachel.*

Suddenly, a mighty surge of confidence rose up in me. I marched over to my friend and tapped her on the shoulder. "We need to talk," I said.

She turned around, offering a pathetic little smile. "What are ya doin' here? Spoilin' my fun?"

"I have a message from Jon Klein—remember him?"

Her eyes brightened. "Really? What's he want?" she whispered, glancing back at the leathered one.

"I'll tell you if you come with me," I coaxed.

"Excuse me," she said to the guy behind her. And she walked toward Penney's with me.

"Jon wants to see *you*. Tomorrow." I told her where and when.

"A date? Are ya sure?"

"One-hundred-percent-amen sure!" Whew, was I ever glad I could say that and mean it.

"Need a ride?" I asked, having mixed feelings about her coming home with us. Mom might react negatively upon seeing Rachel like this. On the other hand, I was willing to do most anything to get her out of this mall and those wretched clothes!

"Do ya mind?" she said. "I suppose it's 'bout time for milkin.'"

I checked my watch. "Hey, you're right."

All that evening, I thought about Rachel. Couldn't help reliving the astonished look on my mother's face when she saw Rachel dressed as a worldly English girl. Mom was smart, though. She said nothing, instead going off on a tangent about her incredible finds at the antique shop.

Dad was quiet at the table, not his usual self. Mom initiated plenty of conversation, though. Mostly centered around Rachel Zook's "wicked getup."

I didn't blame her for being so upset. She needed to vent her disgust and get it out of her system. I must admit, seeing Rachel with her skirt hiked up past her knees, her eyes catlike from too much eyeliner—the whole freaky package was enough to make any mother cringe.

"What's come over Rachel?" she asked after describing the afternoon's scene for Dad's benefit.

"Rachel's gone berserk, that's what." I couldn't think of a better way to relate it.

"Is she thinking of leaving the Amish, like Levi did?" Mom asked.

Now was my chance to mark the difference between Levi and his silly sister. "Levi's called to be a minister," I insisted.

Dad wiped his mouth with a napkin and looked at me without a reply.

"Rachel has other things on her mind. And it has nothing to do with seeking the Lord for her future, that's for sure."

Mom's brown eyes were serious. "What a shame."

"Not only that—she's confused," I blurted. "Rachel doesn't really know what she wants."

Dad sipped his herbal tea and then said, "I've passed her on the road riding with Matthew Yoder in his courting buggy a time or two."

I nodded. "That's probably the biggest hurt. At least for Matthew. *She's* all mixed up, but *he* loves her."

Mom leaned back in her chair. "Well, most likely your friend will come to her senses in good time."

"I hope so . . . before it's too late." I was thinking about Jon's offer to take her for a soda. Tomorrow! If he could straighten her out, I'd be ever grateful. But if he couldn't, I'd have to push Levi even harder for answers in my next letter. Maybe even tell him outright who was worrying me so.

Worse, I felt truly responsible for the whole mess. If I just hadn't given in to Rachel's first request—taking her picture in the haymow—maybe none of this would be happening.

Chelsea was waiting for me at my locker on Wednesday morning. "What's with the Wizard?" she said.

"Jon?"

She nodded. "He's acting so-o weird."

"What else is new?"

"He's all dressed up, like he's going to church or something," she told me.

Then I knew. "Oh, that."

"What?"

"Hey," I laughed. "That's *my* line."

"So tell me. Why's he wearing a button-down shirt and nice jeans to school?"

"It's Rachel . . . they have a date this afternoon."

She grabbed her throat. "Tell me you're kidding!"

"Actually, I'm not. It was my idea."

She studied me, her eyes narrowing slowly. "You set it up? Are you crazy?"

"For a very good cause," I said. "Trust me."

"Whatever."

We walked to homeroom together, and as we did, I tried to make her understand the strange things going on with Rachel.

"She's freaking out—like a bird let out of a cage for the first time."

"Hmm. I wonder what it would be like, feeling imprisoned like that."

"Well, I'm hoping Jon can help her somehow. At least, that's my plan."

She pushed me aside comically, primping in my tiny locker mirror. "Let's hope he doesn't decide to join up with her People and become Amish." She stepped back, the biggest smile spreading across her face. "Hey! An Amish Alliteration Wizard—not bad."

I laughed, knowing without a shadow of a doubt *that* would never happen.

"Shh! Here he comes now," I said, darting into homeroom. Chelsea followed close behind, and I took great pleasure in scrutinizing Jon's attire.

Chelsea wasn't kidding. He was dressed up really nice. For a split second I felt envious, wishing he'd taken such pains to impress *me*.

He waved and smiled. I did the same, reaching for my assignment notebook, thumbing through its pages. The thought that I had no one to blame but myself for the way I felt continued to haunt me all through homeroom and beyond.

By the end of the school day, I was literally a wreck. Not only that, Jon was absolutely not allowing himself to be sucked into any of my many attempts to get him to alliterate.

"Is it true? Are you really bored with it?" I asked after last-period class.

"Off and on, I guess."

"Well, I don't get it. Just when I—*we*—were about to take you on with the championship and all. How could you bail out on us like that?"

He shrugged, picked up his books, and walked with me to the door. "To be honest with you, Merry, it was more fun when the game was our secret."

"Oh." I hadn't ever considered that *he* would think of such a thing. But I was pleasantly surprised. And thinking back on what he'd just said made my heart skip a beat. Maybe there was still hope for Jon and me.

Then I remembered the after-school tête-à-tête I'd arranged for him with Rachel. What was I thinking?

Sighing, I said good-bye and headed off to my locker.

I was clicking off the numbers on my combination lock when Chelsea came up behind me. "Doing anything this minute?" she asked.

"Going home, that's all. Got tons of homework."

"I have an idea," she said, pushing her thick auburn locks behind one ear. "Since I've got my mom's car for the day, why don't you ride home with me?"

"And?"

"We can do some spying first," she said.

Genius! I saw right through her. "Good idea. Why didn't *I* think of this?" We were off to Pinocchio's, the cozy little corner cafe down the street. "Hey, do you mind if I run and pick up my photos first?"

A big grin stretched across her face. "Do I get a sneak preview?"

"All depends," I said.

"On what?"

"If they turned out."

She snorted. "You mean there's a chance that the incredible photographer Merry Hanson could flub up a photo?"

I laughed with her, rushing into the drugstore.

As it turned out, most of the pictures were pretty good. Chelsea flipped through the stack as we situated ourselves at a table in the far end of Pinocchio's. How we ever got inside without being noticed by either Jon or Rachel, I don't know.

But we'd been very discreet, keeping our faces turned the other way.

Now that I sat here snooping on my friends, I wasn't so sure we should've come. And I told Chelsea so.

"Aw, Merry, don't be a spoilsport," she scolded. "You're enjoying this as much as I am."

I had to admit, part of me was. Until Jon leaned across the table and covered Rachel's hand with his own. Oh, and the lovely smile that burst across her face in response to it!

This wasn't in the plan. Jon was supposed to encourage Rachel to be herself—follow the road of obedience to parents and God, not make her fall in love with him, for pete's sake!

But it was too late. Sparks were flying, and I knew it by the way she never took her blue eyes off him. Soon, she was taking out a pen from the pocket of *my* jeans and writing something—probably her address—on a piece of paper.

I groaned and Chelsea decided it was time to split. "We oughta get going. No need to prolong the torture," she said.

Reluctantly, I agreed, sliding out of the booth before the busy waitress ever got around to taking our orders. "Whatever we do, we can't let Jon and Rachel see us," I warned Chelsea.

Miraculously, we were able to slip away through a back exit. Home free!

———

Hours later, Rachel stopped by to see me. I suppose it was timely, too, because I had lots of pictures to show her.

I was in the middle of a math haze, deep in homework, when Mom called upstairs.

"Send her up." I closed my book, wondering what Rachel wanted with me after having spent the afternoon with Jon. Was she going to fill me in on every detail? I curled my toes in my socks, hoping not.

"Hullo, Cousin Merry," she said, breezing into my room.

"Wanna see some pictures?" I asked, pulling them out of the envelope.

Eyes bright, she sat on my bed, examining each shot, holding them as though they were priceless. Guess I might've felt the same way if I'd never seen myself in a photograph.

"Which one do you like best?" I asked.

She held up the one where her hair was free, without the veiling.

"I should've known you'd pick that one," I said, chuckling.

"This was hilarity, highly hidden. Jah?"

"You like your hair down best?" I asked, wondering why she was talking so weird.

She nodded. "Hanging hair is happy hair."

It hit me. "Did Jonathan teach you something today? A different way to talk?"

She absolutely beamed. "I wrote out words that started with *my* name . . . and his!"

Just great, I thought, frustrated. They'd spent their time playing the word game. And Jon had said he was bored with it. What a line!

She took out a billfold and paid me for the pictures. "Can you give this picture to Jonathan tomorrow?" she asked, still studying the hayloft setting. "He says he's anxious to get it."

I'll bet he is, I fumed. But I didn't say anything.

Here I'd thought getting Jon and Rachel together was the brightest thing I'd ever done. Wrong!

Still, I was stuck. "Sure, I'll give him the picture," I said. Then I got up the nerve to ask, "Did Jon say anything about your outfit, your makeup, or your styled hair?"

She glanced down at her feet. "Ach, not really. But he *did* say something kinda interesting."

"What?"

"He said I should think about going out with him on a real date. If my parents wouldn't mind." Her eyes sparkled as she began to recount the afternoon.

Meanwhile, I was feeling rather limp inside. My plan to "save" Rachel from worldly English influences had completely backfired.

What would Levi think if he knew? I wouldn't be the one to inform him, that was for sure. And Chelsea? She'd be laughing in her soup.

He'd taught Rachel the word game mere minutes after telling me he was bored with it. How could he lie to me that way?

Who could I turn to? And why did life have to be so complicated?

Rachel was right. Jon was thrilled to get her picture the next day. His face lit up like a neon sign as I handed it to him.

Hurt and a little more than mad, I turned to head for my locker.

"Whoa, Merry, wait up," he called after me.

Stunned once again that he hadn't used one of his favorite alliterated nicknames for me—*Mistress Merry* or *Merry, Mistress of Mirth*—I froze in place.

"Merry?"

Slowly, I turned around.

"Merry, what's wrong?"

I glanced down at the photo of my Amish girl friend in his hand. Swallowing the anger away, I put on a smile. "Have fun alliterating—Amish style," I said.

"So . . . you heard?" He looked quite sheepish, as if he'd been caught with his hand in a cookie jar.

"Maybe you're just what Rachel needs to get her through this time in her life." I stared him down—literally. "Well, gotta run."

And I did. Scrambled right through the crowd of students and found a safe haven at my locker.

Right after school, Nancy and Ella Mae Zook, Rachel's younger sisters, showed up at my back door. They had on matching green dresses and black pinafore-style aprons under their long black woolen shawls. "Do ya have a minute?" Nancy, the fourteen-year-old, asked.

"Come in." I led them into the kitchen.

Ella Mae, almost ten, whispered, "Can we go someplace more private?"

Now I was worried. "Is this about Rachel?"

They nodded simultaneously.

Without further comment, I motioned them into the small sitting room off the kitchen. Closing the door behind me, I offered them a seat. I stood, however, bracing myself for what was to come.

Nancy blushed bright red. "We ain't here to point blame at ya, Merry, but, well . . ." She paused, adjusting her shawl.

Ella Mae continued. "Didja give Rachel them modern clothes to wear?"

I shouldn't have been surprised that they suspected me. "I loaned her a pair of jeans and a sweater last Monday, but I don't know where she got that short skirt . . . or that low-cut blouse." I shook my head, staring at the ceiling. "I don't even own clothes like that. Honest."

"Okay, then," Nancy said. "We believe ya."

I took a deep breath, wondering what more they had to ask. Hopefully, neither of them knew about the photo shoot in the hayloft. Or the forbidden visit to my high school.

"Our parents will be comin' home tomorrow," Nancy volunteered. "Rachel oughtn't be struttin' around in such awful getup."

I nodded. "Oh, I'm sure she'll put her Amish dress back on. She wouldn't want to show disrespect to your parents."

"Well, I don't know already," Ella Mae said. "She's been terrible haughty the last couple-a days."

"Jah, I can't figure what's come over her," Nancy replied.

I walked to the window, glancing out, and then turned to face the girls. "You've heard of Rumschpringe, right?"

Nancy's face pinched up. " 'Course. But, Merry, it don't hafta be this way. Not all of us sow wild oats."

"That's true." I knew lots of Plain young people held devotedly to their upbringing. "But . . . does Rachel have a strong faith?"

Ella Mae looked puzzled. "In God?"

"Why, sure she does," Nancy said. "We *all* do. It's part of bein' Amish."

Her answer left me hanging. Sounded to me like Nancy assumed that if you were Amish you were automatically a Christian. "Well, I'm sorry you have to go through this with Rachel. She just seems sorta mixed up, I guess."

"Jah, ferhoodled," Ella Mae muttered.

"You can say that again," Nancy agreed.

I didn't tell them their sister was so out of it that she'd gone out with one of my favorite guy friends. That she was willing to entertain him by spouting off alliterated phrases, sneaking out of the house to meet him at corner cafés.

Thinking they were about ready to head back home, I invited them to have a cup of hot cocoa.

"Denki," they said, staying seated.

Awkwardly, I shuffled my feet and twiddled my thumbs.

Then Nancy, who looked rather glum, spoke up. "To top it off, Matthew Yoder stopped by yesterday," she said. "Such a right nice and thoughtful boy, he is."

"Jah." Ella Mae was shaking her head.

I listened, wondering why these girls thought so much of their big sister's boyfriend.

"He came over in his new open buggy," Nancy whispered.

"Jah, it's unheard of. No fella in his right mind wants to be seen callin' on a girl in broad daylight. Courtin's done in secret—at night."

I chimed in. "So I've heard."

"But Matthew came right up to the front door," Nancy explained. "And Rachel wasn't home."

Because she was having sodas with Jon, I thought.

"What do you think Matthew wanted?" I asked.

"Rachel . . . he wanted to see Rachel. We told him she was off to town." Ella Mae was grinning now, her fingers running along the loose strings of her Kapp.

"Did he come to ask her for a date . . . or whatever?" I said, fumbling for the correct Amish word.

"Ach, he seemed upset—wanted to know why she was actin' so peculiar lately," Nancy said. "Probably wanted to drive her to the next singin' in his new buggy. Jah, that's what he wanted with her."

"But I thought the girl's brother is supposed to take her to the singing." I said.

"The big brothers usually do, but Curly John's married now, so I guess Matthew don't wanna wait around for young Aaron to grow up." Nancy looked sharply at me, and a peculiar expression crossed her face. " 'Course, if Levi were home here where he belongs, *he* could be takin' Rachel . . . and lettin' Matthew drive her home. That's the way it's s'posed to be done."

I shivered a bit. Felt as if they were blaming *me* for Levi not living at home anymore—helping his father farm the land, helping his sister snag a husband. . . .

"It was never my idea for Levi to go away to college," I said softly.

"No . . . no. It's nobody's fault, really." Nancy looked more sad than mad. "Guess we'd best be leavin' now."

The conversation had gone in circles. Nothing had been solved. As far as they were concerned, Rachel had only one night to get her act together—to prepare her clothing and her attitude for her parents' return.

What could I do to talk sense into her?

I struggled with that question long after Rachel's sisters left. Finally, with my head spinning with ideas and more worries than could fill an apple barrel, I put on my jacket and headed outdoors.

Fortunately, Mom was in her sewing room making phone calls to several antique dealers. I found that out when I told her I was going for a walk. She pointed to her long list, smiled, and waved me on.

I must say that I was glad she hadn't happened in on my not-so-friendly discussion with our Amish neighbors just now. *That* was definitely something to be thankful for.

Outside, the air was frosty and sweet. Deciding to walk up the hill toward Chelsea's house, I hummed a worship song. I thought of Jon and how he'd hurt me. Again. When would I ever learn my lesson?

Switching to someone more dependable, I thought of Levi. I could hardly wait for him to write back. He should've gotten my letter by now, I guessed. And surely he'd have some advice for me. Because I was desperate.

Just then, up ahead, I saw a horse and buggy coming toward me. The horse's hooves against the snow-packed road sounded more like muffled thuds than the *clippity-clop*s of summer.

I prepared to wave at whichever Amish neighbor might be coming. What a surprise to see that Matthew Yoder was the driver. And the girl? The girl was definitely *not* Rachel Zook!

Trying to be polite, I smiled, refusing to stare at Rachel's competition. "Hi, Matthew!" I called, waving.

"Hullo, Merry. How are ya?" His voice floated off, out to the cornfield as the carriage passed me.

"Just look what you've gone and done, Rachel," I whispered to myself.

Instantly, I knew why Matthew Yoder was out parading his "date" on SummerHill Lane in broad daylight.

Spinning around, I slid back down the hill. Maybe there was time yet to help Rachel with the afternoon milking. More important, hopefully, there was still time to help her get her head on straight.

I ran all the way through the snow, even taking the shortcut through the willow grove. Rachel looked surprised to see me as I dashed breathlessly into the barn.

The smell of hay was sweet in my nose, but my heart trembled at what I had to do. "Rachel, I have to talk to you."

She stopped wiping down the cow's udder and stood tall, staring at me. "What is it, Merry?"

"I hate to be a bearer of bad tidings, but I think you should know something."

"Jah?"

"It's about your Amish boyfriend." I told her everything—about Matthew and his new buggy and his new girl.

Rachel took the news mighty hard at first. Tears sprang up in her eyes. She turned and tried to conceal them, but I saw them just the same.

She wiped her face on the back of her sleeve, and we talked some more. After rethinking the situation with Matthew and herself out loud, she was more positive.

"Maybe he *was* just tryin' to get my attention. And that other girl—wish I knew who she was."

We started to laugh about it. "Jealousy is a cruel taskmaster," I said, speaking for myself.

She nodded in agreement. "Guess I oughta be thankin' ya, Merry. I'm glad ya told me." Her face was serious and drawn now. "I best be givin' back these jeans of yours," she was quick to say.

I didn't go inside with her when she invited me but said my good-byes out by the milk house. "Hope it's not too late for you and Matthew," I called back.

She shook her head. "Don'tcha worry none."

Running toward the main road, I felt that I'd done the right thing for Rachel—at last! Of course, telling her about Matthew wasn't going to benefit only *her*. Matthew, if he hadn't truly found someone new, might be real glad to take his old girlfriend back. That is, if she decided to forget about her "running around" nonsense and embrace the Old Ways once again. Surely he would if Matthew loved Rachel as much as she thought he did.

After supper, Levi called. "I got your letter, Merry."

I was startled for a moment. "Uh . . . it's nice to hear your voice, Levi, but I didn't expect you to call me." Now I felt funny having written for his advice.

"It's not a problem. Honest, it isn't."

His "ain't" is missing, I thought. The sign of a truly educated man.

"How's everything at school?" I asked.

"I'm always busy with studies, but the Lord is good. I'm learning to trust Him daily."

I couldn't get over how different he sounded, even since I'd last seen him. "I'm glad you're happy there." I really didn't know what else to say.

"About your letter, Merry—I'd be lying to you if I didn't say that I suspect the person in your letter is my sister Rachel."

Surprised at his words, I just listened.

"Rachel's impulsive now, that's all . . . doesn't quite know where she's headed."

"You're probably right, but she'd never forgive me if she knew I told you," I admitted.

He breathed softly into the phone. Then, "My best advice to you is to pray for her."

"Does she ever read the Bible?" I asked, knowing that most Amish read only the Old Testament.

"Now that I'm not home, I couldn't say."

I went on to tell him about her visit to my school. And her interest in modern clothes. "I wish she'd settle down a bit," I said. "I can't get used to *this* Rachel."

He laughed softly. "And to think that you had to go through all this—on some level—with me last summer, Merry."

"Oh, it wasn't so bad."

"My searching brought me to the Lord Jesus. I'm ever so thankful." Then he asked about my dad. "Is he feeling better?"

"Dad's doing fine now, but he's been talking about an early retirement. Actually, I don't know what he's thinking."

"Really? Maybe he'll have time to travel more. He's always wanted to go on at least two mission trips a year," he said.

I grinned. "He told *you* about that?"

"Missionary work is a topic dear to both your dad's and my heart," he remarked.

"Just tonight at the table, Dad suggested that I come with him and Mom on a trip to Costa Rica over spring break."

"Do it!" Levi exclaimed. "You won't be sorry."

"Dad thinks I'd be a good photojournalist for the church."

"I hadn't thought of that, but he's right." His voice grew softer. "Maybe *that's* where your 'call' lies, Merry."

I'd never thought of my "call" from the Lord coming in the form of something I loved to do as a hobby. But now that Levi mentioned it, it made good sense.

"I'll think about it," I told him.

"Good, then. We'll talk soon, I hope."

"Thanks for calling, Levi."

"I miss you, Merry."

My heart nearly stopped. And I knew I missed him, too. More than ever.

"Oh, about talking in alliterated sentences," he added. "I've tried a few myself. I'll e-mail them to you if you give me your address."

Quickly, I did. "I'll look forward to that."

We said good-bye and hung up.

⁓

As promised, I received Levi's e-mail.

Hi, Merry,

Here's my alliteration for the day: Hope for happiness, holiness, humility, and honor—no halfhearted, ho-hum hypocrisy.

—Levi

⁓

I had to call Chelsea. "You'll never guess who's the new Alliteration Wizard!"

"I give up."

"No . . . you have to guess," I insisted.

"C'mon, Merry, I don't have time for games."

"Oh, so you're not playing, either?" I taunted.

"Who else isn't?" she asked.

"Well, not so long ago Jon wasn't. Or at least he said he wasn't."

"That's strange."

"What?"

"He just called here and was babbling baloney," she said.

I laughed. "So the former Wizard's making a comeback!"

"And maybe *you've* got him back?" she asked.

"Oh," I sighed. "I'm not so sure about Jon anymore." I felt the pain anew.

"Oh really?" She was probing for more details, but I had to put her off. Besides, Levi was on my mind. I was dying to tell her how excited I was about *his* call. "Levi Zook's an incredible alliterater."

"How do you know?"

I told her about the e-mail—the many, many *h*'s in a row. "He's truly amazing."

"With words or just in general?" she asked, laughing.

I wasn't ready to divulge any more secrets. Not yet. But I did tell her about my timely encounter with Matthew Yoder on SummerHill Lane. "Rachel's through with running around," I said. "I'm one-hundred-percent-amen sure!"

"If you say so," she replied.

We giggled briefly and then hung up.

Mom wanted to know what was so funny. "Glad you're having such a good week," she commented.

"Well, none of my cats got run over," I said, heading for the stairs and a mountain of homework.

"Honey, you're not making much sense," she pointed out.

"You're right." I rushed to my room before she could call any more comments up to me.

I plopped onto my bed, gathered my furry foursome around me, and thought of Joseph Lapp. "Well, I guess we have him to thank for the total chaos this week," I told them. "I think Rachel and her brother must share some of his genes."

Abednego eyeballed me as if to say, *Look who's talking.*

"Hey, I've been on both sides of the fence—the inside *and* the outside—and you know what?"

He meowed politely.

"It's not so much where you are; it's who you know. And I'm not talking riddles here, boys." I bowed my head. It was time for a personal chat with my heavenly Father—about Rachel and her future, about Levi and his, and about my own uncertainties.

Hide Behind the Moon **Twenty-Two**

Weeks later Dad decided, after all was said and done, that he would take early retirement from the hospital. And he and Mom are planning an overseas trip without me, since I can't miss that much school. Amazingly, Miss Spindler—Old Hawk Eyes, the neighbor lady behind us—has agreed to let me stay with her.

Maybe now I'll have a chance to do some sleuthing over there. I've been dying to know how she keeps such a close eye on everybody in SummerHill.

As for my baby-sitting job, it's earning me some spending money. The best part is getting to see sweet little Mary every weekend.

Levi's coming home for spring break, and it's for sure! I found out yesterday from Rachel, who, by the way, is behaving like her old self once again. In fact, I can hardly remember what she looked like in a short skirt and lipstick.

She's wearing her veiled covering consistently—*reverently*—and seems more content with being Plain. "I'm where I belonged all along," she told me recently.

Matthew Yoder forgave her in an instant. Last I heard, they'll start taking the required baptismal classes together come late July. I wouldn't be surprised if there's another wedding coming up in a year or so.

Now, if I can just get my favorite jeans back from her sometime. Souvenirs of wayward days probably aren't the best thing to keep around. I've told Rachel that, but she only smiles and says, "Looking at them and Joseph Lapp's secret picture every so often are what help keep me Amish."

I don't ask "What?" in response. Instead I listen sincerely with my heart and pray . . . and try to understand. That's the best a friend can do, with or without the moon.

Windows on the Hill

For
Julie Witner,
who loves cats as much as
Merry Hanson.

"For the eyes of the Lord run to and fro throughout the whole earth . . ."

—2 CHRONICLES 16:9 KJV

I'll never forget the day my sweet and sassy Abednego disappeared. The afternoon was unseasonably warm and sultry. Too warm for the middle of April.

Perched on the garden bench under our backyard maple, I played with the lens cap on my digital camera. I'd loaded it with freshly charged batteries for today's special event—a retirement party for my dad. Actually, the party was an open house, a come-and-go sort of thing. I wouldn't have admitted it to my parents, but I was bored out of my mind.

My cat quartet—Shadrach, Meshach, Abednego, and Lily White—gathered around my feet. I figured they were horribly hot and uncomfortable inside their heavy fur coats. Fidgety, they rolled around in the cool grass, pawing at one another.

I leaned back and gazed up at the pale blue sky. A series of ballooning white clouds sped across the heavens. Mom liked to call them thunderheads. I'd nicknamed them thunderbumpers.

"Looks like rain," I told my feline friends. "Those clouds up there are gonna crash together and make all kinds of racket pretty soon." I didn't realize that what I'd just said would actually happen. And in a very frightening way.

The cats didn't seem too alarmed by my comment. Only Abednego lifted his fat, furry head and stared at me. His eyes blinked slowly. Then he put his head down again and licked his paws.

"What's on your mind, little boy?" I reached down for him, but he hissed back at me. "Abednego! Is that any way to behave?"

He responded by making a beeline for the gazebo, squeezing his plump black belly under the white latticework—his favorite hiding spot. Whenever he was missing, I first checked under the gazebo.

"He's upset about something," I muttered, playing with Lily White, my fluffy white cat, now a year old. Sitting there, I felt a bit miffed at Abednego, not knowing what on earth was on his mind. Maybe he shared my indifference toward the strangers in our yard. Several former colleagues of Dad's had already arrived—emergency room nurses and doctors. They were laughing and sharing stories in the shelter of the large gazebo.

Originally, Mom had decided to book a downtown hotel suite for the occasion. In the end, though, Dad got his way—a simple springtime picnic on the grounds of our one-hundred-year-old farmhouse.

Casually, I looked toward the back porch and noticed Mom motioning from the kitchen window. She called through the screen. "Merry, come and help serve finger food."

I was glad she'd asked—something to do. Quickly, I left my private post, and the three remaining cats insisted on following me up the back steps and into the house.

By the time I arrived in the kitchen, Mom was occupied with the arrangement of carrot sticks, celery, cauliflower, and broccoli on one side of a round tray.

When I caught her eye, I noticed she seemed a bit stressed. "Please pass this tray around outside, honey." She glanced at the sky through the wide kitchen window. "And pray that the weather holds."

Her request was understandable. With temperatures soaring and humidity hovering in the ninety-percent range, the chance of a storm was extremely high. I hoped—and prayed—for both Dad's and Mom's sake that the breeze might blow the ominous clouds far away.

I headed toward the back door, carrying the enormous tray. My mouth watered at the sight of the creamy, homemade buttermilk dressing smack-dab in the center. There were other delicacies, too, and I made note of the barbecued chicken wings and drumsticks, hoping some of them might get passed over so I could have a taste later.

Dad's party was in full swing. The gazebo was filling up with folks offering their best wishes for his early retirement. Gingerly, I carried the tray across the yard and up the white wooden gazebo steps.

"Here's my girl," Dad said. His eyes lit up as he began making introductions. "This is my daughter, Merry. She's quite the photographer, so you may see her roaming the grounds taking candid shots."

"Hello. Nice to meet you," I said, smiling and feeling terribly awkward, yet offering my courtesy.

Dad nodded, obviously pleased that I'd made an attempt to chat. "Merry's making a scrapbook of the afternoon," he commented. "So her old dad will remember this day."

"Oh, Daddy," I said, feeling the heat of embarrassment work its way into my face. "You're not old."

Several of the men agreed.

"My daughter's an optimistic young lady," Dad said, winking at me.

"And she must be very thoughtful, too," added one of the nurses, smiling. She went on to say that she'd attended a creative workshop on scrapbooking recently. "What a wonderful way to record special memories."

She's right about that, I thought, recalling the cherished scrapbooks of my twin sister, Faithie, and me. The long-ago

pictures brought back some of the happiest days of my life—
days before Faithie died of leukemia at age seven.

I kept smiling and playing hostess, taking the tray items
around to fifteen or more people. The finger food vanished
quickly, and I headed toward the house to stock up.

"Merry, honey," Dad called. "Why don't we have a group
picture when you come back out?"

"Okay," I replied and hurried into the kitchen.

"Back so soon?" Mom said, eyeing the empty tray.

I nodded. "People are showing up in droves. Probably because of all the free food."

"Merry, for goodness' sake," Mom scolded. "Your father's
a highly respected doctor in Lancaster County."

"*Was* . . ."

She was shaking her head at me. "C'mon, Merry. You know
what I mean."

"Sorry, Mom. It just came out wrong."

She fell silent, going about the business of scraping more
carrots. I leaned against the fridge, watching Lily White chase
her golden-haired brothers around the corner and into the
family room.

"Are the Zooks coming?" I asked, thinking of our Amish
neighbors and good friends.

Mom answered without looking up. "Abe and Esther and
the children were invited. I'd be very surprised if they didn't
drop in for a while."

"What about Old Hawk Eyes? Do you think *she'll* come?"

Mom's head jerked up. Her deep brown eyes bored into
me. "Merry, now, really."

I wrinkled my nose. "Everyone calls Miss Spindler that . . .
even the Zook kids!"

Mom shook her head. "Does she deserve a nickname like
that?"

"Well, she's always spying on the neighborhood. Always seems to know exactly what's going on in SummerHill, you know."

Mom knew it was true, and she had too many things on her mind to argue with me now. "Ruby Spindler is a lonely old lady, but she has a heart of gold" was all she said.

I bit my tongue—wasn't going to remind Mom unduly of Miss Spindler's nosy behavior. I headed back outside to prepare for the group picture Dad wanted. That's when a crack of thunder like I'd never heard boomed down on the party.

Abednego darted out from under the gazebo as though he'd been shot. He came straight for me across the yard, and if I hadn't stood perfectly still he would've tangled up in my feet and made me fall, camera and all.

Another deafening thunderclap followed, and I ran to the safety of the house. Inside, I set down my camera equipment and raced to the family room windows, hoping to see where my elderly cat had run for cover.

Then I spotted him. His long black tail was pointing straight up as he dashed around the side of the house, heading for the road.

"Yee-ikes!" I said, hurrying back to the kitchen.

"What is it, dear?" Mom asked, scurrying about.

"I think Abednego's completely flipped out." I didn't bother to explain. But I had the strangest feeling that I might never see my beloved baby again.

Two Windows on the Hill

I scrambled to the hall closet and pulled out an old raincoat and hat. Those thunderbumpers had done their job, giving clear warning. The sky opened right up like a burst dam.

My golden-haired cats—Shadrach and Meshach—and Lily White at least had enough sense to come in out of the storm. They'd made a beeline to the stairs that led to my bedroom. Actually, it was sort of *their* room, too, since I allowed all four of my cats to sleep at the foot of my big bed.

Now, standing by the front door, I snapped up my waterproof coat and hat, wondering where to look for Abednego. How could I persuade my old cat to come home?

People poured into the kitchen, located at the back of the house. I could hear Mom's voice mixed in with the swell of animated conversation, the casual comments about it "pouring cats and dogs." The only problem was one of *my* cats was getting drenched out there. And the poor thing was way too old and coddled to survive getting caught in this sort of gully washer.

Without telling Mom or anyone, I ducked my head and ran out into the drenching rain. Rain pellets fell so hard they were like tiny hammers on my rain hat.

"Abednego!" I hollered.

The rain was roaring, coming straight down in fierce sheets. I retraced his steps and dashed back to the gazebo, squatted down, and looked under the latticework, hoping . . . hoping he might've run back here to hide.

"Here, kitty, kitty," I called again and again.

Standing there like a statue in the rain and wind, I wondered which direction to take, thinking he might've headed up Strawberry Lane—the road that ran along the north side of our property. Miss Spindler lived up that road, and Abednego might've gone there to find refuge under the thicket and large trees surrounding her old house.

I hurried across the backyard to Strawberry Lane, leaning my head into the wind. Looking down, I noticed that I'd forgotten to wear rain boots, and my sneakers were soaked and muddy. Nevertheless, I pushed on, arriving at Miss Spindler's stately residence.

I rang the doorbell, and she came quickly, her blue-gray hair and makeup absolutely perfect, as always. In fact, if I wasn't mistaken, it looked as if she'd had her hair recently dyed a shade of cobalt blue. Politely, I squelched a giggle.

"My, oh my, what're you doin' out in this, dearie?" she greeted me. "Goodness me, Merry, you're soakin' wet."

"It's my cat," I blubbered. "Abednego's run off. Have you seen him?"

She shook her head slowly. "There ain't been no sign of man nor beast since this terrible storm came up. But I'll be on the lookout for him," she assured me.

I wondered what she meant by "on the lookout." Maybe she really did have a lookout room somewhere in the house. Was *that* how she spied on everyone and everything?

"Well, thank you, Miss Spindler. I better keep searching for my cat."

She clucked her tongue at me, as if to say I shouldn't be out in such inclement weather, but I couldn't let her discourage me.

"We're gonna have us a good time when you come next week," she said through the screen door.

I smiled at her. "Yes, I'm looking forward to it." Which was actually a true statement. I was eager to discover more about this nosy neighbor of ours!

Stumbling back down Strawberry Lane, I made the turn onto SummerHill Lane at the bottom of the hill. There I scanned the ditches on either side of the road. Tears stung my eyes as I thought of losing my cat to this vicious storm.

With renewed determination, I trudged onward, toward our Amish neighbors' private lane. Where was Abednego? Had he gone for shelter in the Zooks' barn?

Bowed against the ferocious gale, I might've wandered into the path of the oncoming Amish buggy, but the horse neighed loudly enough to penetrate the sound of the pounding rain. Heart thumping, I stopped dead in my tracks.

Not more than a few yards away, one of Abe Zook's driving horses was snorting and stomping and rearing his head. Slowly, I backed away, hoping to calm him so he wouldn't tip over the carriage. "It's just me . . . Merry Hanson," I said, even though I couldn't imagine the horse even heard my voice. Still, I moved back gradually till I sensed he was beginning to relax.

Then I heard Abe Zook speaking to his horse in monotone Pennsylvania Dutch—gentle and composed.

I'm not sure how long I stood there, but I was shivering, that much I knew. My teeth began to chatter, more from the near accident than from the cold.

"Merry, *kumm mit!*" Abe Zook called. "Come along into the buggy. We'll take ya home."

"Thank you!" I was glad for the invitation but still concerned about Abednego. Yet as I settled into the second seat, next to my Plain girl friend, Rachel, I didn't say a word about my runaway pet.

"We're headed over to your pop's retirement party," Rachel said. Her pretty blue eyes glimmered with expectancy.

"It's not such a good day for it, I'm afraid," I said as the carriage creaked and struggled up the muddy hill.

"*Jah*, but it'll pass," she said, smiling. "Bad weather always does."

Her positive, upbeat attitude always left me nearly breathless. The climate outside or inside really didn't matter—the oldest daughter of our Old Order Amish neighbors was usually on top of the world, so to speak.

"What're you doin' out in this rain?" asked Esther from the front seat.

I hesitated to mention my foolish cat. "Well, did you hear those thunderclaps?" I ventured.

They nodded that they had . . . all the kids, too.

"My cat took off running right after that," I said.

"Which cat?" asked seven-year-old Susie, the youngest.

"Abednego, the oldest."

"Ain't he the one always runnin' off?" asked Aaron, the youngest boy.

"Always," I answered.

"Best do something 'bout that," Ella Mae, age nine, spoke up.

"Like what?" asked her older sister Nancy.

"Maybe get him a cage," giggled Susie.

Rachel shushed her. "Now, don't make fun," she said.

I was thankful for my friend's comment. After all, my precious cat was still wandering around out in this nasty weather. Lost!

"Heard you was stayin' over at Old Hawk Eyes' a bit next week," Rachel whispered. "While your parents go on a trip."

"Just three days . . . till my brother gets home from college for his Easter break," I explained.

Susie and Ella Mae were leaning up behind us, their noses poking over the seat where Rachel and I sat. "Why ain'tcha comin' to stay with us?" asked Ella Mae.

"Well, Mom talked about asking you, but then she decided your mama has enough children to keep track of." I wanted to admit that I'd much rather spend three days at their Amish dairy farm than stay with Miss Spindler at all.

Still, there was something I was dying to find out, only I hadn't told a soul. There was a secret waiting inside Old Hawk Eyes' house, probably in her attic. Next week was my chance to find it out.

The guests who came to help Dad celebrate were either Plain or fancy—the phrase used here in Pennsylvania to describe the difference between Amish or Mennonite folk and regular modern people like me and my family.

I took plenty of pictures indoors for the retirement scrapbook, taking care not to capture our Amish acquaintances in any shots. In spite of the rainstorm, my father's former colleagues continued to show up in groups of three or four. None of the medical types were Plain, though. They were highly educated people, unlike the Amish, who abandoned formal schooling after the eighth grade. Higher learning was strongly discouraged by Amish bishops. They believed that if a person searched for knowledge and found it, the risk of straying from the path of the *Ordnung*—the unwritten rules of the Amish community—was too high to keep him in the Old Order.

Dad and I went around the house together, arm in arm, introducing our Amish neighbors, the Abe Zook family, including their homegrown children: Rachel, Nancy, Aaron, Ella Mae, and little Susie.

Levi, their next-to-oldest son, was off in Virginia at a Mennonite college, finding his way in the world of cars and electricity. And Curly John, the Zooks' firstborn, had already settled down to marriage and family with his young bride, Sarah, and their daughter, Mary.

Abe and Esther Zook didn't waste any time locating my mother after introductions were finished. They strolled from the living room right out to the kitchen and made themselves at home.

But Rachel hung back with me, and we found a spot in the family room to chat a bit. "What's your pop gonna do with himself since he ain't workin' no more?" she came right out and asked. Her fingers slid up and down the white strings on her *Kapp*—the head covering she always wore.

I knew the answer to that question. "My dad wants to take a few mission trips overseas, going as a helper to construction missionaries. I think he'll keep plenty busy, especially with building churches and Bible schools. That's what he hopes to do."

"Well, if there's any time when he's twiddling his thumbs, you just send him on over to *Dat*. He'll put him to *gut* use in a hurry." Rachel's rosy face shone under the lamp behind the chair.

I laughed but not too hard. Growing up around Amish helped me understand these good-hearted people. "Sure, I'll tell him. But it wouldn't hurt for your father to do the same, probably."

"Right ya be," Rachel said, smoothing her long blue dress.

Rachel and her sisters were grinning hard at me. I couldn't resist. I had to know what was on their minds. "What's up?" I asked.

They glanced back and forth at one another as they sat on the sofa, like they were too shy to say.

"C'mon, I know you've got something up your sleeves," I urged.

Rachel finally spoke up. "I probably shouldn't say nothing, what with Abednego acting up and all."

I hadn't forgotten my lost cat, not for a single second. But her remark hit home, and I excused myself and got up to look out the window. *Where are you, Abednego?* I wondered.

"We've got us too many kittens," Rachel said, almost abruptly.

Her words hardly registered in my brain. Sadly, I turned away from the window. "What did you say?"

"We got us more cats than we know what to do with," repeated Ella Mae.

Nancy was nodding her head to beat the band. "Dat's gonna hafta shoot 'em if we don't find 'em homes," she said.

"Aw, you're not serious. Would he do that, really?" I shouldn't have asked because I knew Abe was more than eager to lessen the cat population on his dairy farm. Cats had a tendency to get in the way—made farm work difficult, getting all tangled up underfoot.

"I think kitty cats are awful cute," little Susie piped up. "Can't ya take a couple more?"

I shook my head. "My mother's upset about the four cats I already have. She'd never stand for five!"

"*Ach*, what's the difference?" Rachel asked. "Four, five, or twenty—they're all just cats. Makes for good mouse catchin'."

Thinking about that, I realized we hadn't seen a single mouse in over a year. "You're probably right."

"So . . . do ya want another one, then?" Rachel asked, grinning from ear to ear.

I shook my head and sat down again. "Better not even ask my mother. She might drop that big tray of goodies over there." Through the wide doorway, we watched her pick her way through the growing *indoor* crowd of well-wishers.

"Won't it seem funny havin' your pop home all the time?" Rachel asked. Her light brown hair was parted simply down the middle, but specks of light danced prettily on the sides.

"When Dad's home, he'll keep busy with hobbies and volunteer work at the hospital and the church. And there's always my mother's growing fascination with antiques," I explained.

"Your *Mam* likes old furniture?" Rachel asked while her sisters were silent, just smiling.

"She's smitten with antique fever. Next thing I know, she'll be starting up a shop somewhere in this house." I glanced outside at the gazebo. "I wouldn't be surprised at anything."

Rachel pushed the hairs at her neck up into her bun, under the thin white netting. "So . . . you're sure you don't need another cat or two?"

"Not if I want to keep living here," I said, laughing.

"Okay, then. I won't bring it up again." She got up and went to the kitchen with me to get a plate and some finger food. Her sisters followed right along without ever saying a word.

"Wait a minute." I just thought of someone who might be in the market for a kitten. "Have you talked to Miss Spindler? She'd be a good cat person, I think."

Rachel's eyes lit up. "Are ya sure?"

"One-hundred-percent-amen sure!" I said.

"Jah . . . Old Hawk Eyes *does* need a cat," Nancy said out of the blue.

"She must be awful lonely over there in that great big house of hers, don'tcha think so, Rachel?" asked Ella Mae.

I smiled. "Nancy and Ella Mae are probably right." Just then Shadrach and Meshach scampered into the room. "Excuse me," I said quickly. "I'd better round up my cats before Mom says they're spoiling Dad's party."

"Need any help?" asked Rachel.

"Sure!"

We ran around the family room, finally catching up with Abednego's little brothers. It was usually the feisty, fat feline I was chasing. Shadrach and Meshach weren't nearly as adventuresome these days. The farthest they'd ever strayed was the willow grove, the dividing line between the Zooks' property and ours.

But Abednego was another story. He'd been known to wander off as far away as the highway, clear to the east end of SummerHill Lane. I didn't want to think about my cat running that direction. Not with the rain continuing to pour down in buckets.

But I had to admit, I was worried something awful about Abednego being gone this long. Truly worried!

Four *Windows on the Hill*

I don't happen to swallow all that stuff about cats having nine lives. People get carried away with notions sometimes, I think. But if the nine-lives thing were really true, I guess I'd have had higher hopes of Abednego's return.

Yet I continued to stare out my second-floor window into the twilight, missing my fat black cat. My deep affection for him kept me standing there, motionless, remembering all the years spent with the spunkiest cat in all of SummerHill.

Finally I forced myself away from the rain-streaked window. It wasn't that I was giving up on finding him. The night was just so wet and cold. Too blustery to go searching the countryside again. Even Mom had put her foot down about my going back out.

But I had a plan. A pure genius strategy to help locate Abednego. I sat at my desk with pen and paper, beginning to outline my idea.

Soon I was lost in thought when someone knocked softly on my bedroom door. "Say the secret slogan," I said.

Dad peeked his head in. "Hey, honeybunch."

"That's not a password," I replied.

"Close?" He shrugged and cocked his head to one side.

"Not even." I laughed and waved him in.

Opening the door wider, he moseyed inside. He stood near my antique dresser, frowning cautiously. "How're you doing, kiddo?"

Quickly, I looked away.

"You're upset," he said, coming over.

"Abednego's disappeared," I blurted. "I'm worried sick."

"Of course you are, honey. Your cats mean a lot to you."

Shadrach, Meshach, and Lily White perked up and looked at Dad as if they'd heard their own names. I had to smile, wondering what went through those furry little heads at a time like this, with Big Brother lost in the night somewhere.

Dad stood in the middle of the room, eyes soft and gentle. For a moment I thought I saw them glisten. "I wanted to come up and say thanks for helping your mother this afternoon. And for taking all those pictures."

I felt almost shy. "It was a great retirement party, Dad. I was glad to help out."

He shook his head as he sat at the foot of my bed. "I'm having second thoughts."

"About retirement?"

That got a chuckle. "No . . . no, not at all. This old man's eager and ready for a change of pace."

"And scenery, too?" I added quickly, thinking of my parents' Costa Rica trip.

He looked at me with compassionate eyes. "I'm wondering if leaving you with Miss Spindler is the right thing," he began again. "Maybe we should postpone the trip until this summer and go together, as a family."

"I'll be fine, Dad. Miss Spindler's looking forward to having someone around. I'll keep her company."

He nodded as if reevaluating the idea. "And you'll be there only a short time," he admitted.

"Three days." *Enough time to do some snooping*, I thought.

"Then it's settled," he said. "When your brother arrives home, he'll be here for you until we return."

I went to him and offered a hug. "I'm not a child anymore, Dad. You don't have to worry."

He got up and walked to the door, smiling. "Well, I'm glad we had this little talk."

"Me too. Old Hawk Eyes and I will get along okay."

That's when he laughed so loud Mom came and poked her head in the room, too. I didn't feel the need to rehearse the "Old Hawk Eyes" issue again.

"What's so funny?" She leaned against the doorframe.

I glanced at Dad, deciding it was up to him to tell her. He was cool that way—truly understood the need for appropriate nicknames.

The phone rang, and I was more than happy to excuse myself, speeding down the hall to get it.

"Hanson residence," I answered. "Merry speaking."

"Merry *speaking*? When did you change your name?"

I laughed. "Oh, it's *you*."

"So how's the feline freak?" Skip asked.

I could almost visualize my older brother's straight face. He wasn't joking, not one bit. Honestly, he believed that I was cat crazy.

"You'll probably be glad to hear that I'm short one cat at the moment," I informed him.

"Well, that *is* good news." He chortled a bit and then continued. "Let me guess . . . Abednego got run over by an Amish buggy."

"Skip Hanson!"

"Hey . . . just kidding. But it *is* Abednego that's missing, right?"

"You know my cats pretty well," I said but didn't want to continue this line of conversation. "So . . ." I paused. "Why'd you really call?"

"Just checking up on my little Merry" came the saucy reply.

"Aw, how sweet," I said sarcastically.

"Seriously," he said, "how's school? Sophomore year still treating you okay?"

"Sure, what's left of it. The school year's nearly over, remember?"

"Yes, well . . . I hear that you and our nosy neighbor are planning an extended sleepover. *That* should be interesting."

I had to laugh. Skip was so clever with words, and I honestly missed having him around. "If you promise to keep something quiet, I'll tell you a secret."

"You've gotta be kidding." He laughed. "This is definitely a first."

"Hush. If you keep it up, I won't tell you a thing."

"I'm all ears."

I took a deep breath. "Okay . . . here goes. I'm hoping to solve a mystery while I'm over at Old Hawk Eyes' place."

He was snorting now. "Let me guess. You're going to check out her high-powered telescope, right?"

"Count on me."

"My sister, the super sleuth," he teased.

"I'm approaching adulthood, I'll have you know. In case you forgot, I'm going to be sixteen and a half in three days . . . April twenty-second."

"That's the most ridiculous thing I've ever heard. Nobody celebrates midyear birthdays."

"Well, *I* do."

"Figures."

I ignored his flippant response. We talked a few more minutes before he asked to speak to Mom. "I'll see you next Thursday afternoon," he added.

"Remember, now—what you promised?" I reminded him of our secret.

"Won't breathe a word," he replied. "But I'll want a full report of your findings the minute I get home."

"Deal."

" 'Bye, little girl," he said.

If Mom hadn't suddenly come into the hall, I probably would've chewed him out for yet another "little girl" comment. Enough was enough.

Still, I couldn't wait for Skip to come home. Especially now that he showed signs of wanting to be a true confidant, someone trustworthy to share in the results of my Spindler visit.

I handed the phone to Mom and headed back to my room and to my three remaining cats. Settling down on my bed, I thought of my brother's return home. Actually, I could hardly wait to see him again. Mainly because it seemed like such a long time since Christmas break—almost four months!

But Skip wasn't the only one coming home. Levi Zook— Rachel's brother—was, too. Truth was, I'd tried *not* to think of Levi's return. He liked me. Maybe too much.

Scooting off the bed, I went to my desk to think through my plan to locate my cat—the project I'd started before Dad knocked on my door. It would never do to sit around and wonder about Levi, anyway. He'd be here soon enough.

As for Jonathan Klein, the sometime object of my affections, he and I weren't exactly on the best terms lately, which was one-hundred-percent fine with me.

I picked up my pencil and made several attempts to create a lost-cat poster. But I was stuck for creative ideas—all because thoughts of Levi Zook had crowded into my brain.

"Abednego's missing," I told my girl friends after church the next day.

"Again?" Chelsea Davis asked, frowning. "Does he ever stay home?"

. She *would* say that. After all, Abednego was known for disappearing off and on.

I sighed. "Actually, he got scared yesterday during that horrible storm."

"Oh, I remember," said Ashley Horton, our pastor's daughter, wide-eyed and obviously worried.

Lissa Vyner blinked her sad blue eyes at me. "Can we help?" she asked softly.

I nodded. "Maybe. I sorta thought of a plan."

"Like what?" asked Ashley.

"Well, it didn't turn out to be much, really," I said.

"C'mon, Mer, *tell* us. We're your closest friends," Chelsea insisted.

So I told them. I described how I'd sat at my desk last night till close to midnight, halfway waiting for Abednego to wander home a drenched and frightened ball of fur, and halfway trying to make clever and eye-catching flyers to distribute around SummerHill.

"Your poster idea is positively terrific," Ashley said, her eyes smiling. Gushing was her trademark, and over time I'd learned to put up with it.

"So . . . tell us about your flyers," Chelsea said, twisting her auburn hair around her finger.

Lissa was silent, waiting with eyes fixed on me.

"Promise not to laugh," I said. "Honestly, I tried the alliteration thing, you know, for a catchy phrase or two, but I wasn't very successful. Abednego starts with *A*, and that's a hard letter to work with."

"No kidding," said Ashley.

"What about the Alliteration Wizard?" Chelsea inquired, mentioning the very person who'd first challenged me to talk in alliteration-eze, back when it was our private game. "Have you talked to Jon?"

"Forget *him*," I spouted, glancing around to make sure Jon wasn't within earshot.

Chelsea's deep green eyes tunneled through me. "I can't believe you still feel that way. After everything you two have been through together."

I turned to go. "Not now, Chelsea."

⸻

It was Lissa who followed me out the church doors and down the steps. The day was breezy and bright, with the promise of everlasting clear skies. A perfect day to walk home from church. And if I'd spotted my parents right at that moment to let them know, I would've set out for SummerHill Lane on foot.

"Merry, please don't be upset," Lissa said, hurrying to keep up. "Chelsea didn't mean it. Not really."

I whirled around. "Of course she meant it! You were there— you heard what she said."

"No . . . no, I think you misunderstood" came the reply.

Shaking my head, I studied my wispy friend. Her wavy blond hair drifted softly around her shoulders, but it was the set of her lips that convinced me of her concern.

"Oh," I groaned. "This is truly horrible."

"It'll be okay," she said sympathetically. "You'll see."

But I felt dreadful. "Why do I have to get so freaked out over a boy?"

Lissa looked up from below her long lashes. "Maybe it's because you still like him. Way down deep in your heart."

I couldn't bear to hear it, especially from her. After all, late last spring Lissa had fallen hard for Jon. And at the time, I'd considered him all mine. But now I wasn't one bit interested. At least, that's what I kept telling myself.

"Can we *not* talk about this here?" I snapped.

"Fine with me," she said softly.

I knew I'd offended her. "Look, why don't you come over this afternoon. We'll talk then."

"Okay, I'll call you after lunch," she said, turning to go.

Almost instantly, Ashley and Chelsea were on either side of me. "We'll come help you make flyers," Chelsea volunteered.

"Okay with you?" Ashley asked.

I shrugged. "Sure, come on over."

"All right! Another alliteration affair," Chelsea announced.

I couldn't believe how good she was getting. "Wow, you've really caught on," I said.

"Amazingly well," Ashley said.

"So . . . watch out, Jon!" Chelsea said with thumbs up. "I'm ready to take you on."

Ashley grinned. "Hey, that rhymed."

"Shh! There he is," I whispered, pointing to a group of guys spilling into the courtyard.

Chelsea's face dropped. "I hope he didn't hear me."

"Let's not take any chances," I said.

"Meaning?" said Chelsea.

"I think we'd better split," I suggested, waving to the girls. "Call me about this afternoon."

They glanced over their shoulders at Jon and then grinned back at me.

Yee-ikes! I rushed to the parking lot. My parents were waiting in the car, windows down.

"Sorry," I muttered. "Got tied up talking."

"No problem," Dad said with a smile and started the car.

As he drove home, I leaned back against the seat, gazing at the cloudless sky and replaying the weird exchange between Chelsea and me.

After all these months, I still hadn't figured things out. Why did I have to get so mixed-up just talking about Jon Klein? Especially when I couldn't care less.

Not only did we make flyers, my girl friends and I, we tromped all over the SummerHill area that Sunday afternoon, searching the bushes and asking neighbors if they'd seen Abednego.

Chelsea came up with the catchiest wording for our flyers. *Missing: a fussy, fat black feline—an amazing animal named Abednego*, it read. *Please contact Merry Hanson (owner), corner of Strawberry and SummerHill Lanes.*

The flyer was far better than anything I could've come up with—probably because my brain wasn't functioning up to par. I was too caught up in the loss of my beloved pet. Sadly, the chances of finding him seemed more dismal with every passing hour.

I'd even cried myself to sleep the night of Dad's retirement party, wishing the storm had never happened. Wishing something else, too—that Abednego wasn't such an exasperating pet, forever running off. Anguished, I'd stared hard at the long wall near my bed, unable in the dark to make out the mini gallery of my own framed photography. Several pictures featured Shadrach, Meshach, and Abednego—my very first, and oldest, cats. Lily White had come into my life one year ago this month, so she was still the baby of the bunch.

"Where's your head, Merry?" called Ashley from across SummerHill Lane.

I snapped back to attention. "Uh, sorry, guess I was just daydreaming . . . about Abednego."

Unknowingly, I'd stopped at a quaint little springhouse off the side of the road. It was the most serene place, almost like a playhouse made of old hand-hewn stone. Delicate willows draped their branches low, creating a leafy green-fringed frame. The ideal setting for a country picture.

Ashley came running, followed by Chelsea and Lissa. "We have another idea," she said.

I was ready for a new approach . . . anything! We'd knocked on every neighbor's door within a one-mile radius. No one had seen Abednego. Not a single soul.

Ashley's hair was pulled back in a long ponytail, and her face shone with this most recent brainstorm. "Your neighbor is Old Hawk Eyes, right?"

"What about her?" I asked.

She paused, as if rethinking what she was about to say. Chelsea and Lissa hung on, waiting for Ashley's idea. "So . . . spill it out," Chelsea said.

Ashley took a dramatic deep breath. "Have you ever come right out and asked Miss Spindler how she keeps track of everyone?"

"Well, no," I answered. "She's a very private person. Seems a bit nosy, if you know what I mean . . . but . . . why do you ask?"

We all looked at Ashley, waiting for her response.

Ashley raised one eyebrow in a questioning slant. "Well, I just thought the old lady might be able to find out where your cat is, that's all."

Chelsea chuckled. "Yeah, she does seem to know the most intimate details about nearly everyone around here."

I nodded. "You can say that again."

."So what do you think?" Ashley said, eyes eager. "Why don't you ask her how she keeps tabs on things?"

I gave her a sideways glance. "Well, I've thought of doing that but never followed through."

"Why not?" asked Chelsea.

"Because it's like asking her to let me in on a big secret." I sighed, frustrated. "How *does* she spy on all of us?"

All three girls shrugged—nobody knew for sure. Quiet now, we began to walk back up SummerHill Lane. The sky was filling up with fluffy white cloud balls, reminding me of cats. Lots of beautiful alabaster cats.

Ashley got the Miss Spindler question rolling again. "You *did* ask her to keep an eye out for Abednego, right?"

"I sure did. In fact, Old Hawk Eyes' home was the first place I went during the storm."

That seemed to satisfy her, and we set out for my house. On the way, I glanced at my watch. "If we hurry, there might still be a few chocolate chip cookies left," I said. "My mom made a big batch yesterday after Dad's retirement party."

The prospect of homemade cookies made us pick up our pace, and we scurried past one Amish farm after another. Today was an off Sunday for the SummerHill Old Order church district, so lots of Plain folk were out visiting relatives and friends—the reason for the many buggies clattering up and down the road.

"Do you ever get tired of meeting up with the Amish?" asked Lissa.

"On the road, you mean?" I studied her, trying to figure out what she was really asking.

"Well, you know." She was clamming up on me.

"No, I don't," I replied. "Spell it out."

She shook her head, recoiling like she'd been hit.

"Look, Lissa. I can't read your mind. How can I know what you're thinking if you don't explain?" I asked gently. She'd suffered years of abuse at the hands of her father, and although he was taking therapy seriously and steadily improving, she still showed the emotional scars of a girl who'd been through the mill, so to speak.

She shook her head. "It's not important," she insisted.

"Yes, it *is* if you said it," Chelsea spoke up.

Ashley was nodding her head, encouraging Lissa to continue.

It looked as if we'd have to drag the question out of her. Finally, after repeated pleas, she told us what she'd meant to say all along. "I'm curious about Levi Zook—his coming home for college break and all," she said.

I bristled at the comment. "If you're asking how I feel about him, I'm cool with our relationship," I confessed. "That's all I'm saying."

Chelsea ran her fingers through her hair. "But isn't Levi, like, in love with you or something?" As soon as she realized what she'd let slip, Chelsea covered her mouth, her eyes wide. "Oh . . . I'm sorry, Mer, I shouldn't have said anything."

I laughed it off. Had to. If I made too big a deal of it, she—*all* of them—would get the wrong idea. So I simply said, "Levi's a dear."

"And what about Jon? He's a dear, too, right?" Ashley piped up.

That got Lissa and Chelsea laughing. I joined in, hoping none of them would notice my cheeks growing warmer by the second. Truth was, I liked both boys, in spite of the pain Jon had put me through in the past. But as far as I was concerned, there was no rush to choose either one.

"Does Rachel Zook ever talk about Jon to you?" Chelsea asked, which surprised me to no end.

"Never," I said. "After all, she's got a beau."

"Is a beau what I think it is?" asked Chelsea.

"Yep, and his name's Matthew Yoder. I wouldn't be surprised if she ends up marrying him in a year or two."

The girls fell silent, and for the first time since we left the house, I heard birds singing.

"Rachel's pretty young to be thinking about settling down with a husband, but that's the way Amish do things. The younger you're married, the more children you'll be able to have," I explained.

"So . . . if you married Levi, would you have a whole houseful of kids, like the Amish?" Lissa asked.

I felt my cheeks blushing. "Do we *have* to discuss this?"

"C'mon, Merry," Ashley spoke up. "Don't avoid the question. You know you're fond of Levi."

Fond? Where'd she ever get that idea? I wondered.

"Well, I can see this conversation is way out of hand," I told my friends. "Let's talk about someone else's romantic interests for a change."

Ashley's eyes darted away from my gaze, and Chelsea flung her long, thick hair to one side without saying a word. Lissa, on the other hand, just pursed her lips, trying not to smile.

Glancing down the road, I noticed Abe and Esther Zook pulling out of their dirt lane, the boxlike gray carriage filled with children. Rachel was along, too.

"Look, there's your future mode of transportation," Lissa informed me with a stifled snicker. "If you marry an Amishman, that is."

It was high time to set them straight, once and for all. "Levi is no longer Amish," I said. "In fact, he never took the baptismal vow to join his parents' church. He's Mennonite now, studying to be a preacher at Bible school."

"Oh" was all Lissa said.

"Case closed," I said, waving to the Zooks as their horse and buggy approached us.

Ashley ignored my comment. "What's Jon Klein want to be?"

"You mean when he grows up?" added Lissa.

381

I shook my head in playful disgust. "You three are every bit as mischievous as my wayward cat."

Chelsea clutched her throat. "Oh, tell me it isn't so!"

We burst into giggles and ran to my house.

At first I thought it was my lost cat jumping onto my bed, but then my bedroom burst to life with the early morning rays of the sun. Another too-real dream. One of many.

Mom called for me to "rise and shine" from her end of the hall. "Day's a-wasting," she added.

"I'm getting up!" Sliding out from under the lightweight blanket, I let my legs dangle off the side of the bed.

Shadrach, Meshach, and Lily White remained asleep, all three of them curled up tight against the dawn.

"Maybe today's the day Abednego comes home," I said, hoping it would be true.

Meow. Shadrach was all ears. And Meshach and Lily White leaped off the bed, stretched, and padded into the walk-in closet with me.

"You're truly lonely for Abednego, aren't you?" I whispered to my cat trio. "Well, I'm not giving up, so don't you worry your furry heads, okay?"

Lily White rubbed against my bedroom slipper, and Meshach hung around like he hardly knew what to do with himself. Shadrach waited, intense eyes blinking only occasionally.

"Count on me to find him," I promised. But I had no idea what my next move would be. Abednego had already been gone for two days.

Meshach seemed terribly insecure and followed me to the bathroom door. "This is where I draw the line," I said, picking him up and kissing his soft, warm head. "I take showers *alone*."

Meow. It was as if he was pleading to be with me, and the sad expression on his face broke my heart anew. "We'll talk this afternoon when I get home from school," I told him.

I knew we wouldn't have much time to "talk"—Meshach and I—because as soon as the school bus dropped me off, I'd have to get myself packed and head over to Miss Spindler's.

In the shower, all I could think of was Abednego, possibly struck by lightning or drowned . . . or maybe only half alive.

———

Downstairs, Mom had something akin to a royal feast prepared for breakfast. It was her typical Saturday morning brunch fare, except today was Monday. She'd gone to lots of trouble to cook up her favorite recipes because she and Dad were leaving for Costa Rica this afternoon.

"I want this to be a breakfast to remember," Mom declared as she served up little pancakes, cheese omelets with onions and green peppers, German sausage, and French toast with powdered sugar and maple syrup.

"You outdid yourself," I said, placing my napkin in my lap.

Dad raised his eyebrows. "Better be thankful, kiddo," he said. "I doubt Miss Spindler will come close to spoiling you like this."

I nodded, waiting for Mom to join us.

She dried her hands and then sat down, smiling across the table at me. "Ruby Spindler is an extraordinary cook, so I'm positive you won't go hungry."

Then I knew why Mom had chosen our eccentric neighbor to watch over me. She wanted someone to dote on me—look after me with meticulous care. "Oh, Mom, for pete's sake. Miss Spindler doesn't have to baby me." I was laughing.

"Well, she'd better give it her best shot," Dad said, winking at me.

I bowed my head for the prayer, grateful to have such thoughtful parents. Dad gave thanks for the meal in his deep voice, and I knew I'd miss them. Even though they'd be gone only for six days.

Later, we hugged our good-byes. "Don't worry about me. I'll be just fine," I assured them. "And have a great trip."

Dad whispered in my ear, "Be kind to Old Hawk Eyes."

I giggled, trying not to distract Mom from her packing. Glancing at my watch, I grabbed my school bag and headed down the front stairs to the door. "My bus is coming," I called to them.

"Have a good day at school," Mom said from the top of the steps. "Remember to set the lamp timers before you leave for Miss Spindler's this afternoon."

"I'll remember."

"And take your cats along with you," Mom reminded.

"Naturally," I called up to her. Didn't she know I wouldn't leave my precious babies alone in an empty house?

I headed out the front door and down the steps, thinking again of Abednego. My emotions were hanging by a thread—I missed him that much. And when I spied Chelsea on the bus, we talked of my runaway cat from the time I sat down until we scrambled to our lockers.

"We'll find him, Mer," she said, trying to soothe me.

"I truly hope so." I opened my locker and rummaged through the chaos in the bottom. "Because if I don't . . ." I paused.

"If you don't . . . *what*?" She leaned over and gawked at me with those deep-set sea-green eyes of hers.

Tears welled up and began to spill down my cheeks. "Oh great. I'm losing it at school," I bawled.

Chelsea draped her arm over my shoulder, and we huddled there near the bottom shelf of my locker. "It'll be okay," she kept saying over and over.

I wished my emotions hadn't run away with me, because just then I heard a familiar male voice. Jon Klein's.

"Everything fine here?" he asked.

I gulped, wiping my eyes and taking a deep breath. Chelsea and I stood up together. "Hi, Jon," Chelsea said.

"You two look upset," he replied.

Chelsea nodded, glancing at me. "Have you ever lost something super significant?" she said—in alliteration-eze, no less.

Jon stepped back, blinking his brown eyes. "How significant are we talking?"

Chelsea waved him away. "Never mind, you wouldn't understand."

"Try me," he said, coming closer . . . looking at me.

I straightened up. "What Chelsea's trying to say is . . ." I stopped, thinking how it would sound to blurt out that I was mourning my lost cat, wondering how Jon would react.

So far, he was smiling. "Mistress Merry, make me marvel."

I couldn't believe it. He wanted to play the Alliteration Game—now!

"What letter?" I mumbled.

"*C*'s," he replied, shifting his books from one arm to the other.

"Okay, here goes." I took a deep breath and began. "My crazy cat commands constant care," I said.

Chelsea jumped in. "Merry's cunning cat can't catch cold . . . he's old."

I turned around to face her. "Hey, that rhymed—and with alliteration, too!"

Jon was grinning. Not at Chelsea, at me! "So . . . let me get this straight," he said. "Your cat's both suffering and absent?"

"In plain English, yes," I said.

"So sorry . . . sad story," Jon alliterated and rhymed.

"Hey, what's with this?" I asked. "Is this the expanded version of the word game?"

Jon shrugged, his eyes still on me. "Could be."

Just when I thought I might fall in love with him, standing there sounding so charming, the bell rang for first period.

"Later, ladies," he said, heading down the hall.

Chelsea was giggling into my locker. "Didn't I tell you, Mer? This is so incredible!"

I grabbed my three-ring binder. "Keep it to yourself," I told her. "No one, and I mean *no one*, needs to know."

"C'mon! Jon likes you and you like—"

"Don't say it!" I interrupted and rushed off to homeroom.

Right after school, Chelsea dragged me off to the bus stop, probably so I wouldn't end up alone with Jon. But since he rode the same bus we did, there wasn't any real way to avoid seeing him.

"What're you doing?" I whispered, pulling away from her at the curb.

"Trying to save you your share of heartache," she said.

"What's that supposed to mean?"

"You know." She motioned her head slightly toward the left of me.

"Jon?" I mouthed the word silently.

She nodded.

"Pretend we didn't see him," I whispered.

"Okay, quick! Open your English book."

But by that time, I could see Jon out of the corner of my eye. Still, I shuffled through my book, going along with her request.

No use. Jon came right up to us and stood next to me. His sleeve actually touched my arm. "So what's with the expanded word-game notion?" he asked.

I smiled, not saying a word.

"I'll take you on," he said.

Chelsea started howling. "You're kidding! You aim to alliterate *and* rhyme . . . at the same time?"

I nearly choked. Chelsea was too good at this. A natural.

"What's the good word, Mistress Merry?" Jon asked, smiling down at me.

I shrugged, closing my English book. "It'll pose problems— take plenty of practice, probably." I watched the school bus head our way. "But then, so did alliteration-eze at first."

"Too true," said Chelsea, grinning at me.

The bus doors swooshed open and we climbed on, one after the other, like three blind mice—three very smart ones.

It turned out that Jon sat in front of Chelsea and me, turning around to talk with us the whole way home. In no time, the three of us had decided the extended word game was a truly good challenge—the alliterated rhyme—but we hadn't decided what to call the game yet.

Strangely enough, I had a powerful feeling that Jon wanted this to be a special game—exclusive—between him and me. He never came right out and said it, of course, but it was the way he kept looking at me whenever we discussed it.

Chelsea, on the other hand, was having a great time observing the two of us. I was afraid she was reading too much into things, though. And I let her know so as we got off the bus at the willow grove, just down the hill from my house.

"Please don't get any ideas about Jon and me," I told her.

She was silent, her eyes twinkling.

"I'm not kidding, Chelsea!"

"What's not to get? I'm not totally dense. You're nuts for Jon—ditto for him."

I kicked a pebble, wishing for a different topic, anything but speculative talk about Jon Klein!

Chelsea kept babbling about how perfect he and I were together. I couldn't stand for her or anyone else declaring such things. That was my business and a very private matter, to say the least.

Finally we reached my house. Chelsea waved good-bye with a silly know-it-all grin, and I checked the mailbox. To tell the truth, I was glad for the solitude. Glad, too, that Chelsea hadn't asked to come in and help me pack. Miss Spindler would be waiting for me.

I thumbed through the stack of mail on the way up the walk. Hardly any bills or ads this time, but I noticed several pieces of personal mail. Two for Mom—one from Aunt Teri and the other from an old friend in the antiques business in Vermont. The third letter was from Levi Zook, addressed to me.

"Perfect timing," I muttered as I went around the house to the kitchen door.

My three remaining cats were waiting for me in the kitchen, near their bowl. Placing the unopened letter on the counter, I knelt down to stroke them.

"Ready for a snack?" I asked, which usually brought gleeful smiles.

But today all they wanted was my gentle touch. I fed them Kitty Kisses anyway, and they enjoyed the treat all the more because I sat on the kitchen floor with them.

"You guys are spoiled worse than rotten." I stroked Lily White, hoping she'd overlook my use of the male gender. "I love my prissy little lady, too," I said for her benefit.

While they ate, I stared at the envelope, high on the counter. Levi's letters had come fast and frequent right after his Christmas visit, but more recently they'd slowed down. *He's probably busy with his college work*, I thought.

I was busy, too. This last semester of school had been truly tough. Epecially the amount of homework—almost more than I could keep up with sometimes, even with Dad's voluntary assistance. Skip and everyone else had warned me that my first year in high school would be a big transition. I just hadn't expected it to last clear into spring.

There was only one full month of school left, and I could hardly wait for summer. But first things first. Tomorrow was my sixteenth-and-a-half birthday. Miss Spindler had no idea about it, but I was going to celebrate. Probably just me and my cats somewhere outside with my camera, a blue sky, and a sunny meadow filled with buttercups.

Then I thought of Abednego again. The pain of loss stabbed my heart. The worst of it was not knowing if he was dead or alive, sick or his robust self. *Where, oh where, can he be?* I wondered.

Meshach came over and nestled into my lap, taking up every inch of space. It was time for our talk.

"Your brother's out there somewhere," I assured him. "The Lord sees Abednego this very minute. I know He does." I sighed and continued. "If God can take care of an ordinary sparrow, He'll take care of our Abednego."

Meshach began licking his paws, and I knew my words, whether he understood or not, had calmed him.

Leaning back on my elbows, I stared at Levi's letter as Lily White rubbed against my arms. Shadrach curled up against my hip, nose to nose with Meshach. "Are we ready to stay with Auntie Hawk Eyes?"

At that, Lily White coughed hard and spit up a furball. I couldn't help myself; I started laughing. It almost sounded like Shadrach and Meshach were chortling a bit, too.

The phone rang in the middle of our hilarity. Gently, I lifted Meshach off my lap. "Sorry," I said, getting up. I reached for the wall phone.

"How's every little thing, dearie?" It was Miss Spindler.

"Things are fine," I said, touching Levi's letter. "I just got home from school and gave my cats a snack."

"Aw, the darlings," she cooed.

"Yes, they're pretty excited about coming to see you," I told her. I didn't say my cats were wildly anticipating the prospect of sampling *her* assortment of mice.

"Well, you come on over whenever you're ready, hear?"

I glanced at the wall clock. "Give me about an hour."

"That's right fine," she said.

I hung up the phone and picked up the letter, taking it to the privacy of my bedroom. Of course, there was no need, really. The house was void of humans.

Still, I sat on my bed, surrounding myself with plenty of huggable pillows. When I was completely settled, I opened the letter and began to read.

Dear Merry,

I hope you're enjoying the warm springtime weather there in SummerHill. Surely the farmers are busy plowing these days. Sometimes I miss farming and working with God's fertile soil. Now I'm tilling a different kind of soil and sowing the seeds of the Word. I've never been so happy, Merry. Coming here to Bible college was the best thing I ever set out to do.

The last time I phoned you, I said I'd be home for my Easter break, but just this week I've decided differently. Something's come up, and after much fervent prayer, I believe that my staying here is the Lord's will.

As for this summer, I will be taking more classes but hope to get home for a quick visit with my family, maybe around the Fourth of July. I'll look forward to seeing you then.

Meanwhile, please greet your mother and father for me.

Your friend,
Levi

I folded the letter, staring out the window. Levi was right about plowing season, all right. The days had been warm, accompanied by frequent afternoon showers. Perfect for enticing Amish farmers and their mules out at the crack of dawn. Hyacinths and daffodils were blooming everywhere, including those in my mom's flower beds.

Getting up, I went to my desk and opened the center drawer. *Your friend,* Levi had signed off this time.

I slid the letter into the drawer. Levi had found himself a new girlfriend. I was almost positive.

I suppose I should've reread his letter, double-checking my suspicions, but all I really needed to do was ask Rachel. She'd know, probably. At least, I guessed she would. But big brothers didn't *always* divulge their romantic game plans to younger sisters. Firsthand, I knew that to be true.

Sighing, I gathered up my school clothes for the next three days, as well as my pajamas, robe, and my camera. Even though I tried not to let the news from Levi sadden me, I felt nearly hollow inside when I coupled the news with the loss of Abednego.

"When it rains it pours," I spouted into my closet. "Why'd he have to go and do this now?" But the more I thought about it, the more I realized I preferred the letter over having Levi call me, stuttering around, trying to explain why he wasn't coming home this week.

Still, it hurt. And I was honestly glad to be going to Miss Spindler's. Too bad her lookout room or telescope, or whatever, couldn't see clear out to Virginia, to a Mennonite Bible college . . . and to Levi Zook.

Nine *Windows on the Hill*

Miss Spindler was humming to her vegetable garden in the side yard as I hauled my suitcase up Strawberry Lane. Followed by my three devoted cats, I saw—on further observation—that she had every right to be truly captivated by her prim rows of onions and radishes.

"Another green spring day in SummerHill," I said when she spotted me and my parade of pets.

"My, oh my, there you are." She smiled, eyeing the cats. "And those furball critters of yours."

"We're all here, except Abednego," I said, hoping she wouldn't change her mind about the cats staying.

She shook her head. "The poor thing hasn't shown up?"

"Not yet," I said, glancing down at my cats. "But I haven't given up hope."

"We can only hope he's safe somewhere," she said. "Let's go inside and get you settled, dearie." She turned and marched up to the back stoop and opened the door. "We'll have some right good fun, I say."

I smiled, calling for the cats to follow.

Indoors, the kitchen smelled of delectable things, and I thought of Mom's wish for me to be well taken care of while she and Dad were out of the country. There were several pies laid out on a sideboard near the round dining room table.

Through the doorway, I could see the old-fashioned parlor, overflowing with quaint furniture from the past—fringed shades on tall floor lamps, a black steamer trunk doubling as a coffee table, and an old pump organ. Overstuffed chairs and a large sofa were draped with white sheets, as if someone were remodeling. The formal living room had remained exactly the same since I'd first seen this house at age five, when my twin sister and I would visit for tea and apple pie with Mom.

"Well, come along, now. I'll show you to your room, Merry."

I followed Miss Spindler up the steps to the second floor, keeping my eyes peeled for any clues about her spy tactics. Skip had asked for a full report, and I intended to give him the scoop. That is, if I could just steal away to the attic unattended.

"This is the guest room," said Miss Spindler, showing me into a spacious, wide room complete with a fireplace and two large dormer windows.

"What a pretty place," I said, spotting the lavender-and-blue Amish Spring Flower quilt pattern, probably made by Esther Zook and her relatives.

Miss Spindler's face was aglow with pleasure. I could see she was thrilled to have me and my cats share her home, if only for a few days. "It's not many who come stay with me," she explained, frowning slightly. "Oh, I have my friends—a good many, too—but not much overnight company anymore."

"Thank you for having me," I said politely.

She showed me where there were extra hangers in the closet for my clothes. "There're empty drawers in the dresser, too," she said, sliding them out to show me, one after another.

"You've gone to too much trouble." I put my suitcase down.

"No . . . no, I always keep drawers empty, just a-waiting for folks. Don'tcha worry none about that." She smiled broadly, showing her teeth briefly—for a moment I thought she was going to hug me, too. But she came close and picked up my suitcase, carrying it over to the closet. She pulled out a foldable rack and placed my suitcase on top. "There you be, dearie."

Again I said, "Thanks," and began unpacking while she tiptoed away. I waited till her footsteps faded, then I slipped out of the room. Glancing around the hallway and second-floor landing, I wondered where the attic steps might be located. But I didn't feel comfortable heading off to do serious snooping just yet. I had to unpack first and then get the lay of the land, so to speak. Besides, my cats were antsy. I wouldn't risk having one of them interfere with my scheme to investigate Old Hawk Eyes' attic. Still, I was prickle-skinned with expectation.

Miss Spindler's supper went far beyond delicious. Her Waldorf salad, homemade rolls, and chicken and dumplings were topped off with two kinds of pie—Dutch apple and cherry, with vanilla ice cream.

I chose the apple, and she warmed it up ever so slightly, enough to make the scoop of ice cream slide off the side.

When we were finished eating, Miss Spindler seemed altogether pleased with herself. "Well, looks like we ate for clear weather, didn't we," she said, clucking.

Carrying my dishes over to the sink, I offered to help. "Why don't you sit down and I'll clean up."

She waved her hand at me as though shooing a fly. "Aw, dearie, I'm sure you have something better to do—like homework or whatnot."

"I finished my homework in study hall."

"Well, what about that there retirement scrapbook your mama told me about? What about working on *that* tonight?" she said.

I'd brought along prints of the best pictures, all right, but I still wanted to do my fair share in the kitchen. And I told her so.

"Nonsense." Her blue-gray bob shimmered under the sink light. "While you're here, you're my guest." She flashed a smile at me. "I want you to come again sometime, you know."

I nodded, feeling at a loss for words. The old woman was bullheaded, that was for certain. She got something set in her mind and nobody but nobody was going to persuade her differently.

"If I can't help tonight, what about breakfast?" I offered. "You'd be surprised what a good cook I am—and even better at cleaning up!"

She nodded her petite head up and down as she stooped over the deep, two-sided sink. "Nothin' doing," she protested, and the finality of her words was clear. She was standing her ground. Old Hawk Eyes was like a thick-shelled Brazil nut—too tough to crack.

I wondered how tough it would be to find her attic and see for myself what was going on up there.

It turned out that I did work on Dad's scrapbook a while, and after about an hour of that, Miss Spindler and I played a rousing game of checkers. Not that she was so much better than I—she was just so shrewd and cautious of every move.

At last, it was bedtime. I knelt beside the bed and prayed for my parents and the building project in South Central America. I prayed for Levi, too, but only in passing. It was hard to focus in on someone I'd cared so much about, knowing his feelings were changing toward me, or already had.

Jon Klein showed up in my nighttime requests, but I only asked the Lord to help me not freak out so much in front of him. Nothing else.

My concerns for Abednego concluded my prayers. "Please, Lord," I whispered into the darkness, "keep my big, old cat safe. Send someone along to find him if he's hurt—to take care of him until *I* can again. Thank you for hearing my prayer. Amen."

Windows on the Hill Ten

The next day dawned sparkling bright, and morning birds warbled to their hearts' content. First thing, I thought of Abednego and prayed that today he might find his way back home.

I got up early on purpose so I'd have time to stop in and visit Rachel Zook before heading off to the school. Miss Spindler didn't seem to understand why I wasn't all that hungry, so I told her where I was headed. I didn't tell her today was my midyear birthday, though. Most older folk don't understand that sort of thing. Guess they forget what it's like being a teenager. "Between twelve and twenty's a precarious spot," Dad had teased last September on my sixteenth birthday.

"I'll look after your cats for you," Miss Spindler called to me.

"Thanks, and keep an eye out for Abednego . . . just in case!" I hurried down over her sloping backyard, crisscrossing to my own, and stopped to check on the house. Searching under the gazebo first—and not finding him there—I continued looking everywhere, in the back and side yards, and around the front porch. But Abednego was nowhere to be seen.

Inside, I dashed to my room, thinking if he'd returned through the kitty door in the garage, he might be curled up on my bed, fast asleep.

"Kitty, kitty, are you here?" I called, going from room to room upstairs.

In my parents' bedroom, I noticed the narrow door leading to the attic steps was ajar. Quickly, I closed it without thinking anything about it.

Not till later.

I was on my way to Rachel Zook's house, cutting through the willow grove, when it dawned on me where to look for Miss Spindler's attic steps. In her bedroom, of course.

But how would I get there without being caught?

Dismissing the discouraging thought, I ran across the open meadow, over the white wooden fence, through the pasture-land, and down the side yard, to the barn. There I found Rachel cleaning up from the morning's milking.

She seemed surprised to see me. "Cousin Merry! What're *you* doin' over here so early?"

I had to laugh every time I heard her refer to me that way—as a cousin. But it was absolutely true, in a distant sort of way, at least. We had traced our roots back to common ancestors. Sure enough, we *were* cousins.

Looking around, I felt uneasy now that I was here. What would Rachel think if I inquired after Levi this morning, clear out of the blue?

I went up close to her, glancing this way and that, making sure no one was around. "Have you heard from Levi?" I asked hesitantly.

"Jah, we had a letter from him yesterday," my friend replied.

"So he must've told you that he's staying in Virginia this week?" I phrased my question carefully. I didn't want to come right out and state anything too presumptuous.

She kept her head turned, facing the cow. "S'pose he's too busy to bother with us during his school break," she said.

I didn't comment on her reply, and it was probably a good thing because in walked young Aaron with his father. Rachel surely must've sensed that I didn't want to discuss Levi with her father and younger brother in such close proximity, pitching hay to the mules a few yards away.

Thank goodness she didn't expect me to help sweep out the barn. I was already showered and dressed for school. There'd be no time to run back to Miss Spindler's and change before the bus lumbered down SummerHill Lane if I did happen to get my clothes dirty.

I checked my watch. Plenty of time left to chat with my Amish friend, but this wasn't a private enough atmosphere for it.

"What're you doing this afternoon?" I whispered to Rachel.

"Weedin' our Charity Garden, probably," she said. "Wanna help?"

I considered her invitation, but what I really wanted to do was go explore a meadow of yellow-faced daisies or maybe ride my bike over to the sun-dappled trees surrounding the springhouse a mile or more down the road. "It's . . . well, sort of a special day for me," I said, dawdling.

She grinned back, and her blue eyes lit up. "Jah, I know."

"You do?"

"It's April twenty-second, right?" she said, wiping her hands on her long gray apron.

"Uh-huh."

"So then ya must be turnin' sixteen-and-a-half," she said, as if she'd known all along.

"That's right."

She gave me a quick hug. "We oughta do somethin' right nice, Cousin Merry. A wonderful-gut walk in the woods or whatever you say."

I had to smile. Rachel knew me almost as well as Faithie had.

"Are you sure you won't be missed in your garden?" I asked, not wanting to take her away from chores.

"Ach, I can weed after lunch. You just come on over after school's out. We'll have us a nice time together."

We walked outside into the sunlight. "Thanks for being such a good friend, Rachel," I said, giving her another hug.

"Is Abednego back?" she asked suddenly.

I shook my head. "Not yet . . . but soon."

She frowned, her blue eyes more serious now. "Shall we go searching for your cat today?"

"My school friends and I spent Sunday afternoon combing the area. Nobody's seen him anywhere," I told her.

"He's probably out having himself a mouse-eating party," she said with a hopeful grin. "Jah, maybe we'll find Abednego today."

"That would be a good half-birthday present." I had to laugh because it was so true.

"Well, happy half birthday," she said, grinning at me.

"See you after a bit," I called, running down the Zooks' dirt lane to the road.

My heart thumped *Jon Klein, Jon Klein* ninety miles an hour as I headed down the crowded school hallway. I couldn't figure out what was causing me to feel this way. Chelsea was absolutely right—saying that Jon and I had been through a lot together. Mostly rough times. He'd hurt me by flirting with both Lissa and Ashley over the past eighteen months—even Rachel Zook, last February. Still, that was two months ago already.

I sighed. Guess it was time to relinquish my grudge, if that's what it was. But I was worried. Could I really and truly trust the Alliteration Wizard?

"Merry, you're right on time," Jon said, waiting for me at my locker.

"What's up?" I asked, willing my heart to slow its pace.

"The game . . . the new one, remember?" His light brown hair was combed neatly, and I spied the gold flecks in his eyes. Funny, he was getting more handsome every time I saw him.

I remembered the game, all right. "I doubt I'll be able to hold my own," I said. "Creating alliterated *and* rhyming phrases all in the same breath, well . . . I don't know. Maybe Chelsea and you should try."

He was shaking his head slowly, eyes fixed on me. "I'm asking *you*, Merry."

It seemed strange not hearing his alliterated nickname for me—Mistress of Mirth or Mistress Merry. But there was something truly sweet about the way he'd said my name without fuss and frills.

The bell for homeroom rang before we could continue. In a way, I was glad. Mainly because I hadn't fully decided if I was up to the task. Alliteration-eze was one thing, but this rhyming idea . . . well, I didn't know for sure.

I asked Chelsea about it in algebra, and she was all smiles. "Let's go for it. I'm up for the challenge," she said, choosing the seat next to me.

"Maybe it's *your* thing," I said. "Yours and Jon's."

"Oh, Mer, how can you say that? You're the one who's the *real* wit around here." She opened her notebook. "I'm only the tagalong."

I wanted to debate her comment, but the teacher stood up and began discussing our homework assignment from yesterday.

Word Game Plus would have to wait.

If Jon hadn't seemed so interested in getting me involved, I might've blown the whole thing off. Let Chelsea and Jon have their fun. But I knew by the look in Jon's eyes, he wanted me to participate. To tell the truth, though, I was more interested in digging up clues in Old Hawk Eyes' attic than dreaming up another word game.

"Give me some sleuthing ideas," I said to Chelsea as we waited for the bus after school.

"What kind of sleuthing are we talking?" Her eyes were wide with intrigue.

I hadn't wanted to completely divulge my plan to snoop in Miss Spindler's attic. Skip's knowing was enough of a risk.

"Okay, Mer, level with me. What're you planning over at Old Hawk Eyes'?" asked Chelsea.

"Well . . ." I looked around to see if Jon or anyone else might be around to hear. "It's time someone found out the truth."

Her eyebrows jerked up. "The truth about what?"

"About . . . *you know*." I began to whisper. "How Ruby Spindler does it—spying on everyone."

She shrugged her shoulders and sighed. "Oh that."

"Yes, *that*!"

Her eyes narrowed and she peeked at me with an inquisitive gaze. "I'd say you're extremely caught up in this."

"Too caught up? I'm a human being, for pete's sake!"

"A too-curious one, I'd say." Chelsea glanced over her shoulder. "I wonder what Jon would say about this idea of yours."

I pulled on her arm, yanking her back. "Don't tell him or anyone else, you hear?"

She started cackling. "Man, you sound as backwoodsy as Old Hawk Eyes herself. Rachel Zook, too."

Something rose up in me. It was one thing to poke fun at my elderly, eccentric neighbor. It was quite another to belittle my Old Order Amish girl friend—one of the dearest and closest friends of my life.

"Rachel is who she is, and that has nothing to do with being backward or woodsy."

Chelsea stepped back slightly. "Well, aren't we the defensive one."

More than anything, I wished we weren't having this tiff. It was ridiculous, really, especially since months had passed since Chelsea had abandoned atheism and started reading the Bible, even regularly attending Sunday school and church with me. What was going on between us at the moment was entirely unnecessary. Yet I had no idea why she was being so sarcastic.

"I didn't mean for us to fuss," I said softly.

The bus pulled to a stop, and we boarded without further comment. Chelsea slid into our usual seat and stared out the window.

We rode along, not speaking for several miles. Then she turned to me and said, "I don't know what got into me, Merry. I'm not the least bit jealous of Rachel. Honest, I'm not."

"You don't have any reason to be," I replied.

She shook her head and then answered my original question at last. "Seems to me you ought to be able to distract Miss Spindler somehow."

"Like how?"

"What do you want to investigate?" she asked me point-blank.

"Her attic."

"Good idea."

I smiled.

"Maybe someone should give her a call, divert her attention, you know. Get her out of the house," Chelsea commented.

"I thought of that."

She stacked up her pile of books neatly. "But you simply can't get caught . . . that's the main thing."

"You're right. You want to give her a call sometime?" I asked, wondering what she'd say.

"Maybe." Chelsea had a faraway look in her eyes. "What I'd give to check out her attic with you."

"You're kidding. Really?"

She was nodding and grinning.

"Here's what I'll do," I said, thrilled we were seeing eye-to-eye again. "I'll take pictures—lots of them, okay?"

"Great idea!" Chelsea was delighted.

"Aren't you glad I'm a world-class photographer?" I joked.

"Very glad . . . *silly.*"

We stood up for our bus stop, and with a fleeting look out the window, I saw Rachel Zook weeding her mother's flower garden. All of a sudden, I could hardly wait to run away to a beautiful, private setting; I wanted to celebrate the midway point between sixteen and seventeen with my longtime Amish friend.

But first things first. I had an attic to attend to. And an old lady to visit with, as well.

Sure enough, Miss Spindler was waiting for me at her back door. "How's every little thing today?" she asked.

"School was fine."

"Easy too?"

I had to think about that. "History and math weren't very easy," I admitted. "But most all my other subjects were." I didn't go on to say that socializing in the hall with a certain person wasn't all that easy, either.

"Any sign of Abednego?" I asked, hoping she had seen my funny feline.

"I thought you'd be asking about him," she said, a quizzical smile spreading over her wrinkled face. "So I done put my feelers out all over."

Feelers?

"What'd you do?" I asked, dying to know how she pried into the affairs of the world of SummerHill.

"Trust me, dearie. I'm doing my dead-level best to find that there kitty cat of yours." She clammed up after that—went right over and opened her fridge. I figured there was no point in pushing the question.

Shadrach, Meshach, and Lily White were excited to see me, but not so eager that they didn't make a beeline to their milk dish after a few friendly comments and strokes.

On the table, a plate of peanut butter cookies and a tall, cold glass of milk awaited me. "You're gonna spoil me, Miss Spindler," I said, sitting down.

She smiled, making even more lines in her ancient face. "There, there, dearie," she said. "You've been studying your heart out all day at school, now, haven't you?" She didn't wait for me to answer. "You deserve a nice treat, I daresay."

"Thank you," I said, remembering my manners as I chose a cookie from the offered plate. "Mm-m, they're still warm."

She nodded silently, her eyes glistening. I wondered how lonely she was, living in this big house by herself.

"Ever think about getting a pet to keep you company?" I asked between mouthwatering bites.

"A pet? Well, my, oh my, I haven't ever thought of such a thing."

"The Zooks have some new kittens to give away," I mentioned.

She leaned her bony elbow on the table, looking into my eyes. "Now, what on earth would an old lady like me do with a couple of frisky kittens?"

"Maybe you could start with one and see how you like it," I suggested, taking another cookie.

She sighed, gazing at my three cats having a snack of their own. "Well, I suppose it might be a good idea. Just don't rightly know where I'd put the dear thing."

"Cats like to wander the house," I told her. "They need plenty of roaming room. You have a two-story house . . . and an attic, too, right?"

She nodded, oblivious to my sneaky statement. "My attic's off limits to a cat, I'm afraid."

My ears perked right up. "Oh, why's that?"

Her eyebrows arched high over her eyes. "Well, now, a lady oughta have herself some privacy in a house this size, don'tcha think?"

Surprised that she'd nearly come out and admitted to having a hideaway for meddling, I thought it best to drop the subject. Didn't want her to think I was prying, especially about something of great interest to me.

I thanked her for the after-school treat before heading upstairs to change clothes for the afternoon.

"Tomorrow we'll have oatmeal and raisin cookies," she spoke up quickly.

"You don't have to bake a new batch just for me." I felt uneasy about her going out of her way for me. After all, she was no spring chicken.

"I'd be downright honored," she insisted.

So I left it at that.

On the way to my room, I took time to locate Miss Spindler's large bedroom. Stepping inside the doorway, I scanned the room briefly until I heard her rickety voice from below.

"Merry, dearie, I forgot to tell you that your parents phoned this morning after you left for school."

"They must be in Costa Rica . . . safe and sound?" I called, leaving her bedroom.

"They wanted you to know," she answered, her footsteps on the stairs.

Worried that I was about to be caught, I turned and fled to my room.

Twelve *Windows on the Hill*

The meadow near the banks of Deer Creek was the perfect spot to spend the rest of the afternoon. That is, *after* we went scouring the bushes and underbrush in the willow grove for Abednego.

When we didn't find him there, we headed out to the highway, way at the east end of SummerHill Lane. He must have run far away to escape the lightning bolts and the crashing thunder.

"Maybe Abednego thought the noise and the lightning was coming from near the house," I told Rachel, wondering what might've been going through his furry head during the storm.

"Jah, maybe," Rachel said, out of breath.

We walked back toward her house and then cut across the north pasture to the meadow. There we sat in the tall grasses, encircled by golden buttercups and white and yellow daisies. We watched a pair of swallows flitter and dive after insects in flight.

"Has anyone ever seen Old Hawk Eyes' attic?" I asked, shielding my eyes from the light of the sun.

Rachel played with the strings on her prayer cap and shook her head. "Nobody seems to know a thing about how she keeps up with all that gossip of hers."

"It's like she's connected somehow," I said, letting myself fall back in the grass. "She just knows so much . . . about all of us."

"Jah, plugged in to the gossip line, I'd hafta say."

We talked about what it would be like for us to turn seventeen next fall and how much Rachel enjoyed going to barn singings on weekends.

"How's Matthew Yoder these days?" I asked, staring up at her silhouette blocking the sun.

She giggled and her cheeks turned crimson. "Ach, ya ain't s'posed to be askin' that sort of thing, Merry."

"So you *do* still like him?"

"Matthew's the beau for me," she said softly. "We'll be going to baptismal classes together come July. It's very important."

"Does this mean what I think it means?" I asked, anxious to know if she'd be joining the Amish church this year.

"I'm planning my future, jah. It's what's expected of me, I s'pose." She leaned back in the grass next to me, her cap askew.

"Then, you're not sure if it's the right thing . . . is that what you're saying?" It was nosy of me, but I had to ask.

"If I want to be Matthew's wife someday, I'll join the church. It's the only way to marry an Amish boy."

I turned to face her, the grass tickling my neck. "Are you saying he's already proposed?"

"Sorry, Cousin Merry, you know our traditions about going for steady. It's always kept a secret till two weeks before the weddin'."

I smiled. "Can't fool me. You're practically engaged, and you know it!"

With that, she got up and ran across the meadow. I chased her, laughing like a young child as ribbons of sunbeams floated all around us.

Later, after we'd worn ourselves out, we sat with our bare feet splashing in the creek. It was then that I asked her about Levi. "I have this feeling, you know."

"Far as I know, he ain't got a new girlfriend," Rachel said. "But then again, I could be wrong. Things like that can happen so fast. Almost overnight, sometimes."

"I know, and that's okay . . . really it is."

She turned to me and reached to touch my hand. "It ain't okay, Cousin Merry, and you know it. Ach, not knowin' for sure is burning up your heart, and ya can't think of much else. Am I right?"

I didn't dare fess up. Not to Levi's sister, of all people.

She pulled her feet up out of the cool stream and dried them against the wild grass. "I was hopin' all along that someday you'd be my sister-in-law, ya know."

Any other time, I might've smiled at that. Pete's sake, I'd heard it enough times from her. But today I sat as still as the boulders along the creek bed, watching sunlight dance like teardrops on the water. "Someday's so far off when you're only sixteen," I whispered, still gazing at the little stars of light skipping and playing on the brook.

"You're sixteen and a half," she reminded me. "That's why we're here today . . . remember?" Picking up a pebble, she tossed it into the water.

"Caught between twelve and twenty," I muttered.

———

Before going to bed, I decided to write Levi a note.

April 22
Dear Levi,

Thanks for writing again. You must be very busy at school, so I understand if you can't write as often as before. I've been busy, too.

*I'm staying with Miss Spindler for a few days while my parents
are in Costa Rica. Remember, they talked about going during
MY Easter break? Anyway, it didn't work out, so they went this
week, and I would've gone with them—to take pictures, like
you suggested one time—but I couldn't miss that much school.
So here I am.*

*Skip's coming home on Thursday afternoon to stay with me till
Mom and Dad return on the weekend. My brother has a job near
his college campus, so even though he's on Easter break this week,
he's not getting much of a vacation from school, after all.*

*Today Rachel and I went looking for my ornery cat, Abed-
nego. He's the one who's always running off. Well, I don't know
for sure, but it seems he's not coming back this time, and I miss
him. Only the Lord knows where he is now.*

*Maybe I'll see you this summer. Take care, and God bless
you.*

Your friend,
Merry

I read what I'd written and realized the note had a stiff sort
of feel to it. I wondered if Levi would notice. I hadn't meant
to be standoffish toward him just because he wasn't coming
home as promised. I was shielding myself, I guess. Didn't want
to be hurt.

It wasn't long before Miss Spindler was calling me for supper. "Coming in a minute," I said, hoping to locate her attic
stairs before heading down.

Once inside her bedroom, I opened two doors,
both of which turned out to be closets. On the third
try—bull's-eye!

I was absolutely baffled by what I saw. My eyes roamed
up the steep beige *carpeted* steps. "Truly amazing," I
whispered.

It looked to me as if Miss Spindler's attic had been finished
in as pretty a style as the rest of her house. Tomorrow, without

fail, I would talk to Chelsea about setting up a time to phone Miss Spindler to occupy her time. I *had* to see this attic.

"Merry, dearie!" I was being paged.

Silently, I closed the attic door and hurried downstairs for supper.

Tomorrow!

Chelsea Davis was absent from school the next day. I realized she was probably sick when she wasn't on the school bus, seated and smiling in her usual spot.

Later, when I asked Ashley and Lissa about her, Ashley said she'd called and asked for prayer last night. "She had a high fever, she said. Her parents were getting ready to take her to the emergency room," Ashley explained.

My heart sank. "Did your dad pray with her on the phone?"

Ashley nodded, sporting a grin. "Daddy was quite thrilled to pray for her. And something else."

"What?" I asked.

"Chelsea called Daddy her pastor."

"Really?" I was truly excited about that but concerned about Chelsea's physical problems.

"Has anyone called to check on her this morning?" I asked.

Lissa looked at her watch. "I doubt that you have time to now."

I knew she was right. "Maybe during lunch."

The girls hurried off to their lockers just as I spied the Alliteration Wizard. Tall, lean, and relaxed, he strolled up to my locker. I honestly had to tell myself to cool it. He was only a guy, for pete's sake. Sure, he was an exceptionally good-looking one, but that was beside the point. There were oodles of cute boys at James Buchanan High. Still, why did my heart have to pound so hard when he came near?

"Mistress Merry," he said, greeting me with his usual nickname.

Funny, but I wished he'd revert back to calling me just plain Merry. Like yesterday.

We talked about Chelsea being sick and my lost cat. There was no mention made of his brain wave about alliterating and rhyming in one breath. I was actually relieved. It was enough to wonder where Abednego had gone and contemplate my next move with Miss Spindler and her attic—especially now that Chelsea wouldn't be able to distract her with a phone call—let alone ponder if I was up to the task of expanding my cerebellum by adding yet another facet to Jon Klein's word game.

"I wonder . . . could you do me a favor?" I blurted.

His gaze and smile made me almost forget what I was about to say. "Whatever you wish," he said.

"You've met Miss Spindler, right?"

He frowned, thinking. "Not really . . . not formally, at least."

I wondered if this was such a good idea, after all.

"What's the favor?" he prodded.

"Could you give her a call after school today?"

"Old Hawk Eyes?" He chuckled, reaching up and smoothing his hair back with one hand. "You want me to call an old woman I don't remember ever meeting?"

"Would you, *please*?"

"Only if you give me some ideas—you know, what I should say to her," he insisted.

I sighed. "Well, let's see. You could talk about her vegetable garden or . . . her need for a pet. That's it! Tell her you know of someone—that would be Rachel Zook—who has way too many cats. I've already put a bug in her ear about that. What do you think? Nice topic for conversation, right?"

He offered a slight smile. "I think you better tell me what this is about, Merry, because I have a feeling you're up to something."

Jon was absolutely right. So I told him what I planned to do while he kept Miss Spindler on the phone.

He shook his head, laughing. "You're going to be upstairs in her attic?"

"Uh-huh."

"Doing what?"

"Just spying a little."

He seemed interested. "Checking out her attic for what?"

The bell rang, and we had to conclude our talk.

"I'll fill you in at lunch," I promised.

He was still in a daze. I saw confusion in his eyes.

Then it hit me.

Oh great, I thought, *this is the dumbest thing I've ever done!*

It turned out that something must've come up for Jon over lunch hour, because he never showed up. I told Ashley and Lissa about my quick chat with Chelsea's mom before lunch. "Chelsea's really sick."

They listened, wide-eyed, as I filled them in. "Chelsea's got scarlet fever and won't be back to school for over a week."

"Scarlet fever?" Lissa gasped. "Don't people die from that?"

I tried to calm her down, explaining that back in the olden days people didn't have strong antibiotics to kill the virus.

"Hey, wait a minute," Ashley said, clutching her throat. "It's contagious . . . and haven't we been exposed to her?"

"You're right. Especially Sunday, when all of us went looking for Abednego together," I said, thinking back to whether Chelsea had complained of a sore throat or anything else. "The best thing to do if you've never had scarlet fever is get plenty of rest and drink lots of water," I told them what Chelsea's mom had just advised me over the phone. "And take extra vitamin C—that might help you, too."

My comments seemed to satisfy Ashley's concern. Lissa, however, was still frowning. "Someone will have to take Chelsea's homework to her, right?"

I shrugged it off. "I'll take it. I'm not afraid."

"You sure that's a good idea?" Ashley asked.

"I'll be fine. Don't worry." I meant it. "When I was little I had a mild case of scarlet fever."

"You remember?" Lissa asked.

"Barely, but yeah."

"Well, then, you're the girl for the job," Ashley said.

"Say that with all *j*'s," I dared her. But she didn't even try.

I excused myself and got up from the table. "Have to find where Jon's hiding out. He and I have something to settle." I didn't want to say more.

Lissa's eyes blinked ninety miles an hour. "Uh, really? Is this something *we* oughta know about?"

I brushed off her comment. Didn't need to let her in on my wild scheme. Maybe later, but not now.

"Are you and Jon getting . . . you know, back together?" Lissa asked out of the blue.

I almost choked. "We were never 'together' in the first place." *Except in my heart*, I thought.

"But you and he—"

"Nope, we were always just friends." I paused, remembering the days when he and I were strictly alliteration buddies. Back before anyone else knew about the word game. "Just good friends," I repeated.

"So then, what's the big secret?" Ashley came right out and asked.

I debated whether to divulge my plan. Students all around us were eating and chattering, some laughing and making jokes at their tables, others cramming for tests—spreading homework out in front of them.

"Merry?" said Lissa. "Does it have something to do with Miss Spindler?"

I couldn't hold it in another second. "You're right. It's about Old Hawk Eyes . . . and her attic."

"How does Jon fit in?" Ashley asked, reaching for her soda.

"Very carefully" was all I would say.

"Aw, tell us," Ashley persisted.

"Gotta run," I said, leaving the table, their pleadings ringing in my ears.

Fourteen *Windows on the Hill*

After school, I took Chelsea's homework assignment to her house and gave it to her mother at the door. It was good to see Mrs. Davis looking so fit and perky, her cheeks rosy and eyes bright again. She'd been through quite an ordeal last fall, and I knew God had answered many prayers.

"Thank you, Merry," she said. "I'll be sure to tell Chelsea you dropped by."

"Give her this, too." I held out a get-well card I'd made during study hall. "It's from Ashley, Lissa, and me."

"How sweet of you. You're very kind."

I waved and headed down the front steps to the road. Running down SummerHill Lane was easy from Chelsea's house to mine. It was the steep slope that turned left at Strawberry Lane that took the wind out of me.

At precisely 4:15 the phone rang at Miss Spindler's. I held my breath, leaning over the banister upstairs, listening.

"This is Ruby Spindler," I heard her answer the telephone. Then, for the longest time, there was silence on her end.

Johnny-on-the-spot, I dashed to her bedroom and checked the caller ID on the bedside phone table. Sure enough, Jon Klein had come through for me, exactly as we'd secretly concocted at my locker after school.

Cupping my hand over my mouth, I held in the giggle that threatened to spill out. Quickly and quietly, I approached the door that led to the attic, thinking that I'd love to know what Jon was saying right now! Was he showing off his alliteration-eze for her?

Once I was on the other side of the door with my foot on the first step, I turned and closed the door behind me. Silent as springtime.

Then, climbing the stairs two at a time, I sprang up into the attic, taking in the wood-paneled walls, finished ceiling, and flecked beige carpet.

What I saw at the top of the steps, I'd never have believed in a million years if I wasn't seeing it with my own eyes. This was an old lady's attic, for pete's sake!

I looked around, amazed. Here was a room high in the eaves, completely set up as an office, with built-in oak cupboards and a wide computer desk.

"A computer? What's Old Hawk Eyes doing with a computer?" I muttered.

Truly incredible.

I crept closer to the sight before me. Surely, this was an outlandish dream. But my eyes told a different story. This was *not* a dream. My fingers were touching the desk, the top of the computer, and the small desk lamp, declaring the reality of the whole setup.

Miss Ruby Spindler must've had a professional come in and install the computer for her. It was the weirdest thing. Why on earth did an old woman need all this high-tech equipment?

Wait'll Rachel hears about this, I thought. *And Levi!*

Yes, Levi would get a big charge out of this. So would Jon and all my girl friends at school. In fact, they'd have a hard time believing this place really and truly existed.

That's when I remembered my digital camera. I'd forgotten to bring it along. *What were you thinking?* I reprimanded myself.

Turning to go down the steps to retrieve it, I heard my name being called. I froze in place, looking every which way—wondering where I might hide.

"Merry, dearie," Miss Spindler called from what sounded like her own bedroom. Just below the attic room!

Yee-ikes! I had no idea what to think or do.

"Merry? Can you hear me?" she said again.

My heart was pounding in my ears so hard, I couldn't begin to think of a solution to my plight. The old lady wanted a reply, and if she didn't get one soon, she might come looking in the attic. I couldn't have that. There had to be another way!

Glancing around the long, narrow room, I noticed a small closet door smack-dab in the center. An odd place for a door, to be sure.

Without a second thought, I darted inside. I was surprised to see the door led to more steps, straight to the roof of the house and to a hinged, double-swing door. The latch was unlocked, so I pushed hard and it opened easily.

Standing up, I saw that the roof was actually a widow's walk perched on top of the main roof of the house. I paced off the flat, square area, flabbergasted at this incredible lookout. Taking in the sweet springtime air, I stopped to lean on the wooden railing that surrounded the observation platform, letting my eyes roam the expanse of sky and landscape below. "Of course," I said to the air and trees, "this is how Old Hawk Eyes sees so much!" But honestly, I'd never noticed the widow's walk from our house. Probably because the enormous trees blocked it from view.

I saw clearly the road that ran in front of my parents' home and all the way down past the Zooks' private lane. I saw the white gazebo in my own backyard, where strangers had slipped a baby in a basket and left her there, and the willow grove where Lissa had waited for me on that moonlit November night so long ago.

Sighing, I knew, sure as anything, how the nosy old lady had spotted little Susie Zook being harassed by tourists last summer. How she'd seen me riding with Levi in his courting buggy, too.

Beneath me, there were noises coming from the attic, and I assumed Miss Spindler was still searching for me. But I remained silent, not wanting her to know that I'd discovered her secret. At least, part of it.

"Merry, are you up there?" she called.

She was on her way up! I was going to be caught whether I liked it or not.

What should I do? I glanced over the side of the railing, determining if I could jump to the lower roof level. Carefully surveying the distance, I decided not to risk a broken leg or two. I wasn't *that* stupid.

"Merry?" There she was again. Miss Spindler was coming. I was burnt toast!

There was no other choice but to answer. And I was opening my mouth to call to her when I heard a chiming sound, like beautiful orchestral bells.

Whatever the sound was, it silenced Miss Spindler. She actually stopped calling! Not sure whether to shout for joy or hold my breath, I sat on the railing and looked out over the valley below. Rachel Zook was coming in from the barn, followed by Aaron and her younger sisters. They were finished with afternoon milking, most likely.

To the south of me, I scanned the soon-to-be acres and acres of cornfield across SummerHill Lane from the front of my house. To the west, I enjoyed the leafy tops of maple, spruce, and elm trees. I could not see as far up the hill as Chelsea Davis's house, though. It was situated on the crest of the hill, higher than even the roof of Miss Spindler's house. Back to the north, I could see the sun-dappled meadow where Rachel and I had spent our afternoon together yesterday.

I'm queen of the mountain, I thought. Checking my watch, I suddenly realized I hadn't heard a sound from Miss Spindler for quite some time.

Now might be as good a time as any to head back into the attic. Maybe, just maybe, I could sneak back down to my room and she'd never have to know where I'd been.

On tiptoes, I inched my way back into the attic, peeking through the crack in the door before heading inside.

The place was deserted.

Whew! I was home free!

Just as I crept past the computer desk, though, the chimes I'd heard before *dinged* again. I glanced toward the screen.

Wonder of wonders! Miss Spindler, it said, had an e-mail message. I stepped closer for a better look. No, it said she had *five* new e-mails! Truly amazing. Old Hawk Eyes was as thoroughly modern as any person I knew.

Not wanting to pry, I noticed a note pad lying near the mousepad on the desk. To my surprise, I saw a long list of names. *E-mail pals*, it read, and at the top were printed the words, *Windows on the Hill*.

"What's going on?" I whispered, investigating further— snooping around the desk area but not reading her e-mail messages. "Wait'll Skip hears about this!"

Miss Spindler was truly plugged in and turned on. She was in touch with the world in a way I'd never dreamed possible. *Never!*

But what could "Windows on the Hill" mean?

I had to find out!

Stepping inside Miss Spindler's attic and seeing her computer setup, e-mail and all, was one thing. Trying to decipher what was actually going on up there was something else altogether.

It turned out I had no time to find out for sure. The supper bell was ringing downstairs mighty powerfully. I had to scoot. And fast.

After supper dishes were cleared away, Miss Spindler asked if I'd had a nice after-school nap.

"A nap?"

"Why, yes, dearie, I called and called to you. I figured you were fast asleep . . . poor thing, tired from all that there book learnin'. " Her eyes were smiling, as if she knew I hadn't been sleeping at all. To tell the truth, it seemed as if she was playing a little game with me.

"I wasn't napping," I said.

"Oh?" She tilted her head to one side. "Well, I was mistaken, then, I do suppose."

"Yes" was all I said, but I was dying to ask her about Jon Klein's phone call. Since I wasn't supposed to know anything about it, I'd have to wait till she brought it up on her own. *If* she did.

So I tried to be patient all through a game of Scrabble. She simply rearranged her wooden tiles, one after the other, taking her sweet time, not talking about Jon's phone call. All the while, I stewed. What *had* he said to her during that time? *Maybe he taught her how to speak alliteration-eze*, I thought comically and almost laughed while Miss Spindler racked up a triple-word score.

"Well, now, dearie, let's see if you can top that." She'd said it with a spirit of determination—and victory.

Now what was I to do?

Shuffling my tiles, frustrated at the appearance of a *q* without an accompanying *u*, I planned my pathetic move.

"What's the matter tonight, Merry?" she asked, sticking a pencil into her blue-gray puff of hair.

I glanced at the clock. "I'd better get to my homework."

She was shaking her head. "Nothin' doing, dearie. Not before you take your turn. Then we'll tally up the score."

There was no way out. I had to follow her wishes. After all, I was the guest here. Still, I *had* to know about that elaborate computer setup of hers. And her conversation with Jon.

I took my turn and counted up a measly eight points. Before I left for my room, Miss Spindler added up the score. She was the winner. "Thank you, Merry, for being such a right good sport," she said as I pulled out my chair. "But I'm wondering if there might be something else on your mind, dearie?"

I wasn't rude, but I dodged the question. "One of my school friends is waiting for me to call," I said. "Do you mind?"

"No, no, I'll put the game away. You run along."

Deciding it would be best to call Jon from my cell phone, I darted up the stairs to my room and dialed. Thank goodness, he answered on the first ring. "You'll never guess what I found in Miss Spindler's attic," I said, not even saying who I was.

Jon was all ears. "I'm listening, Merry."

"On second thought, I'd better wait to tell you at school," I said, thinking I shouldn't reveal anything over the phone. "But it's big . . . I mean *big*."

"Okay, I'll meet you at your locker, first thing."

"That's nothing new," I said, chuckling.

"Oh really? Well, if that's the case, let's not stop now." His laugh was warm and encouraging.

I was anxious to hear about his phone call. "What did you and Miss Spindler talk about this afternoon?"

He paused. "Maybe I should make *you* wait till tomorrow, too."

"Aw, don't be a spoilsport," I said. "It's not such a secret, is it?"

"Might be, Mistress Merry." It was his cue for me to play the word game.

"*M*'s?" I asked.

"Maybe," he said.

I stopped to think. "Might Merry make many more mindless mistakes?"

"Wow—great stuff."

"That's not *m*'s," I insisted. "Start again."

"Nope, I give up. You win today. You win for always."

"What?" This was truly amazing.

"You heard me, Merry. You're the Alliteration Queen. I pronounce you the victor."

"You're kidding, right?" After all this time, he was naming *me* winner?

His voice grew soft just then. "I'm tired of it."

"Alliteration-eze?"

"That and the idea to add rhymes to everything." He stopped, and I could hear his breathing. "You know what I'd really like, Merry?"

I was breathless—could hardly speak.

He didn't wait for me to answer, and I was glad. "I want to start talking to you normally. It's too hard to make real sense of things when you're all tongue-tied over *t*'s . . . or, well, you know."

I knew exactly what he meant. But I wasn't feeling so articulate at the moment. I had a funny feeling he was trying to tell me something very important.

"Merry . . . you still there?"

"I'm here," I said softly.

"Good. I'll see you tomorrow."

"At my locker, right?"

"No . . . better yet, I'll save you a seat on the bus."

My tongue felt permanently tied, for sure. All I could do was mumble something totally unintelligible when he said good-bye.

Hanging up the phone, I honestly felt a bit dizzy. I'd been waiting nearly forever for this moment, and I could hardly breathe.

My cats were sympathetic enough. We snuggled, the four of us, on top of the old feather bed. "Somebody likes me," I told them softly. *Very* softly.

Leaning back against the fat, over-plump pillows, I daydreamed of walking down the halls of James Buchanan High with Jonathan Klein at my side.

"There's only one other thing that would make me as happy as this," I said to Shadrach, Meshach, and Lily White. "Finding Abednego would be truly great."

They seemed to understand—at least the brothers agreed with my remark. I wasn't so sure about Lily White. She seemed entirely satisfied sharing the attention with one less cat.

"Tomorrow I'm going to search for him again," I told them. "Cats as big and black as Abednego don't just vanish from the face of the earth."

His brothers must've understood because both of them hopped off the bed and leaped up to adjacent wide windowsills and peered out into the darkness.

"We go home tomorrow afternoon," I told Lily White. "You'll get to see Skip again. Won't that be nice?" I cuddled her close to my face, and her purring was strong and steady.

"Miss Spindler's got herself a computer . . . and e-mail, too," I whispered against the soft, furry head. "Isn't that the tallest tale you ever heard?"

When I said the word *tale*, Lily White flapped her delicate white one against my arm. "Okay, kitty-girl, down you go."

It was then I remembered something Old Hawk Eyes had said. *"I done put my feelers out all over."* Had she e-mailed lost-cat messages to her computer pals? Is that what "putting feelers out" meant?

Sixteen Windows on the Hill

Jon's broad smile lit up the entire school bus. I tried not to show my giddiness, and he was polite and slid over next to the window as I sat down.

Fortunately, Chelsea was nowhere in sight. Had she been on the bus, saving a seat as she always did, I would've had some big explaining to do.

"Who goes first?" Jon said.

I couldn't help but smile. He was more than eager to hear of Miss Spindler's attic hideaway. "I've got the most incredible news for you." And I told him about the old lady's computer setup, complete with e-mail capability.

"Wow, that *is* news," he said.

"What I wonder is how she's kept it a secret."

Jon nodded. "Who knows how long she's been using e-mail to keep tabs on people."

I gasped. "So that's it! She must be sending mail to the SummerHill neighbors up and down the road, getting the scoop on everyone that way."

Grinning, Jon leaned against the window, turning to face me. "She told me about some of those neighbors yesterday on the phone. You'll be surprised when you hear who they are."

"Really? Like who?"

"For starters, Matthew Yoder's dad owns a computer."

"You're kidding—Rachel's boyfriend's dad?"

"He can't have it in the house because the Amish bishop won't allow it. But Mr. Yoder has permission to use the computer for his cabinet-making business."

I was shocked. "But they're Old Order Amish!"

"I was surprised, too. But Miss Spindler says she and Matthew's mother exchange e-mail almost every day, along with a lot of other Plain folk, including Ben Fisher's mom, way down at the end of SummerHill Lane." His eyes were on me as he shared this amazing tidbit of information.

"This is so crazy," I said, leaning on my book bag. "How'd you get her to tell you this?"

He glanced down at his books for a moment. "I guess she wanted to talk. She's a lonely old lady, you know."

I shook my head at him. "I think you'd better level with me, Jonathan Klein! What did you *really* say to her?"

"Let's just say I charmed Old Hawk Eyes."

Charmed? I laughed out loud.

"I'll bet you did." I stared at him, knowing full well he wouldn't divulge his tactics. At least not without some prompting. "So . . . did you charm her with alliteration?"

"Only for a while, but soon she was intrigued with the word game, so she decided to try it herself."

I laughed. "Miss Spindler and you?"

"Hey, everyone else is speaking it. Why not?" His eyes were twinkling mischief. "The old lady knew all along where you were, Merry," he said. "She figured you were checking out her attic yesterday when I called."

"What?"

"Miss Spindler went along with it . . . guess she didn't want to spoil your fun."

One wacky revelation after another! "So . . . does she want me to ask her about what I saw in the attic?"

"Not only is she restless to tell you, she's hoping you'll help her sift through all her e-mail messages," he replied.

"Why me?"

"For some reason, she seems to think she can trust you, Merry." He paused, looking right at me. "And something else."

"There's more?"

"She has trouble seeing her monitor with her trifocals—makes her neck stiff, she said. So maybe she'll ask you to help her out sometime."

"Why's she getting so much e-mail, do you think?" I asked.

"She's enjoying all her new friends, I guess."

The bus pulled into the school parking lot and stopped at the appointed curb. My most miraculous moment was about to end. I wanted it to last forever, sitting here beside the cutest boy in the whole school. No, the whole county.

Suddenly, I realized I hadn't taken Levi Zook into consideration. Guess I thought of him less as a boy and more as a young man. Maybe . . .

"See you to your locker?" Jon asked. His smile was as blissful as it was big.

"Okay." And we walked into the school together.

Later, when the bell rang, my yesterday's daydream came true. The former Alliteration Wizard and the reigning Alliteration Queen walked side by side down the swarming, yet seemingly silent, hallway.

———

After school, my cats helped me pack. Well, they didn't actually do anything except curl up in the golden sunbeams that spilled into the guest room from each of the dormer windows.

"We're going home," I sang, trying not to think about Abednego. Here it was Thursday, nearly a week since the storm had scared him away. I missed him terribly, ornery and spiteful as he was.

Looking in all the empty drawers, on the closet floor, and under the bed, I made sure nothing was left behind. Then I realized what a wonderful, old-fashioned bedroom this really was. For a fleeting moment, I actually thought I might miss this quaint place.

"Come on, little ones," I said to my snoozing, perfectly contented cats. "We have to tell Miss Spindler good-bye."

Surprisingly, they got up, stretched, and followed me downstairs, where Miss Spindler was waiting, all smiles.

"I hope you had a right nice time, dearie," she said, filling my backpack with a plastic container of homemade cookies.

"Oh yes, I did." I glanced down at my cats. "I should say *we* did. Thanks again. I know it took a lot of worry off my parents' minds while they're gone." I paused. Now was a good time to apologize for sneaking around in the old woman's house. "I shouldn't have gone snooping in your attic, Miss Spindler. My parents would die if they knew about it. I'm sorry," I said, meaning every word.

"Forget it, dearie," she said and patted the box of cookies through the backpack. "Remember, now, there's more where these came from . . . and you and your brother are gonna be all alone over there. If you need anything at all, give me a holler. Dessert, ice cream . . . you name it. I'll even bake you up some pie."

I was chuckling. "And the same goes for you, Miss Spindler. If ever you need anything, just let me know."

That's when her eyes got big and round, like coat buttons. "Come to think of it, Merry, dear, there *is* something I could use some help with." Then she waved her hand, shooing me off for home. "Aw, shucks, it'll wait till you get yourself settled in again. Tell that big brother of yours hello from this here neighbor, ya hear?"

"I will," I promised, eager to find out if what she needed help with was her e-mail messages. I don't know why it intrigued me—her pushing eighty and doing the high-tech thing. But then again, this was the same old lady who drove a hot red sports car all over SummerHill.

My brother was more excited to hear about the attic "find" than he was glad to see me, I think. He got all caught up in my story right off.

"Won't Mom and Dad freak?" Skip said, face aglow. "I mean, this has gotta be the biggest story in all of Lancaster County. Except maybe that drug bust among the Amish out east of town."

"Hey, I wonder if we should call up the newspaper?"

Skip sat at the kitchen table. "The media would be more than happy to sensationalize a story like this." He helped himself to some of Miss Spindler's cookies. "I can see the headlines now: 'Plain Folk Chat With Hot-Rodding Spinster on Net.' "

Laughing, I poured him a tall glass of milk. "I think we'd better keep the media out of it and just enjoy the wackiness ourselves."

He pulled out a kitchen chair for me, and I was surprised at his gentlemanly gesture. "Who else knows about this?" he asked, breaking the stillness.

"Only Jon." I thought about it. "And some of my girl friends."

"They knew about your investigating Old Hawk Eyes' attic?"

I nodded. "But they haven't heard what I found. Least, not my girl friends."

Skip drank half the glass of milk straight down. "Are you still doing that weird word thing with Jon?" he asked.

"How'd *you* know about that?"

Leaning back on the chair, he devoured another cookie. "Jon's sister talks about it every now and then."

"Oh, so you and Jon's sister are still writing love letters? Or are they e-mails?" I teased.

He couldn't contain the pink color that crept into his face. "That's none of your business," he said flatly.

"Well, it's gonna be my business if Nikki's my sister-in-law someday!"

He sneered—his old self was showing through. "And if I marry her and you marry Jon, our kids will be brousins—closer than cousins. Get it?"

I shook my head at him. This was a pitiful conversation. "I'm going upstairs," I said, getting up from the table.

"Who's cooking tonight?" he asked, looking worried.

"You are." With that, I disappeared up the kitchen flight of stairs and headed to my room. I made myself comfortable on the bed and spread out the scrapbook of my dad's retirement party. Time to finish my project. I wanted Dad *and* Mom to be surprised when they arrived home this Saturday.

The phone rang an hour later, but I ignored it, letting Skip get it for a change. When he didn't call for me right away, I figured it must be for him. *Probably Nikki*, I thought. She had always been one to chase after my brother.

"Merry, it's for you," Skip hollered up to me.

"I'll be right there!" Scurrying down the hall to Mom and Dad's bedroom, I picked up the phone. "Hello?" I said, out of breath.

"Merry, dear, it's Miss Spindler."

"Oh hi. Is everything all right over there?"

She snickered. "That's *my* line, dearie." *How's every little thing* was what she always said first off.

"Yes . . . well, I forgot. Sorry."

"Oh my, there's no need to apologize," she said. "I just thought I'd call and check with you about supper plans."

Supper plans?

Then I remembered my brother was in charge of the kitchen. At least, I'd told him he was cooking tonight. "Uh . . . yes, we're open to suggestions," I said rather quickly.

"That's what I hoped to hear," said Miss Spindler. "I made a ravioli casserole that's downright too big—family size, I daresay—and, well, since there ain't much of a family over here, I thought I'd invite myself to supper."

I looked up to see Skip standing comically in the doorway, motioning for me to say yes. Which I was more than happy to do.

"Aren't you the lucky one," I told Skip as I hung up the phone. "Somebody who can actually cook is bringing pasta for supper."

"Hallelujah!" he sang.

I was mighty glad about it, too. But I couldn't help wondering what Miss Spindler had on her mind. Surely there was something.

Quickly, I dialed Ashley Horton. I filled her in on everything she'd missed since my snooping expedition in the refurbished attic across the yard from me.

"I'm not one bit surprised," Ashley said. "Anyone that old who still likes to drive fancy cars is probably a good candidate for the computer age. Don't you think so?"

Leave it to Ashley to throw in her homegrown philosophy. In the short time I'd known her, she always managed to pick exactly the right time to insert her strange-but-true comments.

"Curiosity killed the cat, right?" she said, laughing.

"Excuse me?"

"Your curiosity got the best of you," she began to summarize. "So you nosed around in Miss Spindler's attic."

"Right."

"Merry, you really can't expect to be too surprised at the result, can you?"

"I'm not dead, am I?"

"No . . . no, that's not what the old proverb means." Once again, she tried to get me to see the light. "What you did—out of pure inquisitiveness, of course—was bound to get you into trouble in the long run."

"But I'm *not* in trouble," I insisted.

"Well, I think you might be if Miss Spindler ever finds out."

I proceeded to tell her that Miss Spindler knew all—and about the old lady's e-mail pals. "I guess you could say she wanted to be found out. Maybe she wanted us to know that she's a truly 'with it' old lady."

"She's cool, all right. And I'll be the first to congratulate her," Ashley said.

"Well, I don't know if that's such a good idea."

"Why not?"

"Because she doesn't realize that very many of us know yet."

Ashley's sigh came through to my end of the phone. Loud and long. "Now I'm completely confused."

"I don't blame you." I was dying to tell her that I wouldn't be playing the Alliteration Game anymore. (The thought was triggered by the *c* words she'd used.) But I thought better of it and decided to keep that decision secret—just between Jon Klein and me.

Miss Spindler came for supper with bells on. She was all dolled up—a touch of lipstick and pinkish cheeks. She wore a long, floral broomstick skirt and a hot-pink blouse to match the rosebuds in her flowing skirt.

"Now, dearies, I brought along Parmesan cheese to sprinkle on the pasta and enough warm garlic bread to feed every last one of our Amish neighbors." She said this with a playful smile on her wrinkled face.

"You're getting to know lots of them?" I blurted without thinking.

"Who's that, dear?" she asked.

"Our Amish neighbors," I repeated.

Skip was trying not to explode in the corner of the kitchen between the wall and Mom's African violet plants. I could tell by the way he was smashing his lips together—and that silly grin on his face. Man, was I crazy to bring this up, or what?

"As a matter of fact, I *have* been getting myself acquainted with a whole bunch of Plain folk, come to think of it," she said.

"Oh?" I had to play dumb. I wasn't supposed to know this.

"I'm sure your nice young man—that Jonathan Klein, was it?—told you all about my little chat with him yesterday afternoon." Her beady eyes were on me now. I had a mighty powerful feeling that there was no way out. I had to fess up.

"Well, first of all"—I said this for Skip's sake—"Jon's not my nice young man. I don't mean that he's *not* nice, just not mine. At least, not yet." I was sliding deeper and deeper, right to where Skip was most interested, no doubt.

She ignored the explanation and placed the casserole dish on the table. Then she called my brother over. "The food's hot, but not for long. We'd best get started."

After the prayer, I asked if I could start again. "Please do," Skip had the gall to say. Grinning, no less.

Sighing, I decided to back up to the real point of Miss Spindler's earlier comment. "I was very surprised to hear about your e-mail friends," I began. "And, yes, Jon did fill me in on that."

A beautiful smile, pure and sweet, spread across her face. "Ah, Merry, dearie, I'm ever so glad to have dreamed up such a right fine name for my cozy attic office," she said. "It's *Windows on the Hill*, you know."

I knew but didn't dare let on.

"My, oh my, I've met a good many folk on the Web."

I had to work hard at chewing my food—keeping it in my mouth—and not spraying it across the table. But the laugh insisted, and I grabbed for my napkin.

Miss Spindler looked worried. "What is it, Merry?"

I was shaking my head, patting my chest. "I'm all right, really I am."

Now she had the most peculiar look on her face. Like she thought she must've said something quite comical. "Well, I daresay my sense of humor must surely be improving."

I was nodding, eyeballing Skip. He started nodding his head, too. We talked awhile longer about computers and how easy it was to connect unknowingly with weirdos and strangers who might not be good for us. Miss Spindler agreed and said that she was being careful of that.

During dessert, Skip brought up the subject of Abednego. "Did he ever show up?"

I slouched sadly. "Don't get me started. Honestly, I thought I'd never give up on him, but I have to admit I'm starting to wonder if God had other plans for my old cat."

Skip's eyebrows rose, and he pursed his lips. "He was always such a crafty creature."

"*Was?* Don't say it that way. It sounds like you think he's already dead."

"Hold on, now, Merry," Miss Spindler was saying, reaching over and patting my hand. "We don't know yet, now, do we?"

"He's been missing for six days—unbearable days. Cats always come home after a storm, don't they?"

Miss Spindler was quiet for a moment. "They do, I suppose, unless someone comes along and claims them for their own."

I sat up in my chair. "Do you really think someone stole my Abednego?"

Skip leaned his head into his hands and rubbed his face, while Miss Spindler tried to calm me down. "Wouldn't that be far better than finding out the poor thing had up and died?"

I thought about that. Miss Old Hawk Eyes Spindler was right. Still, I found it terribly confusing when she insisted that I come right home with her after supper dishes were finished. "Let's talk some more about that lost cat of yours," she said.

As I walked with our quirky old neighbor across the backyard and up the slope of her own property—all that time—I could see my brother's ridiculous smile in my mind.

"You sit here, dearie." Miss Spindler stepped aside so I faced her computer screen directly.

"Where will *you* sit?" I asked.

She was already one step ahead of me, pulling a folding chair across the attic's carpeted floor. "Here we are," she said.

She asked me to click onto her e-mail program, which I did. "Now," she said, "I was hoping you'd read each of this week's messages to me."

This week's. There were thirty messages!

"Oh, I have such a hard time," she explained, taking off her thick glasses and showing me where the trifocal line began. "You have no idea just how difficult it is to see the words."

"Maybe you should order a software program with larger letters." I'd heard of such things, especially for folks who suffered from partial blindness.

"Well, for now, I've got *you* here," she said. "Thank you for agreeing to help this old lady."

I began to read her personal messages, feeling a bit awkward. The first was from an Amishwoman who said she lived north of the Davises on SummerHill Lane. She described her busy day—washing and hanging out the clothes to dry, baking, cleaning, sewing, and gardening. On and on.

The writer signed off with: *Nobody's seen hide nor hair of a big black cat.*

"You asked her about Abednego?" I said, turning to face Miss Spindler.

"Oh yes, I've asked every one of my e-mail friends."

"Is that why you wanted me to come help you?"

She responded with a quick smile. "Keep on reading," she said, moving her hands.

I read the next five, but none of the writers had seen my cat. We were clear down to the next to the last message. An Amish lady two houses down from the Fishers' place—out near the highway—wrote to say that she'd spotted a large animal prowling around her house.

If it's a house cat, it's a very big one, she wrote. *I daresay that one would take a batch of field mice to keep full.*

"Sounds like Abednego!" I said, eager to read on.

Last night, we put out a bowl of milk for him. Fast as a wink, he drank it down. My grandson put out another bowl, and that one was gone in nothing flat. If ya wanna come and see for yourself about this here mouse catcher, I'll hang on to him for ya, just a bit.

I was clapping my hands. "Can we go, Miss Spindler? Please?"

"It's getting late," she said, reminding me that Amish folk head for bed about eight-thirty. "I'll tell you what, dearie, we'll drive on over there. If the oil lamps are burnin' in the kitchen, we'll know they're still up."

Thrilled beyond belief, I closed down the Windows on the Hill. Miss Spindler was truly amazing.

———

"Don't get your hopes up too high, dearie," she told me as we rode down SummerHill Lane.

Crickets were chirping to beat the band, and the moon was starting to rise in the east. I sat in the front seat of the fanciest sports car this side of the Susquehanna River, praying that Abednego would be waiting on the front porch for us.

Miss Spindler pulled slowly into the driveway when we found the house. "See any lights?" I whispered.

"Not a one," she said.

I opened the car door. "I'm gonna go look for him."

"No . . . no, you mustn't be impatient, now. All good things come to those who wait."

I argued. "But I've been waiting nearly a week. Can't I at least walk around the house and call for him?"

She shook her head. "Not on your life, dearie. That's trespassing, pure and simple."

"I know, but—"

"No buts. We'll come back tomorrow."

"Abednego might be gone by then," I insisted.

"Not if these good folk are feeding him milk every day, he won't."

She had a point. Still, I wanted Abednego in my arms tonight!

"Here, kitty, kitty," I called softly. "It's Merry come to get you, baby. Come on, now, you know your Merry's here."

Miss Spindler was beside herself. "Get in the car," she said. "We best be goin'. "

"I promise not to trespass," I said, moving to the front of the car. "It's Merry . . . Merry's here. Come on, little boy, you know you wanna go home."

The sky was dotted with shimmering silver flecks of light. All around me I heard the sounds of nightfall.

"You want some Kitty Kisses?" I said softly. "Merry's gonna give her little boy some treats."

I waited some more, listening for the slightest clue. The tiniest sound of a cat.

"Psst, Merry," called Miss Spindler. "We'll try again tomorrow." She flicked her headlights on and turned on the ignition.

Just then a light came on in the back of the house. "Look!" I said. "Someone's up." My heart was thumping with anticipation.

Miss Spindler was out of the car, catching up with me as I hurried around to the back door of the farmhouse. "Best let me handle this," she said, opening the screen door and knocking on the inside door.

"Jah, who's there?" said an Amishman, peering out at us.

"It's Ruby Spindler, your wife's friend up the road a piece. She wrote something about finding a stray cat."

The man was nodding his head, his gray beard bumping his chest each time he did. "Jah, we know of such a cat."

"He's here?" I asked excitedly. "Abednego's here?"

Looking quite perplexed, the man frowned and shook his head. "I never heard of that name—not for a cat."

"But it's him, isn't it?" I could hardly stand there, aching to know if they had him or not.

"Ach, I think ya must be mistaken. We saw no such tag on the cat—not nowhere." The man was beginning to close the door.

"Please," I said, "may I have a look at the cat you found?"

He paused, as if he wasn't sure whether he should invite us in.

Then behind me I heard a stirring in the bushes, followed by *meow*.

"Wait! I'd know that sound anywhere," I said, turning and scooping up my beloved baby into my arms. "Oh, you're safe, Abednego! You're truly safe."

I heard Miss Spindler thank the man.

"Well, that takes care of that," he said, closing the back door.

All the way home, I cuddled my cat. "Hey, I think you're fatter than before," I told him.

Abednego didn't talk back; instead, he purred like a motorboat and leaned his head against my arm.

"How can I ever thank you, Miss Spindler?" I asked.

She kept driving, probably deciding what she ought to say to me. Then it came. The cutest thing I'd heard all year. "Guess Old Hawk Eyes ain't so awful bad, now, is she?"

I sucked in a little breath, shocked that she knew her nickname. "I won't ask where you heard that," I said, giggling. "It's really none of my business, is it?"

Her head went back with hearty laughter. And I snuggled with my newly found pet.

It was a night to remember.

Miss Spindler was kind enough to let me take pictures of her attic computer room so I could show all my girl friends. And my new boyfriend. That's right, Jon Klein and I are officially going out. It's a dream come true, and I only wish Faithie were alive to witness my joy.

I haven't written Levi about it yet. I figure I can wait till he comes home this summer. Besides, he should feel relieved to hear the news, especially if he has someone new himself.

Dad and Mom are back from Costa Rica, and all they talk about is taking Skip and me the next time. "You'd love the people," Dad says. "They're so hungry for Jesus."

Speaking of hunger, Abednego has never been so interested in his regular kitty food. He learned a hard lesson by running away. But now that he's back home, his behavior is improving. Even Skip has noticed how placid and cooperative my wayward cat is now.

As for Chelsea, she's completely well and back to school. She says she's sorry she missed the day Jon and I sat together on the bus. She said she'd give anything to have been there. Of course, he and I still sit together, but Chelsea's right there, too. Either in front of us or right across the aisle.

The Alliteration Word Game is history, a thing of the past—for Jon and me, at least. Chelsea, Ashley, and Lissa are still going strong, and occasionally Miss Spindler tries her hand at alliterating. Jon and I are much better communicators without the limitation of having to match up every word in a sentence. I must admit, I've never been so happy.

Rachel Zook and I *finally* talked Miss Spindler into taking one of the gray kittens as a pet. When the light is just right, the sweet little thing matches Old Hawk Eyes' blue-gray hair!

Most of all, I'm thankful that God's eyes were on Abednego during those six worry-filled days. And I know something else: He used Old Hawk Eyes' curiosity and turned it into something good.

I'm thinking it might be time for a new nickname for my neighbor. Or maybe none at all.

Shadows Beyond the Gate

Special thanks
to
Gordon and Betty Bernhardt,
who shared with me
the story of Buttercup,
the *real* twin lamb.

For
Julie Arno,
who heralds herself a
"Sincere SummerHill Secrets Series Fanatic."

Hide me in the shadow
of your wings . . .

—Psalm 17:8

Right off the bat, I'll admit that I'd only *thought* I was over the loss of my twin sister. Some days, Faithie's death seems like a long time ago. Other days, it's like yesterday that the leukemia came and took her away.

But the day everything got stirred up again—or got me "all but ferhoodled," as my Amish girl friend would say—was as perfect as any Pennsylvania springtime. It was late May, and the remnants of my sophomore year at James Buchanan High were fading all too quickly. Not a single cloud cluttered the clear blue sky.

Rachel Zook came running up SummerHill Lane just as I stepped off the school bus. I took one look at her and knew something was wrong. Her white head covering had tipped a bit off center, and her usual long gray apron was mussed. Nearly breathless and eyes wide, she sputtered her request, "Can ya come . . . help me out, Merry?"

"You can count on me." I scurried down the road toward the long dirt lane that led to the Zooks' farmhouse, trying to keep up with Rachel, the hem of her skirt flapping in the warm breeze.

"My twin lamb's gonna die, I'm afraid," she said as we ran.

"What's wrong with her?"

"Well, her mama died yesterday morning, hours after she birthed the twins . . . and then 'twasn't long and the first twin lamb up and died, too." Rachel stopped running as we neared the barnyard. Catching our breaths, we strolled over to the white plank fence.

I shaded my eyes with my hand as I scanned the grassy, fenced area. "Where is she?"

We searched the corral with our eyes. At last, Rachel located her. "*Ach*, of all things—she's right here."

Peering down through the fence slats, I spied a single baby lamb, all fluffy and white. "Oh, she's so adorable."

"Adorable, *jah*, but she's all alone in the world. Won't eat nothin', neither," Rachel said, her voice soft and low. "We can't get her to take milk, not even from Ol' Nanna."

I was surprised to hear it because I'd seen Ol' Nanna with her own babies. The older sheep was gentle and loving—the way a good foster mother ought to be.

Rachel pointed to Ol' Nanna grazing by herself across the meadow. "She doesn't mind sharin' her milk with young'uns that ain't hers. I can't begin to count the number of orphan lambs we've bonded on to her. And plenty-a time, too." Rachel shook her head. "But not *this* time. It just ain't workin' out."

I stared down at the poor little creature. Her fleece was creamy white, like detergent suds. Made you want to reach down and pick her up—cuddle her like a human baby. My heart went out to the lost lamb. "Why do you think she won't eat?" I asked.

Rachel's fingers trailed down the long white strings of her *Kapp*, the prayer veiling she always wore. She moved close to me, whispering. "If ya want my opinion, I think she's dyin' of loneliness."

I looked out over the enclosure where at least twenty sheep roamed the pastureland, wondering how on earth the lamb could be lonely. "But look at all her relatives. She's got oodles of aunts, uncles, and cousins . . . doesn't she?"

Rachel didn't smile. She frowned instead. "It's the oddest thing, really. But I think she downright misses her twin . . . and her mama." Rachel's voice grew even softer. "If something doesn't change, and soon, I'm afraid she'll lie down and die. Just plain give up."

Squatting to get closer, I stroked the animal's soft wool coat. Seemed to me, Rachel might be right. "See how her eyes plead?"

"Like she needs someone to help her, ain't so?" Rachel said. "That's why I asked ya over here, Merry. I thought you could coax her to take some milk . . . from this baby bottle, maybe." She handed the bottle to me.

"Me?"

"Jah." She paused, and a peculiar look swept across her pretty face. "If ya think on it, I'm sure you'll understand why." She didn't say more but headed off toward the barn, waving that she'd be back "awful quick."

I had to stop and really ponder what Rachel had just said. Kneeling in the grass, I was nearly nose to nose with the adorable animal. "You're such a pretty thing," I said through the fence. I stroked the fleecy coat, cooing at her like I often did to each of my four cats.

Then, while I continued to pet the lamb, I realized exactly what my Amish girl friend meant. It struck me like lightning hits a tree. I *was* a good choice for her lamb project. A very good one, in fact. Because I, too, had suffered great loss. Of course, my twin hadn't died at birth, or even close to it, but Faithie was gone all the same.

I kept watch over the poor, suffering lamb, observing her sad face, the way she could hardly raise her eyes to look at me. She seemed too downhearted to think about living, let alone care about drinking milk from a bottle.

"You poor thing," I said softly, offering the baby bottle. When the lamb wasn't interested, I didn't coax. "I think I know what you need."

Setting the bottle down, I turned and sat in the grass. "I think you need a pretty name—one to match who you are."

After a good deal of thinking on my part, an idea came. I whispered the name into the air, imagining the warm breeze picking it up and carrying it high over the silo on the Zooks' bank barn, on past the pond with its bottomless holes, and beyond the creaky windmill.

Yes, it might well be the perfect name. And one way to cheer up a sad little lamb. Sighing, I said, "I think your name should be . . . Jingle Belle. Jingle, for short. What do you think of that?"

At first, I wondered if I might be dreaming, because Jingle responded to her new name. I actually thought she was beginning to smile. Well, sort of, because I guess lambs don't really smile. Unless, of course, they want to.

Jingle shook her head playfully, which rang the tiny bell at her neck. A sweet, cheerful ringing sound. *Jingle Belle.* What a terrific name. One-hundred-percent-amen wonderful!

It was the sweetest thing—the absolutely nicest thing that had happened to me in a while. Sitting there in the thick green grass, I leaned against the fence and knew that Rachel would be delighted, too. Yep, things were about to change for her little lamb.

And something else. I couldn't be sure, but I had a funny feeling that things were about to change for me, too. Because deep inside, where no one ever sees but God, I still longed for Faithie. It was as if a shadow covered everything on the path of my future.

"Only time will heal that kind of wound," Dad gently reminds me every so often. But I honestly didn't see how that could ever be. Half of me is gone. Faithie's absence is like thick pollen in springtime, scattered everywhere.

Leaning my head against the fence, I felt Jingle's soft wool on my forehead. Sweet and comforting, she nuzzled me.

Closing my eyes, I allowed my tears to spill out. "I know how you feel, Jingle," I whispered. "And I'm going to help you. I promise."

Two Shadows Beyond the Gate

On a really warm day, you ought to be able to sit outside in pajamas and play with your cats. Soak up some sunshine. At least, that was my idea of a lazy Saturday morning in SummerHill. But my mother had other plans for me, and I worried that spring would slip through my fingers before I had a chance to do anything truly frivolous.

"We'll sit in the sun another time, little boys," I told Shadrach, Meshach, and Abednego, the cat brothers. I discarded my bathrobe and headed into my walk-in closet to see what to wear.

When I was dressed for the day, I noticed Lily White—the only lady of the feline group—still lying at the foot of my bed. She opened her tiny eyes and blinked beore succumbing again to morning drowsiness. I laughed at her, ignoring her disinterest. "I know, I know . . . you're not a morning person." Then, catching myself, I realized what I'd said. "Yee-ikes! You're not a *person* at all!"

To that, she opened both eyes wide, stretched her petite hind legs, and jumped off my bed, padding slowly toward me.

"Well, what's this?" I said, still laughing at my adorable white cat. "Are you up for good?"

She followed me down the hall to my parents' bedroom, where my mother was busy gathering up laundry. The washing was probably the reason Mom had nixed my idea of whiling away the morning in the sun. Laundry, it seemed, could never wait. It *had* to be attended to in a timely manner. Which meant the notion that dirty clothes might merely lie patiently in a hamper until a designated weekly wash day—like the Amish folk do it—was out of the question. At least at our house. If so much as two days of washing piled up, Mom was on to it like a cat after a mouse.

"Let's get our work done before noon, what do you say?" Mom suggested, her hair neatly combed. She wore her pretty blue blouse and her best casual pants. I had a feeling she was going out later.

"What's the rush?" I asked.

"Oh, there's an antique show in the area," she muttered, her arms filling up with Dad's shirts. "That's all."

That's all.

Funny she said it that way, because I knew about Mom's great fascination with antiques. There was no hiding it. Her interest had become stronger with the passing of each year.

I stumbled after her, my own arms loaded down. "Are you looking for a specific piece?"

"Not for me personally," she said as we made our way downstairs through the kitchen toward the cellar steps.

It seemed to me she didn't really want to say what she was looking for. So I changed the subject. "After I help with the laundry, is it okay if I just hang out for the rest of the afternoon?"

"Hang out?" She pushed Dad's shirts into the washer. "As in *hang out* the clothes to dry?" She wore an affected smile, which quickly faded.

I should've known Mom would think I was volunteering. In her opinion, there was not a more pleasant smell than clothing dried by the fresh air and sunshine.

"Hang out the clothes? Well, no," I said, "that's not what I meant, but . . ."

She eyed me curiously. "You didn't mean to say that you were going to *waste* away your Saturday afternoon, did you?"

I wondered if my mother would ever understand that what I said most of the time didn't have anything to do with what I *meant* to say. I sighed. "I thought I'd spend some time with Rachel Zook today. That's all."

"Well, why didn't you say so?" Mom replied, turning on the washer and pouring in a cup of detergent.

The suds reminded me of Rachel's little lamb, but I couldn't bring myself to tell Mom about yet another "mammal mission," as she so often referred to my attraction to strays or other needy creatures.

I thought more about Jingle Belle. Such a sad situation. But it wasn't like I wanted to offer the lamb a roof over her fleecy head. I couldn't have her sleep at the bottom of my bed with the cats, and I certainly didn't want to have her following me around inside the house all day. No, I simply wanted to help give her the courage to live. Somehow.

"Okay, Merry," Mom said, jolting me out of my thoughts. "I think it's time we have some breakfast."

If you've never had Saturday breakfast at our house, you have no idea what Mom's idea of "breaking a fast" was all about. To her, it meant cooking up more than enough food for the entire rest of the day!

So while the washing machine did its thing, Mom whipped up waffle batter, fried German sausage and eggs, and made French toast in the oven. I set the table and arranged the homemade jellies and jams, gifts from Esther Zook, Rachel's mother. Then I scurried off to check on my cats . . . and Dad.

I found him reading the paper in his study, still wearing a bathrobe. "I hope you're hungry," I whispered, poking my head around the corner.

He looked up and grinned at me. "Is your mother cooking up a storm?"

"It's Saturday, right?" I laughed, settling into the chair across from his desk. "She'll expect us to sample everything, you know."

Folding his paper, he focused his attention on me. "Your mother has some very interesting plans for herself."

"Yeah, she told me. She's off to an antique show."

He nodded his head. "I didn't mean her plans for *today*."

"What, then?"

"She's talking of converting our potting shed into an antique shop."

This was news to me. Not once since Dad's early retirement had I ever stopped to think that we might need additional money each month. But with my older brother, Skip, off at college, maybe we *were* short of cash. "Are we . . . I mean, does Mom need to work?"

His hearty laugh brought some relief for me. "No, no, your mother doesn't need to work. We're fine, honey." He paused, getting up and standing near his chair. "I think your mother's just getting her second wind. That's all."

Not sure what he was talking about, I waited for more.

"She's a bit restless at this stage of her life, I guess you could say. You and your brother are nearly raised, so her interests are beginning to broaden."

"But she's always loved antiques, so this is nothing new."

He fell silent, still holding the folded newspaper in his hands.

"Why would she want an antique shop in our backyard? Doesn't she realize it could be an absolute nightmare—tourists tromping all across our lawn," I spouted. "What's this *really* about?"

Dad came and pulled me up out of the chair gently. "I think your mother's ready to compete with our Amish neighbors."

I was the one chuckling this time. Amish roadside stands couldn't be the reason. "Mom's not going to sell jams and jellies or make quilts, is she?"

"Who knows what she'll sell in her shop." Dad seemed somewhat guarded about Mom's ambitions.

"But this is her idea, right?"

He hugged me and guided me down the hall toward the kitchen. "We'll talk more later, okay?"

"Sure," I said, my curiosity piqued. "Later."

The morning was balmy, with a hint of a shower in the air. Rachel and her sisters, Nancy, Ella Mae, and little Susie, were outside urging the tiny lamb to drink when I arrived at the Zooks' farm.

"How's Jingle doing?" I asked, leaning on the fence post.

"About the same," Nancy said. But the somber look on her face gave her away. The Amish sisters were as worried as before.

"So . . . nothing's changed?" I pressed.

Rachel shook her head. "Here, *you* try, Merry. Let's see if Jingle will drink for you."

I shrugged, accepting the baby bottle. Hesitant to hunker down and force the poor thing to eat in front of an insistent group, I sat in the grass about two feet from the fence. "Has she ever been let out?" I asked, referring to the fenced area.

Little Susie gasped, cupping her hand over her mouth in horror. "Ach no, Merry! Jingle might run away and get herself lost. We wouldn't want that to happen, now, would we?"

"No, Susie," Rachel said quickly, comforting her small sister.

Clearly, the youngest Zook was not in favor of my idea. "I didn't mean that Jingle should run loose," I explained to Susie. Then, turning to Rachel, I asked, "What if the lamb came outside the fence—right here with me?" I patted the grass.

Rachel was nodding. Her smile spread across her tan face. "I'd say it's an awful *gut* idea, Cousin Merry." She liked to call me "cousin" because of our distant connection to the same Plain relative.

Usually, I had to smile at her reference to our remote kinship, but not today. Today, something very important was on my mind—more vital than my mother's idea to run an antique shop out of a backyard shed. Right now *I* hoped to get a lonely and dying lamb's full attention. Because maybe today Jingle Belle would nurse from the bottle for me. I could only hope . . . and pray.

Three *Shadows Beyond the Gate*

Before she embarked on her antique adventure, Mom stopped by the Zooks' house. There was a familiar glint in her eye as she leaned her head out the car window. "Merry, honey, I thought you'd like to know that Jonathan Klein called as I was leaving the house."

Jon! My heart jittered.

"What did he want?" I asked.

She touched one delicate blue earring, a grin adding even more pizzazz to her outfit. "He wanted to talk to *you*. But since I told him you were over here, he said he'll call you later, in about an hour."

I glanced at my watch. "Good . . . that's perfect." I would be sure to make it home by then.

Mom looked tired. No, she looked totally wiped out. I watched her drive the car forward, creeping into the barnyard area. As she came back around, I flagged her down, stopping her. "You okay?" I asked, leaning on the car window.

"Just a little tired," she said, shrugging. "I'll take a nap later."

A nap? Mom *never* took naps!

"Will you please take it easy?" I asked.

She nodded. "Don't miss your phone call," she said, blowing a kiss. She headed down the long dirt road and was still waving out the car window as she made the turn onto SummerHill Lane.

I giggled at her girlish approach to *my* love life. Yep, Mom was on to something, tired or not. Most likely she'd guessed how much I liked the former Wordplay Wizard from James Buchanan High. Jon and I had discarded our alliteration absurdity. Yet I still found myself creating phrases with matching vowels or consonants, almost without will. The difference was that I wasn't constantly *trying* to alliterate when Jon and I were together. And neither was Jon. Our friendship was secure and strong, much better now that we weren't hung up on trying to impress each other with our wits.

Turning back to the task at hand, I was glad Rachel and her sisters had slipped away into the house. I suspected they were helping their mother with baking bread and pies for church. Tomorrow was their turn to have Preaching service at their house.

Meanwhile, I had loosely tied the newborn lamb to one of the fence posts. It was the post nearest a young willow tree. A nearly eleven-year-old tree, to be exact. I knew its age to the day because I'd sat in the grass the afternoon it had been planted—though by accident.

I'd never heard of a fishing pole becoming a tree. Stories like that came from tall tales. Some of the Old Order Plain folk were known for such entertaining yarns, but the truth was this: Faithie's willow stick—her fishing pole—actually grew into a tree. I never forgot the surprise on her delighted face, weeks later, when that skinny pole began to sprout in our Amish neighbors' yard!

The long-ago August day had been so exciting for Faithie and me—two little English girls spending the day on an Amish dairy farm. We'd gone fishing with the older Zook kids, hoping to bring home at least one small fish for our mother to cook in the frying pan. After all, Levi and his big brother, Curly John, caught fish like that all the time.

On that particular day, Levi—a year older than my sister and me—helped us hook our bait. He and Rachel showed us the best place to cast our lines. But it was my twin sister's determination to catch a fish that spurred me on. By afternoon's end, neither one of us had caught anything, but that didn't dampen Faithie's spirits. She wanted to come back and try the next day. Except that was the Lord's Day, so we knew better than to ask Daddy's permission.

"We'll go fishin' again next week," Levi had said, wearing Curly John's baggy hand-me-downs.

"I think my willow stick's too green," Faithie had told us, laughing as we tromped toward the barn, away from the pond.

"Maybe that's why the fish wouldn't bite today," I said, not knowing for sure. After all, we were young—just one month shy of six years old.

"Better get yourself a sturdier stick next time," Rachel offered, pointing to a hint of green beneath the bark.

"Jah, gut thinkin'," Levi said, waving as he headed for the house.

Rachel stood and talked with us a bit longer, lingering near the fenced area. There weren't any new lambs that year—at least I don't remember them. If there had been, I'm sure Faithie and I would've leaned on the fence, coaxing one of the soft little ones over so we could pet it. Faithie and I were both crazy about animals.

When Rachel's mother called for supper, Rachel hurried off to the house. I figured we'd be heading home soon. But for some reason, Faithie wanted to sit in the grass and "watch the sheep."

"What for?" I'd asked, sitting next to her.

"Just 'cause."

So we sat there, gawking at the Zooks' sheep. Faithie told me a strange story that afternoon. Not a tall tale or anything like that. But she shared something of her young heart with me while she fooled with her fishing pole, pushing it down . . . down ever so slowly into the ground.

"Know what, Merry?" she began.

"What?"

"Last night I dreamed we had our tenth birthday."

I giggled at that. "That's silly."

"Ten's a long time away, isn't it?" Faithie said, still pushing on her fishing pole.

Turning ten *had* seemed a lifetime away! Besides that, girls who were ten were nearly grown-up. At least, it seemed that way. We didn't talk about that so much, though. It was the passing of years that was most heavy on Faithie's mind.

"Birthdays are weird," she continued.

"Huh?"

"You change to a new number." She sighed, letting go of the fishing pole. "But when you're seven, you're still six inside. And five and four and three—all the *old* birthdays wrapped up in the next number. Uncle Tim was in my dream, too. He explained all this to me."

I didn't really get what she was saying. Besides, it seemed weird to me, especially because our uncle was dead. "What do you think Uncle Tim meant?"

"He *told* me when you're six or seven or eight, you're still five and four and three inside." She looked frustrated, as if she was struggling to explain.

I thought about what she'd said. "Do you mean sometimes you wanna cuddle your teddy bear . . . so it's like you're still two years old or even only one?"

Faithie started giggling. "That's it! When you act like a three-year-old, you still *are* that number. And when you set the table for Mommy and do something more grown-up, you're four or five, too. All at the same time."

"How old will we feel when we're ten, I wonder?"

Suddenly, her eyes were big and round. "Maybe we won't feel different at all."

"We'll have to just wait and see," I said.

She looked pleased with herself. Like she'd finally made her dream clear to me. "Birthdays are like tiny puzzle pieces that all fit together. Uncle Tim said one year goes inside the next."

"Wow. Uncle Tim's very smart since he's gone to heaven."

"I think so, too." Then she kissed me all over my face, knocking me down in the tall green grass.

"What age are you now?" I teased.

By the time we left for home, the fishing pole was stuck in the hole. "Leave it there," Faithie had said, patting the ground around it. "Maybe it'll sprout someday."

I laughed, wondering where on earth my sister had gotten such an idea.

A clap of thunder startled me, and I rushed to get the lamb back inside the fence. Jingle had taken only a small amount of milk from the bottle. That didn't mean she wouldn't eventually get used to the bottle, though, because I was *not* giving up!

After getting the lamb back inside the fold, I ran to take shelter. On the Zooks' front porch, I watched the rain come pelting down, spawned by a determined cloudburst. The lone willow swayed, keeping company with the wind.

Maybe we won't feel different at all. . . .

How sad that Faithie hadn't lived to experience her tenth birthday; not even her eighth. And yet the seven years we had together were mighty strong in me. I would never forget them. Or her.

More than that, I felt incomplete without my sister. Like a tree that has shed its leaves in the autumn, I still felt bare without her. Something would always be missing for me. I'd read that all twins feel that way if separated at birth or if one of them dies. Well, it was definitely one-hundred-percent-amen true!

Staring out over the grassy meadow, I spotted the frail little lamb. Her ribs poked through her sides. It pained me to see how scrawny she was. Sighing, I understood how she must feel, losing both her mother and twin sister. She needed a reason to live, to want to take nourishment.

It was then, as I stood on the Zooks' long white front porch, in the midst of a midday thundershower, I knew exactly what I must do. As soon as possible!

Four Shadows Beyond the Gate

I borrowed Rachel's umbrella for the walk home. The rain was still coming down fast, but I couldn't let it stop me. I was anxious to get home for Jon's phone call, so I hurried down the Zooks' lane as the dirt quickly turned into a muddy path.

While I was removing my muddy shoes at our back door, I heard the phone ring. Dad would answer. No rush.

"I'm home if it's for me!" I called, coming inside.

Sure enough, the ringing stopped in the middle of the second ring. I waited, holding my breath . . . hoping. Was it Jon calling?

When I didn't hear my name, I assumed the call was for Dad and headed upstairs to my room. I removed my soggy socks and greeted my cats. All four of them were huddled inside my closet. I didn't blame them for hiding, not after those amazingly powerful claps of thunder. And poor Abednego . . . well, I'm sure it brought back harrowing memories of the day he ran away from home. All because of a vicious storm.

"You okay, kitties?" I cooed, getting down on my hands and knees to nuzzle each of them. "Thunder never hurt anybody."

Abednego was trembling so hard, I picked him up, fat and heavy as he was. "Aw, little man, it'll be all right. Merry's here with you."

Lily White wasn't impressed with the attention my eldest cat was receiving. She pushed her face against my hand, and I decided it was time to dish out equal time. So I sat on the floor of my closet, with the only light filtering in from the bedroom, talking baby talk to my cats. "Let's pretend we're only three years old," I caught myself saying. "So it's okay if we're scared, right?"

Of course, I wasn't really frightened by the thunder or the storm. But it comforted the cats to see me calm and in control.

While I petted Lily White, I glanced up at the shelf above me. Scrapbooks of Faithie and me stood neatly in a row. Did I dare open them today? Stir up even more memories? I wondered if possibly my memories of Faithie's illness might help me nurse Jingle Belle back to health. Maybe I *should* take a peek, I decided. It had been quite a while since I'd cozied up with one of the scrapbooks.

Just as I was putting Lily White down, I heard Dad calling up the stairs. "Merry! Kiddo, the phone's for you."

I could hardly believe my ears. Had Dad been talking to Jon Klein all this time?

"Coming," I said, leaving my cat foursome to deal with the storm on their own. I hurried to Skip's bedroom, just down the hallway from my room. Not wanting to sound too eager, I counted to five before I picked up the phone.

Jon was happy to hear my voice. At least, he *sounded* upbeat and happy. "Hi, Merry. What're you doing today?"

"Hanging with my cats right now. Before that, I was over at Rachel Zook's."

"That's cool."

I had to know, so I asked. "Were you talking to my dad, uh, before?"

"Yeah, he was giving me some pointers on my new camera. Nice guy, your dad." Then Jon began to tell me about his latest photography project. "This class I'm taking is really great. Mostly outdoor shots . . . nature, trees . . . stuff like that."

"Sounds fun," I replied, thinking that he should come out to SummerHill and take pictures of the new lamb. But no, I didn't want to invite him. Not yet.

"Would you like to go with me—with the youth group—next Tuesday night?" he asked.

"Where to?"

"Hiking. I thought we could go out afterward for ice-cream sundaes."

I wasn't sure what shape Rachel's lamb might be in by then. "I'll have to see," I said, holding back.

He was silent for a second. "Everything okay?"

"It's just that I might be busy, that's all."

"Too busy for a hike and ice cream?" There were more questions in his voice, but he didn't push.

"I'll have to let you know," I said. "Thanks for calling."

After we hung up, I worried that he might've thought I didn't want to go. But I wasn't concerned enough to call back.

And at church the next day, I didn't say a word about the lamb, either. I guess I felt it was my thing . . . this sickly lamb and me. My thing and God's.

The next time Jon called was Monday evening. I'd totally forgotten to get back to him about the hike. But I wasn't home when he called, so Mom took another message.

"Are things all right between you and your friend?" Mom asked, her eyes searching mine. "Seems like you're playing phone tag."

I went to the sink to wash my hands. "I've got other things on my mind," I said.

"Not Levi, I hope," Mom shot back.

Why she had that idea, I didn't know. "Levi's off at college," I reminded her.

"I heard he's coming home for a visit." Mom pulled a chair away from the table and sat down. No doubt she wanted to talk this through.

"Are you sure? Because last I heard, he wasn't."

She frowned. "Miss Spindler told me today that he was."

"She oughta know!" Miss Spindler seemed to know everything there was to know in the neighborhood, usually before it even happened. Now that I knew how she kept up on all of us in SummerHill, I didn't pursue things with Mom. I'd play it safe and keep quiet.

"Is it classified information that's keeping you so busy over at our Amish neighbors' farm?" Mom asked gently—not probing, really, just terribly interested.

"I'm helping Rachel care for one of the new lambs."

"Oh?"

"The lamb's sickly . . . an orphan. She won't take to the bottle very well."

Mom's eyes were wide. "How very sad."

"That's why I'm going over there so much."

Mom nodded her head, taking a deep breath. "Well, I'm glad to know this isn't about Rachel's brother."

"Oh, Mom," I laughed it off, "you can relax about Levi. He has a new girlfriend, I'm pretty sure."

Our conversation ended quickly enough, but another was soon to take place. The prelude to it occurred when I bumped in to Dad on my way past his study.

"Hi, Dad," I said, glad to see him. "What have you been doing all day?" I followed him up the steps.

"I think it's time to finish our talk," he said. "I'll meet you in the backyard at the gazebo in, say, ten minutes?"

I checked my watch. "Sure, but first I have to make a phone call."

He smiled faintly, and I hurried to my brother's room, where I dialed Jon Klein. "Hi, Jon," I said when he answered. "It's me, Merry."

"Hey!" He was truly glad to hear from me. "I hope you're coming tomorrow."

"I'd really like to, but I promised to help Rachel after school."

"Oh." A weighty silence followed. He probably wanted an explanation and deserved one. But how could I tell him I was choosing a sick and possibly neurotic animal over him? I couldn't. He might not understand, and I didn't want to risk losing my friendship with him. Besides, I could feel it in my bones—I was getting closer to a breakthrough with little Jingle Belle.

"Maybe I'll go the next time," I spoke up.

"How about next week?" he persisted.

"Why, what's happening then?"

"Some people from my photography class are going down to the banks of the Susquehanna River. We'll shoot some pictures, walk along the river . . . enjoy the surroundings."

"Church friends?" I asked, knowing how picky Dad was.

"Two are." The others were school friends of Jon's, ones I didn't know very well.

I was pretty sure Dad would say I couldn't go. "I guess not. And I'm sorry about tomorrow."

"Will you let me know sooner . . . next time?" He sounded annoyed.

"Yeah, I can do that." Truth was, I could've let him know *this* time but didn't. I'd treated his invitation with reckless indifference.

Again, we hung up on a slightly sour note. I truly hoped Jon would understand about Rachel's lamb once I told him the whole story. If he'd just be patient long enough.

By the time I met Dad at the gazebo, he was looking out through the white latticework. "What took you so long?" he joked.

"Jonathan Klein."

"Great kid . . . I like him." Dad was grinning now, raising his eyebrows at me.

"He seems to like you, too," I said, eager to know what was on his mind. "So what are we talking about?"

"Your mother," he said.

My breath caught in my throat. "She's not sick, is she?" Illness was always the first thought to come to mind. Because of Faithie.

He shook his head, turning to lean against the wood railing so that he was now facing me. "Your mom's going through what's commonly known as a midlife crisis, although *I* don't think it's anything to worry about." He paused, raking his fingers through his hair. "I think her antique shop idea is an excellent one. It'll keep her busy."

"Is there anything I can do? I mean, to make Mom feel better?"

"Maybe there is," he said more softly. "Why don't you talk to her . . . about Faithie. Share your memories of your twin sister."

"Would she want to? I mean, are you sure about this?"

He nodded, eyes glistening. "Mom still misses Faith terribly. We all do."

"*We all do.*" His words tumbled over and over in my brain.

I don't honestly know how I got from where I was standing across the gazebo to my father's arms. Somehow, I managed through a mist of tears. Dad wrapped me in his strong embrace, and I smelled his subtle cologne fragrance and felt the texture of his golf shirt on my cheek. "Oh, Dad," I cried. "I miss Faithie, too."

Five Shadows Beyond the Gate

I would've offered to ride along with Mom after school the next day. I had actually planned to go antique browsing with her, but Rachel Zook was sitting on the white gazebo steps when I came bounding up the back walk. Wisps of her light brown hair had slipped out from under her head covering. It looked like she'd run all the way through the willow grove to get here.

"Hi, Rachel," I said, observing her black dress and gray apron. Looked like Amish mourning clothes to me. "Jingle didn't die, did she?" I barely got the words out.

"No . . . no, no," she said, glancing down at her drab clothing. "But I don't blame ya for thinkin' that." Her face broke into a small smile. "But Jingle's still only takin' enough nourishment to keep her alive. *Dat* has got her on tube feeding now."

The muscles in my jaw began to relax. "You had me worried for a minute."

"Jah, I 'spect I did."

I invited her inside for lemonade and freshly baked cookies. I assumed there would be some ready and waiting on the kitchen counter, because that was Mom's usual after-school snack for me in the spring and summer.

We weren't disappointed. Mom had gone the extra mile and not only made oatmeal cookies but an apple crumb cake, too, along with a pitcher filled with sweet lemonade.

"Your mom's an awful gut cook," Rachel said, sitting down at the table with me.

"That's a compliment, coming from you," I replied, knowing what an incredible cook *her* mother was.

Then, out of the blue, Rachel said, "Jingle's bein' shunned by the flock."

I sat up straight in my chair. "Why, what's happened?"

"The rest of the sheep sense her troubled state."

"Maybe you should keep force-feeding her," I suggested.

Rachel shook her head. "Dat and *Mam* think it's just a matter of days and she'll be gone. Unless . . ." Her voice faded away.

"Unless what?"

"Well, if it ain't God's will for her to go yet."

I should've known Rachel would say that. God's sovereign will covered all His creation; it was I who hadn't thought to invite the Lord into the situation. "Let's ask God to help us with Jingle," I said, ready to pray right then.

She didn't answer, but her blue eyes were serious. "Talkin' like that to God is up to you . . . and Levi," she said softly.

"Levi?" I was startled to hear her mention his name.

"He's home for a visit. Arrived not more than an hour ago."

So Miss Spindler was right. Once again, she knew what she was talking about. "Has Levi prayed for the lamb yet?" I asked.

"Not that I know of, but he's looked her over real gut. 'Tween you and me, I doubt he's as concerned 'bout Jingle as we are."

"What do you mean?"

Her eyes took on an almost distant look. "S'posin' his distraction is understandable."

I listened, waiting for more.

"Levi brought a girl home . . . to meet us," Rachel sputtered out the words.

"His girlfriend from the Mennonite college?"

"Jah."

So I was right all these weeks about my suspicions. No wonder his letters had stopped. Quickly, I remembered my manners. "Well, I'm happy for him. For you, too, Rachel."

"Me?" Rachel blinked her eyes. "Ya know, I was hopin' *you'd* be my sister-in-law someday, Cousin Merry."

I laughed softly. "Oh, things are over between Levi and me. He's all grown-up now, and a Mennonite, too. I never would've fit very well in his Plain world."

"I s'pose not," she whispered, head down. "But it was awful nice to hope."

Getting up, I carried the pitcher of lemonade to the table. "You know, I just realized Levi hasn't heard the news about Miss Spindler's secret."

"Don'tcha mean Old Hawk Eyes?" Rachel asked.

"To me she's simply Miss Spindler now. I don't think she deserves a nickname anymore. Never did, really." Miss Spindler had turned out to be a remarkably astute old lady. Outsmarting all of us.

"I'm sure Levi's gonna want to see you while he's home," Rachel said before she left.

My heart actually stayed put hearing that. I guess I surprised myself, too. Maybe I was truly over any romantic interest in my lifelong friend. "I'd like to meet his girlfriend sometime," I told her.

"You mean you'd like to *approve* of her?"

We literally howled at that, and since parting for us was always next to impossible, I walked all the way out to the lane and down to the willow grove shortcut with her.

The branches above us mushroomed over our heads like a giant tent. Deep in the willows, we found our secret place, more beautiful than one could imagine. The place had belonged to Faithie and me first. After her death, Rachel and I had claimed it as our own. Only one adult had ever visited here. My mother. That was two months shy of a year ago, the day I'd discovered baby Charity abandoned in our gazebo.

Beyond the willow grove was pure sunshine. Golden rays bounced off the grassy meadow to the west of the Zooks' barnyard. And out behind the barn, the pond was aglow with dancing light. Summer was almost here!

"It won't be long and I'll be joining the Amish church, Merry." Rachel's face was serious as she said it, and her eyes shone.

"You sure now?"

"Jah, it's the right way for me," she said reverently. "Matthew and I will both take our kneelin' vow this September."

"I'm not surprised."

She smiled, her dimples showing. "A gut many young people will be joining church this fall. Oh my, and Dat's ever so glad 'bout it."

I thought of Abe Zook's disappointment over his second son, Levi, joining ranks with the Mennonites. "Makes up for certain ones *not* joining, I guess."

"Jah. Dat thinks it's high time we Amish take back our children from the clutches of the world," Rachel said unexpectedly. "He's started speakin' out more and more 'bout raising the standard for our young people."

"Does he plan to talk to Levi about returning to his Amish roots?"

"Well, yes and no. It's a right touchy situation, with Martha around and all."

"Martha?"

"Levi's girlfriend—Martha Martin."

For a second, I nearly laughed, thinking of the alliteration. "Is she staying at your house?" I asked, composing myself.

She nodded sheepishly. "I'm sharing my room with her."

"You'll get acquainted real quick that way."

"Well, ain't that the truth!"

I watched her turn and head out of the willow grove, her slender form flitting through the trees and the underbrush as the sun twinkled down on her.

"I'll be right over after I change clothes," I hollered to her, remembering the dear little lamb who needed me.

"Make it snappy!" she called over her shoulder.

I would hurry, all right. Because I was sure I knew what to do to get Jingle's attention. I could hardly wait to try!

On the way back up the hill, I saw Mom driving out of our lane, then make the turn onto Strawberry Lane. Where was she headed? She never went into town that way. It was the opposite direction!

Quickening my pace, I shot through the front and side yards. Just in time, too, because when I peered through the trees, I saw Mom pulling into our neighbor's driveway. "What's she doing at Miss Spindler's?" I wondered aloud.

Mom and Ruby Spindler had been casual friends for as long as I remembered. Our elderly neighbor seemed to enjoy doting on our family, sharing her freshly baked pies and other pastries. But never had she and Mom been close friends. So this was a surprise! In fact, if I hadn't had an ailing lamb to tend to, I would've schemed to get to the bottom of Mom's visit with our eccentric neighbor. But I had more important things on my mind. Today, I intended to change the course of Jingle Belle's life!

The afternoon sky had begun to turn overcast by the time I changed clothes and headed toward the Zooks' farm. Because of the gray clouds, I felt somewhat gloomy. But I was determined to help Jingle Belle, so I tried to ignore the discouraged feeling.

When I saw Rachel, I told her only a select part of my idea. "I've been thinking of doing something. It might sound a little weird. But . . . it just might save Jingle's life."

She gave me a sidelong glance, but I ignored it. We waited near the fence for the orphaned lamb to wander over. The tiny bell tinkled its sweet sound, and we petted Jingle's soft coat.

A lump caught in my throat when I saw how pitiful she was. Like a shadow of herself. "She's pining away, all right," I whispered.

"An awful shame," Rachel replied.

I considered my unconventional idea, pondering it over and over in my mind. Then I got brave and made my intention known, so I wouldn't get cold feet and back out. "Do you think it's safe for me to go inside the fence?" I asked Rachel at last.

"Well, Merry, whatever for?"

"I want to try to enter Jingle's world, so to speak. Honestly, I think she'll take the nursing bottle better if I do."

"I don't know . . ."

"Isn't it worth a try?" I insisted.

Rachel scanned the area, shading her eyes with one hand. "Ach, just a minute! Looks to me like Dat and Levi let the rams out to the back pasture." It was true, only the ewes and smaller sheep—and Jingle Belle—remained in the enclosure. "It *might* well be safe enough for ya," she said, still surveying things.

"Maybe this is providential," I spoke up. "With the rams let out and all."

Rachel seemed to like my mention of "providential." Delight was written on her face. "Jah, maybe it's not such a bad idea, after all." And she ran to get the bottle of milk.

While she was gone, I prayed that God would help me connect with the starving lamb. "Somehow, Lord, please let Jingle take more nourishment today," I prayed under my breath. "Please . . ."

My eyes caught sight of the willow tree, the one that had grown from the simple fishing pole. *If Faithie were alive, she'd be right here, helping me,* I thought. But I knew better than to talk to my sister, who'd gone to heaven. It was God who would help me now.

"Here you are," Rachel said, running toward me with the bottle of milk.

I tested the nipple, squirting a thin stream of milk on Jingle's nose by accident. Then I climbed over the plank fence. "Hello, sweet girl," I whispered, sitting down next to Jingle. "I'm here, baby, just for you."

She began to nuzzle next to me, making the saddest, yet dearest sounds. Jingle Belle was crying. Someone had cared enough to crawl over the fence. To *her* side!

Almost at once, the clouds seemed to part, allowing the sun to break through for a moment. When I offered the milk bottle, there was no hesitation from Jingle. The lamb drank heartily.

"That-a girl," I whispered, holding hard to the bottle.

Rachel was nearly breathless with excitement. "Wait'll I tell Dat and Mam," I heard her say, and then she flew off toward the house.

"You're the best little lamb I know," I cooed to Jingle, who didn't seem to mind my dinner talk. "We'll fatten you up and get you well, don't you worry."

There were only the contented sounds of Jingle's suckle. No sorrowful bleatings. I was overjoyed! "Thank you, Lord" was all I could say.

By the time Rachel arrived, bringing along her mother, Esther, and the rest of the children, Jingle had come close to draining the bottle dry.

"Let's get her more milk!" young Nancy exclaimed.

"Jah, and hurry up about it," Mrs. Zook said, clapping her hands.

The second bottle disappeared almost as quickly, and Jingle began to nod her head up and down. "Look, she's thankin' you, Merry," little Susie said.

I climbed out of the fence and stood there with the Zooks, admiring the lamb on the other side.

"I should say, I believe she's gonna live," Esther announced under a sky that seemed bluer than before. "Well, I do declare."

"Wait'll we tell Levi," said Nancy and Ella Mae.

"Praise be!" little Susie said, and the younger girls scampered off.

"We're ever so grateful to you," Rachel said, throwing her arms around me in a jubilant hug.

"I'm glad it turned out this way," I said.

" 'Merry had a little lamb, it's fleece was white as snow,' " Rachel's mother recited comically.

Rachel herself finished the verse. " 'And everywhere that Merry went, the lamb was sure to go.' "

We had a good laugh, but there was more to it. A precious animal's life had been saved. Right before our eyes!

Later that night, as I dressed for bed, I thought of Jingle and her world of the sheep corral. What had made me think to crawl over the fence and join her there? More than that, why had it worked?

The night sky was evident through the curtains. White fog had begun to descend on Lancaster County. I went to stand at one of the windows, looking out at the ancient maple in our front yard. Far sturdier than the frail weeping willow near the sheep fence, this tree had shaded our lawn for more than a hundred and fifty years, providing refuge on hot days and now lending support for a wooden swing, too. It was also the tree Lissa Vyner, my dear friend, had crouched under, calling me out of bed one moonlit night a year and a half ago. I hadn't know it then, but along the way—since that night—God had made me aware of my "helping" gift. First stray cats, then an abused girl friend, an autistic boy, an abandoned baby, and now a sickly lamb.

Often, I worried that I got too caught up in my "Miss Fix-It" mentality. But I'm coming to understand myself better these days. I'm not so hard on myself, I guess. Losing Faithie may have gotten the helper thing going. I don't know for sure. It really doesn't matter. What counts is that I'm depending on the Lord for heavenly help.

Before slipping into bed, I thanked God again for letting Jingle live. "That dear little lamb is a lot like I was after Faithie died. For years, I couldn't cry over her. Remember, Lord? But when I finally did, I started to heal."

I brushed my tears away. "I think when Jingle drank all that milk today, she began to heal, too," I continued my prayer. "Thank you, God, for giving me the idea about going into *her* world . . . the way Jesus did for us when He left heaven and came to earth."

I hadn't thought of the connection before—between what God did for humanity and what I'd done for Jingle—but it got me wound up. I really couldn't sleep a wink, I was that excited.

Instead of wasting time tossing in bed, I got up and went to my desk and turned on the light. Now was a good time to double-check my English assignment for tomorrow, and while I was at it, I scrutinized my math and history homework, too.

I thought of my school and church friends: Lissa Vyner, Chelsea Davis, and Ashley Horton. All three would be giggling if they could see me now.

It turned out that I only stayed up till just past eleven. Then, I fell into a delicious, deep sleep. I dreamed I was a tall, sturdy maple tree, planted near a river—like the one in the first psalm. My roots reached far down into the soil, and nothing could shake me.

When I awakened hours later, my arms were stiff and nearly numb, like frozen tree branches in winter. I sat up in bed, moving my arms to get the blood circulating. Yet the tree dream lingered in my mind, the most peculiar dream ever.

Seven Shadows Beyond the Gate

The rain stopped sometime in the wee hours, Mom told me at breakfast. And the ominous white fog dissipated by the time I left the house to stand along SummerHill Lane, waiting for the school bus. I had a good feeling that this was going to be a beautiful day.

To start with, Jon saved a place for me on the bus next to him. Chelsea, in her regular spot, sat across the aisle from us, her nose in a book. She looked up briefly when I got on, pushed her thick auburn locks behind one ear, and then flipped back through the pages in her book.

"What's she reading?" I asked Jon, smiling at him.

"Must be something very deep" came his answer, far less ecstatic than usual.

I knew why. I'd hurt Jon by not going on the hike with him. Taking a deep breath, I made an attempt at smoothing things over. "I'm really sorry about yesterday," I managed, but my words came out flat.

"The hike?" He shrugged. "Forget it."

I didn't dare ask if he had a good time, or even if he went at all. The thought crossed my mind that he might've wanted to ask someone else, since I didn't go. It wasn't as if he and I were in an exclusive dating relationship. Not at my age—going on seventeen.

We rode in silence all the way to school. I stared straight ahead, looking out the wide dash window up front, feeling very awkward about the tension between Jon and me.

When we arrived, I could hardly wait to get off the bus. I scurried to the shelter of my locker without another word to Jon.

Chelsea followed close behind. "You two aren't exactly humming today. Is it because you stood him up?"

"Chelsea Davis, I did *not*!"

"Well, what do you call it?" Her green eyes flashed.

I was no dummy. She'd definitely heard *someone's* version of the story. I wondered how many other people Jon had told.

"You stood him up," Chelsea accused me again.

"I'm late for homeroom," I blurted.

"We just got here, remember?"

"I must be late for something." I reached for my three-ring binder, and a landslide of books followed behind. "Yee-ikes! Look what you made me do!" I hollered, causing students to gawk.

"I'm outta here," she said, launching into the tidal wave of humanity in the hallway.

I fumed, wishing Chelsea hadn't said what she'd said. Wishing, too, I hadn't retaliated and treated her horribly. I gathered my books and stuffed them back in my locker. I wished something else, too—that I had been completely honest with Jon. What on earth had kept me from telling him about Rachel's lamb? Why was I protecting my experience with a helpless animal, keeping it from a close friend like Jon?

I don't know how long I stood there, staring and fuming into my locker. It must've been long enough to lose myself in my anger, because, suddenly, I heard a voice behind me.

"What're you doing, Mer?"

Turning around, I saw Lissa Vyner frowning at me. "Hey, what's up, Liss?"

"Asked you first."

I sighed. "Whatever."

"So?" I figured she wouldn't leave me alone till I spilled out my problems to her. Lissa was like that—she could pretty much read my facial expressions and know when I was really upset.

"I was a jerk to Chelsea," I admitted.

"No kidding. News like that travels with the speed of sound." She nodded solemnly. "It's not like you, Merry," she said quietly.

"I know, and I'm sorry. It's just that . . ."

"Is it about you and Jon?" she asked.

I couldn't bear to hear any of this. Not from meek and mild Lissa. "Who all knows about this, for pete's sake?"

She shrugged, taking a step closer to me. "Jon thinks you like Levi Zook *again*. He thinks that's why you're spending so much time at the Amish farm."

I shook my head. "I haven't even seen Levi."

"Then he *is* back?" Her eyes were wider than I'd seen them in a long time.

"His sister said he was visiting, and I heard he was working with his dad, but, honestly, I have *not* seen him." I paused, closing my locker. "Please tell Jon that Levi and I are ancient history!"

She smiled, hugging me. "That's all I wanted to hear."

The first-period bell rang, and we parted ways.

No wonder Jon was so quiet on the bus, I thought. He was freaked over Levi's return. But Jon had nothing to fear. Levi had a college girlfriend now. He was in love with someone new.

Then I felt it, my first twinge of uncertainty. It definitely wasn't jealousy or anything like that. I slid into my home-room desk and glanced at my assignment notebook. Browsing through my schedule for the day, I realized the twinge had become more of a stabbing pain. I could never, ever reveal this to my girl friends. And I would keep it secret from Jon, too. No one needed to know. Because this was totally absurd.

Yet the more I thought of Levi in love with Martha Martin, whoever she was, the more I cringed. My toes even curled up inside my shoes, and I felt the tension in my jaw. But I had no choice—I'd have to deal with it. Besides, it was too late now; I'd stuck my neck out, for sure. Why had I told Rachel I wanted to meet Levi's girlfriend?

What *was* I thinking?

I groaned so loudly, several students turned around and glared at me. Sadly for me, the day was turning out to be less than beautiful.

Eight *Shadows Beyond the Gate*

The house was filled with music when I arrived home. The CD player was blaring with the likes of Mozart and Haydn. The cats didn't seem to mind the classical racket. Actually, they were busy scarfing down their usual afternoon snack.

"What's with the music?" I asked, giving Mom a quick hug.

"I'm attempting to raise the cats' level of intelligence." Her eyes twinkled.

"By playing the classics?" This was too weird.

"I read that it works for human babies, so why not cats?"

"You can't be serious," I said, getting down on the floor to pet my favorite kitties.

"Oh yes, I am." She carried a plate of warm cookies to the kitchen table. "And . . . I'm practicing my ability to soothe customers while I'm at it."

I looked up from my vantage point on the floor. Mom was absolutely radiant. She didn't seem in need of a heart-to-heart talk, like Dad had said. Maybe he was mistaken. On second thought, maybe he was right. Maybe Mom was submerging her sorrow in planning a business.

"Miss Spindler's agreed to be my partner. She and I have already discussed things, and we're definitely having soft music piped into our little antique shop."

"Dad told me you wanted to fix up the shed—start an antique business."

She nodded. "Yes, and I've already begun to sort through old things, mostly junk that can be hauled away."

"Are you actually going to do this?"

"Oh, Merry, honey, I'm so excited!" She gave me an impulsive hug.

"Did Dad mention the possibility of tourists trampling your flower beds?" I couldn't see how any of this was a good idea.

"Oh, nonsense," and she waved her hand as if tourists were not a concern. "The stone walkway will lead right to the shop. No trampling worries."

I was surprised at her response. "Better ask Rachel and her mother about some of the rude folks they've encountered."

But Mom was insistent. She was determined to open a cozy shop in the backyard. She was going to focus on antiques—the past—in order to handle the present, and possibly her future, too: life minus Faithie. I was convinced more than ever that losing Faithie was behind all this talk.

I finished my homework in two hours—record time. Then I called Chelsea. My lousy behavior had begun to gnaw at my conscience. I wanted to apologize for my outburst at school. But she wasn't at home, so I called Lissa. "Any idea where Chelsea is?" I asked.

"How should I know?"

"She's gotta be around SummerHill somewhere," I mumbled into the phone. It made no sense for me to ask Lissa where Chelsea was because Chelsea Davis lived up the hill from *me*. And Lissa lived miles away.

"Why don't you just call Jon?" Lissa suggested. "That's who you *really* want to talk to, right?"

Lissa knew me well. I smiled into the phone. "I don't know what to say to him. He wasn't very talkative on the bus today . . . morning or afternoon."

"Start with Levi Zook. Get it out in the open. Let Jon hear it from you that Levi's out of the picture."

"I thought you told Jon in study hall," I said.

"Sure, but—"

"What did Jon say?"

Lissa sighed into the phone. "To tell you the truth, Mer, he only nodded his head."

"Like he didn't believe you?"

"You could say that." She paused, then continued. "I really think you should call him."

I was surprised at Lissa's persistence. This was very different for her. "Okay, I will . . . later. Right now I've got something important to do."

"More important than your *boyfriend*? I can't believe this. What could be so important?" She really wanted to know, but I wasn't telling. "I thought we were super close, Mer," she said, sounding less confident.

"We are," I assured her. "Lighten up, Lissa."

She was silent for a moment, then giggled a little. "Did you say what I think you said?"

"Yeah. So?"

"But you quit the Alliteration Game, right?"

"Yeah, I quit."

"Except you just did it . . . again."

She was right. "Oh that. Well, for some reason it seems to fly out of my mouth automatically every now and then."

"Maybe that's because it's a part of who you are after all this time."

Funny how Lissa's comment fit right into what I'd been thinking about Levi Zook.

After all this time . . .

Levi was a big part of my life, too. How could I let him slip out of it, smack-dab into Martha's?

I could hear Lissa's mom calling her in the background, so we said good-bye and hung up. I was glad our conversation ended with Lissa's explanation of why she thought I was still alliterating my words. Much better than pleading with me for answers. I hadn't told her the cool thing Jon had said not too long ago. *"You're the Alliteration Queen,"* he'd announced one day. Where that particular thought came from, I didn't know. Anyway, it was small consolation at the moment.

Fact was, both Jon and Levi had been a huge part of my life. And for a very long time. Levi and I, however, went back a few years further than Jon and I. Still, it was terribly unnerving to care so much for two boys. At the same time!

Rachel Zook came over before supper. "Jingle won't take the bottle from any of us," Rachel said, her blue eyes earnest as can be. "She needs you, Merry."

"I'm coming," I said and then called to Mom over my shoulder. "I'll be back in an hour or so."

"Where are you going?" she said, coming into the kitchen.

"I'm 'on call' at the Zook farm," I told her, laughing.

The air was as sweet and clean as fresh laundry hung out to dry. And as Rachel and I ran through the yard to SummerHill Lane and then into the willow grove, a peculiar thought hit me. What would Mom do about her clothesline if customers were coming and going at her antique shop? Would she give up one of life's simple pleasures to accommodate shoppers? I couldn't imagine her dumping clothes into an electric dryer, except during inclement weather. I made a mental note to ask her.

"Something on your mind?" Rachel asked halfway through the abundant thicket of willow trees and vegetation.

"Oh, it's my mother. She's having some sort of a midlife crisis."

"What's *that*?"

"Well, she's almost fifty. Thinks life is passing her by, I guess. That's how my dad explained it."

Rachel slowed her pace to a stroll. We walked single file down past the tallest trees, turning toward the meadow that led to the Zooks' barnyard. "Never heard of such a thing, really," Rachel said. "Maybe it's something *Englischers* get."

"You're probably right," I said with a chuckle. Middle-aged Amish folk didn't have time to feel sorry about their children growing up and going to college. They were too busy raising the tail end of a long line of children. No empty-nest syndrome till the grandchildren started coming on. Besides that, most of their young people never went off to college because the bishops didn't allow education past the eighth grade. A Plain wife didn't have to worry about early retirement for her husband. Amish farmers, carpenters, and blacksmiths worked up until God called them home. Or until they couldn't physically work any longer. That's the way it was in the Anabaptist community.

"Is your mother gonna be all right?" asked Rachel. "Is she seein' a doctor?"

I stifled a laugh. "It's not as serious as that. Mom's going to start up an antique shop in our backyard. It'll give her something to keep her mind off herself."

"That doesn't sound so bad," Rachel replied, looking more confused than before. "Maybe I can help tend the store sometimes."

Leave it to Rachel to offer. "I'm sure Mom would love to have some expert help."

"Expert?"

"Well, you know, all the experience you have from your fruit and vegetable stands."

"Oh, I see what you're sayin'."

We climbed over the fence that divided the open pasture-land from the side yard. That's when I spied a Mennonite girl hanging out clothes on the line behind the Zooks' farmhouse. "Is that Levi's girlfriend?" I whispered.

"Jah," answered Rachel. "Come, I'll introduce you."

I felt myself holding back, feeling suddenly shy. I wasn't sure why, but I put on a smile. "Sure, that'd be nice," I said, following Rachel to the wide backyard.

We walked right up to the clothesline. The young woman was clearly a strict Mennonite. The hem of her floral print dress came well below her knees. Her hair was a lighter brown than Rachel's, more like the color of ripened wheat. And her bright brown eyes—you couldn't help but notice the sparkle.

"Martha, I want you to meet my friend Merry Hanson," said Rachel. "Merry lives past the willow grove across the way." She pointed toward my house, to the west, then turned to me. "And, Merry, this is Martha Martin from the Mennonite college in Virginia, where Levi goes to school."

"Hello, Merry," Martha Martin said, extending her hand.

"Nice to meet you," I said, wondering why Rachel hadn't simply said Martha was Levi's girlfriend.

"SummerHill is a beautiful place," Martha was saying. Her smile was contagious. Actually, everything about her was delightful. I could see why Levi had fallen in love. "How long have you lived here, Merry?" she asked.

"My whole life, pretty much."

"Then you've been friends with Rachel for a long time?"

I glanced at Rachel, who was nodding and grinning at me. "Since we were toddlers, I guess you could say."

Rachel spoke up. "All us kids were good friends with Merry and her brother, Skip."

"And Faithie, too," I added.

Rachel's eyes softened, and she tilted her head against the sun. "Faithie was Merry's twin sister," she said.

It was uncanny, because Martha really didn't have to be told that Faithie had died. I guess the way Rachel said "Faithie *was* Merry's twin sister" gave it away.

"I'm sorry about your sister," Martha replied. She was so sweet and gentle spirited. As much as I might've wanted to be upset with her for latching on to Levi, I simply couldn't be. She was the perfect choice for a former Amish boy called into the ministry.

After I gave Jingle her nursing bottle—and she drank every drop—I headed home, alone. This time, I stopped in the middle of the willow grove and sat on a dead tree stump in the secret place. I thought about meeting Martha Martin, the amazing Mennonite maid.

When I saw Levi again, I would tell him what a wonderful girl she was. I would congratulate him, too.

It was really the weirdest thing, but my twinges and stabs were actually starting to go away. How could I be so back and forth about things?

I caught up with Chelsea at Wednesday night Bible study, before church in the girls' rest room. "I tried to call you after school," I said.

She didn't bother to turn away from the mirror, but our eyes caught all the same.

"Look, I don't blame you for being upset," I continued. "I shouldn't have freaked out like that."

"No kidding," she muttered.

"I'm sorry, Chelsea. It won't happen again."

She smirked.

Several girls and their mother came in then. I knew we'd have to finish the one-sided conversation later. Anyway, it was obvious Chelsea wasn't in the mood to forgive me any time soon.

"Can we talk later?" I pleaded.

She acted as if she hadn't heard me, same as before.

"Chelsea?"

She turned and glared at me. "Tomorrow," she whispered and left.

I washed my hands without ever looking in the mirror.

It was late in the day when I went outside in my pajamas and looked up at the sky. Shadrach and Meshach had followed me. I knew it wouldn't be long before the other cats would come, too. It was almost completely dark as I sat on the back steps, thinking about what the future held for me. For my friends, too.

Rachel and Matthew Yoder were following the traditional Amish courting rituals. I was pretty sure they'd marry within a year of this coming November, during wedding season. Levi and Martha Martin were probably headed in the same matrimonial direction.

Stars were beginning to appear, one at a time, like city lights. Cicadas and crickets began singing their night songs, calling back and forth. First in one clump of bushes, then another group joined in, until an entire choir of nighttime insects' sounds mingled with the dark blue dusk.

Would I be sitting here if Faithie were alive tonight? I asked myself. *Would I be contemplating my future?*

I pictured the two of us sitting on the steps, pointing out one star after another, maybe even spotting a planet or two. She would be wearing different pajamas than mine, though. Even as a little girl, she'd had strong opinions about our not looking exactly alike—doing our hair different, wearing distinct outfits. I was pretty sure, though, that we'd be barefoot if we were here together. Letting the cool green grass tickle our feet was something we always liked to do in the evening hours when the day was dying down. And she would've liked cuddling up with the cats. As for her taking in strays, I doubt it.

If Faithie had continued as she was—much more like Mom—she probably would've shied away from having so many pets. She might've turned out to be intolerant toward my cats, the way Mom often was. Then again, maybe I wouldn't have needed so many cats, or any at all, if Faithie had lived.

"Oh, Lord, I wish I could get past the hurdle of my sister's death. It's like a shadow shrouding the gateway to my future."

I thought of Jingle Belle, how she would only take her milk when I held the nursing bottle. What did it mean? Could she sense my great personal loss?

Sitting outside under the vast sky, it was easy to feel sorry for myself, being the surviving twin. I often wondered why God hadn't let Faithie live instead of me. Why *not* her? Was it because she was born first—twenty minutes before me? She always had to be the first to show Mom and Dad her report card, first to wrap her Christmas presents, and first in most any footrace. Did she have to outdistance me and beat me to heaven, too?

I leaned back on my elbows, staring hard at the sky. It was turning slate gray, and the stars seemed brighter than before. In the stillness, I wondered what the insects were saying to each other. Were they calling back and forth, "We can sing louder than you"? "No, *we* can . . . we can . . ." Were they debating the time of tomorrow's sunrise?

Sighing, I listened till the choristers blended into one clamorous cadenza. The half moon surprised me when it appeared, floating up over the trees, its light clinging to the east side of the gazebo. A lonely owl hooted into the chaos of the night chorus, and I felt a slight chill.

One thing I knew for sure: Rachel's lamb had stirred up everything about Faithie's death. Jingle and I had connected somehow. We were linked with a common cord. And God had answered my prayer for the sick baby animal.

I sighed, looking down as I felt two furry bodies pushing into my lap. Just as I thought, Abednego and Lily White had made their presence known. They didn't want to miss out on getting attention.

"Where have you been?" I asked, petting them both. "Did you think I'd gone and left you?"

Mew. Abednego had the audacity!

"Don't you know I'd never do that," I insisted. "You can count on me!"

"I will not leave you comfortless . . ." The verse in John's gospel popped into my mind. It had been one of the Scripture readings at Faithie's funeral. Our pastor had said God would never abandon us in our sorrow. He would take care of us in our loneliness, in our sadness.

"God cares more about me than I care for my cats," I said aloud, surprising myself.

God cares . . .

I stayed outside another fifteen minutes or so, letting the truth sink in. The insects had calmed down. I hadn't been aware of the silence until now. No more competitive chirping and singing back and forth between bushes.

The moon's light had shifted. Now it lay across the back steps, where I was surrounded by cats. The beauty of the night and the stillness made me feel like crying. The tears came for all the days and nights I had missed Faithie. All the life experiences we might've shared together.

I wiped my nose on the hem of my pajama top, something my twin would *never* have done. Realizing that, I began to snicker.

Getting up, I opened the door and headed back into the house. Without saying good-night to either of my parents, I made a beeline to my room and fell on my knees beside my bed.

Would God answer my prayer and lift my burden? Was it too much to ask?

I should've known Mom would have a hefty breakfast spread out when I came downstairs. Several days had passed since she'd last made waffles. Scrambled eggs, bacon, and jelly toast were her usual fare, even when things were rushed. But today it was the works, and I reminded her that it was only Thursday. "Not Saturday brunch."

"It's your next-to-last week of school before summer vacation," she said, which made absolutely no sense to me. "You need a good breakfast to keep you going."

"I don't get it, Mom. You don't have to knock yourself out making all this food. It's just breakfast, for pete's sake."

She ignored my comments and set about pouring orange juice in her best juice glasses. "Your father and I are going to Bird-in-Hand to talk to a Mennonite antique dealer today."

"Have fun," I said offhandedly.

Mom must've picked up on the tone of my remark. She turned, and then I noticed she was still wearing her bathrobe. "What's the matter, Merry?" she asked.

Since Mom hardly ever wore her bathrobe downstairs, I guess I might've been staring at her. "What . . . what did you say?"

"The antique business," she stated. "You seem opposed to the idea."

"Oh, I don't really care," I answered, wondering how I should proceed. "I guess it's not the coolest thing, dealing in ancient history. That's all."

Mom sat across the table from me. Her face was crestfallen. "Merry, honey, I'd like to say something."

I nodded, feeling lousy now. Dad had asked me to please reach out to Mom, not alienate her with flippant remarks.

She sighed audibly. "You may not realize this, but I happen to like the idea of selling antiques. It's one of my goals . . . something I've wanted to do for a very long time."

"Since Skip went to college?" I asked, hoping it was the right thing to say.

"Long before that," she replied, pushing her hair behind her ear. "I'd say I've wanted to do the antique thing ever since you and Faithie were born."

Faithie . . .

So I was right.

"Authentic antiques have a unique quality." She paused, smiling faintly. "I feel renewed when I'm surrounded by the past."

"Old things won't bring Faithie back," I said softly.

Her eyes widened, her forehead creased into a deep frown. "Excuse me?"

I shook my head. "Oh nothing."

"No . . . you said something quite startling, Merry. I think we should talk about this."

Glancing at my watch, I saw that we didn't have time for a knockdown, drag-out conversation. Unfortunately, I had a desperate feeling that's what it might turn out to be. "Can it wait till after school?"

We both heard Dad's footsteps at the same time. "Perhaps," she said, sounding worse than forlorn. She was heartbroken. Thanks to me.

Once again, I'd made a fatal error. First Jon, then Chelsea, and now Mom. "I'm sorry," I managed to say before Dad came in and sat down. He reached for the newspaper and opened it, which was a good thing. For now, he wouldn't see the sadness in Mom's eyes.

I, on the other hand, observed her grief all too well.

To top things off, Chelsea was sitting next to Jon when I boarded the bus. They were having a lively conversation, so I walked past them and sat farther back, where I could observe them in private. I had no idea what was going on. But Chelsea was up to something—I could count on it!

Several times during the ride to school, Jon glanced back at me. I managed to divert my eyes so that he wouldn't think I was watching them. It had nothing to do with jealousy because I knew Chelsea had no interest in Jon Klein. And even if she had, I knew perfectly well how Jon felt about me. He and I had been good friends since elementary school, and only recently had we decided to go out.

Chelsea actually waited for me to get off the bus. "Can we talk now?" *She* was asking me! She fell into step with me, and I kept my eye on Jon as he hurried into the school ahead of us. "I'll be straight with you, Merry," she began.

"What?"

"You've got plenty of competition, in case you don't know."

"What're you talking about?" I said.

"Jon wants to know why you stood him up for the hike."

I felt the same resentment as yesterday when she accused me of the same thing. "I told you, I didn't stand him up."

She waved her hand. "Call it what you like. Truth is, you've been ignoring him."

"Why should *you* care?"

"Jonathan's my friend," she replied. "I'm not going to stand by and watch you hurt him."

I had no idea where she was going with this. "Jon and I will work it out," I told her. "Stay out of it."

She gave me a severe frown and flounced off.

Immediately, I headed for Jon's locker. Before I could think twice and chicken out, I walked right up to him and said, "I don't think it's fair what you're saying about me."

He turned to look at me, his brown eyes thoughtful. His shirt was a soft yellow, which brought out the gold flecks in his eyes, and his gorgeous brown hair shone. "I really just want us to get along, Merry."

"How is that possible with you spreading things around behind my back?"

"I don't want anyone else getting in the way," Jon answered.

"Who're you talking about?" I said right out. "Is there someone you'd rather ask out? Is that it?"

He was shaking his head. "No, I hope *you'll* spend time with me, Merry."

I knew I had to set the record straight. He suspected Levi and I were getting too friendly. "You don't have to second-guess me, Jon. If you want to know why I've been spending so much time at Zooks', it's because of an orphan lamb."

His eyes softened. "A lamb?"

"That's right, and her name is Jingle Belle. She was desperate—dying—for a name, among other things. . . ."

By the time the homeroom bell rang, I'd told him the entire sad story. How Jingle needed me, how she wouldn't eat much for anyone else. How she was mourning her family.

"This is incredible," he said. "Why didn't you tell me Monday?"

"I should've . . . I know."

He reached for my hand and held it. "Oh, Merry, forgive me?"

My heart nearly flipped out of my chest as he continued to hold my hand there in the hallway as the entire population of James Buchanan High filed by. "I'm sorry, too."

On my way to homeroom, I wondered how I could smooth things over with both Mom and Chelsea. I would definitely try. Still, I couldn't help but think Chelsea had meant to interfere. I was going to find out the truth. At lunch!

I would give it my best shot with my outspoken girl friend. Chelsea was a new Christian, so I knew I must be very understanding toward her. I would close my mouth and open my ears—hear her out completely.

Searching the cafeteria, I saw her sitting alone. "Thank goodness, I found you," I said, nearly breathless as I scooted in next to her.

She kept chewing her sandwich, glancing at me out of the corner of her eyes.

"I don't know why you were so upset about the hike thing . . . and Jon and me," I began. "But it's okay now, he and I are cool. We talked."

She turned toward me. "It's just that I know how crazy you were over him for such a long time. I couldn't stand by and let the two of you self-destruct." She went on to say that there were other girls in the youth group at church. "They've got their eyes on Jon."

"Plenty of girls do. I'm not stupid."

Chelsea nodded. "He's always been so 'out there'—on another planet somewhere—when it came to the opposite sex. I honestly thought he'd never figure out the girl-boy thing. But now with you and him together . . . well, it's almost too good to be true."

I agreed. "You don't have to worry. I haven't been avoiding Jon. He knows where I've been hanging out all week." Then I told *her* the lamb story.

She laughed out loud. "I don't believe this! You've been lamb-sitting?"

After further explanation, she seemed to understand. "I don't know about you, Mer. You've always been a little strange, but this . . . ?"

"Sometimes even I don't know about me," I muttered.

She didn't catch the tone of my remark, and I was glad. I really didn't care to explain my present mournful state. Knowing Chelsea, she might not understand that, either.

After school, Jon showed up at my locker. He waited for me to collect my books, and then we walked to the bus. We sat together and talked all the way to SummerHill. When the bus stopped, I stood up to get off.

Jon jumped up. "Mind if I walk you home?"

I knew if he did, he'd have a long walk to his own house. "You don't have to," I said.

"But I *want* to, Merry." His smile softened my heart.

"Okay." Inside, I was secretly thrilled beyond words.

We took our sweet time walking up the hill that led to my parents' hundred-year-old farmhouse. Old, gnarled trees and the willow grove to the north surrounded us as we talked. "My sister used to think it would be fun to live in the woods," I told him.

"Faithie was really special," he replied. "I remember, in kindergarten, she painted a picture of a tree house."

I was shocked that he remembered. "You remember *that*?"

He nodded, his eyes smiling. "That, and lots more." He paused for a second. "Mostly I remember *you*, Mistress Merry."

"We've known each other nearly forever," I said, looking down at the road.

"I'm glad about that." He seemed shy just then.

"Me too," I said.

We talked of other school memories. Funny things that happened, and some not so funny. Later, Jon brought up the lamb at the Zooks'. "Sometime, I'd like to see her," he said.

"I thought you might want to take some pictures of Jingle. You know, for your photography class."

"That would be cool." He surprised me and reached for my hand. I have to admit I couldn't believe how fantastic it felt, holding hands with Jon again. At school and now here, on SummerHill Lane. I'd dreamed of this since forever, and now it was happening. I could hardly believe he'd decided to walk me home today. And I was pretty sure my mom would invite him in for her usual cookies and lemonade after-school menu.

"I'll ask Rachel if you can take some farm shots for your class next time I see her."

"That'd be great. Thanks."

"I don't think the Zooks will mind."

"Just so I don't focus on *them*, right?" Jon said.

I agreed that it was a good idea to aim the lens only at the sheep. "You know how the Amish are about cameras. They despise having their pictures taken."

He laughed. "I've heard."

We slowed our pace as we approached the front yard of my house. At the mailbox, he stopped. "Merry, I think of you as my best friend." His eyes were shining. "I have for a long time."

"That's the nicest thing anyone's said to me." I felt completely comfortable admitting it.

"I think the Alliteration Game helped make the friendship connection stronger with you. You have no idea how shy I was back then—sorta had my head in the clouds, too. I'm glad we've moved on to a different level of friendship."

"Me too."

"You don't miss the word game, do you?" he asked, his eyes searching mine.

"Sometimes, but talking like this is much better."

I loved hearing his soft laughter. "You're the *best* friend I've ever had, Merry . . . or ever hoped to have."

I couldn't honestly say that back to him because of Faithie. She'd been my best friend, of course. "I've been hoping you'd say that ever since we sat across from each other in fourth grade."

He nodded. "Yeah, I remember. Guys don't really notice girls, I guess, till later on."

"Well, we found each other. That's what matters," I said, matching his stride as we headed up the front lawn and around the side to the back door. He gave my hand a gentle squeeze before letting go.

Mom was waiting on the back steps, smiling to beat the band. "Merry . . . Jon! Please come inside."

"You'd better be hungry," I whispered.

He chuckled and followed me into the kitchen.

I would've expected Mom to still be a little ticked at me. Instead, I was surprised by her enthusiasm. She seemed positively delighted to see me. And Jon, too.

The reason for her joy was forthcoming. Mom and Dad had spent their entire day discussing at length the ins and outs of running an antique dealership. And now my mother was sharing every conceivable tidbit of information with Jon and me—whether we wanted to hear about it or not.

"It's going to be quite a venture," she said, offering the plate of cookies to Jon for the second time.

He was polite, of course, and listened to her babble on. Several times his gaze caught mine, and we shared a furtive glance. I was sure he was bored out of his mind, yet he sat there listening intently.

"Rachel Zook said she would help with your store if you ever need her," I said, making small talk.

"How sweet of her," Mom said. Then, quite unexpectedly, she added, "Speaking of Rachel, her brother dropped by this afternoon."

I gulped inwardly. *Not now, Mom!* I thought. *Don't talk about Levi in front of Jon!*

"Was Martha with him?" I asked, hoping she'd take the hint.

She looked puzzled, slowly catching on, I could only hope. "I didn't see her, no."

"Well, she's here visiting Levi's family," I managed to say. "Rachel thinks Levi and his girlfriend will soon be engaged."

Mom smiled at this news. "How lovely."

But it wasn't so lovely, her bringing up the subject of Levi Zook. Not today. Not after everything Jon and I had been through!

Still, the question remained: Why had Levi come here? Mom hadn't made that clear. But I remembered Rachel saying she was sure Levi would want to see me.

Sooner or later, I'd have to address the sticky situation with Jon. If I wanted to continue as his best friend, I'd have to. It just wasn't fair otherwise. Besides, I knew I wanted to see Levi again. For more than one reason.

"Mom, how *could* you?" I wailed the second Jon left. "I don't get it. You seemed relieved before that Levi was out of my life, and then you bring him up . . . in front of Jon! It doesn't make any sense!"

She turned to the refrigerator and stood in the doorway for the longest time without speaking. "I'm sorry, Merry." She closed the refrigerator door and stood there, the gloomiest expression on her face. A stark contrast to the jovial face she'd worn minutes before while telling Jon and me about her day.

I wished I knew what to do. Stay and try to patch things up with Mom? Dad would probably say that was a good idea. But I was so angry with her. So terribly confused, too.

It would be easier for me to wander over to the Zooks' and busy myself there. Maybe check on Jingle Belle. Or, who knows, maybe bump into Levi.

"What did Levi say when he came over?" I asked, more cautious now.

Mom ran some water and drank a sip out of a glass before answering. "It was quite obvious he was eager to see you, Merry. That's why he came."

"But why did you have to say anything in front of Jon?" I still saw no logical reason for it.

She shook her head. "You had just mentioned Rachel, and my mind leaped to Levi." She went to the table and sat down. "I don't know what's come over me lately." She began to whimper. "Sometimes I make the silliest mistakes—forget things, too. I'm worn out most of the time, but my doctor says it's typical."

Her doctor?

Suddenly, I felt truly horrible. I had no idea Mom was dealing with something physical. Dad had said it was a midlife crisis. Whatever that was. But by the sound of it, Mom was experiencing something worse. Why hadn't Dad told me?

"Oh, Mom, it's okay to cry," I said, going to her and stroking her hair. "I'm sorry . . . about everything. Honest. I shouldn't have talked to you that way at breakfast. I didn't know."

She blubbered her response, and I had no idea what she said. But the air was definitely cleared between us. I had several more cookies and a glass of milk to wash them down. Before I left for the Zooks' farm, I kissed her. "I love you, Mom," I said.

"I love you, too, honey." Her tears were gone.

I felt much better, too.

Rachel met me halfway between my house and hers. She said she'd been watching for me. Strands of hair at her neck were coming loose from her bun, and she was out of breath. "Merry, I was hopin' you'd come over." She seemed anxious.

"Everything all right?"

She shook her head. "Jingle's missing. Somehow, she got out of the fence."

I wondered if that was the reason for Levi's visit. But I didn't mention it. "Where'd you see her last?"

"She was near Ol' Nanna, like she might nurse from her . . . and then she just disappeared." Rachel hurried, her gait longer and faster than mine.

I scrambled to keep up with her. "Is there a place in the fence where she might've pushed through?"

"Honestly, I think she got out through the gate . . . maybe when Dat fed the older sheep."

"There aren't any wolves or other predators around, are there?" I asked.

She seemed more concerned about the lamb wandering too far away, forgetting how to get home. Maybe even starving to death. "Sheep are so dumb, ya know?"

I didn't know from experience, only from what I'd read in the Bible. "They're followers, right? They need a leader—a shepherd."

She nodded. "That's why we keep ours fenced in. At least, we *try* to."

The sun grew hotter as we ran together to the north meadow, out past the barn, beyond the pond. It was the same grassland where Rachel and I often gathered daisies and sat in the tall grass, sharing secrets. A wide expanse of land. Not the best place for a new lamb to roam freely. It was obvious why the entire Zook family had joined together to comb this section of land.

Just ahead, in the deepest grass, Levi and Martha were searching the meadow. To the right of them, Nancy, Ella Mae, and little Susie had joined hands, calling, "Jingle Belle, can you hear us?" over and over. Rachel's father and younger brother, Aaron, were looking, too. It would take hours to scour every inch of land. Most of the meadow remained untouched.

Rachel stopped to wipe her forehead. "How will we ever find Jingle?"

"We won't give up, that's how," I replied, forging ahead. I called out the name I'd chosen for the dear lamb. "Jingle, where are you? Where *are* you?"

We kept at it, plodding through patches of meadow, even skirting the edge of the woods, looking, calling louder. I spotted a variety of wild and useful herbs and other plants along the way. I imagined Jingle's white wooly coat showing up clearly under the powerful spotlight of the sun's rays. If we could just find her before dark!

"Where would a baby lamb wander off to?" I said, stopping to catch my breath.

Rachel shook her head sadly. "That's the thing . . . it's hard to know, really."

"She's got a mind of her own, that's for sure."

"Sheep are like that," she reminded me. Not giving up, Rachel kept moving through the grass. Her skirt hem brushed the tops of the foliage, and she kept her eyes on the ground.

I, on the other hand, glanced up ahead every so often. Occasionally, I caught sight of Levi and his girlfriend. They were working the field as a team. So were Rachel's younger sisters. Abe Zook and Aaron were way off in the outskirts of the meadow, still calling to the wayward lamb.

Suddenly, I thought of the Pied Piper. In a way, the lost lamb had been an invisible guide, leading us through the thickest grasses and trees. We were trying to follow an unseen trail. Then it occurred to me to look for a narrow path through the grass. "Wouldn't it be a good idea to look for smashed-down meadow grass?" I asked Rachel.

" 'Course it would. Gut thinking!"

So we turned around and did exactly that. We gazed back at the meadow from this side of the pond. I hoped to spot something to indicate that Jingle had wandered through the tallest grass.

"Do you see anything?" I asked.

"Nothin' at all." Rachel sounded discouraged.

"We'll find her," I assured her. "Count on me."

It was getting close to suppertime. My mother would be worried, especially if I didn't come home and she went to the Zooks' and found all of us gone. Except Esther, of course. Thank goodness, Rachel's mother had stayed behind. My mom would get the facts from her—where we were and why.

In the distance, I could see the north side of the Zooks' bank barn and pastureland. The willow grove was to the right of their property, creating a ridge—an obvious dividing line between their land and ours. It was an amazing sight. "It's glorious here," I said, scanning the horizon.

"Jah, the best part of livin' in the country. The wide, open spaces . . . and the woods."

I thought, just then, of the strange dream I'd had. Of being a maple tree, strong and true. No matter the wind or the weather, a tree like that stands tall. Was I *that* hardy? I truly wondered.

Thirteen Shadows Beyond the Gate

Low, slinky rain clouds hung in the sky on the far edge of SummerHill. Thunderbumpers, I'd nicknamed them. Soon, there would be distant thunder, but a change in weather was the furthest thing from my mind. A rain shower wouldn't spoil our search efforts, most likely. I, for one, wouldn't let some moisture dampen my spirits. If need be, we could race the weather all the way home. We were going to find Jingle Belle if it took all night!

Another hour and a half passed quickly. Abe and Aaron and the younger girls headed back across the meadow toward the farmhouse. I wondered if Levi and Martha would do the same, but they persevered. So did Rachel and I. Dusk was coming on fast, and my stomach was growling out of control. It wouldn't be long till nightfall.

"We'd better head back. It's getting too dark now," Rachel said.

"You go ahead," I said. "I want to keep looking."

She peered up at the darkening sky. "Soon, you'll need a flashlight or a lantern."

"I have eyes like a cat. I can see in the dark." Then I remembered the moon. It had appeared just last night while I sat with my cats on the back step. "The moon's due out any minute."

"Not if those clouds keep comin," she replied. There was apprehension in her voice.

"I'll be all right." I glanced up to see Levi and Martha still searching. "I'm in good company."

She smiled a weak smile and touched my arm. "You won't mind if I go, then?"

"I'm fine, honest."

She gave me a quick hug. "Maybe Jingle's wandered back to the corral already."

"Wouldn't someone ring the bell to let us know?"

"Jah, you're right." She turned to go, and I watched her for a few seconds before hurrying across the meadow. I decided to go in the opposite direction, away from Levi and Martha. It would be darker in the woods, but Jingle might've lost her way in there.

Time passed quickly. I lost track of how long it had been since Rachel left, and I couldn't see my watch anymore. Dusk had come, and I could barely see where I was walking. Still, I was one-hundred-percent-amen sure I'd be able to see a flash of white wool, given the chance.

A long rumble of thunder rolled across the sky. There was no lightning, though, which would've helped me see. If only for an instant.

I thought of my cats, probably hiding under my bed or in my closet about now. Oh, they hated the sound of thunder! A fleeting, yet frightening thought crossed my mind. Who would comfort my cats if something happened to me—if I lost my way forever? If no one ever found *me*? I couldn't imagine Dad or Mom, either one, taking on the job of caring for my cat quartet. And my brother had always made fun of my need to take in strays. Skip didn't call me cat breath for nothing!

I could almost feel the dark clouds overhead, and I wished for a flash of lightning. Anything to guide me. "Jingle!" I called, again and again. "Can you hear me?"

There was not a sound but the crack of thunder following a welcome flash of lightning. I forced myself to concentrate on finding the lost lamb. "I'm here for you, little girl," I said, clenching my fists. "I'm going to find you!"

The wind began to hit my face, and then came the pelting rain. In no time, my face and hair were drenched. Thankfully, I was spared the full force of the pounding because of the dense trees. I knew better than to plant myself under one of them, though. The rainstorm was fierce, with flashes of light now cracking out of the sky like jagged white fingers. I was determined to find Jingle, yet I wanted to do the wise thing. I had to get far enough away from the trees and keep low to be safe from the lightning.

The thunder made my knees feel like rubber. Was I lost? I couldn't have wandered that far away. Could I?

In the underbrush, I heard a sound. The low bleating of an animal not far from me. "Jingle? Is that you?"

I followed the whimpering, determined to find her. A steady flicker of lightning aided me. There, in the thicket—caught in the brushwood not more than three yards from me—was the little lamb.

"Oh, baby," I cried, crawling to her. "You'll be okay now. I'm here. Merry's here."

Her cries broke my heart, and I struggled to free her from the jungle of sharp vines. "Lord, help me," I whispered, snapping the briar that held her at last. In the process, I cut my fingers. But I couldn't determine how badly; I only felt the blood slowly oozing from my fingertips.

I sat on the wet ground, holding the lamb in my arms. Both of us were shaking hard. "Don't worry," I said, stroking her, holding her close. But my heart was beating ninety miles an hour.

After a time, Jingle began to relax. I continued to pet her and talk softly to her. The warmth of the lamb's body against my own comforted me. "The storm can't last forever," I said. "Storms never do."

That's when I remembered what Dad had said so often to me over the years. *"Only time will heal that kind of wound."*

"Time and . . . God's love, if we're patient," I said into Jingle's soft coat.

I remembered my vivid dream about being a maple tree. My roots were deep, grounded in the soil of God's Word. Thanks to my parents' spiritual training and the teaching I'd received at church, nothing could knock me down. "Not even Faithie's death," I said aloud.

God had reminded me in a very unique way. Teamed up with Him, I was sturdy enough to face the future without my twin. I could trust God, just as this precious lamb in my lap could count on me to care for her through this truly horrible storm.

The storm won't last forever. . . .

My own words! And what truth they held for me. It was time to let go of the past. I had the ability, with God's help, to move past the shadows. The truth hit me harder than the rain falling on my face.

"Thank you, Lord," I prayed, holding on to the lamb for dear life.

Fourteen Shadows Beyond the Gate

How long I sat there, I couldn't tell. After what seemed like hours, the rain finally slowed to a drizzle. It was still mighty dark, but I could see the shadow of the moon behind a cloud. I watched the sky, waiting breathlessly for the moon to become fully visible.

"We'll go home soon," I told Jingle. "We'll walk under the wonderful white moon."

For as long as it took—till we were rescued—I decided to play the Alliteration Word Game. Alone.

"God is here—hovering, holy, helpful," I began. "We'll be glad to get going—gleeful, giddy, and grateful to be home."

The familiar wordplay comforted me. Far better than focusing on the frightening flashes far overhead, not to mention what foreign forest friends—or foes—might be furtively lurking.

Hugging the lamb in my arms, I continued. "Jingle Belle is beautiful, blessed, on her best behavior, both bright and brainy." I was running out of *b* words.

So I tried *f*, thinking jovial Jon would be jubilant just now. "Faithie was fantastic, fun-loving, fast, faithful, full of life . . ." I couldn't go on. Saying descriptive words about my twin made me cry. My tears mingled with the rain on my face till it was impossible to tell which was which.

I thought of the summertime flowers that had refused to bloom after she died. And the horrible drought that followed. Most everything green had turned an ugly brown. When the rain finally did come that year, it had seemed to come in buckets. Soon, life flowered around us again. Just as I believed my life without Faithie was going to blossom . . . from this night on.

It was getting late. A hoot owl startled me in a tree nearby, and I could hear rustling in the underbrush. Noises that were not the wind. I could only imagine what snakes and other crawling things might be out here.

Scared, I began to hum a song from church, wondering what songs they might play at my funeral if I should die here tonight. Purposely, I forced those thoughts out of my mind. I focused, instead, on God's sovereign will covering all His creation. That meant me, too! Merry Hanson trapped in a ferocious storm . . . lost in a deep and dark woods, alone and afraid. Yet God's will covered me. I took true comfort in that.

Just then, a glimmer of light caught my eye. It was coming toward us, bobbing through the woods! Then I heard my name ringing through the trees. "Merry, can you hear me?"

It was Levi's voice! Courageous and strong.

"Over here!" I called back, still clinging to the lamb.

"Merry!"

Louder, I called back. "Levi . . . I'm here!"

Once the moon came out, he found me. His flashlight helped, too. "Oh, Merry," he said, bending down and shining the light in my face. "Are you all right?"

"My socks are soggy and most of me is soaking wet. But I found Jingle . . . and she's safe, too."

He reached down and helped me up, lamb and all. Faintly, I could see his face in the moonlight. "I was awful worried, Merry."

"I didn't think *you'd* come for me," I said, totally amazed.

"Both your father and mine are searching, too. You gave us a fright, really you did."

"I'm okay, honest."

But he kept looking at me, as if he had to see for himself. "You've been crying, Merry . . ." Then, without waiting for me to answer, he brushed away my tears with the pads of his thumbs. "There," he whispered, "much better." Then, unexpectedly, he pulled me close, along with the lamb, into his arms. "I prayed you'd be all right," he was saying. "We all did."

"And I am," I assured him.

Levi released me gently, and we began to hike out of the woods, his flashlight guiding the way. His consoling hug had been a brotherly one. The old feelings, the romantic ones, had been replaced with something new.

He took the lamb from me, carrying her away from the woods toward the meadow. And as we walked, we talked of many things—my present school year . . . and his. How his brother Curly John and sister-in-law, Sarah, and their little Mary were doing. He also mentioned that his father had asked him again to consider "joining church."

"But you're Mennonite," I insisted.

"Dat's stubborn as the day is long. Wants *all* his children in the Amish church."

"I'm sure you can understand why."

"But I've made a stand for the Lord by becoming a follower of Christ instead of the *Ordnung*." He was adamant about growing in his newfound faith, and I was truly glad. Adjusting the lamb in his arms, he explained, "My father's from the Old Order—the old Amish way of doing things. He only knows what his father and grandfather before him passed on to him."

"And the bishop?"

"The bishop, too." He was quiet for a moment. "The fact is, unless someone witnesses to Old Order folk, it's awful hard for them to hear the fullness of the Gospel. For one thing, the

People aren't allowed to read the entire Bible. Only certain passages are encouraged, and those are preached over and over."

"How sad," I spoke up. "The Word of God holds all the answers to life's problems."

"And that's the truth!"

I remembered then that he'd dropped by to see me earlier. "Mom said you came over to the house."

"I couldn't leave SummerHill again without talking to you, Merry. Like the old days."

It was dear of him. "But those days are nearly gone," I gently reminded.

We kept our pace, moving through the tallest grassland now. "Martha said she met you," he said.

"Yes . . . and she's really terrific."

He laughed his joyful laugh—that warm and contagious chuckle I'd come to know so well. "Martha likes you, too."

"Maybe we'll become good friends," I said, hoping so.

"That might be difficult, since we're praying about going to South America as missionaries."

"When?"

"After graduation." He paused. "And after I marry Martha."

The news didn't jolt me, not in the least. But it was mighty nice to hear it directly from Levi. "I know you'll be happy together," I said softly. "She's right for you, Levi."

The lamb jostled in his strong arms. "I hope you'll forgive me. I never wanted to hurt you."

I understood. "We were mistaken about the kind of feelings we had for each other," I said. "I should've known you were more like a wonderful big brother. Nothing can change that."

"Still, I was wrong to lead you on. I said certain things . . . and I'm sorry."

"We're still friends, so don't worry."

"I'm glad you feel that way," he said, and I noticed he patted the lamb's head.

"Jingle's so adorable," I said. "She taught me many things about myself . . . on the farm and back there in the woods. God allowed Jingle to come into my life for a reason. He allowed tonight's storm to happen, too. So I could learn to trust Him to quiet another, much bigger storm."

Levi listened patiently as I recounted my discoveries. He was kind, as always, and put up with my chattering.

Once we were midway across the meadow, we started calling. Hollering, really. "Dad, I'm okay!" I shouted.

We wanted my dad and Levi's, too, to know I'd been found.

"Merry's with me," Levi said, putting his free arm around my shoulder.

Merry's with me. . . .

A year ago, I might've replayed those words and this moment a thousand times in my mind. Tonight, I knew better. Levi was, and always would be, very special to me. But in time, Martha was to be his life mate. I was truly happy for them.

───────

We stopped to let the lamb roam freely for a while, waiting for my dad and Abe Zook to catch up with us. "Miss Spindler's hooked up and turned on to the computer age," I told Levi. "Did Rachel tell you?"

He sat in the grass near the pond. "Well, she tried to, but honestly she lost me. Sounds like you finally did some snooping, though."

"I sure did." I had to stop and laugh, recalling all the top-secret sleuthing that had gone on at my elderly neighbor's. "With her permission, I even took a picture of her high-tech attic to prove it."

"Speaking of pictures, I have a request."

"Shoot."

"Well, I don't know how to ask this."

I had no idea what he was going to say.

"Would you be willing to take a picture of Martha and me for our engagement photo?"

I chuckled, not at the question, but at the idea of asking *me*. "A professional photographer might be a better choice, really. But thanks for the vote of confidence."

He shone his flashlight on Jingle, watching her play. "I've seen your work, Merry. You're very good."

"Well, if you're sure, then I'll be happy to take the picture."

"Would tomorrow work for you, near Mam's rose garden?"

"That'll be such a pretty backdrop. I'll come over after school. Count on me," I said.

Our chatter turned to Miss Spindler again. "I notice you're not calling her your favorite nickname," he said.

"Not anymore." I couldn't wait to tell him why. "Sure, she's a little peculiar. But I have to tell you, she was wonderful to me when I lost Abednego last month. I don't know how I would've found my cat without her help."

"Sounds like things are changing mighty fast around SummerHill," he said, getting up and chasing Jingle playfully.

Well, I had news for him. Miss Spindler wasn't the only one. "My mom wants to start an antique shop," I told him. "Can you believe it?"

"Rachel said something about that. Sounds interesting."

"I'm trying to get used to the idea. It's a little strange, I have to admit."

"How's your friend Jon Klein?" he asked out of the blue.

I wondered how to describe Jon to Levi without sounding like a girl in love. "Well, let's see . . ."

Levi carried the lamb over and sat down beside me again. "I'm all ears."

"Jon's not the Alliteration Wizard anymore, so that's another change. We're done with word games. But he's taking a photography class, which means we have cameras and lenses and pictures in common."

"You're skirting the issue," said Levi, laughing. "I asked a simple question."

"And you want a simple answer, right?"

I looked up at the sky, wondering if tonight was the right time. "This is between you and me, okay?"

"I promise."

I took a deep breath. These were precious words. "I think Jon and I are becoming best friends."

"That's just what I hoped you'd say, Merry."

I was one-hundred-percent-amen happy!

⸻

Dad and I walked home the rest of the way together. I thought of the events of the evening. How I'd lost my way trying to find a missing lamb. I thought, too, of the changes occurring between Levi and me. Between Levi and his own dear family.

Some of the biggest changes had taken place inside me. And I knew I was ready to talk to Mom about Faithie. I could hardly wait!

Mom was terribly worried about the cuts on my fingers. She hovered near me as I ran cold water over them at the kitchen sink. Then she insisted on using antibiotic ointment to cleanse away any possible infection. On top of that, she made me get out of my drenched clothes and put on warm, dry ones. All this before we ever sat down to a late supper.

My cats seemed happier than usual to see me, too. "Guess I should get caught in a rainstorm more often," I teased.

Mom gave me a sideways look, which meant my comment was ridiculous. "Let's pray and eat," she said.

With bandaged fingers, I took my place at the table. Leave it to Mom to keep the meal hot for all this time. I could tell Dad was mighty glad. He stopped to relish almost every bite. Mom got a big kick out of it. But more than that, she seemed eager to dote on me, obviously thrilled that I was safe. "I'm so glad you're home, Merry," she went on and on.

"What a night to remember," I said, grinning at both Dad and Mom.

Mom shook her head. "Well, I can't imagine being lost out in that vicious storm . . . and wandering around in the woods!"

"God answered our prayers for Merry," Dad said, interjecting a positive remark.

"We're so glad He did!" Mom offered me more mashed potatoes and gravy. Instead of refusing, I actually took a second helping, recalling how cold and lonely—and terribly frightened—I'd felt only a few hours before.

It was truly good to be home.

⁓

While Mom and I cleaned up the kitchen, I brought up the subject of her clothesline. "I wondered if you'd thought about it . . . with customers coming, and all."

"I don't mind if *they* don't," she said. Then, smiling at me, she added, "Even if they object, it's staying!" She tossed a dish towel at me, and I began to dry the pots and pans. I wanted to make it easy for Mom to talk about Faithie but hesitated, hoping for the right time.

"Your friend Ashley Horton called during the storm," Mom said.

"I don't believe this! Every time I'm gone, someone calls."

"You have a busy life . . . and that's a good thing."

"What's on her mind?" I asked.

"She's having a sleepover this weekend. She said Chelsea and Lissa were planning to go."

"What'd you tell her?"

She stopped to look at me, her deep brown eyes now very serious. "I told her that you are your own social planner. That you'd return her call."

"Thanks, Mom. You're so cool."

Her eyes widened. "So . . . I'm evolving? To *cool*?"

"Yep."

"Well, hearing that makes my day," she said, turning back to the sudsy sink.

I finished drying one of the pans. Then, all at once, tears began to cloud my vision. I sniffled a little, trying to keep them under control. "Mom, you made *my* day," I said, "the day you gave birth to Faithie and me. . . . "

"Oh, honey." She dropped her dishcloth and wrapped me in her arms.

"I thought I was the one . . . who hurt the most . . . when my sister died," I said, sobbing. "But Faithie and I grew inside you. You gave us life. *You* lost your baby girl!"

Both of us were crying now. Thank goodness Dad didn't stroll through the kitchen just then. Except, if he had, he would've discovered a mother and daughter sharing their deepest pain. Their loss. And best of all, their most precious memories.

I openly talked to Mom about Faithie. Even grabbed her hand and took her upstairs. I closed the door in my room and sat her down on my bed, propping her up with pillows. At first, she wasn't too thrilled about having the cats join us for a tender look back into the past. Our past.

But it didn't take long before she was oblivious to the cats curled up around her. What a long time since I'd invited Mom or anyone to see my scrapbooks. So I took things slow and easy, sharing each memory—even the tiniest one—as it came to me.

Mom, too, had meaningful things to say about each picture. Some things I'd completely forgotten or, better yet, never known. "Faithie insisted on parting her hair on the opposite side to yours," Mom said, pointing to a picture to demonstrate the point.

I nodded, staring at it. "Sometimes I actually got the feeling Faithie resented being a twin."

Mom's arm was around me again. "Your sister was a very independent little girl. But she adored you. And you must surely know that is true."

"I wish I had more gumption," I confessed. "Like Faithie did."

Mom turned to the next page. "God made the two of you unique. No one knows that better than your father and I. And we loved you both dearly." She went on to recite various incidents when Faithie had exerted her strong will.

I slid around the side of the bed so I could look at Mom as she talked. In the end, I spent more time gazing at her face than at the scrapbook. After all, I'd nearly memorized the pages. But it had been a long time since I'd concentrated on my mother.

"This storm is coming to an end, isn't it?" I recalled the words I'd said to comfort the lamb in the forest.

Mom was very still. Then she got up and walked across the room to my bookcase. She reached for my Bible and opened to Psalm seventy-one. "Listen to this, honey," she said, reading to me. " 'For you have been my hope, O Sovereign Lord, my confidence since my youth. From birth I have relied on you; you brought me forth from my mother's womb. I will ever praise you . . . you are my strong refuge.' "

I let the words sink in. How amazing they were!

Our eyes met and locked. "God is our refuge in the storms of life," she said. "He protected us, as He always will." She sighed, closing the Bible. "Yes, Merry, I believe the storm is past."

Jingle Belle took her milk from Ol' Nanna on Friday afternoon. She had graduated from the nursing bottle to a new "mama." A triumph!

I asked Rachel if Jon Klein could come for a visit "to take some pictures around the farm."

She agreed. "That's fine. Anyone who's a friend of yours is welcome here."

I was almost sure she'd feel that way. "Jon's eager to see Jingle," I told her, following her around the side of the brick farmhouse.

"Sounds like her fame is spreading," she replied, straightening her long apron. "I'd say we've got ourselves a perty gut little lamb, don'tcha think?"

"She's healthy . . . she survived the storm. And now, looks like Ol' Nanna's just what the doctor ordered."

"Jah, Dr. Merry." Giggling about it, Rachel took me around the side of the house. We strolled past colorful flower beds of petunias, marigolds, and pansies of every imaginable hue. But it was in Esther Zook's rose garden that Levi and Martha were waiting to have their picture taken.

I made sure the sun was at my back, even though it shone in their eyes a bit. From experience, I knew that kind of lighting would produce the best results. "I never take only one shot," I explained.

Rachel said, "She's right," but didn't say how she knew. Truth was, I'd taken numerous pictures of her last winter before she decided to settle down and follow the Amish ways. Levi, of course, had other plans—ones that didn't include the Old Order rules and regulations. So he posed nicely with his bride-to-be, and I snapped away. Not once did I feel a twinge of sadness for losing my friend Levi to Martha Martin. As the Plain folk liked to say, their love for each other was ever so *providential*.

I found Mom and Miss Spindler cleaning out the potting shed when I returned. They'd already swept out the dirt and cobwebs—shined up the windows, too. Dad was nailing up window boxes all around, and I spied the red geranium plants just itching to be planted. The place was going to be as quaint and cute as any antique shop in Lancaster County.

"Merry, dearie," Miss Spindler called. "Come have a look-see at this here curtain fabric."

I stepped inside the shed-turned-store. She was holding up a soft yellow-striped fabric in one hand, a busy floral in the other. Her blue-gray hair was perfectly coifed in her usual puffed-up do. Her face shone with a radiant joy, the same sort of delight she'd displayed last month when Rachel presented her with a gray kitten.

I eyed the fabric. It was an easy choice. "Definitely the stripes," I said, imagining the room painted and furnished with display tables.

"Merry's partial to stripes," Mom told Miss Spindler.

Miss Spindler tilted her head. "Oh, is that so?"

I nodded. "You should see my room. Stripes are everywhere."

"Well, to tell you the honest truth, I think the floral material is a bit too much." Ruby Spindler grinned broadly.

Mom was smiling, too. "Thanks for your input, Merry."

"Anything else I can help with?" I offered, noticing Miss Spindler's kitten had wandered into the yard and was about to encounter Abednego—king of kitties! "Yee-ikes," I said, buzzing off to avert a *cat*astrophe!

Quickly, I scooped up the kitten. My big cat arched his black furry back and hissed. "That's not polite," I scolded him. "You've got company today."

Meow! Abednego protested, still arched and ready for a hissy fit.

"You need to mind your manners, young man," I continued. "We're going to have many more visitors pretty soon. *Customers.*"

My oldest cat wasn't too wild about that information. He turned and slinked low like he was checking around for a mouse-y meal. Then he made a beeline for the gazebo. His favorite hideout.

"Sorry about that," I whispered to the kitty. "Abednego thinks he simply *has* to be top dog at all times."

"Who're you talking to?" Mom said, poking her head out of one of the windows in her new shop.

I held up the kitten. "Miss Spindler's kitty cat. What's her name, anyway?" I asked.

Mom disappeared momentarily. Soon, both Mom and Miss Spindler were smiling at me. "She doesn't have a name yet," our neighbor said. "What's she look like to *you*, dearie? Is she a Gertie or a Missy?"

"Neither one," I said, taking a good look at her. "Shadow. She looks like a shadow."

Mom clapped her hands. "You're right!"

Miss Spindler agreed. "Then *Shadow* it is."

I sat in the grass, soaking up the sunshine with Shadow in my lap. "Life is full of sunshine and shadows," I said. "You're a good reminder for all of us."

The kitten looked up at me and smiled. Well, at least, I *think* it was a smile.

Ashley Horton gave me the biggest hug ever when I arrived at her house for the sleepover. "We're going to play the Word Game tonight," she announced.

Chelsea was nodding, her arms folded across her chest. "She's not kidding, Mer. Ashley's not going to let us sleep till we each come up with at least four words in a row."

"They have to make a sentence," Lissa said, her hair in a perky ponytail.

I put down my overnight case. "Well, let's see . . ."

"Wait a minute. There's one minor detail missing from this assignment," Ashley said, twirling her hair with her finger. "The alliteration has to be about a boy."

"Oh, not *that*!" Chelsea pretended to choke herself.

I let the others play the game for a while, thinking back to all the energy I'd put into the word wars with Jon for almost two years. The girls might not understand why I'd abandoned the bantering, but it had nothing to do with them.

As I listened to Lissa trying to alliterate four words, I couldn't wait to invite Jon to see Jingle. To take pictures of the darling lamb and Ol' Nanna. Maybe I'd take my camera, too, and secretly shoot Jon taking a picture! What a great photo that would be!

I must've been smiling because Ashley threw a pillow at me. "You're daydreaming, Merry. So . . . it's your turn!"

I thought for a moment. Could I do it?

"Remember, it has to be about a boy," Ashley reminded me, sitting cross-legged on the floor.

"Levi loves life lots," I said.

Lissa burst out laughing, but Ashley was silent. "How does she do that?" Ashley said.

Chelsea looked solemn. "Levi's leaving?"

"Mennonite Martha Martin may be marrying my man...."

"*Your* man?" Lissa gasped. "Surely you don't mean—"

"No, I'm not brokenhearted. Not at all," I explained, abandoning the game. "I'm actually happy for Levi and Martha."

"So . . . are you saying you met her?" Chelsea asked.

"I took their engagement pictures in the Zooks' rose garden this afternoon," I said.

"No way," Chelsea replied.

They were all bug-eyed. Like they couldn't believe it.

"Make some alliteration about Jon Klein," Ashley said, eyes wide.

I shook my head. "I could, but I won't. How I feel about Jon is private stuff."

Lissa and Chelsea were grinning at me. "*Oooh*, I guess we know where Merry stands with the Klein-man," Chelsea teased.

They burst into laughter, but I didn't mind. Tomorrow I would invite Jon to meet Jingle Belle. And if it was an exceptionally beautiful day, I would take my tripod along and make a picture of the three of us.

I could just see it now....

When all was said and done, we talked and giggled and ate popcorn till we were so tired we couldn't keep our eyes open anymore.

As for Jon, I had the best time showing him around the Zooks' dairy farm the next day. We explored every nook and cranny in the barn. And my favorite place in the world: the hayloft. He took oodles of pictures—mules, hand-hewn plows, even the barn rafters. I had to laugh, wondering if maybe Jon was becoming a little *too* interested in farm life.

He and I spent an hour playing with Jingle Belle. He also helped me set up the tripod for a picture. It turned out so well, Mom suggested I frame it. So I'm going to hang it in my photo gallery, on my bedroom wall. That way, I'll never forget the special day.

I have a feeling there are lots more days like that ahead. Jon and I are truly becoming best friends. "A deep and caring friendship is a good, solid basis for a serious dating relationship," Dad said the other night.

Mom smiled her agreement.

I'm going along with Jon and his photography club to the Susquehanna River, after all. He asked if I'd bring *my* camera, too. "You could be president of the club, Merry. You're a natural," he said, flashing his winning smile.

Dad says I'm old enough to start making decisions about who I spend time with. It's great to know he trusts me. And I won't disappoint him or Mom, that's for sure.

The Antique Shoppe is darling, and we've already had more than twenty customers in just three days. Not a single one has mentioned the clothesline. In fact, my mother puts it to good use, displaying old doilies and quilted table runners. Pure genius!

Nearly every evening, I spend time with Mom. She and I have gotten much closer this summer. We've been baking zucchini bread and selling it. When I told Rachel about some of the baked goods we were marketing, she raised her eyebrows. I guess we *are* giving our Amish neighbors some competition.

Skip's home from college for the summer. It's actually great having my brother underfoot again. He still calls me names that allude to my cat obsession, but overall he's becoming a cool guy. Guess that's what growing up does for an obnoxious older brother.

Last I heard, Levi formally proposed to Martha Martin. The *Lancaster New Era* ran their engagement announcement, complete with the photo I took of them. I'm a bona-fide published photographer at last!

One of the Zooks' cats had another litter. Rachel brought over a darling yellow kitten as a thank-you for nursing Jingle back to health. I knew better than to ask Mom. Still, the kitten reminds me of a drop of sunshine. I'm thinking of talking to Miss Spindler about taking another pet. It would be so cute: Sunshine and Shadow, purring together under the same roof.

Sunshine and Shadow . . . That's also the name of a very popular Pennsylvania Amish quilt pattern. It says a lot about life.

I've accepted my share of shadows. Without them, I probably wouldn't appreciate the sunshine. With God's help, I've come a long way since I set up the before-and-after pictures in a SummerHill cemetery.

A truly long way.

From Beverly . . . To You

I'm delighted that you're reading SUMMERHILL SECRETS. Merry Hanson is such a fascinating character—I can't begin to count the times I laughed while writing her humorous scenes. And I must admit, I always cry with her.

Not so long ago, I was Merry's age, growing up in Lancaster County, the home of the Pennsylvania Dutch—my birthplace. My grandma Buchwalter was a Mennonite, as were many of my mother's aunts, uncles, and cousins. Some of my school friends were also Mennonite, so my interest and appreciation for the Plain folk began early.

It is they, the Mennonite and Amish people—farmers, carpenters, blacksmiths, shopkeepers, quiltmakers, teachers, schoolchildren, and bed-and-breakfast owners—who best assisted me with the research for this series. Even though I have kept their identity private, I am thankful for these wonderfully honest and helpful friends.

To learn more about my writing, sign up for my e-newsletter, or contact me, visit my Web site, *www.beverlylewis.com*.

Looking for More Good Books to Read?

You can find out what is new and exciting with previews, descriptions, and reviews by signing up for Bethany House newsletters at

www.bethanynewsletters.com

We will send you updates for as many authors or categories as you desire so you get only the information you really want.

Sign up today!